Praise for

'Bridget Jones's phenomenal success is not just because of her creator's brilliant wit, comic timing and social observation, but because she *captures* what – alas – it is like to be female . . . I laughed out loud many times while reading *The Edge of Reason*. Fielding is excellent at a mixture of perception and comedy, capturing thoughts everyone has but hasn't actually expressed'

Sally Emerson, *Daily Mail*

'Bridget is probably the most successful comic creation of this decade, the most controversial and talked-about female fictional character since Lolita . . . Bridget terminology has slipped into comon parlance . . . She is still on superb form'

Stephanie Merritt, *Observer*

'Could *Bridget Jones: The Edge of Reason* really be as funny as its predecessor? The answer is yes . . . Bridget, the original Singleton, is on ripping form in the sequel . . . But she is far more than the patron saint of single women: she is everyman, or rather, everyperson'

Virginia Blackburn, *Express*

'Like that other gifted commentator Woody Allen, she makes modern urban neuroses, if not art, then at least very, very funny'

Carla Power, *Newsweek*

'Fielding has produced a genuinely original fictional voice. Like Anita Loos before her or, perhaps more pertinently, E. M. Delafield in her *Diary of a Provincial Lady*, she has created a devastatingly funny parody of her life and times . . . Any woman of a certain age can recognize elements of Bridget in herself and will have enormous fun trying to spot them in the book'

Rachel Simhon, *Daily Telegraph*

'Bridget Jones is no mere fictional character, she's the Spirit of the Age'

Melanie McDonagh, *Evening Standard*

'Austen, as before, in Fielding's model, radically but affectionately updated . . . There is, to be honest, a bit of Bridget Jones in a lot of women and men of a certain generation, and to have those aspects so affectionately rendered, and both ridiculed and subversively celebrated, is a welcome treat'

Robert Potts, *TLS*

Bridget Jones's Diary
and
Bridget Jones: The Edge of Reason

Helen Fielding was born in Yorkshire. She worked for many years in London as a newspaper and TV journalist, travelling as wildly and as often as possible to Africa, India and Central America. She is the author of four novels, *Cause Celeb* (1994), *Bridget Jones's Diary* (1996), *Bridget Jones: The Edge of Reason* (2000) and *Olivia Joules and the Overactive Imagination* (2003), and co-wrote the screenplays for the movie of *Bridget Jones's Diary* and the sequel based on *The Edge of Reason*. She now works full-time as a novelist and screenwriter and lives in London and Los Angeles.

Also by Helen Fielding

Cause Celeb

Olivia Joules and the Overactive Imagination

HELEN FIELDING

Bridget Jones's Diary

and

Bridget Jones: The Edge of Reason

PAN BOOKS

Bridget Jones's Diary first published 1996 by Picador.
First published in paperback 1997 by Picador.
Bridget Jones: The Edge of Reason first published 1999 by Picador.
First published in paperback 2000 by Picador.

This omnibus first published 2008 by Pan Books
an imprint of Pan Macmillan Ltd
Pan Macmillan, 20 New Wharf Road, London N1 9RR
Basingstoke and Oxford
Associated companies throughout the world
www.panmacmillan.com

ISBN 978-0-330-45784-2

1 3 5 7 9 8 6 4 2

A CIP catalogue record for this book is available from the British Library.

Printed and bound in Great Britain by
Mackays of Chatham plc, Chatham, Kent

Bridget Jones's Diary

To my mum, Nellie, for not being like Bridget's

Acknowledgements

With particular thanks to Charlie Leadbeater for first suggesting the column at the *Independent*. Thanks too to Gillon Aitken, Richard Coles, Scarlett Curtis, the Fielding family, Piers, Paula and Sam Fletcher, Emma Freud, Georgia Garrett, Sharon Maguire, Jon Turner and Daniel Woods for inspiration and support, and especially, as ever, to Richard Curtis.

Contents

New Year's Resolutions 1

JANUARY An Exceptionally Bad Start 5

FEBRUARY Valentine's Day Massacre 35

MARCH Severe Birthday-Related Thirties Panic 63

APRIL Inner Poise 87

MAY Mother-to-Be 113

JUNE Hah! Boyfriend 139

JULY Huh 161

AUGUST Disintegration 179

SEPTEMBER Up The Fireman's Pole 205

OCTOBER Date with Darcy 225

NOVEMBER A Criminal in the Family 251

DECEMBER Oh, Christ 283

New Year's Resolutions

I WILL NOT

Drink more than fourteen alcohol units a week.

Smoke.

Waste money on: pasta-makers, ice-cream machines or other culinary devices which will never use; books by unreadable literary authors to put impressively on shelves; exotic underwear, since pointless as have no boyfriend.

Behave sluttishly around the house, but instead imagine others are watching.

Spend more than earn.

Allow in-tray to rage out of control.

Fall for any of following: alcoholics, workaholics, commitment phobics, people with girlfriends or wives, misogynists, megalomaniacs, chauvinists, emotional fuckwits or freeloaders, perverts.

Get annoyed with Mum, Una Alconbury or Perpetua.

Get upset over men, but instead be poised and cool ice-queen.

Have crushes on men, but instead form relationships based on mature assessment of character.

Bitch about anyone behind their backs, but be positive about everyone.

Obsess about Daniel Cleaver as pathetic to have a crush on boss in manner of Miss Moneypenny or similar.

Sulk about having no boyfriend, but develop inner poise and authority and sense of self as woman of substance, complete *without* boyfriend, as best way to obtain boyfriend.

I WILL

Stop smoking.

Drink no more than fourteen alcohol units a week.

Reduce circumference of thighs by 3 inches (i.e. 1½ inches each), using anti-cellulite diet.

Purge flat of all extraneous matter.

Give all clothes which have not worn for two years or more to homeless.

Improve career and find new job with potential.

Save up money in form of savings. Poss start pension also.

Be more confident.

Be more assertive.

Make better use of time.

Not go out every night but stay in and read books and listen to classical music.

Give proportion of earnings to charity.

Be kinder and help others more.

Eat more pulses.

Get up straight away when wake up in mornings.

Go to gym three times a week not merely to buy sandwich.

Put photographs in photograph albums.

Make up compilation 'mood' tapes so can have tapes ready with all favourite romantic/dancing/rousing/feminist etc. tracks assembled instead of turning into drink-sodden DJ-style person with tapes scattered all over floor.

Form functional relationship with responsible adult.

Learn to programme video.

JANUARY

An Exceptionally Bad Start

Sunday 1 January

9st 3 (but post-Christmas), alcohol units 14 (but effectively covers 2 days as 4 hours of party was on New Year's Day), cigarettes 22, calories 5424.

Food consumed today:

2 pkts Emmenthal cheese slices
14 cold new potatoes
2 Bloody Marys (count as food as contain Worcester sauce and tomatoes)
⅓ Ciabatta loaf with Brie
coriander leaves – ½ packet
12 Milk Tray (best to get rid of all Christmas confectionery in one go and make fresh start tomorrow)
13 cocktail sticks securing cheese and pineapple
Portion Una Alconbury's turkey curry, peas and bananas
Portion Una Alconbury's Raspberry Surprise made with Bourbon biscuits, tinned raspberries, eight gallons of whipped cream, decorated with glacé cherries and angelica.

Noon. London: my flat. Ugh. The last thing on earth I feel physically, emotionally or mentally equipped to do is drive to Una and Geoffrey Alconbury's New Year's Day Turkey Curry Buffet in Grafton Underwood. Geoffrey and Una Alconbury are my parents' best friends and, as Uncle Geoffrey never tires of reminding me, have known me since I was running round the lawn with no clothes on. My mother rang up at 8.30 in the morning last August Bank Holiday and forced me to promise to go. She approached it via a cunningly circuitous route.

'Oh, hello, darling. I was just ringing to see what you wanted for Christmas.'

'*Christmas?*'

'Would you like a surprise, darling?'

'No!' I bellowed. 'Sorry. I mean . . .'

'I wondered if you'd like a set of wheels for your suitcase.'

'But I haven't got a suitcase.'

'Why don't I get you a little suitcase *with wheels attached*. You know, like air hostesses have.'

'I've already got a bag.'

'Oh, darling, you can't go around with that tatty green canvas thing. You look like some sort of Mary Poppins person who's fallen on hard times. Just a little compact case with a pull-out handle. It's amazing how much you can get in. Do you want it in navy on red or red on navy?'

'Mum. It's eight thirty in the morning. It's summer. It's very hot. I don't want an air-hostess bag.'

'Julie Enderby's got one. She says she never uses anything else.'

'Who's Julie Enderby?'

'You know *Julie*, darling! Mavis Enderby's daughter. Julie! The one that's got that super-dooper job at Arthur Andersen . . .'

'Mum . . .'

'Always takes it on her trips . . .'

'I don't want a little bag with wheels on.'

'I'll tell you what. Why don't Jamie, Daddy and I all club together and get you a proper new big suitcase *and* a set of wheels?'

Exhausted, I held the phone away from my ear, puzzling about where the missionary luggage-Christmas-gift zeal had stemmed from. When I put the phone back she was saying: '. . . in actual fact, you can get them with a compartment with bottles for your bubble bath and things. The other thing I thought of was a shopping trolley.'

'Is there anything *you'd* like for Christmas?' I said desperately, blinking in the dazzling Bank Holiday sunlight.

'No, no,' she said airily. 'I've got everything *I* need. Now, darling,' she suddenly hissed, 'you will be coming to Geoffrey and Una's New Year's Day Turkey Curry Buffet this year, won't you?'

'Ah. Actually, I . . .' I panicked wildly. What could I pretend to be doing? '. . . think I might have to work on New Year's Day.'

'That doesn't matter. You can drive up after work. Oh, did I mention? Malcolm and Elaine Darcy are coming and bringing Mark with them. Do you remember Mark, darling? He's one of those top-notch barristers. Masses of money. Divorced. It doesn't start till eight.'

Oh God. Not another strangely dressed opera freak with bushy hair burgeoning from a side-parting. 'Mum, I've told you. I don't need to be fixed up with . . .'

'Now come along, darling. Una and Geoffrey have been holding the New Year Buffet since you were running round the lawn with no clothes on! Of course you're going to come. And you'll be able to use your new suitcase.'

11.45 p.m. Ugh. First day of New Year has been day of horror. Cannot quite believe I am once again starting the year in a single bed in my parents' house. It is too humiliating at my age. I wonder if they'll smell it if I have a fag out of the window. Having skulked at home all day, hoping hangover would clear, I eventually gave up and set off for the Turkey Curry Buffet far too late. When I got to the Alconburys' and rang their entire-tune-of-town-hall-clock-style doorbell I was still in a strange world of my own – nauseous, vile-headed, acidic. I was also suffering from road-rage residue after inadvertently getting on to the M6 instead of the M1 and having to drive halfway to Birmingham before I could find anywhere to turn round. I was so furious I kept jamming my foot down to the floor on the accelerator pedal to give vent to my feelings, which is very dangerous. I watched resignedly as Una Alconbury's form – intriguingly deformed through the ripply glass door – bore down on me in a fuchsia two-piece.

'Bridget! We'd almost given you up for lost! Happy New Year! Just about to start without you.'

She seemed to manage to kiss me, get my coat off, hang it over the banister, wipe her lipstick off my cheek and make me feel incredibly guilty all in one movement, while I leaned against the ornament shelf for support.

'Sorry. I got lost.'

'Lost? Durr! What are we going to do with you? Come on in!'

She led me through the frosted-glass doors into the lounge, shouting, 'She got lost, everyone!'

'Bridget! Happy New Year!' said Geoffrey Alconbury, clad in a yellow diamond-patterned sweater. He did a jokey Bruce Forsyth step then gave me the sort of hug which Boots would send straight to the police station.

'Hahumph,' he said, going red in the face and pulling his trousers up by the waistband. 'Which junction did you come off at?'

'Junction nineteen, but there was a diversion . . .'

'Junction nineteen! Una, she came off at Junction nineteen! You've added an hour to your journey before you even started. Come on, let's get you a drink. How's your love-life, anyway?'

Oh *God*. Why can't married people understand that this is no longer a polite question to ask? We wouldn't rush up to *them* and roar, 'How's your marriage going? Still having sex?' Everyone knows that dating in your thirties is not the happy-go-lucky free-for-all it was when you were twenty-two and that the honest answer is more likely to be, 'Actually, last night my married lover appeared wearing suspenders and a darling little Angora crop-top, told me he was gay/a sex addict/a narcotic addict/a commitment phobic and beat me up with a dildo,' than, 'Super, thanks.'

Not being a natural liar, I ended up mumbling shamefacedly to Geoffrey, 'Fine,' at which point he boomed, 'So you *still* haven't got a feller!'

'Bridget! What *are* we going to do with you!' said Una. 'You career girls! I don't know! Can't put it off for ever, you know. Tick-tock-tick-tock.'

'Yes. How does a woman manage to get to your age without being married?' roared Brian Enderby (married to Mavis, used to be president of the Rotary in Kettering), waving his sherry in the air. Fortunately my dad rescued me.

'I'm very pleased to see you, Bridget,' he said, taking my arm. 'Your mother has the entire Northamptonshire constabulary poised to comb the county with toothbrushes for your dismembered remains. Come and demonstrate your presence so I can start enjoying myself. How's the be-wheeled suitcase?'

'Big beyond all sense. How are the ear-hair clippers?'

'Oh, marvellously – you know – *clippy*.'

It was all right, I suppose. I would have felt a bit mean if I hadn't turned up, but Mark Darcy . . . Yuk. Every time my mother's rung up for weeks it's been, 'Of course you remember the *Darcys*, darling. They came over when we were living in Buckingham and you and Mark played in the paddling pool!' or, 'Oh! Did I mention Malcolm and Elaine are bringing Mark with them to Una's New Year's Day Turkey Curry Buffet? He's just back from America, apparently. Divorced. He's looking for a house in Holland Park. Apparently he had the most terrible time with his wife. Japanese. Very cruel race.'

Then next time, as if out of the blue, 'Do you remember Mark Darcy, darling? Malcolm and Elaine's son? He's one of these super-dooper top-notch lawyers. Divorced. Elaine says he works all the time and he's terribly lonely. I think he might be coming to Una's New Year's Day Turkey Curry Buffet, actually.'

I don't know why she didn't just come out with it and say, 'Darling, do shag Mark Darcy over the turkey curry, won't you? He's *very* rich.'

'Come along and meet Mark,' Una Alconbury sing-songed before I'd even had time to get a drink down me.

Being set up with a man against your will is one level of humiliation, but being literally dragged into it by Una Alconbury while caring for an acidic hangover, watched by an entire roomful of friends of your parents, is on another plane altogether.

The rich, divorced-by-cruel-wife Mark – quite tall – was standing with his back to the room, scrutinizing the contents of the Alconburys' bookshelves: mainly leather-bound series of books about the Third Reich, which Geoffrey sends off for from Reader's Digest. It struck me as pretty ridiculous to be called Mr Darcy and to stand on your own looking snooty at a party. It's like being called Heathcliff and insisting on spending the entire evening in the garden, shouting 'Cathy' and banging your head against a tree.

'Mark!' said Una, as if she was one of Santa Claus's fairies. 'I've got someone nice for you to meet.'

He turned round, revealing that what had seemed from the back like a harmless navy sweater was actually a V-neck diamond-pattern in shades of yellow and blue – as favoured by the more elderly of the nation's sports reporters. As my friend Tom oftens remarks, it's amazing how much time and money can be saved in the world of dating by close attention to detail. A white sock here, a pair of red braces there, a grey slip-on shoe, a swastika, are as often as not all one needs to tell you there's no point writing down phone numbers and forking out for expensive lunches because it's never going to be a runner.

'Mark, this is Colin and Pam's daughter, Bridget,' said Una, going all pink and fluttery. 'Bridget works in publishing, don't you, Bridget?'

'I do indeed,' I for some reason said, as if I were taking

part in a Capital radio phone-in and was about to ask Una if I could 'say hello' to my friends Jude, Sharon and Tom, my brother Jamie, everyone in the office, my mum and dad, and last of all all the people at the Turkey Curry Buffet.

'Well, I'll leave you two young people together,' said Una. 'Durr! I expect you're sick to death of us old fuddy-duddies.'

'Not at all,' said Mark Darcy awkwardly with a rather unsuccessful attempt at a smile, at which Una, after rolling her eyes, putting a hand to her bosom and giving a gay tinkling laugh, abandoned us with a toss of her head to a hideous silence.

'I. Um. Are you reading any, ah . . . Have you read any good books lately?' he said.

Oh, for God's sake.

I racked my brain frantically to think when I last read a proper book. The trouble with working in publishing is that reading in your spare time is a bit like being a dustman and snuffling through the pig bin in the evening. I'm halfway through *Men are from Mars, Women are from Venus*, which Jude lent me, but I didn't think Mark Darcy, though clearly odd, was ready to accept himself as a Martian quite yet. Then I had a brainwave.

'*Backlash*, actually, by Susan Faludi,' I said triumphantly. Hah! I haven't exactly read it as such, but feel I have as Sharon has been ranting about it so much. Anyway, completely safe option as no way diamond-pattern-jumpered goody-goody would have read five-hundred-page feminist treatise.

'Ah. Really?' he said. 'I read that when it first came out. Didn't you find there was rather a lot of special pleading?'

'Oh, well, not *too* much . . .' I said wildly, racking my

brains for a way to get off the subject. 'Have you been staying with your parents over New Year?'

'Yes,' he said eagerly. 'You too?'

'Yes. No. I was at a party in London last night. Bit hungover, actually.' I gabbled nervously so that Una and Mum wouldn't think I was so useless with men I was failing to talk to even Mark Darcy. 'But then I do think New Year's resolutions can't technically be expected to begin on New Year's Day, don't you? Since, because it's an extension of New Year's Eve, smokers are already on a smoking roll and cannot be expected to stop abruptly on the stroke of midnight with so much nicotine in the system. Also dieting on New Year's Day isn't a good idea as you can't eat rationally but really need to be free to consume whatever is necessary, moment by moment, in order to ease your hangover. I think it would be much more sensible if resolutions began generally on January the second.'

'Maybe you should get something to eat,' he said, then suddenly bolted off towards the buffet, leaving me standing on my own by the bookshelf while everybody stared at me, thinking, 'So that's why Bridget isn't married. She repulses men.'

The worst of it was that Una Alconbury and Mum wouldn't leave it at that. They kept making me walk round with trays of gherkins and glasses of cream sherry in a desperate bid to throw me into Mark Darcy's path yet again. In the end they were so crazed with frustration that the second I got within four feet of him with the gherkins Una threw herself across the room like Will Carling and said, 'Mark, you must take Bridget's telephone number before you go, then you can get in touch when you're in London.'

I couldn't stop myself turning bright red. I could feel it

climbing up my neck. Now Mark would think I'd put her up to it.

'I'm sure Bridget's life in London is quite full enough already, Mrs Alconbury,' he said. Humph. It's not that I wanted him to take my phone number or anything, but I didn't want him to make it perfectly obvious to everyone that he didn't want to. As I looked down I saw that he was wearing white socks with a yellow bumblebee motif.

'Can't I tempt you with a gherkin?' I said, to show I had had a genuine reason for coming over, which was quite definitely gherkin-based rather than phone-number-related.

'Thank you, no,' he said, looking at me with some alarm.

'Sure? Stuffed olive?' I pressed on.

'No, really.'

'Silverskin onion?' I encouraged. 'Beetroot cube?'

'Thank you,' he said desperately, taking an olive.

'Hope you enjoy it,' I said triumphantly.

Towards the end I saw him being harangued by his mother and Una, who marched him over towards me and stood just behind while he said stiffly, 'Do you need driving back to London? I'm staying here but I could get my car to take you.'

'What, all on its own?' I said.

He blinked at me.

'Durr! Mark has a company car and a driver, silly,' said Una.

'Thank you, that's very kind,' I said. 'But I shall be taking one of my trains in the morning.'

2 a.m. Oh, why am I so unattractive? Why? Even a man who wears bumblebee socks thinks I am horrible. Hate the

New Year. Hate everyone. Except Daniel Cleaver. Anyway, have got giant tray-sized bar of Cadbury's Dairy Milk left over from Christmas on dressing table, also amusing joke gin and tonic miniature. Am going to consume them and have fag.

Tuesday 3 January

9st 4 (terrifying slide into obesity – why? why?), alcohol units 6 (excellent), cigarettes 23 (v.g.), calories 2472.

9 a.m. Ugh. Cannot face thought of going to work. Only thing which makes it tolerable is thought of seeing Daniel again, but even that is inadvisable since am fat, have spot on chin, and desire only to sit on cushion eating chocolate and watching Xmas specials. It seems wrong and unfair that Christmas, with its stressful and unmanageable financial and emotional challenges, should first be forced upon one wholly against one's will, then rudely snatched away just when one is starting to get into it. Was really beginning to enjoy the feeling that normal service was suspended and it was OK to lie in bed as long as you want, put anything you fancy into your mouth, and drink alcohol whenever it should chance to pass your way, even in the mornings. Now suddenly we are all supposed to snap into self-discipline like lean teenage greyhounds.

10 p.m. Ugh. Perpetua, slightly senior and therefore thinking she is in charge of me, was at her most obnoxious and bossy, going on and on to the point of utter boredom about latest half-million-pound property she is planning to buy with her rich-but-overbred boyfriend, Hugo: 'Yars, yars, well it *is* north-facing but they've done something frightfully clever with the light.'

I looked at her wistfully, her vast, bulbous bottom swathed in a tight red skirt with a bizarre three-quarter-length striped waistcoat strapped across it. What a blessing to be born with such Sloaney arrogance. Perpetua could be the size of a Renault Espace and not give it a thought. How many hours, months, years, have I spent worrying about weight while Perpetua has been happily looking for lamps with porcelain cats as bases around the Fulham Road? She is missing out on a source of happiness, anyway. It is proved by surveys that happiness does not come from love, wealth or power but the pursuit of attainable goals: and what is a diet if not that?

On way home in end-of-Christmas denial I bought a packet of cut-price chocolate tree decorations and a £3.69 bottle of sparkling wine from Norway, Pakistan or similar. I guzzled them by the light of the Christmas tree, together with a couple of mince pies, the last of the Christmas cake and some Stilton, while watching *EastEnders*, imagining it was a Christmas special.

Now, though, I feel ashamed and repulsive. I can actually feel the fat splurging out from my body. Never mind. Sometimes you have to sink to a nadir of toxic fat envelopment in order to emerge, phoenix-like, from the chemical wasteland as a purged and beautiful Michelle Pfeiffer figure. Tomorrow new Spartan health and beauty regime will begin.

Mmmm. Daniel Cleaver, though. Love his wicked dissolute air, while being v. successful and clever. He was being v. funny today, telling everyone about his aunt thinking the onyx kitchen-roll holder his mother had given her for Christmas was a model of a penis. Was really v. amusing about it. Also asked me if I got anything nice for Christmas in rather flirty way. Think might wear short black skirt tomorrow.

Wednesday 4 January

9st 5 (state of emergency now as if fat has been stored in capsule form over Christmas and is being slowly released under skin), alcohol units 5 (better), cigarettes 20, calories 700 (v.g.).

4 p.m. Office. State of emergency. Jude just rang up from her portable phone in flood of tears, and eventually managed to explain, in a sheep's voice, that she had just had to excuse herself from a board meeting (Jude is Head of Futures at Brightlings) as she was about to burst into tears and was now trapped in the ladies' with Alice Cooper eyes and no make-up bag. Her boyfriend, Vile Richard (self-indulgent commitment phobic), whom she has been seeing on and off for eighteen months, had chucked her for asking him if he wanted to come on holiday with her. Typical, but Jude naturally was blaming it all on herself.

'I'm co-dependent. I asked for too much to satisfy my own neediness rather than need. Oh, if only I could turn back the clock.'

I immediately called Sharon and an emergency summit has been scheduled for 6.30 in Café Rouge. I hope I can get away without bloody Perpetua kicking up.

11 p.m. Strident evening. Sharon immediately launched into her theory on the Richard situation: 'Emotional fuckwittage', which is spreading like wildfire among men over thirty. As women glide from their twenties to thirties, Shazzer argues, the balance of power subtly shifts. Even the most outrageous minxes lose their nerve, wrestling with the first twinges of existential angst: fears of dying alone and being found three weeks later half-eaten by an Alsatian. Stereotypical notions of shelves, spinning wheels and sexual scrapheaps conspire to make you feel stupid, no matter how much time you spend thinking about Joanna Lumley and Susan Sarandon.

'And men like Richard,' fumed Sharon, 'play on the chink in the armour to wriggle out of commitment, maturity, honour and the natural progression of things between a man and a woman.'

By this time Jude and I were going, 'Shhh, shhh,' out of the corners of our mouths and sinking down into our coats. After all, there is nothing so unattractive to a man as strident feminism.

'How dare he say you were getting too serious by asking to go on holiday with him?' yelled Sharon. 'What is he *talking* about?'

Thinking moonily about Daniel Cleaver, I ventured that not all men are like Richard. At which point Sharon started on a long illustrative list of emotional fuckwittage in progress amongst our friends: one whose boyfriend of thirteen years refuses even to discuss living together; another who went out with a man four times who then chucked her because it was getting too serious; another who was pursued by a bloke for three months with impassioned proposals of marriage, only to find him ducking out three weeks after she succumbed and repeating the whole process with her best friend.

'We women are only vulnerable because we are a pioneer generation daring to refuse to compromise in love and relying on our own economic power. In twenty years' time men won't even dare start with fuckwittage because we will just *laugh in their faces*,' bellowed Sharon.

At this point Alex Walker, who works in Sharon's company, strolled in with a stunning blonde who was about eight times as attractive as him. He ambled over to us to say hi.

'Is this your new girlfriend?' asked Sharon.

'Well. Huh. You know, she thinks she is, but we're not going out, we're just sleeping together. I ought to stop it really, but, well . . .' he said, smugly.

'Oh, that is just such crap, you cowardly, dysfunctional little schmuck. Right. I'm going to talk to that woman,' said Sharon, getting up. Jude and I forcibly restrained her while Alex, looking panic-stricken, rushed back, to continue his fuckwittage unrumbled.

Eventually the three of us worked out a strategy for Jude. She must stop beating herself over the head with *Women Who Love Too Much* and instead think more towards *Men are from Mars, Women are from Venus*, which will help her to see Richard's behaviour less as a sign that she is co-dependent and loving too much and more in the light of him being like a Martian rubber band which needs to stretch away in order to come back.

'Yes, but does that mean I should call him or not?' said Jude.

'No,' said Sharon, just as I was saying, 'Yes.'

After Jude had gone – because she has to get up at 5.45 to go to the gym and see her personal shopper before work starts at 8.30 (mad) – Sharon and I were suddenly filled with remorse and self-loathing for not advising Jude simply to get rid of Vile Richard because he is vile. But then, as Sharon pointed out, last time we did that they got back together and she told him everything we'd said in a fit of reconciliatory confession and now it is cripplingly embarrassing every time we see him and he thinks we are the Bitch Queens from Hell – which, as Jude points out, is a misapprehension because, although we have discovered our Inner Bitches, we have not yet unlocked them.

Thursday 5 January

9st 3 (excellent progress – 2lb of fat spontaneously combusted through joy and sexual promise), alcohol units 6 (v.g. for party), cigarettes 12 (continuing good work), calories 1258 (love has eradicated need to pig out).

11 a.m. Office. Oh my God. Daniel Cleaver just sent me a message. Was trying to work on CV without Perpetua noticing (in preparation for improving career) when `Message Pending` suddenly flashed up on top of screen. Delighted by, well, anything – as always am if is not work – I quickly pressed `RMS Execute` and nearly jumped out of my skin when I saw `Cleave` at the bottom of the message. I instantly thought he had been able to tap into the computer and see that I was not getting on with my work. But then I read the message:

Message Jones
You appear to have forgotten your skirt. As I think is made perfectly clear in your contract of employment, staff are expected to be fully dressed at all times.
Cleave

Hah! Undeniably flirtatious. Thought for a little while whilst pretending to study tedious-beyond-belief manuscript from lunatic. Have never messaged Daniel Cleaver before but brilliant thing about messaging system is you can be really quite cheeky and informal, even to your boss. Also can spend ages practising. This is what sent.

Message Cleave
Sir, am appalled by message. Whilst skirt could reasonably be described as a little on the skimpy side (thrift being ever our watchword in editorial), consider it gross misrepresentation to describe said skirt as absent, and considering contacting union.
Jones

Waited in frenzy of excitement for reply. Sure enough. Message Pending quickly flashed up. Pressed RMS:

Will whoever has thoughtlessly removed the edited script of KAFKA'S MOTORBIKE from my desk PLEASE have the decency to return it immediately.
Diane

Aargh. After that: zilch.

Noon. Oh God. Daniel has not replied. Must be furious. Maybe he was being serious about the skirt. Oh God oh

God. Have been seduced by informality of messaging medium into being impertinent to boss.

12.10. Maybe he has not got it yet. If only could get message back. Think will go for walk and see if can somehow go into Daniel's office and erase it.

12.15. Hah. All explained. He is in meeting with Simon from Marketing. He gave me a look when walked past. Aha. Ahahahaha. Message Pending:

> Message Jones
> If walking past office was attempt to demonstrate presence of skirt can only say that it has failed parlously. Skirt is indisputably absent. Is skirt off sick?
> Cleave

Message Pending then flashed up again – immediately.

> Message Jones
> If skirt is indeed sick, please look into how many days sick leave skirt has taken in previous twelvemonth. Spasmodic nature of recent skirt attendance suggests malingering.
> Cleave

Just sending back:

> Message Cleave
> Skirt is demonstrably neither sick nor abscent. Appalled by management's blatently sizist attitude to skirt. Obsessive interest in skirt suggests management sick rather than skirt.
> Jones

Hmm. Think will cross last bit out as contains mild accusation of sexual harassment whereas v. much enjoying being sexually harassed by Daniel Cleaver.

Aaargh. Perpetua just walked past and started reading over shoulder. Just managed to press `Alt Screen` in nick of time but big mistake as merely put CV back up on screen.

'Do let me know when you've finished reading, won't you?' said Perpetua, with a nasty smirk. 'I'd hate to feel you were being *underused*.'

The second she was safely back on the phone – 'I mean frankly, Mr Birkett, what *is* the point in putting three to four bedrooms when it is going to be obvious the second we appear that bedroom four is an airing cupboard?' – I got back to work. This is what I am about to send.

```
Message Cleave
Skirt is demonstrably neither sick nor
abscent. Appalled by management's
blatentLy sizist attitude to skirt.
Considering appeal to industrial tribunal,
tabloids, etc.
Jones.
```

Oh dear. This was return message.

```
Message Jones
Absent, Jones, not abscent. Blatantly, not
blatently. Please attempt to acquire at
least perfunctory grasp of spelling. Though
by no means trying to suggest language fixed
rather than constantly adapting, fluctuat-
ing tool of communication (cf Hoenigswald)
computer spell check might help.
Cleave
```

Was just feeling crestfallen when Daniel walked past with Simon from Marketing and shot a very sexy look at my skirt with one eyebrow raised. Love the lovely computer messaging. Must work on spelling, though. After all, have degree in English.

Friday 6 January

5.45 p.m. Could not be more joyous. Computer messaging re: presence or otherwise of skirt continued obsessively all afternoon. Cannot imagine respected boss did stroke of work. Weird scenario with Perpetua (penultimate boss), since knew I was messaging and v. angry, but fact that was messaging ultimate boss gave self conflicting feelings of loyalty – distinctly un-level playing field where anyone with ounce of sense would say ultimate boss should hold sway.

Last message read:

```
Message Jones
Wish to send bouquet to ailing skirt over
weekend. Please supply home contact no asap
as cannot, for obvious reasons, rely on
given spelling of 'Jones' to search in file.
Cleave
```

Yesssss! Yesssssss! Daniel Cleaver wants my phone no. Am marvellous. Am irresistible Sex Goddess. Hurrah!

Sunday 8 January

9st 2 (v. bloody g. but what is point?), alcohol units 2 (excellent), cigarettes 7, calories 3100 (poor).

2 p.m. Oh God, why am I so unattractive? Cannot believe I convinced myself I was keeping the entire weekend free to work when in fact I was on permanent date-with-Daniel standby. Hideous, wasted two days glaring psychopathically at the phone, and eating things. Why hasn't he rung? Why? What's wrong with me? Why ask for my phone number if he wasn't going to ring, and if he was going to ring surely he would do it over the weekend? Must centre myself more. Will ask Jude about appropriate self-help book, possible Eastern-religion-based.

8 p.m. Phone call alert, which turned out to be just Tom, asking if there was any telephonic progress. Tom, who has taken, unflatteringly, to calling himself a hag-fag, has been sweetly supportive about the Daniel crisis. Tom has a theory that homosexuals and single women in their thirties have natural bonding: both being accustomed to disappointing their parents and being treated as freaks by society. He indulged me while I obsessed to him about my unattractiveness crisis – precipitated, as I told him, first by bloody Mark Darcy then by bloody Daniel at which point he said, I must say not particularly helpfully, 'Mark Darcy? But isn't he that famous lawyer – the human-rights guy?'

Hmmm. Well, anyway. What about my human right not to have to wander round with fearsome unattractiveness hang-up?

11 p.m. It is far too late for Daniel to ring. V. sad and traumatized.

Monday 9 January

9st 2, alcohol units 4, cigarettes 29, calories 770 (v.g. but at what price?).

Nightmare day in office. Watched the door for Daniel all morning: nothing. By 11.45 a.m. I was seriously alarmed. Should I raise an alert?

Then Perpetua suddenly bellowed into the phone: 'Daniel? He's gone to a meeting in Croydon. He'll be in tomorrow.' She banged the phone down and said, 'God, all these bloody girls ringing him up.'

Panic stricken, I reached for the Silk Cut. Which girls? What? Somehow I made it through the day, got home, and in a moment of insanity left a message on Daniel's answerphone, saying (oh no, I can't believe I did this), 'Hi, it's Jones here. I was just wondering how you are and if you wanted to meet for the skirt-health summit, like you said.'

The second I put the phone down I realized it was an emergency and rang Tom, who calmly said leave it to him: if he made several calls to the machine he could find the code which would let him play back and erase the message. Eventually he thought he'd cracked it, but unfortunately Daniel then answered the phone. Instead of saying, 'Sorry, wrong number,' Tom hung up. So now Daniel not only has the insane message but will think it's me who's rung his answerphone fourteen times this evening and then, when I did get hold of him, banged the phone down.

Tuesday 10 January

9st 1, alcohol units 2, cigarettes 0, calories 998 (excellent, v.g., perfect saint-style person).

Slunk into the office crippled with embarrassment about the message. I had resolved totally to detach myself from Daniel but then he appeared looking unnervingly sexy and started making everyone laugh so that I went all to pieces.

Suddenly, `Message Pending` flashed up on the top of my computer screen.

```
Message Jones
Thanks for your phone call.
Cleave.
```

My heart sank. That phone call was suggesting a date. Who replies by saying 'thanks' and leaves it at that unless they . . . but after a little thought, I sent back:

```
Message Cleave
Please shut up. I am very busy and
important.
Jones.
```

And after a few minutes more, he replied.

```
Message Jones
Sorry to interrupt, Jones, pressure must be
hellish. Over and out.
PS. I like your tits in that top.
Cleave
```

. . . And we were off. Frantic messaging continued all

week, culminating in him suggesting a date for Sunday night and me dizzyingly, euphorically, accepting. Sometimes I look around the office as we all tap away and wonder if anyone is doing any work at all.

(Is it just me or is Sunday a bizarre night for a first date? All wrong, like Saturday morning or Monday at 2 p.m.)

Sunday 15 January

9st (excellent), alcohol units 0, cigarettes 29 (v.v. bad, esp. in 2 hours), calories 3879 (repulsive), negative thoughts 942 (approx. based on av. per minute), minutes spent counting negative thoughts 127 (approx.).

6 p.m. Completely exhausted by entire day of date-preparation. Being a woman is worse than being a farmer – there is so much harvesting and crop spraying to be done: legs to be waxed, underarms shaved, eyebrows plucked, feet pumiced, skin exfoliated and moisturized, spots cleansed, roots dyed, eyelashes tinted, nails filed, cellulite massaged, stomach muscles exercised. The whole performance is so highly tuned you only need to neglect it for a few days for the whole thing to go to seed. Sometimes I wonder what I would be like if left to revert to nature – with a full beard and handlebar moustache on each shin, Dennis Healey eyebrows, face a graveyard of dead skin cells, spots erupting, long curly fingernails like Struwelpeter, blind as bat and stupid runt of species as no contact lenses, flabby body flobbering around. Ugh, ugh. Is it any wonder girls have no confidence?

7 p.m. Cannot believe this has happened. On the way to the bathroom, to complete final farming touches, I noticed the answerphone light was flashing: Daniel.

'Look, Jones. I'm really sorry. I think I'm going to have to give tonight a miss. I've got a presentation at ten in the morning and a pile of forty-five spreadsheets to get through.'

Cannot believe it. Am stood up. Entire waste of whole day's bloody effort and hydro-electric body-generated power. However, one must not live one's life through men but must be complete in oneself as a woman of substance.

9 p.m. Still, he is in top-level job. Maybe he didn't want to ruin first date with underlying work-panic.

11 p.m. Humph. He might have bloody well rung again, though. Is probably out with someone thinner.

5 a.m. What's wrong with me? I'm completely alone. Hate Daniel Cleaver. Am going to have nothing more to do with him. Am going to get weighed.

Monday 16 January

9 st 2 (from where? why? why?), alcohol units 0, cigarettes 20, calories 1500, positive thoughts 0.

10.30 a.m. Office. Daniel is still locked in his meeting. Maybe it *was* a genuine excuse.

1 p.m. Just saw Daniel leaving for lunch. He has not messaged me or anything. V. depressed. Going shopping.

11.50 p.m. Just had dinner with Tom in Harvey Nichols Fifth Floor, who was obsessing about a pretentious-sounding 'freelance film maker' called Jerome. Moaned to him about Daniel, who was in meetings all afternoon and only managed to say, 'Hi, Jones, how's the skirt?' at 4.30. Tom said not to be paranoid, give it time, but I could tell he was not concentrating and only wanted to talk about Jerome as suffused with sex-lust.

Tuesday 24 January

Heaven-sent day. At 5.30, like a gift from God, Daniel appeared, sat himself on the edge of my desk, with his back to Perpetua, took out his diary and murmured, 'How are you fixed for Friday?'

Yessssss! Yessssss!

Friday 27 January

9st 3 (but stuffed with Genoan food), alcohol units 8, cigarettes 400 (feels like), calories 875.

Huh. Had dream date at an *intime* little Genoan restaurant near Daniel's flat.

'Um . . . right. I'll get a taxi,' I blurted awkwardly as we stood in the street afterwards. Then he lightly brushed a hair from my forehead, took my cheek in his hand and kissed me, urgently, desperately. After a while he held me hard against him and whispered throatily, 'I don't think you'll be needing that taxi, Jones.'

The second we were inside his flat we fell upon each other like beasts: shoes, jackets, strewn in a trail across the room.

'I don't think this skirt's looking at all well,' he murmured. 'I think it should lie down on the floor.' As he started to undo the zip he whispered, 'This is just a bit of fun, OK? I don't think we should start getting involved.' Then, caveat in place, he carried on with the zip. Had it not been for Sharon and the fuckwittage and the fact I'd just drunk the best part of a bottle of wine, I think I would have sunk powerless into his arms. As it was, I leapt to my feet, pulling up my skirt.

'That is just such crap,' I slurred. 'How dare you be so fraudulently flirtatious, cowardly and dysfunctional? I am not interested in emotional fuckwittage. Goodbye.'

It was great. You should have seen his face. But now I am home I am sunk into gloom. I may have been right, but my reward, I know, will be to end up all alone, half-eaten by an Alsatian.

FEBRUARY

Valentine's Day Massacre

Wednesday 1 February

9st, alcohol units 9, cigarettes 28 (but will soon give up for Lent so might as well smoke self into disgusted smoking frenzy), calories 3826.

Spent the weekend struggling to remain disdainfully buoyant after the Daniel fuckwittage débâcle. I kept saying the words, 'Self-respect' and 'Huh' over and over till I was dizzy, trying to barrage out, 'But I lurrrve him.' Smoking was v. bad. Apparently there is a Martin Amis character who is so crazily addicted that he starts wanting a cigarette even when he's smoking one. That's me. It was good ringing up Sharon to boast about being Mrs Iron Knickers but when I rang Tom he saw straight through it and said, 'Oh, my poor darling,' which made me go silent trying not to burst into self-pitying tears.

'You watch,' warned Tom. 'He'll be gagging for it now. Gagging.'

'No, he won't,' I said sadly. 'I've blown it.'

On Sunday went for huge, lard-smeared lunch at my parents'. Mother is bright orange and more opinionated than ever, having just returned from week in Albufeira with Una Alconbury and Nigel Coles' wife, Audrey.

Mum had been to church and suddenly realized in a St Paul-on-road-to-Damascus-type blinding flash that the vicar is gay.

'It's just laziness, darling,' was her view on the whole homosexuality issue. 'They simply can't be bothered to relate to the opposite sex. Look at your Tom. I really think if that boy had anything about him he'd be going out with you properly instead of all this ridiculous, "friends" nonsense.'

'Mother,' I said. 'Tom has known he was a homosexual since he was ten.'

'Oh, darling! Honestly! You know how people get these silly ideas. You can always talk them out of it.'

'Does that mean if I talked to you really persuasively you'd leave Dad and start an affair with Auntie Audrey?'

'Now you're just being silly, darling,' she said.

'Exactly,' Dad joined in. 'Auntie Audrey looks like a kettle.'

'Oh, for heaven's sake, Colin,' Mum snapped, which struck me as odd as she doesn't usually snap at Dad.

My dad, somewhat bizarrely, insisted on giving my car a full service before I left, even though I assured him there was nothing wrong with it. I rather showed myself up by not remembering how to open the bonnet.

'Have you noticed anything odd about your mother?' he said in a stiff, embarrassed way as he fiddled around with the oil stick, wiping it with rags and plunging it back in a not unworrying manner, if one were a Freudian. Which I am not.

'You mean apart from being bright orange?' I said.

'Well yes, and . . . well, you know, the usual, er *qualities*.'

'She did seem unusually aerated about homosexuality.'

'Oh no, that was just the Vicar's new vestments which set her off this morning. They *were* a little on the frou-frou side, to tell the truth. He's just come back from a trip to Rome with the Abbot of Dumfries. Dressed from head to toe in rose pink. No, I mean did you notice anything different from *usual* about Mummy?'

I racked my brains. 'I can't say I did, to be honest, other than seeming very sort of blooming and confident.'

'Hmmm,' he said. 'Anyway. Best get off before it gets dark. Send my love to Jude. How's she doing?'

Then he hit the bonnet in an off-you-go sort of way – but so hard that I had a feeling he might have broken his hand.

Thought all would be resolved with Daniel on Monday but he wasn't there. Nor yesterday. Work has become like going to a party in order to get off with someone and finding they haven't turned up. Worried about own ambition, career prospects and moral seriousness as seem to reduce everything to level of scout disco. Eventually managed to worm out of Perpetua that Daniel has gone to New York. He will clearly by now have got off with thin American cool person called Winona who puts out, carries a gun and is everything I am not.

On top of everything else, must go to Smug Married dinner party at Magda and Jeremy's tonight. Such occasions always reduce my ego to size of snail, which is not to say am not grateful to be asked. I love Magda and Jeremy. Sometimes I stay at their house, admiring the crisp sheets and many storage jars full of different kinds of pasta, imagining that they are my parents. But when they are together with their married friends I feel as if I have turned into Miss Havisham.

11.45 p.m. Oh God. It was me, four married couples and Jeremy's brother (forget it, red braces and face. Calls girls 'fillies').

'So,' bellowed Cosmo, pouring me a drink. 'How's your love-life?'

Oh no. Why do they do this? Why? Maybe the Smug Marrieds only mix with other Smug Marrieds and don't known how to relate to individuals any more. Maybe they really do want to patronize us and make us feel like failed human beings. Or maybe they are in such a sexual rut they're thinking, 'There's a whole other world out there,' and hoping for vicarious thrills by getting us to tell them the roller-coaster details of our sex lives.

'Yes, why aren't you married yet, Bridget?' sneered Woney (babytalk for Fiona, married to Jeremy's friend Cosmo) with a thin veneer of concern whilst stroking her pregnant stomach.

Because I don't want to end up like you, you fat, boring, Sloaney milch cow, was what I should have said, or, *Because if I had to cook Cosmo's dinner then get into the same bed as him just once, let alone every night, I'd tear off my own head and eat it*, or, *Because actually, Woney, underneath my clothes, my entire body is covered in scales*. But I didn't because, ironically enough, I didn't want to hurt her feelings. So I merely simpered apologetically, at which point someone called Alex piped up, 'Well, you know, once you get past a certain age . . .'

'Exactly . . . All the decent chaps have been snapped up,'

said Cosmo, slapping his fat stomach and smirking so that his jowls wobbled.

At dinner Magda had placed me, in an incestuous-sex-sandwich sort of way, between Cosmo and Jeremy's crashing bore of a brother. 'You really ought to hurry up and get sprogged up, you know, old girl,' said Cosmo, pouring a quarter of a pint of '82 Pauillac straight down his throat. 'Time's running out.'

By this time I'd had a good half-pint of '82 Pauillac myself. 'Is it one in three marriages that end in divorce now or one in two?' I slurred with a pointless attempt at sarcasm.

'Seriously, old girl,' he said, ignoring me. 'Office is full of them, single girls over thirty. Fine physical specimens. Can't get a chap.'

'That's not a problem I have, actually,' I breathed, waving my fag in the air.

'Ooh. Tell us more,' said Woney.

'So who is it, then?' said Cosmo.

'Getting a bit of a shag, old girl?' said Jeremy. All eyes turned to me, beadily. Mouths open, slavering.

'It's none of your business,' I said hoity-toitily.

'So she hasn't got a man!' crowed Cosmo.

'Oh my God, it's eleven o'clock,' shrieked Woney. 'The babysitter!' and they all leapt to their feet and started getting read to go home.

'God, sorry about that lot. Will you be OK, hon?' whispered Magda, who knew how I was feeling.

'Wanta lift or anything?' said Jeremy's brother, following it up with a belch.

'Actually, I'm going on to a nightclub.' I trilled, hurrying out into the street. 'Thanks for a super evening!'

Then I got into a taxi and burst into tears.

Midnight. Har har. Just called Sharon.

'You should have said "I'm not married because I'm a *Singleton*, you smug, prematurely ageing, narrow-minded morons,"' Shazzer ranted. '"And because there's more than one bloody way to live: one in four households are single, most of the royal family are single, the nation's young men have been proved by surveys to be *completely unmarriageable*, and as a result there's a whole generation of single girls like me with their own incomes and homes who have lots of fun and don't need to wash anyone else's socks. We'd be as happy as sandboys if people like you didn't conspire to make us feel stupid just because you're jealous."'

'Singletons!' I shouted happily. 'Hurrah for the Singletons!'

Sunday 5 February

Still no word from Daniel. Cannot face thought of entire Sunday stretching ahead with everyone else in the world except me in bed with someone giggling and having sex. Worst of it is, only a week and a bit to go till impending Valentine's Day humiliation. No way will I get any cards. Toy with idea of flirting energetically with anyone I think might be induced to send me one, but dismiss as immoral. Will just have to take total indignity on the chin.

Hmm. I know. Think I'll go and see Mum and Dad again as am worried about Dad. Then will feel like caring angel or saint.

2 p.m. The last remaining tiny bathmat of security has been pulled from under my feet. Magnanimous offer to pay caring surprise visit met by odd-sounding Dad on end of phone.

'Er . . . I'm not sure, dear. Could you hang on?'

I reeled. Part of the arrogance of youth (well, I say 'youth') is the assumption that your parents will drop whatever they are doing and welcome you with open arms the second you decide to turn up. He was back. 'Bridget, look, your mother and I are having some problems. Can we ring you later in the week?'

Problems? What problems? I tried to get Dad to explain but got nowhere. What is going on? Is the whole world doomed to emotional trauma? Poor Dad. Am I to be the tragic victim of a broken home now, on top of everything else?

Monday 6 February

8st 12 (heavy internal weight completely vanished – mystery), alcohol units 1 (v.g.), cigarettes 9 (v.g.), calories 1800 (g.).

Daniel will be back in the office today. I shall be poised and cool and remember that I am a woman of substance and do not need men in order to be complete, especially not him. Am not going to message him or indeed take any notice of him whatsoever.

9.30 a.m. Humph. Daniel does not seem to be here yet.

9.35 a.m. Still no sign of Daniel.

9.36 a.m. Oh God, oh God. Maybe he's fallen in love in New York and stayed there.

9.47 a.m. Or gone to Las Vegas and got married.

9.50 a.m. Hmmm. think will go inspect make-up in case he does come in.

10.05 a.m. Heart gave great lurch when got back from loos and saw Daniel standing with Simon from Marketing at the photocopier. The last time I saw him he was lying on his sofa looking completely nonplussed while I fastened my skirt and ranted about fuckwittage. Now he was looking all sort of 'I've been away' – fresh faced and healthy-looking. As I passed he looked pointedly at my skirt and gave me a huge grin.

10.30 a.m. `Message Pending` flashed up on screen. Pressed `RMS` to pick up message.

```
Message Jones
Frigid cow.
Cleave.
```

I laughed. I couldn't help myself. When I looked across to his little glass office he was smiling at me in a relieved and fond sort of way. Anyway, am not going to message him back.

10.35 a.m. Seems rude not to reply, though.

10.45 a.m. God, I'm bored.

10.47 a.m. I'll just send him a tiny friendly message, nothing flirtatious, just to restore good relations.

11.00 a.m. Tee hee. Just logged on as Perpetua to give Daniel a fright.

```
Message Cleave
It is hard enough as it is, trying to meet
your targets without people wasting my
team's time with non-essential messages.
Perpetua
P.S. Bridget's skirt is not feeling at all
well and have sent it home.
```

10 p.m. Mmmm. Daniel and I messaged each other all day. But there is no way I am going to sleep with him.

Rang Mum and Dad again tonight but no one answered. V. weird.

Thursday 9 February

9st 2 (extra fat presumably caused by winter whale blubber), alcohol units 4, cigarettes 12 (v.g.), calories 2845 (v. cold).

9 p.m. V. much enjoying the Winter Wonderland and reminder that we are at the mercy of the elements, and should not concentrate so hard on being sophisticated or hardworking but on staying warm and watching the telly.

This is the third time I have called Mum and Dad this week and got no reply. Maybe The Gables has been cut off by the snow? In desperation, I pick up the phone and dial my brother Jamie's number in Manchester, only to get one of his hilarious answerphone messages: the sound of running water and Jamie pretending to be President Clinton in the White House, then a toilet flushing and his pathetic girlfriend tittering in the background.

9.15 p.m. Just called Mum and Dad three times in a row, letting it ring twenty times each time. Eventually Mum picked it up sounding odd and saying she couldn't talk now but would call me at the weekend.

Saturday 11 February

8st 13, alcohol units 4, cigarettes 18, calories 1467 (but burnt off by shopping).

Just got home from shopping to message from my dad asking if I would meet him for lunch on Sunday. I went hot and cold. My dad does not come up to London to have lunch with me on his own on Sundays. He has roast beef, or salmon and new potatoes, at home with Mum.

'Don't ring back,' the message said. 'I'll just see you tomorrow.'

What's going on? I went round the corner, shaking, for some Silk Cut. Got back to find message from Mum. She too is coming to see me for lunch tomorrow, apparently. She'll bring a piece of salmon with her, and will be here about 1 o'clock.

Rang Jamie again and got 20 seconds of Bruce Springsteen and then Jamie growling, 'Baby, I was born to run . . . out of time on the answerphone.'

Sunday 12 February

8st 13, alcohol units 5, cigarettes 23 (hardly surprising), calories 1647.

11 a.m. Oh God, I can't have them both arriving at the same time. It is too Brian Rix for words. Maybe the whole lunch thing is just a parental practical joke brought on by over-exposure of my parents to Noel Edmonds, popular television and similar. Perhaps my mother will arrive with a live salmon flipping skittishly on a lead and announce that she is leaving Dad for it. Maybe Dad will appear hanging upside-down outside the window dressed as a Morris dancer, crash in and start hitting Mum over the head with a sheep's bladder; or suddenly fall face downwards out of the airing cupboard with a plastic knife stuck in his back. The only thing which can possibly get everything back on course is a Bloody Mary. It's nearly the afternoon, after all.

12.05 p.m. Mum called. 'Let *him* come, then,' she said. 'Let him bloody well have his own way as usual.' (My mum does not swear. She says things like 'ruddy' and 'Oh my godfathers'.) 'I'll be all right on my bloody own. I'll just clean the house like Germaine sodding Greer and the Invisible Woman.' (Could she possibly, conceivably, have been drunk? My mum has drunk nothing but a single cream sherry on a Sunday night since 1952, when she got slightly tipsy on a pint of cider at Mavis Enderby's twenty-first and has never let herself or anyone else forget it. 'There's nothing worse than a woman drunk, darling.')

'Mum. No. Couldn't we all talk this through together over lunch?' I said, as if this were *Sleepless in Seattle* and lunch was going to end up with Mum and Dad holding hands and me winking cutely at the camera, wearing a luminous rucksack.

'Just you wait,' she said darkly. 'You'll find out what men are like.'

'But I already . . .' I began.

'I'm going out, darling,' she said. 'I'm going out to get *laid*.'

At 2 o'clock Dad arrived at the door with a neatly folded copy of the *Sunday Telegraph*. As he sat down on the sofa, his face crumpled and tears began to splosh down his cheeks.

'She's been like this since she went to Albufeira with Una Alconbury and Audrey Coles,' he sobbed, trying to wipe his cheek with his fist. 'When she got back she started saying she wanted to be paid for doing the housework, and she'd wasted her life being our slave.' (*Our* slave? I knew it. This is all my fault. If I were a better person, Mum would not have stopped loving Dad.) 'She wants me to move out for a while, she says, and . . . and . . .' He collapsed in quiet sobs.

'And what, Dad?'

'She said I thought the clitoris was something from Nigel Coles's lepidoptery collection.'

Monday 13 February

9st 1, alcohol units 5, cigarettes 0 (spiritual enrichment removes need to smoke – massive breakthrough), calories 2845.

Though heartbroken by my parents' distress, I have to admit parallel and shameful feeling of smugness over my new role as carer and, though I say it myself, wise counsellor. It is so long since I have done anything at all for anyone else that it is a totally new and heady sensation. This is what has been missing in my life. I am having fantasies about becoming a Samaritan or Sunday school teacher, making soup for the homeless (or, as my friend Tom suggested, darling mini-bruschettas with pesto sauce), or even retraining as a doctor. Maybe going out with a doctor would be better still, both sexually and spiritually fulfilling. I even began to wonder about putting an ad in the lonely hearts column of the *Lancet*. I could take his messages, tell patients wanting night visits to bugger off, cook him little goats cheese soufflés, then end up in a foul mood with him when I am sixty, like Mum.

Oh God. Valentine's Day tomorrow. Why? Why? Why is entire world geared to make people not involved in romance feel stupid when everyone knows romance does not work anyway. Look at royal family. Look at Mum and Dad.

Valentine's Day purely commercial, cynical enterprise, anyway. Matter of supreme indifference to me.

Tuesday 14 February

9st, alcohol units 2 (romantic Valentine's Day treat – 2 bottles Becks, on own, huh), cigarettes 12, calories 1545.

8 a.m. Oooh, goody. Valentine's Day. Wonder if the post has come yet. Maybe there will be a card from Daniel. Or a secret admirer. Or some flowers or heart-shaped chocolates. Quite excited, actually.

Brief moment of wild joy when discovered bunch of roses in the hallway. Daniel! Rushed down and gleefully picked them up just as the downstairs-flat door opened and Vanessa came out.

'Ooh, they look nice,' she said enviously. 'Who are they from?'

'I don't know!' I said coyly, glancing down at the card. 'Ah . . .' I tailed off. 'They're for you.'

'Never mind. Look, this is for you,' said Vanessa, encouragingly. It was an Access bill.

Decided to have cappuccino and chocolate croissants on way to work to cheer self up. Do not care about figure. Is no point as no one loves or cares about me.

On the way in on the tube you could see who had had Valentine cards and who hadn't. Everyone was looking round trying to catch each other's eye and either smirking or looking away defensively.

Got into the office to find Perpetua had a bunch of flowers the size of a sheep on her desk.

'Well, Bridget!' she bellowed so that everyone could hear. 'How many did you get?'

I slumped into my seat muttering, 'Shud-urrrrrrp,' out of the side of my mouth like a humiliated teenager.

'Come on! How many?'

I thought she was going to get hold of my earlobe and start twisting it or something.

'The whole thing is ridiculous and meaningless. Complete commercial exploitation.'

'I *knew* you didn't get any,' crowed Perpetua. It was only then that I noticed Daniel was listening to us across the room and laughing.

Wednesday 15 February

Unexpected surprise. Was just leaving flat for work when noticed there was a pink envelope on the table – obviously a late Valentine – which said, 'To the Dusky Beauty'. For a moment I was excited, imagining it was for me and suddenly seeing myself as a dark, mysterious object of desire to men out in the street. Then I remembered bloody Vanessa and her slinky dark bob. Humph.

9 p.m. Just got back and card is still there.

10 p.m. Still there.

11 p.m. Unbelievable. The card is still there. Maybe Vanessa hasn't got back yet.

Thursday 16 February

8st 12 (weight loss through use of stairs), alcohol units 0 (excellent), cigarettes 5 (excellent), calories 2452 (not v.g.), times gone down stairs to check for Valentine-type envelope 18 (bad psychologically but v.g. exercise-wise).

The card is still there! Obviously it is like eating the last Milk Tray or taking the last slice of cake. We are both too polite to take it.

Friday 17 February

8st 12, alcohol units 1 (v.g.), cigarettes 2 (v.g.), calories 3241 (bad but burnt off by stairs), checks on card 12 (obsessive).

9 a.m. Card is still there.

9 p.m. Still there.

9.30 p.m. Still there. Could stand it no longer. Could tell Vanessa was in as cooking smells emanating from flat, so knocked on door. 'I think this must be for you,' I said, holding out the card as she opened the door.

'Oh, I thought it must be for you,' she said.

'Shall we open it?' I said.

'OK.' I handed it to her, she gave it back to me, giggling. I gave it back to her. I love girls.

'Go on,' I said, and she slit open the envelope with the kitchen knife she was holding. It was rather an arty card – as if it might have been bought in an art gallery.

She pulled a face.

'Means nothing to me,' she said, holding out the card.

Inside it said, 'A piece of ridiculous and meaningless commercial exploitation – for my darling little frigid cow.'

I let out a high-pitched noise.

10 p.m. Just called Sharon and recounted whole thing to her. She said I should not allow my head to be turned by a cheap card and should lay off Daniel as he is not a very nice person and no good will come of it.

Called Tom for second opinion, particularly on whether I should call Daniel over the weekend. '*Nooooooo*!' he yelled. He asked me various probing questions: for example, what Daniel's behaviour had been like over the last few days when, having sent the card, he had had no response from me. I reported that he had seemed flirtier than usual. Tom's prescription was wait till next week and remain aloof.

Saturday 18 February

9st, alcohol units 4, cigarettes 6, calories 2746, correct lottery numbers 2 (v.g.).

At last I got to the bottom of Mum and Dad. I was beginning to suspect a post-Portuguese-holiday Shirley-Valentine-style scenario and that I would open the *Sunday People* to see my mother sporting dyed blonde hair and a leopardskin top sitting on a sofa with someone in stone-washed jeans called Gonzales and explaining that, if you really love someone, a forty-six-year age gap really doesn't matter.

Today she asked me to meet her for lunch at the coffee place in Dickens and Jones and I asked her outright if she was seeing someone else.

'No. There is no one else,' she said, staring into the distance with a look of melancholy bravery I swear she has copied from Princess Diana.

'So why are you being so mean to Dad?' I said.

'Darling, it's merely a question of realizing, when your father retired, that I had spent thirty-five years without a break running his home and bringing up his children—'

'Jamie and I are your children too,' I interjected, hurt.

'—and that as far as he was concerned his lifetime's work was over and mine was still carrying on, which is exactly how I used to feel when you were little and it got to the weekends. You only get one life. I've just made a decision to change things a bit and spend what's left of mine looking after me for a change.'

As I went to the till to pay, I was thinking it all over and trying, as a feminist, to see Mum's point of view. Then my eye was caught by a tall, distinguished-looking man with grey hair, a European-style leather jacket and one of those gentleman's handbag things. He was looking into the café, tapping his watch and raising his eyebrows. I wheeled round and caught my mother mouthing, 'Won't be a mo,' and nodding towards me apologetically.

I didn't say anything to Mum at the time, just said goodbye, then doubled back and followed her to make sure I wasn't imagining things. Sure enough, I eventually found her in the perfume department wandering round with the tall smoothie, spraying her wrists with everything in sight, holding them up to his face and laughing coquettishly.

Got home to answerphone message from my brother Jamie. Called him straight away and told him everything.

'Oh, for God's sake, Bridge,' he said, roaring with laughter. 'You're so obsessed with sex if you saw Mum taking communion you'd think she was giving the Vicar a blow-job. Get any Valentines this year, did you?'

'Actually, yes,' I breathed crossly. At which he burst out laughing again, then said he had to go because he and Becca were off to do Tai Chi in the park.

Sunday 19 February

8st 13 (v.g. but purely through worry), alcohol units 2 (but the Lord's Day), cigarettes 7, calories 2100.

Called Mum up to confront her about the late-in-life smoothie I saw her with after our lunch.

'Oh, you must mean Julian,' she trilled.

This was an immediate giveaway. My parents do not describe their friends by their Christian names. It is always Una Alconbury, Audrey Coles, Brian Enderby: 'You know David Ricketts, darling – married to Anthea Ricketts, who's in the Lifeboat.' It's a gesture to the fact that they know in their hearts I have no idea who Mavis Enderby is, even though they're going to talk about Brian and Mavis Enderby for the next forty minutes as if I've known them intimately since I was four.

I knew straight away that Julian would not turn out to be involved in any Lifeboat luncheons, nor would he have a wife who was in any Lifeboats, Rotaries or Friends of St George's. I sensed also that she had met him in Portugal, before the trouble with Dad, and he might well turn out to be not so much Julian but Julio. I sensed that, let's face it, Julio *was* the trouble with Dad.

I confronted her with this hunch. She denied it. She even came out with some elaborately concocted tale about 'Julian' bumping into her in the Marble Arch Marks and Spencer, making her drop her new Le Creuset terrine dish on her foot and taking her for a coffee in Selfridges from which sprang a firm platonic friendship based entirely on department store coffee shops.

Why, when people are leaving their partners because

they're having an affair with someone else, do they think it will seem better to pretend there is no one else involved? Do they think it will be less hurtful for their partners to think they just walked out because they couldn't stand them any more and then had the good fortune to meet some tall Omar Sharif-figure with a gentleman's handbag two weeks afterwards while the ex-partner is spending his evenings bursting into tears at the sight of the toothbrush mug? It's like those people who invent a lie as an excuse rather than the truth, even when the truth is better than the lie.

I once heard my friend Simon cancelling a date with a girl – on whom he was really keen – because he had a spot with a yellow head just to the right of his nose, and because, owing to a laundry crisis he had gone to work in a ludicrous late-seventies jacket, assuming he could pick his normal jacket up from the cleaner's at lunchtime, but the cleaners hadn't done it.

He took it into his head, therefore, to tell the girl he couldn't see her because his sister had turned up unexpectedly for the evening and he had to entertain her, adding wildly that he also had to watch some videos for work before the morning; at which point the girl reminded him that he'd told her he didn't have any brothers or sisters and suggested he come and watch the videos at her place while she cooked him supper. However, there were no work videos to take round and watch, so he had to construct a further cobweb of lies. The incident culminated with the girl, convinced he was having an affair with someone else when it was only their second date, chucking him, and Simon spending the evening getting hammered alone with his spot, wearing his seventies jacket.

I tried to explain to Mum that she wasn't telling the truth, but she was so suffused with lust that she had lost sight of, well, everything.

'You're really becoming very cynical and suspicious, darling,' she said. 'Julio' – aha!' ahahahahahaha! – 'is just a friend. I just need some *space*.'

So, it transpired, in order to oblige, Dad is moving into the Alconburys' dead granny's flat at the bottom of their garden.

Tuesday 21 February

V. tired. Dad has taken to ringing up several times in the night, just to talk.

Wednesday 22 February

9st, alcohol units 2, cigarettes 19, fat units 8 (unexpectedly repulsive notion: never before faced reality of lard splurging from bottom and thighs under skin. Must revert to calorie-counting tomorrow).

Tom was completely right. I have been so preoccupied with Mum and Dad, and so tired from taking Dad's distraught phone calls, I have hardly been noticing Daniel at all: with the miraculous result that he has been all over me. I made a complete arse of myself today, though. I got in the lift to go out for a sandwich and found Daniel in there with Simon from Marketing, talking about footballers being arrested for throwing matches. 'Have you heard about this, Bridget?' said Daniel.

'Oh yes,' I lied, groping for an opinion. 'Actually, I think it's all rather petty. I know it's a thuggish way to behave, but as long as they didn't actually set light to anyone I don't see what all the fuss is about.'

Simon looked at me as if I was mad and Daniel stared for a moment and then burst out laughing. He just laughed and laughed till he and Simon got out and then turned back and said, 'Marry me,' as the doors closed between us. Hmmmm.

Thursday 23 February

8st 13 (if only could stay under 9st and not keep bobbing up and down like drowning corpse – drowning in fat), alcohol units 2, cigarettes 17 (pre-shag nerves – understandable), calories 775 (last-ditch attempt to get down to 8st 7 before tomorrow).

8 p.m. Blimey. Computer messaging somehow whipped itself up to fever pitch. At 6 o'clock I resolutely put my coat on and left, only to meet Daniel getting into my lift on the floor below. There we were, just him and me, caught in a massive electrical-charge field, pulled together irresistibly, like a pair of magnets. Then suddenly the lift stopped and we broke apart, panting, as Simon from Marketing got in wearing a hideous beige raincoat over his fat frame. 'Bridget,' he said smirkily, as I involuntarily straightened my skirt, 'you look as if you've been caught throwing matches.'

As I left the building Daniel popped out after me and asked me to have dinner with him tomorrow. Yessss!

Midnight. Ugh. Completely exhausted. Surely it is not normal to be revising for a date as if it were a job interview? Suspect Daniel's enormously well-read brain may turn out to be something of a nuisance if things develop. Maybe I should have fallen for someone younger and mindless who would cook for me, wash all my clothes and agree with everything I say. Since leaving work I have nearly slipped a disc, wheezing through a step aerobics class, scratched my naked body for seven minutes with a stiff brush; cleaned the flat; filled the fridge, plucked my eyebrows, skimmed the papers and the *Ultimate Sex Guide*, put the washing in and waxed my own legs, since it was too late to book an appointment. Ended up kneeling on a towel trying to pull off a wax strip firmly stuck to the back of my calf while watching *Newsnight* in an effort to drum up some interesting opinions about things. My back hurts, my head aches and my legs are bright red and covered in lumps of wax.

Wise people will say Daniel should like me just as I am, but I am a child of *Cosmopolitan* culture, have been traumatized by supermodels and too many quizzes and know that neither my personality nor my body is up to it if left to its own devices. I can't take the pressure. I am going to cancel and spend the evening eating doughnuts in a cardigan with egg on it.

Saturday 25 February

8st 10 (miracle: sex proved indeed to be best form of exercise), alcohol units 0, cigarettes 0, calories 200 (at last have found the secret of not eating: simply replace food with sex).

6 p.m. Oh joy. Have spent the day in a state I can only describe as shag-drunkenness, mooning about the flat, smiling, picking things up and putting them down again. It was so lovely. The only down points were 1) immediately it was over Daniel said, 'Damn. I meant to take the car into the Citroën garage,' and 2) when I got up to go to the bathroom he pointed out that I had a pair of tights stuck to the back of my calf.

But as the rosy clouds begin to disperse, I begin to feel alarm. What now? No plans were made. Suddenly I realize I am waiting for the phone again. How can it be that the situation between the sexes after a first night remains so agonizingly imbalanced? Feel as if I have just sat an exam and must wait for my results.

11 p.m. Oh God. Why hasn't Daniel rung? Are we going out now, or what? How come my mum can slip easily from one relationship to another and I can't even get the simplest thing off the ground. Maybe their generation is just better at getting on with relationships? Maybe they don't mooch about being all paranoid and diffident. Maybe it helps if you've never read a self-help book in your life.

Sunday 26 February

9st, alcohol units 5 (drowning sorrows), cigarettes 23 (fumigating sorrows), calories 3856 (smothering sorrows in fat-duvet).

Awake, alone, to find myself imagining my mother in bed with Julio. Consumed with repulsion at vision of parental, or rather demi-parental sex; outrage on behalf of father; heady, selfish optimism at example of another thirty years of unbridled passion ahead of me (not unrelated to frequent thoughts of Joanna Lumley and Susan Sarandon); but mainly extreme sense of jealousy of failure and foolishness at being in bed alone on Sunday morning while my mother aged over sixty is probably just about to do it for the second . . . Oh my God. No. I can't bear to think about it.

MARCH

Severe Birthday-Related Thirties Panic

Saturday 4 March

9st (what is point of dieting for whole of Feb when end up exactly same weight at start of March as start of Feb? Huh. Am going to stop getting weighed and counting things every day as no sodding point).

My mother has become a force I no longer recognize. She burst into my flat this morning as I sat slumped in my dressing gown, sulkily painting my toenails and watching the preamble to the racing.

'Darling, can I leave these here for a few hours?' she trilled, flinging an armful of carrier bags down and heading for my bedroom.

Minutes later, in a fit of mild curiosity, I slobbed after her to see what she was doing. She was sitting in front of the mirror in an expensive-looking coffee-coloured bra-slip, mascara-ing her eyelashes with her mouth wide open (necessity of open mouth during mascara application great unexplained mystery of nature).

'Don't you think you should get dressed, darling?'

She looked stunning: skin clear, hair shining. I caught sight of myself in the mirror. I really should have taken my make-up off last night. One side of my hair was plastered to my head, the other sticking out in a series of peaks and horns. It is as if the hairs on my head have a life of their own, behaving perfectly sensibly all day, then waiting till I drop off to sleep and starting to run and jump about childishly, saying, 'Now what shall we do?'

'You know,' said Mum, dabbing Givenchy II in her cleavage, 'all these years your father's made such a fuss about doing the bills and the tax – as if that excused him from thirty years of washing-up. Well, the tax return was overdue, so I thought, sod it, I'll do it myself. Obviously I couldn't make head nor tail of it so I rang up the tax office. The man was really quite overbearing with me. "Really, Mrs Jones," he said. "I simply can't see what the difficulty is." I said, "Listen, can *you* make a brioche?" He took the point, talked me through it and we had it done inside fifteen minutes. Anyway, he's taking me out to lunch today. A tax man! Imagine!'

'What?' I stammered, grabbing at the door frame. 'What about Julio?'

'Just because I'm "friends" with Julio doesn't mean I can't have other "friends",' she said sweetly, slipping into a yellow two-piece. 'Do you like this? Just bought it. Super lemon, don't you think? Anyway, must fly. I'm meeting him in Debenhams coffee shop at one fifteen.'

After she'd gone I ate a bit of muesli out of the packet with a spoon and finished off the dregs of wine in the fridge.

I know what her secret is: she's discovered power. She has power over Dad: he wants her back. She has power over Julio, and the tax man, and everyone is sensing her power and wanting a bit of it, which makes her even more irresistible. So all I've got to do is find someone or something to have power over and then . . . oh God. I haven't even got power over my own hair.

I am so depressed. Daniel, though perfectly chatty, friendly, even flirty all week, has given me no hint as to what is going on between us, as though it is perfectly normal to sleep with one of your colleagues and just leave it at that. Work – once merely an annoying nuisance – has become an agonizing torture. I have major trauma every time he disappears for lunch or puts his coat on to go at end of day: to where? with whom? whom?

Perpetua seems to have managed to dump all her work on to me and spends the entire time in full telephonic auto-witter to Arabella or Piggy, discussing the half-million-pound Fulham flat she's about to buy with Hugo. 'Yars. No. Yars. No, I *quite* agree. But the question is: does one want to pay another thirty grand for a fourth bedroom?'

At 4.15 on Friday evening Sharon rang me in the office. 'Are you coming out with me and Jude tomorrow?'

'Er . . .' I silently panicked, thinking, *Surely Daniel will ask to see me this weekend before he leaves the office?*

'Call me if he doesn't ask,' said Shazzer drily after a pause.

At 5.45 saw Daniel with his coat on heading out of the door. My traumatized expression must have shamed even him because he smiled shiftily, nodded at the computer screen and shot out.

Sure enough, `Message Pending` was flashing. I pressed `RMS`. It said:

```
Message Jones
Have a good weekend. Pip pip.
Cleave
```

Miserably, I picked up the phone and dialled Sharon.

'What time are we meeting tomorrow?' I mumbled sheepishly.

'Eight thirty. Café Rouge. Don't worry, we love you. Tell him to bugger off from me. Emotional fuckwit.'

2 a.m. Argor sworeal brilleve with Shazzan Jude. Dun stupid care bout Daniel stupid prat. Feel sicky though. Oops.

Sunday 5 March

8 a.m. Ugh. Wish was dead. Am never, ever going to drink again for the rest of life.

8.30 a.m. Oooh. Could really fancy some chips.

11.30 a.m. Badly need water but seems better to keep eyes closed and head stationary on pillow so as not to disturb bits of machinery and pheasants in head.

Noon. Bloody good fun but v. confused re: advice re: Daniel. Had to go through Jude's problems with Vile Richard first as clearly they are more serious since they have been going out for eighteen months rather than just shagged once. I waited humbly, therefore, till it was my turn to recount the latest Daniel instalment. The unanimous initial verdict was, 'Bastard fuckwittage.'

Interestingly, however, Jude introduced the concept of Boy Time – as introduced in the film *Clueless*: namely five days ('seven', I interjected) during which new relationship is left hanging in air after sex does not seem agonizing lifetime to males of species, but a normal cooling-down period in which to gather emotions, before proceeding. Daniel, argued Jude, was bound to be anxious about work situation, etc., etc., so give him a chance, be friendly and flirty: so as to reassure him that you trust him and are not going to become needy or fly off the handle.

At this Sharon practically spat into the shaved Parmesan and said it was inhuman to leave a woman hanging in air for two weekends after sex and an appalling breach of confidence and I should tell him what I think of him. Hmmm. Anyway. Going to have another little sleep.

2 p.m. Just triumphantly returned from heroic expedition to go downstairs for newspaper and glass of water. Could feel water flowing like crystal stream into section of head where most required. Though am not sure, come to think of it, if water can actually get in your head. Possibly it enters through the bloodstream. Maybe since hangovers are caused by dehydration water is drawn into the brain by a form of capillary action.

2.15 p.m. Story in papers about two-year-olds having to take tests to get into nursery school just made me jump out of skin. Am supposed to be at tea party for godson Harry's birthday.

6 p.m. Drove at breakneck speed feeling like I was dying, across grey, rain-sodden London to Magda's, stopping at Waterstone's for birthday gifts. Heart was sinking at thought of being late and hungover, surrounded by ex-career-girl mothers and their Competitive Child Rearing.

Magda, once a commodity broker, lies about Harry's age, now, to make him seem more advanced than he is. Even the conception was cut-throat, with Magda trying to take eight times as much folic acid and minerals as anyone else. The birth was great. She'd been telling everyone for months it was going to be a natural childbirth and, ten minutes in, she cracked and started yelling, 'Give me the drugs, you fat cow.'

Tea party was nightmare scenario: me plus a roomful of power mothers, one of whom had a four-week-old baby.

'Oh, isn't he *sweet*?' cooed Sarah de Lisle, then snapped, 'How did he do in his AGPAR?'

I don't know what the big deal is about tests for two – this AGPAR is a test they have to do at two minutes. Magda embarrassed herself two years ago by boasting at a dinner party that Harry got ten in his, at which one of the other guests, who happens to be a nurse, pointed out that the AGPAR test only goes up to nine.

Undaunted, however, Magda has started boasting around the nanny circuit that her son is a defecational prodigy, triggering off a round of boast and counter-boast. The toddlers, therefore, clearly at the age when they should be securely swathed in layers of rubberware, were teetering around in little more than Baby Gap G-strings. I hadn't been there ten minutes before there were three turds on the carpet. A superficially humorous but vicious dispute ensued about who had done the turds, following by a tense stripping off of towelling pants, immediately sparking another contest over the size of the boys' genitals and, correspondingly, the husbands'.

'There's nothing you can do, it's a hereditary thing. Cosmo doesn't have a problem in that area, does he?'

Thought head was going to burst with the racket. Eventually made my excuses and drove home, congratulating myself on being single.

Monday 6 March

11 a.m. Office. Completely exhausted. Last night was just lying in nice hot bath with some Geranium essential oil and a vodka and tonic when the doorbell rang. It was my mother, on the doorstep in floods of tears. It took me some time to establish what the matter was as she flopped all over the kitchen, breaking into ever louder outbursts of tears and saying she didn't want to talk about it, until I began to wonder if her self-perpetuating sexual power surge had collapsed like a house of cards, with Dad, Julio and the tax man losing interest simultaneously. But no. She had merely been infected with 'Having It All' syndrome.

'I feel like the grasshopper who sang all summer,' she (the second she sensed I was losing interest in the breakdown) revealed. 'And now it's the winter of my life and I haven't stored up anything of my own.'

I was going to point out that three potential eligible partners gagging for it plus half the house and the pension schemes wasn't exactly nothing, but I bit my tongue.

'I want a career,' she said. And some horrible mean part of me felt happy and smug because I had a career. Well – a job, anyway. I was a grasshopper collecting a big pile of grass, or flies, or whatever it is grasshoppers eat ready for the winter, even if I didn't have a boyfriend.

Eventually I managed to cheer Mum up by allowing her

to go through my wardrobe and criticize all my clothes, then tell me why I should start getting everything from Jaeger and Country Casuals. It worked a treat and eventually she was so much back on form she was actually able to call up Julio and arrange to meet him for a 'nightcap'.

By the time she left it was after ten so I called Tom to report the hideous news that Daniel had not rung all weekend and asked him what he thought about Jude and Sharon's conflicting advice. Tom said I should listen to neither of them, not flirt, not lecture but merely be an aloof, coolly professional ice-queen.

Men, he claims, view themselves as permanently on some sort of sexual ladder with all women either above them or below them. If the woman is 'below' (i.e. willing to sleep with him, very keen on him) then in a Groucho Marx kind of way he does not want to be a member of her 'club'. This whole mentality depresses me enormously but Tom said not to be naïve and if I really love Daniel and want to win his heart I have to ignore him and be as cold and distant to him as possible.

Eventually got to bed at midnight, v. confused, but was woken three times in the night by phone calls from Dad.

'When someone loves you it's like having a blanket all round your heart,' he said, 'and then when it's taken away . . .' and he burst into tears. He was speaking from the granny flat at the bottom of the Alconburys' garden, where he's staying, as he says hopefully, 'Just till things are sorted out.'

I suddenly realize everything has shifted and now I am looking after my parents instead of them looking after me, which seems unnatural and wrong. Surely I am not that old?

Monday 6 March

8st 12 (v.v.g. – have realized secret of dieting is not weighing oneself).

Can officially confirm that the way to a man's heart these days is not through beauty, food, sex, or alluringness of character, but merely the ability to seem not very interested in him.

Took no notice of Daniel whatsoever all day at work and pretended to be busy (try not to laugh). **Message Pending** kept flashing but I just kept sighing and tossing my hair about as if I were a very glamorous, important person under a great deal of pressure. By the end of the day I realized, like a school chemistry lab miracle (phosphorus, litmus test or similar), it was working. He kept staring at me and giving me meaningful glances. Eventually, when Perpetua was out, he walked past my desk, stopped for a moment and murmured, 'Jones, you gorgeous creature. Why are you ignoring me?'

In a rush of joy and affection I was just about to blurt out the whole story of Tom, Jude and Shazzer's conflicting theories, but the heavens were smiling on me and the phone rang. I rolled my eyes apologetically, picked it up, then Perpetua bustled up, knocking a pile of proofs off the desk with her bottom, and bellowed, 'Ah, Daniel. Now . . .' and swept him away, which was fortunate because the phone call was Tom, who said I had to keep up the ice-queen act and gave me a mantra to repeat when I felt myself weakening. 'Aloof, unavailable ice-queen; Aloof, unavailable ice-queen.'

Tuesday 7 March

9st 4, 2 or 5?? alcohol units 0, cigarettes 20, calories 1500, Instants 6 *(poor).*

9 a.m. Aargh. How can I have put on 3lb since the middle of the night? I was 9st 4 when I went to bed, 9st 2 at 4 a.m. and 9st 5 when I got up. I can understand weight coming *off* – it could have evaporated or passed out of the body into the toilet – but how could it be put *on*? Could food react chemically with other food, double its density and volume, and solidify into every heavier and denser hard fat? I don't look fatter. I can fasten the button, though not, alas, the zipper on my '89 jeans. So maybe my whole body is getting smaller but denser. The whole thing smacks of female body-builders and makes me feel strangely sick. Call up Jude to complain about diet failure, who says write down everything you've eaten, honestly, and see if you stuck to the diet. Here is list.

Breakfast: hot-cross bun (Scarsdale Diet – slight variation on specified piece of wholemeal toast); Mars Bar (Scarsdale Diet – slight variation on specified half grapefruit)

Snack: two bananas, two pears (switched to F-plan as starving and cannot face Scarsdale carrot snacks). Carton orange juice (Anti-Cellulite Raw-Food Diet)

Lunch: jacket potato (Scarsdale Vegetarian Diet) and hummus (Hay Diet – fine with jacket spuds as all starch, and breakfast and snack were all alkaline-forming with exception of hot-cross bun and Mars: minor aberration)

Dinner: four glasses of wine, fish and chips (Scarsdale Diet and also Hay Diet – protein forming); portion tiramisu; peppermint Aero (pissed)

I realize it has become too easy to find a diet to fit in with whatever you happen to feel like eating and that diets are not there to be pick and mixed but picked and stuck to, which is exactly what I shall begin to do once I've eaten this chocolate croissant.

Tuesday 14 March

Disaster. Complete disaster. Flushed with the success of Tom's ice-queen theory I began to rather brim over, as it were, into Jude's, and starting messaging Daniel again, to reassure him that I trust him and am not going to become needy or fly off the handle without just cause.

By mid-morning, so successful was the ice-queen combined with *Men are from Mars, Women are from Venus* approach that Daniel walked right up to me by the coffee machine and said, 'Will you come to Prague next weekend?'

'What? Er hahahaha, you mean the weekend after this one?'

'Yeeeeees, next weekend,' he said, with an encouraging, slightly patronizing air, as if he had been teaching me to speak English.

'Oooh. *Yes, please,*' I said, forgetting the ice-queen mantra in the excitement.

Next thing he came up and asked if I wanted to come round the corner for lunch. We arranged to meet outside the building so no one would suspect anything and it was all rather thrilling and clandestine until he said, as we walked towards the pub, 'Listen, Bridge, I'm really sorry, I've fucked up.'

'Why? what?' I said, even, as I spoke, remembering my mum and wondering if I ought to be saying 'Pardon?'

'I can't make Prague next weekend. I don't know what I was thinking about. But maybe we'll do it another time.'

A siren blared in my head and a huge neon sign started flashing with Sharon's head in the middle going, 'FUCK-WITTAGE, FUCKWITTAGE'.

I stood stock still on the pavement, glowering up at him.

'What's the matter?' he said, looking amused.

'I'm fed up with you,' I said furiously. 'I told you quite specifically the first time you tried to undo my skirt that I am not into emotional fuckwittage. It was very bad to carry on flirting, sleep with me then not even follow it up with a phone call, and try to pretend the whole thing never happened. Did you just ask me to Prague to make sure you could still sleep with me if you wanted to as if we were on some sort of ladder?'

'A ladder, Bridge?' said Daniel. 'What sort of ladder?'

'Shut up,' I bristled crossly. 'It's all chop-change chop-change with you. Either go out with me and treat me nicely, or leave me alone. As I say, I am not interested in fuckwittage.'

'What about you, this week? First you completely ignore me like some Hitler Youth ice-maiden, then you turn into an irresistible sex kitten, looking at me over the computer with not so much 'come-to-bed' as just 'come' eyes, and now suddenly you're Jeremy Paxman.'

We stared at each other transfixed like two African animals at the start of a fight on a David Attenborough programme. Then suddenly Daniel turned on his heel and walked off to the pub, leaving me to stagger, stunned, back to the office, where I dived to the loo, locked the door and sat down, staring crazily at the door with one eye. Oh God.

5 p.m. Har har. Am marvellous. Feeling v. pleased with self. Had top-level post-works crisis meeting in Café Rouge with Sharon, Jude and Tom, who were all delighted with the Daniel outcome, each convinced it was because I had followed their advice. Also Jude had heard survey on the radio that by the turn of the millennium a third of all households will be single, therefore proving that at last we are no longer tragic freaks. Shazzer guffawed and said, 'One in three? Nine out of ten, more like.' Sharon maintains men – present company (i.e. Tom) excepted, obviously – are so catastrophically unevolved that soon they will just be kept by women as pets for sex, therefore presumably these will not count as shared households as the men will be kept outside in kennels. Anyway, feeling v. empowered. Tremendous. Think might read bit of Susan Faludi's *Backlash*.

5 a.m. Oh God, am so unhappy about Daniel. I love him.

Wednesday 15 March

9st, alcohol units 5 (disgrace: urine of Satan), cigarettes 14 (weed of Satan – will give up on birthday), calories 1795.

Humph. Have woken up v. fed up. On top of everything, only two weeks to go until birthday, when will have to face up to the fact that another entire year has gone by, during which everyone else except me has mutated into Smug Married, having children plop, plop, plop, left right and centre and making hundreds of thousands of pounds and inroads into very hub of establishment, while I career rudderless and boyfriendless through dysfunctional relationships and professional stagnation.

Find self constantly scanning face in mirror for wrinkles and frantically reading *Hello!*, checking out everyone's ages in desperate search for role models (Jane Seymour is forty-two!), fighting long-impacted fear that one day in your thirties you will suddenly, without warning, grow a big fat crimplene dress, shopping bag, tight perm and face collapsing in manner of movie special-effect, and that will be it. Try to concentrate hard on Joanna Lumley and Susan Sarandon.

Also worried about how to celebrate birthday. Size of flat and bank balance prohibits actual party. Maybe dinner party? But then would have to spend birthday slaving and would hate all guests on arrival. Could all go out for meal but then feel guilty asking everyone to pay, selfishly presuming to force costly and dull evening on others merely to celebrate own birthday – yet cannot afford to pay for everyone. Oh God. What to do? Wish had not been born but immaculately burst into being in similar, though not identical, manner to Jesus, then would not have had to have birthday. Sympathize with Jesus in sense of embarrassment he must, and perhaps should, feel over two-millennium-old social imposition of own birthday on large areas of globe.

Midnight. Have had v.g. idea about birthday. Am going to ask everyone round for cocktails, perhaps Manhattans. Will then have given to guests something in manner of grand society hostess, and if everyone wishes to go to dinner afterwards: why, they may do so. Not sure what Manhattan is, come to think of it. But could buy book of cocktails maybe. Probably won't, to be perfectly honest.

Thursday 16 March

9st 1, alcohol units 2, cigarettes 3 (v.g.), calories 2140 (but mainly fruit), minutes spent doing party guest list 237 (bad).

Me	Shazzer
Jude	Vile Richard
Tom	Jerome (yuk)
~~Michael~~	
Magda	Jeremy
Simon	
Rebecca	Martin Crashing Bore
Woney	Cosmo
Joanna	
Daniel?	Perpetua? (eek) and Hugo?

Oh no. Oh no. What am I going to do?

Friday 17 March

Just called Tom who says, very wisely, 'It is your birthday and you should invite exactly and only who you want.'

So am just going to ask the following:

Shazzer
Jude
Tom
Magda and Jeremy

– and cook supper for everyone myself.

Called Tom back to tell him the plan and he said, 'and Jerome?'

'What?'

'And Jerome?'

'I thought, like we said, I'd just ask who I . . .' I tailed off, realizing if I said 'wanted' it would mean I didn't 'want' i.e. 'like' Tom's insufferable, pretentious boyfriend.

'Oh!' I said, over-compensating madly. 'You mean *your* Jerome? *Course* Jerome's invited, yer ninny. Chuh! But do you think it's OK not to ask Jude's Vile Richard? And Sloaney Woney – even though she had me to her birthday last week?'

'She'll never know.'

When I told Jude who was coming she said perkily, 'Oh, so we're bringing other halves?' which means Vile Richard. Also now that it's not just six I will have to ask Michael. Oh well. I mean nine is fine. Ten. It'll be fine.

Next thing Sharon rang. 'I hope I haven't put my foot in it. I just saw Rebecca and asked her if she was coming to your birthday and she looked really offended.'

Oh no, I'll have to ask Rebecca and Martin Crashing Bore now. But that means I'll have to ask Joanna as well. Shit. shit. Now I've said I'm cooking I can't suddenly announce we're going out to a restaurant or I'll seem both bone idle and mean.

Oh God. Just got home to icy offended-sounding answerphone message from Woney.

'Cosmo and I were wondering what you'd like for your birthday this year. Would you call us back, please?'

Realize I am going to spend my birthday cooking food for sixteen people.

Saturday 18 March

8st 13, alcohol units 4 (fed up), cigarettes 23 (v.v. bad, esp. in two hours), calories 3827 (repulsive).

2 p.m. Humph. Just what I needed. My mother burst into my flat, last week's Grasshopper Who Sang All Summer crisis miraculously forgotten.

'My godfathers, darling!' she said breathily, steaming through my flat and heading for the kitchen. 'Have you had a bad week or something? You look dreadful. You look about ninety. Anyway, guess what, darling,' she said, turning, holding the kettle, dropping her eyes modestly, then looking up, beaming like Bonnie Langford about to embark upon a tap-dancing routine.

'What?' I muttered grumpily.

'I've got a job as a TV presenter.'

I'm going shopping.

Sunday 19 March

8st 12, alcohol units 3, cigarettes 10, calories 2465 (but mainly chocolate).

Hurray. Whole new positive perspective on birthday. Have been talking to Jude about book she has been reading about festivals and rites of passage in primitive cultures and am feeling happy and serene.

Realize it is shallow and wrong to feel that flat is too small to entertain nineteen, and that cannot be arsed to spend birthday cooking and would rather dress up and be taken to posh restaurant by sex-god with enormous gold credit card. Instead am going to think of my friends as a huge, warm, African, or possibly Turkish, family.

Our culture is too obsessed with outward appearance, age and status. Love is what matters. These nineteen people are my friends; they want to be welcomed into my home to celebrate with affection and simple homely fare – not to judge. Am going to cook shepherd's pie for them all – British Home Cooking. It will be a marvellous, warm, Third-World-style ethnic family party.

Monday 20 March

9st, alcohol units 4 (getting into mood), cigarettes 27 (but last day before giving up), calories 2455.

Have decided to serve the shepherds pie with Chargrilled Belgian Endive Salad, Roquefort Lardons and Frizzled Chorizo, to add a fashionable touch (have not tried before but sure it will be easy), followed by individual Grand Marnier soufflés. V. much looking forward to the birthday. Expect to become known as brilliant cook and hostess.

Tuesday 21 March: Birthday

9st, alcohol units 9, cigarettes 42*, calories 4295*. *If can't splash out on birthday, when can I?*

6.30 p.m. Cannot go on. Have just stepped in a pan of mashed potato in new kitten-heel black suede shoes from

Pied à terre (Pied-à-pomme-de-terre, more like), forgetting that kitchen floor and surfaces were covered in pans of mince and mashed potato. It is already 6.30 and have to go out to Cullens for Grand Marnier soufflé ingredients and other forgotten items. Oh my God – suddenly remembered tube of contraceptive jelly might be on side of washbasin. Must also hide storage jars with embarrassing un-hip squirrel design and birthday card from Jamie with picture of little lamb on front which says 'Happy Birthday, Guess which one is you?' Then inside, 'You're the one over the hill.' Humph.

Schedule:

- **6.30.** Go to shop.
- **6.45.** Return with forgotten groceries.
- **6.45–7.** Assemble shepherd's pie and place in oven (oh God, hope will all fit).
- **7–7.05.** Prepare Grand Marnier soufflés. (Actually think will have a little taste of Grand Marnier now. It is my birthday, after all.)
- **7.05–7.10.** Mmm. Grand Marnier delicious. Check plates and cutlery for tell-tale signs of sluttish washing-up and arrange in attractive fan shape. Ah, must buy napkins also (or is it serviettes? Can never remember which one is common).
- **7.10–7.20.** Tidy up and move furniture to sides of room.
- **7.20–7.30.** Make frisse lardon frizzled chorizo thing.

All of which leaves a clear half-hour to get ready so no need to panic. Must have a fag. Aargh. It's quarter to seven. How did that happen? Aargh.

7.15 p.m. Just got back from shop and realize have forgotten butter.

7.35 p.m. Shit, shit shit. The shepherd's pie is still in pans all over the kitchen floor and have not yet washed hair.

7.40 p.m. Oh my God. Just looked for milk and realized have left the carrier bag behind in the shop. Also had the eggs in it. That means . . . Oh God, and the olive oil . . . so cannot do frizzy salad thing.

7.40 p.m. Hmm. Best plan, surely, is to get into the bath with a glass of champagne then get ready. At least if I look nice I can carry on cooking when everyone is here and maybe can get Tom to go out for the missing ingredients.

7.55 p.m. Aargh. Doorbell. Am in bra and pants with wet hair. Pie is all over floor. Suddenly hate the guests. Have had to slave for two days, and now they will all swan in, demanding food like cuckoos. Feel like opening door and shouting, 'Oh, go *fuck* yourselves.'

2 a.m. Feeling v. emotional. At door were Magda, Tom, Shazzer and Jude with bottle of champagne. They said to hurry up and get ready and when I had dried hair and dressed they had cleaned up all the kitchen and thrown away the shepherd's pie. It turned out Magda had booked a big table at 192 and told everyone to go there instead of my flat, and there they all were waiting with presents, planning to buy me dinner. Magda said they had had a weird, almost spooky sixth sense that the Grand Marnier soufflé and frizzled lardon thing were not going to work out. Love the friends, better than extended Turkish family in weird headscarves any day.

Right: for coming year will reactivate New Year's Resolutions, adding the following:

I will

Stop being so neurotic and dreading things.

I will not

Sleep with, or take any notice of, Daniel Cleaver any more.

APRIL

Inner Poise

Sunday 2 April

9st, alcohol units 0 (marvellous), cigarettes 0, calories 2250.

I read in an article that Kathleen Tynan, late wife of the late Kenneth, had 'inner poise' and, when writing, was to be found immaculately dressed, sitting at a small table in the centre of the room sipping at a glass of chilled white wine. Kathleen Tynan would not, when late with a press release for Perpetua, lie fully dressed and terrified under the duvet, chain-smoking, glugging cold *sake* out of a beaker and putting on make-up as a hysterical displacement activity. Kathleen Tynan would not allow Daniel Cleaver to sleep with her whenever he felt like it but not be her boyfriend. Nor would she become insensible with drink and be sick. Wish to be like Kathleen Tynan (though not, obviously, dead).

Lately, therefore, whenever things have risked ranging out of control, I have repeated the phrase 'inner poise' and imagined myself wearing white linen and sitting at a table with flowers on it. 'Inner poise.' No fags for six days now. Have assumed air of dignified hauteur with Daniel and not messaged, flirted or slept with him for three weeks. Only three alcohol units consumed over the last week as grudging concession to Tom, who complained that spending the evening with the new vice-free me was like going out for dinner with a whelk, scallop or other flaccid sea-creature.

My body is a temple. I wonder if it's time to go to bed yet? Oh no, it's only 8.30. Inner poise. Ooh. Telephone.

9 p.m. It was my father, speaking in a weird, disconnected voice, almost as if he were a dalek.

'Bridget. Turn your television set to BBC1.'

I switched channels and lurched in horror. It was a trailer for the Anne and Nick show and there, frozen in a video-effect diamond between Anne and Nick on the sofa, was my mother, all bouffed and made-up, as if she were Katie Bloody Boyle or someone.

'Nick,' said Anne pleasantly.

'. . . and we'll be introducing our new Springtime Slot,' said Nick, "Suddenly Single" – a dilemma being faced by a growing number of women. Anne.'

'And introducing spanking new presenter Pam Jones,' said Anne. '"Suddenly Single" herself and making her TV debut.'

While Anne was speaking my mother unfroze within the diamond, which started whooshing towards the front of the screen, obscuring Anne and Nick, and revealing, as it did so, that my mother was thrusting a microphone under the nose of a mousy-looking woman.

'Have you had suicidal thoughts?' boomed my mother.

'Yes,' said the mousy woman and burst into tears at which point the picture froze, turned on its end and whizzed off into one corner to reveal Anne and Nick on the sofa again looking sepulchral.

Dad was devastated. Mum hadn't even told him about the TV-presenting job. It seems he is in denial and has convinced himself Mum is just having an end-of-life crisis and that she already realizes she has made a mistake but is too embarrassed to ask to come back.

Actually, I'm all for denial. You can convince yourself of any scenario you choose and it keeps you as happy as a sandboy – as long as your ex-partner doesn't pop up on your television screen forging a new career out of not being married to you any more. I tried to pretend it didn't mean there was no hope, and that Mum might be planning their reunion as a really grabby end to the series, but it didn't wash. Poor Dad. I don't think he knows anything about Julio or the man from the tax office. I asked him if he'd like me to come up tomorrow and we could go out and have a nice supper together on Saturday night and maybe go for a walk on Sunday, but he said he was all right. The Alconburys are holding an Olde English supper on Saturday night for the Lifeboat.

Tuesday 4 April

Determined, now, to tackle constant lateness for work and failure to address in-tray bulging with threats from bailiffs, etc. Resolve to begin self-improvement programme with time-and-motion study.

7 a.m. Get weighed.

7.03 a.m. Return to bed in sulk over weight. Head-state bad. Sleeping or getting up equally out of question. Think about Daniel.

7.30 a.m. Hunger pangs force self out of bed. Make coffee, consider grapefruit. Defrost chocolate croissant.

7.35–7.50 a.m. Look out of window.

7.55 a.m. Open wardrobe. Stare at clothes.

8 am. Select shirt. Try to find black Lycra mini-skirt. Pull clothes out of bottom of wardrobe in quest for skirt. Go through drawers and search behind bedroom chair. Go through ironing basket. Go through dirty linen basket. Skirt has vanished. Have cigarette to cheer self up.

8.20 a.m. Dry skin brushing (anti-cellulite), bath and hairwash.

8.35 a.m. Begin selection of underwear. Laundry crisis means only available pants are vast white cotton. Too unattractive to contemplate, even for work (psychological damage). Go back to ironing basket. Find unsuitably small black lacy pair – prickly but better than giant Mummy-pant horror.

8.45 a.m. Start on black opaque tights. Pair one seems to have shrunk – crotch is three inches above knees. Get second pair on and find hole on back of leg. Throw away. Suddenly remember had Lycra mini-skirt on when returned home with Daniel last time. Go to living room. Triumphantly locate skirt between cushions on sofa.

8.55 a.m. Return to tights. Pair three have hole only in toe. Put on. Hole transforms into ladder which will protrude tellingly from shoe. Go to ironing basket. Locate last pair of black opaque tights twisted into rope-like object speckled with bits of tissue. Untangle and purge of tissue.

9.05 a.m. Have got tights on now. Add skirt. Begin ironing shirt.

9.10 a.m. Suddenly realize hair is drying in weird shape. Search for hairbrush. Locate in handbag. Blow-dry hair. Will not go right. Spray with plant spray and blow some more.

9.40 a.m. Return to ironing and discover stubborn stain on front of shirt. All other possible shirts dirty. Panic about time. Try to wash out stain. Entire shirt now soaking wet. Iron dry.

9.55 a.m. V. late now. In despair, have fag and read holiday brochure for calming five minutes.

10 a.m. Try to find handbag. Handbag has vanished. Decide to see if anything nice has come in the mail.

10.07 a.m. Access letter only, about non-payment of minimum payment. Try to remember what was looking for. Restart quest for handbag.

10.15 a.m. Beyond lateness now. Suddenly remember had handbag in bedroom when looking for hairbrush but cannot find. Eventually locate under clothes from wardrobe. Return clothes to wardrobe. Put on jacket. Prepare to leave house. Cannot find keys. Scour house in rage.

10.25 a.m. Find keys in handbag. Realize have forgotten hairbrush.

10.35 a.m. Leave house.

Three hours and thirty-five minutes between waking and leaving house is too long. In future must get straight up when wake up and reform entire laundry system. Open paper to read that convicted murderer in America is convinced the authorities have planted a microchip in his buttocks to monitor his movements, so to speak. Horrified by thought of similar microchip being in own buttocks, particularly in the mornings.

Wednesday 5 April

8st 13, alcohol units 5 (Jude's fault), cigarettes 2 (sort of thing that could happen to anyone – does not mean have started smoking again), calories 1765, Instants 2.

Told Jude today about the inner poise thing and she said, interestingly, that she'd been reading a self-help book about Zen. She said, when you looked at life, Zen could be applied to anything – Zen and the art of shopping, Zen and the art of flatbuying, etc. She said that it was all a question of Flow rather than struggle. And if, for example, you had a problem or things were not working out, instead of straining or becoming angry you should just relax and feel your way into the Flow and everything would work out. It is, she said, rather like when you can't get a key to open a lock and if you wiggle it furiously it gets worse, but take it out, stick a bit of lip gloss on it, then just sort of sense your way and Eureka! But not to mention idea to Sharon because she thought it was bollocks.

Thursday 6 April

Went to meet Jude for quiet drink to talk about Flow some more and noticed a familiar besuited figure with knitting-pattern dark good looks sitting in a quiet corner having dinner: it was Magda's Jeremy. Waved at him and just for split second saw expression of horror cross his face, which instantly made me look to his companion who was a) not Magda b) not yet thirty c) wearing a suit which I have tried on twice in Whistles and had to take off as too expensive. Bloody witch.

I could tell Jeremy was going to try to get away with the sort of quick 'Hello not now' look which acknowledges your close, old and enduring friendship but at the same time demonstrates that this is not the moment to affirm it with kisses and an in-depth chat. I was about to play along with it but then I thought, hang on a minute! Sisters! Under the skin! Magda! If Magda's husband has nothing to be ashamed of in dining with this worthless trollop in *my* suit, he will introduce me.

I altered my path to pass his table, at which he immersed himself deep in conversation with the trollop, glancing up as I walked past and giving me a firm, confident smile as if to say 'business meeting'. I gave him a look which said, 'Don't you business meeting me,' and strutted on.

What should I do now, though? Oh dear, oh dear. Tell Magda? Not tell Magda? Ring Magda and ask if everything's OK? Ring Jeremy and ask him if everything's OK? Ring Jeremy and threaten to tell Magda unless he drops the witch in my suit? Mind my own business?

Remembering Zen, Kathleen Tynan and Inner Poise, I did a version of Salute to the Sun I remembered from distant Yogacise class and centred myself, concentrating on the inner wheel, till the Flow came. Then I resolved serenely to tell no one, as gossip is a virulent spreading poison. Instead I will ring Magda a lot and be there for her so if anything is amiss (which she is bound, with woman's intuition, to sense), she will tell me. Then if, through Flow, it seems the right thing to do, I will tell her what I saw. Nothing of value comes through struggle; it is all about Flow. Zen and the art of life. Zen. Flow. Hmmm, but then how did I happen to bump into Jeremy and the worthless trollop if not through Flow? What does that mean, then?

Tuesday 11 April

8st 11, alcohol units 0, cigarettes 0, Instants 9 (this must stop).

All seems normal with Magda and Jeremy so maybe it was just a business meeting. Maybe the Zen and Flow notion is correct, for there is no doubt that by relaxing and going with the vibes I have done the right thing. Am invited to a glittering literati launch of *Kafka's Motorbike* next week at the Ivy. Determined, instead of fearing the scary party, panicking all the way through and going home pissed and depressed, am going to improve social skills, confidence and Make Parties Work for Me – as guided by article have just read in magazine.

Apparently, Tina Brown of the *New Yorker* is brilliant at dealing with parties, gliding prettily from group to group, saying, 'Martin Amis! Nelson Mandela! Richard Gere!' in a tone which at once suggests, 'My God, I have never been more enchanted to see anyone in my entire life! Have you met the most dazzling person at the party apart from you? Talk! Talk! Must network! Byeee!' Wish to be like Tina Brown, though not, obviously, quite so hardworking.

The article is full of useful tips. One should never, apparently, talk to anyone at a party for more than two minutes. When time is up, you simply say, 'I think we're expected to circulate. Nice to meet you,' and go off. If you get lost for words after asking someone what they do to which they reply 'Undertaker' or 'I work for the Child Support Agency', you must simply ask, 'Do you enjoy that?' When introducing people add a thoughtful detail or two about each person so that their interlocutor has a conversational kicking-off point. E.g., 'This is John – he's from New Zealand and enjoys windsurfing.' Or, 'Gina is a keen skydiver and lives on a barge.'

Most importantly, one must never go to a party without a clear objective: whether it be to 'network', thereby adding to your spread of contacts to improve your career; to make friends with someone specific; or simply 'clinch' a top deal. Understand where have been going wrong by going to parties armed only with objective of not getting too pissed.

Monday 17 April

8st 12, alcohol units 0 (v.g.), cigarettes 0 (v.g.), Instants 5 (but won £2 so total Instants expenditure only £3).

Right. Tomorrow is *Kafka's Motorbike*. Am going to work out clear set of objectives. In a minute. Will just watch adverts then ring up Jude.

Right

1) Not to get too pissed.
2) To aim to meet people to network with.

Hmmm. Anyway, will think of some more later.

11 p.m. Right.

3) To put the social skills from the article into action.
4) ~~To make Daniel think I have inner poise and want to get off with me again. No. No.~~
4) ~~To meet and sleep with sex god.~~
4) To make interesting contacts in the publishing world, possibly even other professions in order to find new career.

Oh God. Do not want to go to scary party. Want to stay home with bottle of wine and watch *EastEnders*.

Tuesday 18 April

9st 0, alcohol units 7 (oh dear), cigarettes 30, calories (cannot bear to think about it), Instants 1 (excellent).

Party got off to a bad start when could not see anyone that I knew to introduce to each other. Found myself a drink then spotted Perpetua talking to James from the *Telegraph*. Approached Perpetua confidently, ready to swing into action but instead of saying 'James, Bridget comes from Northamptonshire and is a keen gymnast' (am going to start going to gym again soon), Perpetua just carried on talking – well beyond the two-minute mark – and ignored me.

I hung around for a while feeling a total git, then spotted Simon from Marketing. Cunningly pretending I had not intended to join Perpetua's conversation at all, I bore down purposefully upon Simon, preparing to say, 'Simon Barnett!' in the style of Tina Brown. When I was almost there, however, I noticed that, unfortunately, Simon from Marketing was talking to Julian Barnes. Suspecting that I might not be able to fully pull off crying, 'Simon Barnett! Julian Barnes!' with quite the required gaiety and *tone*, I hovered indecisively then started to sidle away, at which point Simon said in an irritated superior voice (one you, funnily enough, never hear him use when he is trying to get off with you by the photocopier), 'Did you want something, Bridget?'

'Ah! Yes!' I said, panicking wildly about what it was I could possibly want. 'Ahm.'

'Yeees?' Simon and Julian Barnes looked at me expectantly.

'Do you know where the toilets are?' I blurted. Damn. Damn. Why? Why did I say that? I saw a faint smile hover over the thin-but-attractive lips of Julian Barnes.

'Ah, actually I think they're over there. Jolly good. Thanks,' I said, and made for the exit. Once out of the swing doors I slumped against the wall, trying to get my breath back, thinking, 'inner poise, inner poise'. It was not going particularly well so far, there were no two ways about it.

I looked wistfully at the stairs. The thought of going home, putting my nighty on and turning on the telly began to seem irresistibly attractive. Remembering the Party Objectives, though, I breathed in deeply through my nose, murmured, 'inner poise' and pushed through the doors back into the party. Perpetua was still by the door, talking to her ghastly friends Piggy and Arabella.

'Ah, Bridget,' she said. 'Are you going to get a drink?' and held out her glass. When I returned with three glasses of wine and a Perrier they were in full autowitter.

'I have to say, I think it's disgraceful. All it means in this day and age is that a whole generation of people only get to know the great works of literature – Austen, Eliot, Dickens, Shakespeare, and so on – through the television.'

'Well, quite. It's absurd. Criminal.'

'Absolutely. They think that what they see when they're "channel hopping" between *Noel's House Party* and *Blind Date* actually *is* Austen or Eliot.'

'*Blind Date* is on Saturdays,' I said.

'I'm sorry?' said Perpetua.

'Saturdays. *Blind Date* is on Saturdays at seven fifteen, after *Gladiators*.'

'So?' said Perpetua sneerily, with a sideways glance at Arabella and Piggy.

'Those big literary adaptations don't tend to go out on Saturday nights.'

'Oh look, there's Mark,' interrupted Piggy.

'Oh God, yah,' said Arabella, beadily. 'He's left his wife, hasn't he?'

'What I meant was, there isn't anything any good like *Blind Date* on the other side during the literary masterpieces, so I don't think that many people would be channel hopping.'

'Oh, *Blind Date* is "good", is it?' sneered Perpetua.

'Yes, it's very good.'

'And you do realize *Middlemarch* was originally a book, Bridget, don't you, not a soap?'

I hate Perpetua when she gets like this. Stupid old fartarse bag.

'Oh, I thought it was a soap of a shampoo,' I said, sulkily grabbing a handful of passing saté sticks and shoving them into my mouth. As I looked up I saw a dark-haired man in a suit straight in front of me.

'Hello, Bridget,' he said. I nearly opened my mouth and let all the saté sticks fall straight out. It was Mark Darcy. But without the Frank Bough-style diamond-patterned sweater.

'Hello,' I said through my mouthful, trying not to panic. Then, remembering the article, turned towards Perpetua.

'Mark. Perpetua is . . .' I began and then paused, frozen. What to say? Perpetua is very fat and spends her whole time bossing me around? Mark is very rich and has a cruel-raced ex-wife.

'Yes?' said Mark.

'. . . is my boss and is buying a flat in Fulham, and Mark is,' I said, turning desperately to Perpetua, 'a top human-rights lawyer.'

'Oh, hello, Mark. I know *of* you, of course,' gushed Perpetua as if she were Prunella Scales in *Fawlty Towers* and he were the Duke of Edinburgh.

'Mark, hi!' said Arabella, opening her eyes very wide and blinking in a way she presumably thought was very attractive. 'Haven't seen you for yonks. How was the Big Apple?'

'We were just talking about hierarchies of culture,' boomed Perpetua. 'Bridget is one of these people who thinks the moment when the screen goes back on *Blind Date* is on a par with Othello's "hurl my soul from heaven" soliloquy,' she said, hooting with laughter.

'Ah. Then Bridget is clearly a top post-modernist,' said Mark Darcy. 'This is Natasha,' he said, gesturing towards a tall, thin, glamorous girl beside him. 'Natasha is a top family-law barrister.'

I had the feeling he was taking the piss out of me. Bloody cheek.

'I must say,' said Natasha, with a knowing smile, 'I always feel with the Classics people should be made to prove they've read the book before they're allowed to watch the television version.'

'Oh, I *quite* agree,' said Perpetua, emitting further gales of laughter. 'What a marvellous idea!'

I could see her mentally fitting Mark Darcy and Natasha in with an array of Poohs and Piggies round the dinner table.

'They should have refused to let anyone listen to the World Cup tune,' hooted Arabella, 'until they could prove they'd listened to *Turandot* all the way through!'

'Though in many respects, of course,' said Mark's Natasha, suddenly earnest, as if concerned the conversation was going quite the wrong way, 'the democratization of our culture is a *good thing*—'

'Except in the case of Mr Blobby, who should have been punctured at birth,' shrieked Perpetua. As I glanced involuntarily at Perpetua's bottom thinking, 'That's a bit rich coming from her,' I caught Mark Darcy doing the same thing.

'What I *resent*, though' – Natasha was looking all sort of twitchy and distorted as if she were in an Oxbridge debating society – 'is this, this sort of, arrogant individualism which imagines each new generation can somehow create the world afresh.'

'But that's exactly what they *do*, do,' said Mark Darcy gently.

'Oh well, I mean if you're going to look at it at that level . . .' said Natasha defensively.

'What level?' said Mark Darcy. 'It's not a level, it's a perfectly good point.'

'No. No. I'm sorry, you're *deliberately* being obtuse,' she said, going bright red. 'I'm not talking about a ventilating deconstructionalistic freshness of vision. I'm talking about the ultimate *vandalization* of the cultural framework.'

Mark Darcy looked as if he was going to burst out laughing.

'What I mean is, if you're taking that sort of cutesy, morally relativisitic, "*Blind Date* is brilliant" sort of line . . .' she said with a resentful look in my direction.

'I wasn't, I just really like *Blind Date,*' I said. 'Though I do think it would be better if they made the pickees make up their own replies to the questions instead of reading out those stupid pat answers full of puns and sexual innuendos.'

'Absolutely,' interjected Mark.

'I can't stand *Gladiators,* though. It makes me feel fat,' I said. 'Anyway, nice to meet you. Bye!'

I was just standing waiting for my coat, reflecting on how much difference the presence or absence of a diamond-patterned sweater can make to someone's attractiveness, when I felt hands lightly on my waist.

I turned round. 'Daniel!'

'Jones! What are you doing skulking off so early?' He leaned over and kissed me. 'Mmmmmm, you smell nice,' then offered me a cigarette.

'No thank you, I have found inner poise and given up smoking,' I said, in a pre-programmed, Stepford Wife sort of way, wishing Daniel wasn't quite so attractive when you found yourself alone with him.

'I see,' he smirked, 'inner poise, eh?'

'Yes,' I said primly. 'Have you been at the party? I didn't see you.'

'I know you didn't. I saw you, though. Talking to Mark Darcy.'

'How do you know Mark Darcy?' I said, astonished.

'Cambridge. Can't stand the stupid nerd. Bloody old woman. How do you know him?'

'He's Malcolm and Elaine Darcy's son,' I began, almost going on to say, 'You know Malcolm and *Elaine,* darling. They came over when we lived in Buckingham—'

'Who in the—'

'They're friends of my parents. I used to play with him in the paddling pool.'

'Yes, I bet you did, you dirty little bitch,' he growled. 'Do you want to come and have supper?'

Inner poise, I told myself, inner poise.

'Come on, Bridge,' he said, leaning towards me seductively. 'I need to have a serious discussion about your blouse. It's extremely thin. Almost, when you examine it, thin to the point of transparency. Has it ever occurred to you that your blouse might be suffering from . . . *bulimia*?'

'I've got to meet someone,' I whispered desperately.

'Come on, Bridge.'

'No,' I said with a firmness that rather surprised me.

'Shame,' he said softly. 'See you Monday,' and gave me a look so dirty I felt like throwing myself after him shouting, 'Shag me! Shag me!'

11 p.m. Just called Jude and told her about Daniel incident, also about Malcolm and Elaine Darcy's son, whom Mum and Una had tried to get me off with at the Turkey Curry Buffet, turning up at the party looking rather attractive.

'Wait a minute,' said Jude. 'You don't mean *Mark* Darcy, do you? The lawyer?'

'Yes. What – do you know him as well?'

'Well, yes. I mean, we've done some work with him. He's incredibly nice and attractive. I thought you said the chap at the turkey curry buffet was a real geek.'

Humph. Bloody Jude.

Saturday 22 April

8st 7, cigarettes, 0, alcohol units 0, calories 1800.

Today is an historic and joyous day. After eighteen years of trying to get down to 8st 7 I have finally achieved it. It is no trick of the scales, but confirmed by jeans. I am thin.

There is no reliable explanation. I have been to the gym twice in the last week, but that, though rare, is not freakish. I have eaten normally. It is a miracle. Rang Tom, who said maybe I have a tapeworm. The way to get rid of it, he said, is to hold a bowl of warm milk and a pencil in front of my mouth. (Tapeworms love warm milk, apparently. They love it.) Open my mouth. Then, when the worm's head appears, wrap it carefully round the pencil.

'Listen,' I told him, 'this tapeworm is staying.' I love my new tapeworm. Not only am I thin, but I no longer want to smoke or glug wine.

'Are you in love?' asked Tom in a suspicious, jealous tone. He's always like this. It's not that he wants to be with me, because, obviously, he is a homosexual. But if you are single the last thing you want is your best friend forming a functional relationship with somebody else. I racked my brains, then stopped, shocked by a sudden, stunning realization. I am not in love with Daniel any more. I am free.

Tuesday 25 April

8st 7, alcohol units 0 (excellent), cigarettes 0 (v.v.g.), calories 995 (continuing good work).

Humph. Went to Jude's party tonight in tight little black dress to show off figure feeling v. full of myself.

'God, are you all right?' asked Jude when I walked in. 'You look really tired.'

'I'm fine,' I said, crestfallen. 'I've lost half a stone. What's the matter?'

'Nothing. No, I just thought . . .'

'What? What?'

'Maybe you've lost it a bit quickly off your . . . face,' she trailed off, looking at my admittedly somewhat deflated cleavage.

Simon was the same.

'Bridgiiiiiiiit! Have you got a fag?'

'No, I've given up.'

'Oh blimey, no wonder you look so . . .'

'What?'

'Oh, nothing, nothing. Just a bit . . . drawn.'

It continued all evening. There's nothing worse than people telling you you look tired. They might as well have done with it and say you look like five kinds of shit. I felt so pleased with myself for not drinking but as the evening wore on, and everyone got drunker, I began to feel so calm and smug that I was even irritating myself. I kept finding myself in conversations when I actually couldn't be bothered to say a single word, and just looked on and nodded in a wise, detached manner.

'Have you got any camomile tea?' I said to Jude at one

point as she lurched past, hiccupping happily, at which point she collapsed into giggles, put her arm round me and fell over. I decided I'd better go home.

Once there, I got into bed, put my head on the pillow but nothing happened. I kept putting my head in one place, then another place, but still it wouldn't go to sleep. Normally I would be snoring by now and having some sort of traumatized paranoid dream. I put the light on. It was only 11.30. Maybe I should do something, like, well, er . . . mending? Inner poise. The phone rang. It was Tom.

'Are you all right?'

'Yes. I feel great. Why?'

'You just seemed, well, flat tonight. Everyone said you weren't your usual self.'

'No, I was fine. Did you see how thin I am?' Silence.

'Tom?'

'I think you looked better before, hon.'

Now I feel empty and bewildered – as if a rug has been pulled from under my feet. Eighteen years – wasted. Eighteen years of calorie and fat-unit-based arithmetic. Eighteen years of buying long shirts and jumpers and leaving the room backwards in intimate situations to hide my bottom. Millions of cheesecakes and tiramisus, tens of millions of Emmenthal slices left uneaten. Eighteen years of struggle, sacrifice and endeavour – for what? Eighteen years and the result is 'tired and flat'. I feel like a scientist who discovers that his life's work has been a total mistake.

Thursday 27 April

Alcohol units 0, cigarettes 0, Instants 12 (v.v. bad, but have not weighed self or thought about dieting all day; v.g.).

Must stop doing the Instants but the trouble is I do quite often win. The Instants are much better than the Lottery itself, because the numbers no longer come up during *Blind Date* (it is not on at the moment) and all too often do not have a single one of yours among them, leaving you feeling both impotent and cheated with nothing to be done except screw your ticket up and throw it defiantly on the floor.

Not so with the Instants, which is very much a participation thing, with six cash figures to be scratched off – often quite a hard and skilled job – and never giving you the feeling that you didn't have a chance. Three amounts the same secures a win, and in my experience you always get very close, often with as many as two matching pairs for amounts as great as £50,000.

Anyway, you can't deny yourself all pleasures in life. I'm only on about four or five a day and, besides, I'm going to stop soon.

Friday 28 April

Alcohol units 14, cigarettes 64, calories 8400 (v.g., though bad to have counted. Slimming obsession v. bad), Instants 0.

At 8.45 last night I was running a relaxing aromatherapy bath and sipping camomile tea when a car burglar alarm started up. I have been waging a campaign in our street against car burglar alarms which are intolerable and counter-productive since you are more likely to get your car broken into by an angry neighbour trying to silence the burglar alarm than by a burglar.

This time, however, instead of raging and calling the police, I merely breathed in through flared nostrils and murmured, 'inner poise'. The doorbell rang. I picked up the intercom. A v. posh sheep-voice bleated, 'He's having a *fucking* affair.' Then there was hysterical sobbing. I rushed downstairs, where Magda was outside the flat in floods of tears fiddling under the steering wheel of Jeremy's Saab convertible, which was emitting a 'dowee-dowee-doowee' of indescribable loudness, all lights flashing, while the baby screamed as if being murdered by a domestic cat in the car seat.

'Turn it off!' somebody yelled from an upstairs window.

'I bloody well can't!' shrieked Magda, tugging at the car bonnet.

'Jerrers!' she yelled into the portable phone. 'Jerrers, you fucking adulterous bastard! How do you open the bonnet on the Saab!'

Magda is very posh. Our street is not very posh. It is of the kind which still has posters in the windows saying 'Free Nelson Mandela'.

'I'm not bloody coming back, you bastard!' Magda was yelling. 'Just tell me how to open the fucking bonnet.'

Magda and I were both in the car now, pulling every lever we could find, Magda swigging intermittently at a bottle of Laurent-Perrier. By this time an angry mob was gathering. Next thing, Jeremy roared up on his Harley-Davidson. But instead of turning off the alarm, he started trying to grab the baby out of the back seat with Magda screaming at him. Then the Australian guy, Dan, who lives below me, opened his window.

'Oy, Bridgid,' he shouted. 'There's water pouring through my ceiling.'

'Shit! The bath!'

I ran upstairs, but when I got to my door I realized I'd shut it behind me with the key inside. I started banging my heard against it, yelling, 'Shit, shit!'

Then Dan appeared in the hall. 'Chrisd,' he said. 'You'd biddah have one of these.'

'Thanks,' I said, practically eating the proffered fag.

Several cigarettes and a lot of fiddling with a credit card later we were in, to find water flooding everywhere. We couldn't turn the taps off. Dan rushed downstairs, returning with a spanner and a bottle of Scotch. He managed to turn off the taps, and started helping me to mop up. Then the burglar alarm stopped and we rushed to the window just in time to see the Saab roar off, with the Harley-Davidson in hot pursuit.

We both started laughing – we'd had quite a lot of whisky by now. Then suddenly – I don't quite know how – he was kissing me. This was quite an awkward situation, etiquette-wise, because I had just flooded his flat and ruined his evening, so I didn't want to seem ungrateful. I know that didn't give him licence to sexually harass me, but the complication was quite enjoyable, really, after all the dramas and inner poise and everything. Then suddenly a man in motorbike leathers appeared at the open door holding a pizza box.

'Oh shit,' said Dan. 'I forgod I ordered pizza.'

'So we ate the pizza and had a bottle of wine and a few more cigarettes and some more Scotch and then he restarted trying to kiss me and I slurred, 'No, no, we mushn't,' at which point he went all funny and started muttering, 'Oh, Chrisd. Oh, Chrisd.'

'What is it?' I said.

'I'm married,' he said. 'But Bridged, I think I love you.'

When he'd finally gone I slumped on the floor, shaking, with my back to the front door, chain-smoking butt ends. 'Inner poise,' I said, half-heartedly. Then the doorbell rang. I ignored it. It rang again. Then it rang without stopping. I picked it up.

'Darling,' said a different drunken voice I recognized.

'Go away, Daniel,' I hissed.

'No. Lemme explain.'

'No.'

'Bridge . . . I wanna come in.'

Silence. Oh God. Why do I still fancy Daniel so much?

'I love you, Bridge.'

'Go away. You're drunk,' I said, with more conviction than I felt.

'Jones?'

'What?'

'Can I use your toilet?'

Saturday 29 April

Alcohol units 12, cigarettes 57, calories 8489 (excellent).

Twenty-two hours, four pizzas, one Indian takeaway, three packets of cigarettes and three bottles of champagne later, Daniel is still here. I am in love. I am also now between one and all of the following:

a) Back on thirty a day.
b) Engaged.
c) Stupid.
d) Pregnant.

11.45 p.m. Have just been sick, and as I slumped over the loo trying to do it quietly so Daniel wouldn't hear, he suddenly yelled out from the bedroom, 'There goes your inner poise, my plumptious. Best place for it, I say.'

MAY

Mother-to-Be

Monday 1 May

Alcohol units 0, cigarettes 0, calories 4200 (eating for two).

I seriously think I am pregnant. How could we have been so stupid? Daniel and I were so carried away with euphoria at being back together again that reality seemed to go out of the window – and once you've . . . oh look, I don't want to talk about it. This morning I definitely felt the beginnings of morning sickness, but that could be because I was so hungover after Daniel finally left yesterday that I ate the following things to try to make myself feel better:

2 packets Emmenthal cheese slices.
1 litre freshly squeezed orange juice.
1 cold jacket potato.
2 pieces unbaked lemon cheesecake (very light; also possibly eating for two).
1 Milky Way (125 calories only. Body's enthusiastic response to cheesecake suggested baby needed sugar).
1 chocolate Viennoise dessert thing with cream on top (greedy baby incredibly demanding).
Steamed broccoli (attempt to nourish baby and stop it growing up spoilt).

4 cold Frankfurter sausages, (only available tin in cupboard – too exhausted by pregnancy to go out to shop again).

Oh dear. Am starting to get carried away with idea of self as Calvin Klein-style mother figure, poss. wearing crop-top or throwing baby in the air, laughing fulfilledly in advert for designer gas cooker, feel-good movie or similar.

In the office today Perpetua was at her most obnoxious, spending 45 minutes on the phone to Desdemona, discussing whether yellow walls would look nice with pink-and-grey ruched blinds or whether she and Hugo should go for Blood Red with a floral freize. For one 15-minute interlude she said nothing whatsoever except, 'Absolutely . . . no, absolutely . . . absolutely,' then concluded, 'But of course, in a sense, one could make exactly the same argument for the red.'

Instead of wanting to staple things to her head, I merely smiled in a beatific sort of way, thinking how soon all these things were to be immaterial to me, alongside caring for another tiny human being. Next I discovered a whole new world of Daniel fantasies: Daniel carrying the baby in a sling, Daniel rushing home from work, thrilled to find the two of us pink and glowing in the bath, and, in years to come, being incredibly impressive at parent/teacher evenings.

But then Daniel appeared. I have never seen him look worse. The only possible explanation was that on leaving me yesterday he had carried on drinking. He looked over at me, briefly, with the expression of an axe-murderer. Suddenly the fantasies were replaced by images from the film *Barfly*, where the couple spent the whole time blind drunk, screaming and throwing bottles at each other, or Harry

Enfield's The Slobs with Daniel yelling, 'Bridge. The baby. Is bawlin'. Its 'ead off.'

And me retorting, 'Daniel. I am *avin'* ay fag.'

Wednesday 3 May

9st 2 (Eek. Baby growing at monstrous unnatural rate), alcohol units 0, cigarettes 0, calories 3100 (but mainly potatoes, oh my God).* Must keep eye on weight again, now, for Baby's sake.*

Help. Monday and most of Tuesday I sort of thought I was pregnant, but knew I wasn't really – rather like when you're walking home late at night, and think someone is following you, but know they're not really. But then they suddenly grab you round the neck and now I'm two days late. Daniel ignored me all day Monday then caught me at 6 p.m. and said, 'Listen, I'm going to be in Manchester till the end of the week. I'll see you Saturday night, OK?' He hasn't called. Am single mother.

Thursday 4 May

9st 3, alcohol units 0, cigarettes 0, potatoes 12.

Went to the chemist to discreetly buy a pregnancy test. I was just shoving the packet at the girl on the till, with my head down, wishing I'd thought to put my ring on my wedding finger, when the chemist yelled, 'You want a pregnancy test?'

'Shhh,' I hissed, looking over my shoulder.

'How late's your period?' he bellowed. 'You'd be better with the blue one. It tells you if you're pregnant on the *first day* after your period is due.'

I grabbed the proffered blue one, handed over the eight pounds sodding ninety-five and scuttled out.

For the first two hours this morning I kept staring at my handbag as if it was an unexploded bomb. At 11.30 I could stand it no longer, grabbed the handbag, got in the lift and went to the loos two floors down to avoid the risk of anyone I knew hearing suspicious rustling. For some reason, the whole business suddenly made me furious with Daniel. It was his responsibility too and he wasn't having to spend £8.95 and hide in the toilets trying to wee on a stick. I unwrapped the packet in a fury, shoving the box and everything in the bin and getting on with it, then put the stick upside down on the back of the loo without looking at it. Three minutes. There was no way I was going to watch my fate being sealed by a slowly forming thin blue line. Somehow I got through those hundred and eighty seconds – my last hundred and eighty seconds of freedom – picked up the stick and nearly screamed. There in the little window was a thin blue line, bold as brass. Aargh! Aargh!

After 45 minutes of staring blankly at the computer trying to pretend Perpetua was a Mexican cheeseplant whenever she asked me what was the matter, I bolted and went out to a phone booth to ring Sharon. Bloody Perpetua. If Perpetua had a pregnancy scare she's got so much English establishment behind her she'd be down the aisle in an Amanda Wakeley wedding dress in ten minutes flat. Outside, there was so much traffic noise I couldn't make Sharon understand.

'What? Bridget? I can't hear. Are you in trouble with the police?'

'No,' I snuffled. 'The blue line in the *pregnancy test.*'

'Jesus. I'll meet you in Café Rouge in fifteen minutes.'

Although it was only 12.45 I thought a vodka and orange wouldn't do any harm since it was a genuine emergency, but then I remembered that baby wasn't supposed to have vodka. I waited, feeling like a weird sort of hermaphrodite or Push-me-pull-you experiencing the most violently opposed baby sentiments of a man and a woman both at the same time. On the one hand I was all nesty and gooey about Daniel, smug about being a real woman – so irrepressibly fecund! – and imagining fluffy pink baby skin, a tiny creature to love, and darling little Ralph Lauren baby outfits. On the other I was thinking, oh my God, life is over, Daniel is a mad alcoholic and will kill me then chuck me when he finds out. No more nights out with the girls, shopping, flirting, sex, bottles of wine and fags. Instead I am going to turn into a hideous grow-bag-cum-milk-dispensing-machine which no one will fancy and which will not fit into any of my trousers, particularly my brand new acid-green Agnés B jeans. This confusion, I guess, is the price I must pay for becoming a modern woman instead of following the course nature intended by marrying Abnor Rimmington off the Northampton bus when I was eighteen.

When Sharon arrived I sulkily thrust the pregnancy test, with its tell-tale blue line, at her under the table.

'Is this it?' she said.

'Of course it's it,' I muttered. 'What do you think it is? A portable phone?'

'You,' she said, 'are a ridiculous human being. Didn't you read the instructions? There are supposed to be two lines. This line is just to show the test is working. One line means you're *not* pregnant – you ninny.'

Got home to an answerphone message from my mother saying, 'Darling, call me immediately. My nerves are shot to *ribbons*.'

Her nerves are shot to ribbons!

Friday 5 May

9st (oh sod it, cannot break weighing habit of lifetime, particularly after pregnancy trauma – will get therapy of some kind in future), alcohol units 6 (hurrah!), cigarettes 25, calories 1895, Instants 3.

Spent the morning mooning about in mourning for lost baby but cheered up a bit when Tom called to suggest a lunchtime Bloody Mary to get the weekend off to a healthy start. Got home to find a petulant message from Mother saying she's gone to a health farm and will call me later. I wonder what's the matter. Probably overwhelmed by too many Tiffany's boxes from love-sick suitors and TV presenter job offers from rival production companies.

11.45 p.m. Daniel just called from Manchester.

'Had a good week?' he said.

'Super, thanks,' I said brightly. Super, thanks. Huh! I read somewhere that the best gift a woman can bring to a man is tranquillity, so I could hardly, as soon as we've started properly going out, admit that the minute his back was turned I started having neurotic hysterics over a phantom pregnancy.

Oh well. Who cares. We're seeing each other tomorrow night. Hurray! Lalalala.

Saturday 6 May: VE Day

9st 1, alcohol units 6, cigarettes 25, calories 3800 (but celebrating anniversary of end of rationing), correct lottery numbers 0 (poor).

Awake on VE Day in unseasonable heatwave trying to whip up frenzy of emotion in self about end of war, freedom of Europe, marvellous, marvellous, etc. etc. Feel extremely miserable about whole business, to tell truth. In fact, 'left out' might be the expression I am groping towards. I do not have any grandpas. Dad has got all worked up about a party being hosted in the Alconburys' garden at which, for unexplained reasons, he will be tossing pancakes. Mum is going back to the street she was brought up in in Cheltenham for a whale-meat fritter party, probably with Julio. (Thank God she didn't run off with a German.)

None of my friends are organizing anything. It would seem embarrassingly enthusiastic and all wrong, somehow, suggesting a positive approach to life or that we were trying creepily to annex something that was nothing to do with us. I mean, I probably wasn't even an egg when the war ended. I was just nothing: while they were all fighting and making jam out of carrots or whatever they did.

I hate this idea and toy with calling Mum to see if she had started her periods when the war ended. Do eggs get produced one at a time, I wonder, or are they stored from birth in micro-form until they are activated? Could I have somehow sensed the end of the war as a stored egg? If only I had a grandpa I could have got in on the whole thing under the guise of being nice to him. Oh, sod it, I am going to go shopping.

7 p.m. The heat has made my body double in size, I swear. I am never going in a communal changing room again. I got a dress stuck under my arms in Warehouse while trying to lift it off and ended up lurching around with inside-out fabric instead of a head, tugging at it with my arms in the air, rippling stomach and thighs on full display to the assembled sniggering fifteen-year-olds. When I tried to pull the stupid dress down and get out of it the other way it got stuck on my hips.

I hate communal changing rooms. Everyone stares sneakily at each other's bodies, but no one ever meets anyone's eye. There are always girls who know that they look fantastic in everything and dance around beaming, swinging their hair and doing model poses in the mirror saying, 'Does it make me look fat?' to their obligatory obese friend, who looks like a water buffalo in everything.

It was a disaster of a trip, anyway. The answer to shopping, I know, is simply to buy a few choice items from Nicole Farhi, Whistles and Joseph but the prices so terrify me that I go scuttling back to Warehouse and Miss Selfridge, rejoicing in a host of dresses at £34.99, get them stuck on my head, then buy things from Marks & Spencer because I don't have to try them on, and at least I've bought something.

I have come home with four things, all of them unsuitable and unflattering. One will be left behind the bedroom chair in an M&S bag for two years. The other three will be exchanged for credit notes from Boules, Warehouse, etc., which I will then lose. I have thus wasted £119, which would have been enough to buy something really nice from Nicole Farhi, like a very small T-shirt.

It is all a punishment, I realize, for being obsessed by shopping in a shallow, materialistic way instead of wearing the same rayon frock all summer and painting a line down the back of my legs; also for failing to join in the VE Day celebrations. Maybe I should ring Tom and get a lovely party together for Bank Holiday Monday. Is it possible to have kitsch ironic VE day party – like for the Royal Wedding? No, you see, you can't be ironic about dead people. And then there's the problem of flags. Half of Tom's friends used to be in the Anti-Nazi league and would think the presence of Union Jacks meant we were expecting skinheads. I wonder what would have happened if our generation had had a war? Ah well, time for a little drinky. Daniel will be here soon. Best start preparations.

11.59 p.m. Blimey. Hiding in kitchen having a fag. Daniel is asleep. Actually, I think he's pretending to be asleep. *Completely* weird evening. Realized that our entire relationship so far has been based on the idea that one or other of us is supposed to be resisting having sex. Spending an evening together when the idea was that we were *supposed* to have sex at the end of it was nothing short of bizarre. We sat watching VE Day on television with Daniel's arm uncomfortably round my shoulders as if we were two fourteen-year-olds in the cinema. It was really digging into the back of my neck but I didn't feel I could ask him to move it. Then when it was getting impossible to avoid the subject of bedtime any longer we went all formal and English. Instead of tearing each other's clothes off like beasts, we stood there going, 'Do use the bathroom first.'

'No! After you!'

'No, no, no! After you!'

'Really! I insist.'

'No, no, I won't hear of it. Let me find you a guest towel and some miniature seashell-shaped soaps.'

Then we ended up lying side by side and not touching, like we were Morecambe and Wise or John Noakes and Valerie Singleton in the Blue Peter House. If there is a God I would like to humbly ask Him – whilst making it clear that I am deeply grateful for His suddenly turning Daniel inexplicably into a regular feature after so much fuckwittage – to stop him getting into bed at night wearing pyjamas and reading glasses, staring at a book for 25 minutes then switching off the light and turning over – and turn him back into the naked lust-crazed sex beast I used to know and love.

Thanking you for your kind attention, Lord, regarding this matter.

Saturday 13 May

9st 1lb 8oz, cigarettes 7, calories 1145, Instants 5 (won £2 therefore total Instants expenditure only £3, v.g.), Lottery proper £2, number of correct numbers 1 (better).

How come have put on only 8oz after last night's over-consumption orgy?

Maybe food and weight are the same as garlic and stenchful breath: if you eat several entire bulbs your breath doesn't smell at all, similarly if eat huge amount does not cause weight gain: strangely cheering theory but creates v. bad situation in head. Would welcome removal for thorough valeting. Still, was worth it for delicious night of drunken feminist ranting with Sharon and Jude.

An unbelievable amount of food and wine was consumed since the generous girls, as well as bringing a bottle of wine each, had all brought a little extra something from M&S. Therefore, in addition to the three-course meal and two bottles of wine (1 fizzy, 1 white) I had already bought from M&S (I mean prepared by entire day's slaving over hot stove) we had:

1 tub hummus & pkt mini-pittas.
12 smoked salmon and cream cheese pinwheels.
12 mini-pizzas.
1 raspberry pavlova.
1 tiramisu (party size).
2 Swiss Mountain Bars.

Sharon was on top form. 'Bastards!' she was already yelling by 8.35, pouring three-quarters of a glass of Kir Royale straight down her throat. 'Stupid, smug, arrogant, manipulative, self-indulgent bastards. They exist in a total Culture of Entitlement. Pass me one of those mini-pizzas, will you?'

Jude was depressed because Vile Richard, with whom she is currently split up, keeps ringing her, dropping little verbal baits suggesting he wants to get back together to make sure he keeps her interested, but protecting himself by saying he just wants to be 'friends' (fraudulent, poisoned concept). Then last night he made an incredibly assumptive, patronizing phone call, asking her if she was going to a mutual friend's party.

'Ah well, in that case I won't come,' he said. 'No. It really wouldn't be fair on you. You see, I was going to bring this, sort of, date with me. I mean, it's nothing. It's just some girl who's stupid enough to let me shag her for a couple of weeks.'

'What?' exploded Sharon, beginning to turn pink. 'That's the most repulsive thing I've ever heard anyone say about a woman. Arrogant little *prat*! How dare he give himself licence to treat you any way he likes under the name of friendship, then make himself feel clever by trying to upset you with his stupid new date. If he really minded about not hurting your feelings he'd just shut up and come to the party on his own instead of waving his stupid date under your nose.'

'"Friends?" Pah! The Enemy more like!' I shouted happily, tucking into another Silk Cut and a couple of salmon pinwheels. 'Bastard!'

By 11.30 Sharon was in full and splendid auto-rant.

'Ten years ago people who cared about the environment were laughed at as sandal-wearing beardy-weirdies and now look at the power of the green consumer,' she was shouting, sticking her fingers into the tiramisu and transferring it straight into her mouth. 'In years ahead the same will come to pass with feminism. There won't be any men leaving their families and post-menopausal wives for young mistresses, or trying to chat women up by showing off in a patronizing way about all the other women throwing themselves at them, or trying to have sex with women without any niceness or commitment, because the young mistresses and women will just turn round and tell them to sod off and men won't get any sex or any women unless they learn how to behave properly instead of cluttering up the sea-bed of women with their SHITTY, SMUG, SELF-INDULGENT, BEHAVIOUR!'

'Bastards!' yelled Jude, slurping on her Pinot Grigio.

'Bastards,' I yelled through a mouthful of raspberry pavlova mixed with tiramisu.

'Bloody bastards!' shouted Jude, lighting a Silk Cut with the butt end of the last one.

Just then the doorbell rang.

'I bet that's Daniel, the bloody bastard,' I said. 'What is it?' I yelled into the entryphone.

'Oh, hello, darling,' said Daniel in his gentlest, politest voice. 'I'm really sorry to bother you. I did ring earlier and leave a message on your answerphone. It's just I've been stuck in the most tedious board meeting you can imagine for the entire evening and I so much wanted to see you. I'll just give you a little kiss and then go, if you like. Can I come up?'

'Burr. All right, then,' I muttered grumpily, pressed the buzzer and lurched back to the table. 'Bloody bastard.'

'Culture of Entitlement,' growled Sharon. 'Cooking, succour, beautiful young girls' bodies when they're old and fat. Think women are there to give them what they're bloody entitled . . . Here, have we run out of wine?'

Then Daniel appeared up the stairs, smiling lovingly. He looked tired yet fresh-faced, clean-shaven and very neat in his suit. He was holding three boxes of Milk Tray.

'I bought you all one of these,' he said, one eyebrow raised sexily, 'to eat with your coffee. Don't let me interrupt. I've done the shopping for the weekend.'

He carried eight Cullens carrier bags into the kitchen and started putting everything away.

At that moment the phone rang. It was the mini-cab firm the girls had rung half an hour earlier saying there'd been a terrible multiple pile-up in Ladbroke Grove, plus all their cars had unexpectedly exploded and they weren't going to be able to come for another three hours.

'How far are you going?' said Daniel. 'I'll drive you home. You can't hang around the streets looking for cabs at this time of night.'

As the girls fluttered around finding their handbags and grinning stupidly at Daniel I started eating all the nut, praline, fudge or caramel-based chocolates out of my box of Milk Tray, feeling a bewildering mixture of smugness and pride over my perfect new boyfriend whom the girls clearly wished to have a go at shagging, and furious with the normally disgusting sexist drunk for ruining our feminist ranting by freakishly pretending to be the perfect man. Huh. We'll see how long that lasts, won't we? I thought, while I waited for him to come back.

When he came back he ran up the stairs, swept me up into his arms and carried me into the bedroom.

'You get an extra chocolate for being lovely even when you're squiffy,' he said, taking a foil-wrapped chocolate heart out of his pocket. And then . . . Mmmmmm.

Sunday 14 May

7 p.m. Hate Sunday night. Feels like homework night. Have got to write catalogue copy for Perpetua before tomorrow. Think I will just ring Jude first.

7.05 p.m. No reply. Hmmmph. Anyway, down to work.

7.10 p.m. Think will just call Sharon.

7.45 p.m. Shazzer was annoyed with me for ringing because she had just got in and was about to call 1471 to see if this guy she has been seeing had rung while she was out and now my number will be stored instead.

Consider 1471 to be brilliant invention, instantly telling you the number of the last person who called. It was ironic, really, because when the three of us first found out about 1471 Sharon said she was totally against it, considering it exploitation by British Telecom of the addictive personalities and relationship-breakdown epidemic among the British populace. Some people are apparently calling it upwards of twenty times a day. Jude, on the other hand, is strongly in favour of 1471, but does concede that if you have just split up with or started sleeping with someone it doubles misery potential when you come home: no - number - stored -on-1471-misery, to add to no-message-on-answerphone-misery, or number - stored - turning - out - to - be - Mother's - misery.

Apparently in America the 1471 equivalent tells you *all* the numbers that have rung you since last time you checked and *how many times*. Shudder with horror at the thought of own obsessive calling of Daniel's number in early days being exposed in this way. The good thing over here is that if you dial 141 before you ring, it stops your number being stored on the other person's phone. Jude says you have to be careful, though, because if you have an obsessive crush on someone and ring accidentally when they are in, then ring off and no number is stored they might guess it was you. Must make sure Daniel does not find out about any of this.

9.30 p.m. Decided to nip round corner for cigarettes. On way up stairs heard phone ringing. Suddenly realizing had forgotten to put answerphone back on when Tom rang, tore up stairs, emptied contents of handbag on floor to find key and threw self across from to phone at which point phone stopped. Had just gone into loo when phone rang again. Stopped when got to it. Then started ringing again when went away. Finally got it.

'Oh, hello, darling, guess what?' Mum.

'What?' I said, miserably.

'I'm taking you to have your colours done! And don't keep saying, "what", please, darling. Color Me Beautiful. I'm sick to death of you wandering round in all these dingy slurries and fogs. You look like something out of Chairman Mao.'

'Mum. I can't really talk, I'm expecting . . .'

'Now come along, Bridget. I don't want any silliness,' she said in her Genghis-Khan-at-height-of-evil voice. 'Mavis Enderby used to be all miserable in buffs and mosses, now she's had hers done she comes out in all these wonderful shocking pinks and bottle greens and looks twenty years younger.'

'But I don't want to come out in shocking pinks and bottle greens,' I said, through clenched teeth.

'Well, you see, darling, Mavis is Winter. And I'm Winter, but you might be Summer like Una and then you'll get your pastels. You can't tell till they get the towel on your head.'

'Mum, I'm not going to Color Me Beautiful,' I hissed, desperately.

'Bridget, I'm not listening to any more of this. Auntie Una

was just saying the other day: if you'd had something a bit more bright and cheerful on at the turkey curry buffet Mark Darcy might have shown a bit more interest. Nobody wants a girlfriend who wanders round looking like someone from Auschwitz, darling.' Thought better of boasting to her about having a boyfriend despite being dressed from head to toe in slurry but prospect of Daniel and self becoming hot topic for discussion precipitating relentless stream of feedback folk-wisdom from Mum dissuaded me. Eventually got her to shut up about Color Me Beautiful by telling her I would think about it.

Tuesday 17 May

9st 2 (hooray!), cigarettes 7 (v.g.), alcohol units 6 (so v.g. – v. pure).

Daniel is still being gorgeous. How could everyone have been so wrong about him? Head is full of moony fantasies about living in flats with him and running along beaches together with tiny offspring in manner of Calvin Klein advert, being trendy Smug Married instead of sheepish Singleton. Just off to meet Magda.

11 p.m. Hmmm. Thought-provoking supper with Magda, who is v. depressed about Jeremy. The night of the burglar alarm and screaming row in my street was a result of a remark from Sloaney Woney, who claimed she had seen Jeremy with a girl at the Harbour Club who sounded suspiciously like the witch I saw him with all those weeks ago. After that, Magda asked me at point blank range if I'd heard or seen anything so I told her about the witch in the Whistles suit.

Turned out Jeremy admitted there'd been a flirtation and he'd been very attracted to this girl. They hadn't slept together, he alleged. But Magda was really fed up.

'You should make the most of being single while it lasts, Bridge,' she said. 'Once you've got kids and you've given up your job you're in an incredibly vulnerable position. I know Jeremy thinks my life is just one big holiday, but basically it's extremely hard work looking after a toddler and a baby all day, and it doesn't stop. When Jeremy comes home at the end of the day he wants to put his feet up and be nurtured and, as I imagine all the time now, fantasize about girls in leotards at the Harbour Club.

'I had a proper job before. I know for a fact it's much more fun going out to work, getting all dressed up, flirting in the office and having nice lunches than going to the bloody supermarket and picking Harry up from playgroup. But there's always this aggrieved air that I'm some sort of ghastly Harvey Nichols-obsessed lady who lunches while he earns all the money.'

She's so beautiful, Magda. I watched her toying with her champagne glass despondently and wondered what the answer is for we girls. Talk about grass is always bloody greener. The number of times I've slumped, depressed, thinking how useless I am and that I spend every Saturday night getting blind drunk and moaning to Jude and Shazzer or Tom about not having a boyfriend; I struggle to make ends meet and am ridiculed as an unmarried freak, whereas Magda lives in a big house with eight different kinds of pasta in jars, and gets to go shopping all day. And yet here she is so beaten, miserable and unconfident and telling me I'm lucky . . .

'Ooh, by the way,' she said, brightening, 'talking of Harvey Nicks, I got the most wonderful Joseph shift dress in there today – red, two buttons at one side at the neck, very nicely cut, £280. God, I so much wish I was like you, Bridge, and could just have an affair. Or have bubble baths for two hours on Sunday morning. Or stay out all night with no questions asked. Don't suppose you fancy coming shopping tomorrow morning, do you?'

'Er. Well, I've got to go to work,' I said.

'Oh,' said Magda, looking momentarily surprised. 'You know,' she went on, toying with her champagne, 'once you get the feeling that there's a woman your husband prefers to you, it becomes rather miserable being at home, imagining all the versions of that type of woman he might run into out in the world. You do feel rather powerless.'

I thought about my mum. 'You could seize power,' I said, 'in a bloodless coup. Go back to work. Take a lover. Bring Jeremy up short.'

'Not with two children under three,' she said resignedly. 'I think I've made my bed, I'll just have to lie in it now.'

Oh God. As Tom never tires of telling me, in a sepulchral voice, laying his hand on my arm and staring into my eyes with an alarming look, 'Only Women Bleed.'

Friday 19 May

8st 12½ (have lost 3lb 8oz literally overnight – must have eaten food which uses up more calories to eat it than it gives off e.g. v. chewy lettuce), alcohol units 4 (modest), cigarettes 21 (bad), Instants 4 (not v.g.).

4.30 p.m. Just when Perpetua was breathing down my neck so she didn't end up late for her weekend in Gloucestershire at the Trehearnes' the phone rang.

'Hello, darling!' My mother. 'Guess what? I've got the most marvellous opportunity for you.'

'What?' I muttered sulkily.

'You're going to be on television,' she gushed as I crashed my head on to the desk.

'I'm coming round with the crew at ten o'clock tomorrow. Oh, darling, aren't you *thrilled*?'

'Mother. If you're coming round to my flat with a television crew, I won't be in it.'

'Oh, but you must,' she said icily.

'No,' I said. But then vanity began to get the better of me. 'Why, anyway? What?'

'Oh, darling,' she cooed. 'They're wanting someone *younger* for me to interview on "Suddenly Single": someone pre-menopausal and Suddenly Single who can talk about, well, you know, darling, the pressures of impending childlessness, and so on.'

'I'm *not* pre-menopausal, Mother!' I exploded. 'And I'm not Suddenly Single either. I'm suddenly part of a couple.'

'Oh, don't be silly, darling,' she hissed. I could hear office noises in the background.

'I've got a boyfriend.'

'Who?'

'Never you mind,' I said, suddenly glancing over my shoulder at Perpetua, who was smirking.

'Oh, please, darling. I've told them I've found someone.'

'No.'

'Oh, pleeeeeease. I've never had a career all my life and

now I'm in the autumn of my days and I need something for myself,' she gabbled, as if reading from a cue card.

'Someone I know might see. Anyway, won't they notice I'm your daughter?'

There was a pause. I could hear her talking to someone in the background. Then she came back and said, 'We could blot out your face.'

'What? Put a bag over it?' Thanks a lot.'

'Silhouette, darling, silhouette. Oh, please, Bridget. Remember, I gave you the gift of life. Where would you be without me? Nowhere. Nothing. A dead egg. A piece of space, darling.'

The thing is I've always, secretly, rather fancied being on television.

Saturday 20 May

9st 3 (why? why? from where?), alcohol units 7 (Saturday), cigarettes 17 (positively restrained, considering), number of correct lottery numbers 0 (but v. distracted by filming).

The crew had trodden a couple of wine glasses into the carpet before they'd been in the house thirty seconds, but I'm not too fussed about that sort of thing. It was when one of them staggered in shouting, 'Mind your backs,' carrying an enormous light with flaps on it, then bellowed, 'Trevor, where do you want this brute?' overbalanced, crashed the light through the glass door of the kitchen cupboard and knocked an open bottle of extra virgin olive oil over on to my River Café cookbook that I realized what I'd done.

Three hours after they arrived, filming had still not begun and they were still boshing around saying, 'Can I just cheat you this way a bit, love?' By the time we finally got going, with Mother and I sitting opposite each other in semi-darkness, it was nearly half past one.

'And tell me,' she was saying in a caring, understanding voice I'd never heard before, 'when your husband left you, did you have' – she was almost whispering now – 'suicidal thoughts?'

I stared at her incredulously.

'I know this is painful for you. If you feel you're going to break down we can stop for a moment,' she said hopefully.

I was too livid to speak. What husband?

'I mean, it must be a terrible time, with no partner on the horizon and that biological clock ticking away,' she said, kicking me under the table. I kicked her back and she jumped and let out a little noise.

'Don't you want a child?' she said, handing me a tissue.

At this point there was a loud snort of laughter from the back of the room. I had thought it would be fine to leave Daniel asleep in the bedroom because he never wakes up till after lunch on Saturdays and I'd put his cigarettes on the pillow next to him.

'If Bridget had a child she'd lose it,' he guffawed. 'Pleased to meet you, Mrs Jones. Bridget, why can't you get all done up on Saturdays like your mum?'

Sunday 21 May

My mum is not speaking to either of us for humiliating her and exposing her as a fraud in front of her crew. At least she might leave us alone for a bit now. So much looking forward to the summer, anyway. Will be so lovely having a boyfriend when it is warm. We will be able to go on romantic mini-breaks. V. happy.

JUNE

Hah! Boyfriend

Saturday 3 June

8st 13, alcohol units 5, cigarettes 25, calories 600, minutes spent looking at brochures: long-haul 45, mini-break 87, 1471 calls 7 (g.).

Finding it impossible to concentrate on almost anything in the heat except fantasies about going on mini-breaks with Daniel. Head is filled with visions of us lying in glades by rivers, me in long white floaty dress, Daniel and I sitting outside ancient Cornish waterside pub sipping pints in matching striped T-shirts and watching the sun set over the sea; Daniel and I eating candlelit dinners in historic country-house-hotel courtyards then retiring to our room to shag all hot summer night.

Anyway. Daniel and I are going to a party tonight at his friend Wicksy's, then tomorrow I expect we will go to the park or out to a lovely pub in the country for lunch. It is marvellous having a boyfriend.

Sunday 4 June

9st, alcohol units 3 (g.), cigarettes 13 (g.), minutes spent looking at brochures: long-haul 30 (g.), mini-break 52, 1471 calls 3 (g.).

7 p.m. Humph. Daniel has just gone home. Bit fed up, actually. Was really lovely hot Sunday but Daniel did not want to go out or discuss mini-breaks and insisted on spending all afternoon with the curtains drawn, watching the cricket. Also the party was quite nice last night, but at one point we went over to join Wicksy and a very pretty girl he was talking to. I did notice, as we approached, that she looked rather defensive.

'Daniel,' said Wicksy, 'have you met Vanessa?'

'No,' said Daniel, putting on his most flirtatious seductive grin and holding out his hand. 'Nice to meet you.'

'Daniel,' said Vanessa, folding her arms and looking absolutely livid, 'We've *slept together.*'

God, it's hot. Quite like leaning out of the window. Someone is playing a saxophone in effort to pretend we are all in a film set in New York, and can hear voices all around because everyone's windows are open, and smell cooking from restaurants. Hmm. Think would like to move to New York: though probably, come to think of it, not v.g. area for mini-breaks. Unless mini-break actually is to New York, which would be pointless if one were already in New York.

Will just ring Tom then get down to work.

8 p.m. Just going round to Tom's for a quick drink. Just for half an hour.

Tuesday 6 June

9st 2, alcohol units 4, cigarettes 3 (v.g.), calories 1326, Instants 0 (excellent), 1471 calls 12 (bad), hours spent asleep 15 (bad, but not self's fault as heatwave).

Managed to persuade Perpetua to let me stay at home to work. Certain she only agreed because she wants to sunbathe too. Mmmm. Got lovely new mini-break brochure: 'Pride of Britain: Leading Country House Hotels of the British Isles'. Marvellous. Going through all pages one by one imagining Daniel and me being alternately sexual and romantic in all the bedrooms and dining rooms.

11 a.m. Right: am going to concentrate now.

11.25 a.m. Hmmm, got a bit of a scratchy nail.

11.35 a.m. God. I just started having paranoid fantasy for no reason about Daniel having an affair with someone else and thinking up dignified but cutting remarks to make him sorry. Now why should that be? Have I sensed with a woman's intuition that he is having an affair?

The trouble with trying to go out with people when you get older is that everything becomes so loaded. When you are partnerless in your thirties, the mild bore of not being in a relationship – no sex, not having anyone to hang out with on Sundays, going home from parties on your own all the time – gets infused with the paranoid notion that the reason you are not in a relationship is your age, you have had your last ever relationship and sexual experience ever, and it is all your fault for being too wild or wilful to settle down in the first bloom of youth.

You completely forget the fact that when you were twenty-two and you didn't have boyfriend or meet anyone you remotely fancied for twenty-three months you just thought it was a bit of a drag. The whole thing builds up out of all proportion, so finding a relationship seems a dazzling, almost insurmountable goal, and when you do start going out with someone it cannot possibly live up to expectations.

Is it that? Or is it that there is something wrong with me being with Daniel? Is Daniel having an affair?

11.50 a.m. Hmmm. Nail really *is* scratchy. Actually, if don't do something about it I'll start picking at it and next thing I'll have no fingernail left. Right, I'd better go and find an emery board. Come to think of it, this nail varnish generally is looking a bit scrotty. I really need to take it all off and start again. Might as well do it now while I think about it.

Noon. It is such a bloody bore when the weather is so hot and one's *soi-disant* boyfriend refuses to go anywhere nice with you. Feel he thinks I am trying to trap him into a mini-break; as if it were not a mini-break but marriage, three kids and cleaning out the toilet in house full of stripped pine in Stoke Newington. I think this is turning into a psychological crisis. I'm going to call Tom (can always do the catalogue stuff for Perpetua this evening).

12.30 p.m. Hmmm. Tom says if you go mini-breaking with somebody you are having a relationship with you spend the whole time worrying about how the relationship is going, so it is better just to go with a friend.

Apart from sex, I say. Apart from sex, he agrees. I'm going to meet Tom tonight with brochures to plan fantasy, or phantom mini-break. So I must work really hard this afternoon.

12.40 p.m. These shorts and T-shirt are too uncomfortable in this heat. I'm going to change into a long floaty dress.

Oh dear, my pants show through this dress now. I'd better put some flesh-coloured ones on in case someone comes to the door. Now, my Gossard Glossies ones would be perfect. I wonder where they are.

12.45 p.m. In fact think might put the Glossies bra on to match if I can find it.

12.55 p.m. That's better.

1 p.m. Lunchtime! At last a bit of time off.

2 p.m. OK, so this afternoon I am really going to work and get everything done before the evening, then can go out. V. sleepy, though. It's so hot. Maybe I'll just close my eyes for five minutes. Catnaps are said to be an excellent way of reviving oneself. Used to excellent effect by Margaret Thatcher and Winston Churchill. Good idea. Maybe I'll lie down on the bed.

7.30 p.m. Oh, Bloody Hell.

Friday 9 June

9st 2, alcohol units 7, cigarettes 22, calories 2145, minutes spent inspecting face for wrinkles 230.

9 a.m. Hurrah! Night out with girls tonight.

7 p.m. Oh no. Turns out Rebecca is coming. An evening with Rebecca is like swimming in sea with jellyfish: all will be going along perfectly pleasantly then suddenly you get painful lashing, destroying confidence at stroke. Trouble is, Rebecca's stings are aimed so subtly at one's Achilles' heels, like Gulf War missiles going 'Fzzzzzz whoossssh' through Baghdad hotel corridors, that never see them coming. Sharon says am not twenty-four any more and should be mature enough to deal with Rebecca. She is right.

Midnight. Argor es wororrible. Am olanpassit. Face collapsin.

Saturday 10 June

Ugh. Woke up this morning feeling happy (still drunk from last night), then suddenly remembered horror of how yesterday's girls' night had turned out. After first bottle of Chardonnay was just about to broach subject of constant mini-break frustration when Rebecca suddenly said, 'How's Magda?'

'Fine,' I replied.

'She's incredibly attractive, isn't she?'

'Mmm,' I said.

'And she's amazingly young-looking – I mean she could easily pass for twenty-four or twenty-five. You were at school together, weren't you, Bridget? Was she three or four years below you?'

'She's six months older,' I said, feeling the first twinges of horror.

'Really?' said Rebecca, then left a long, embarrassed pause. 'Well, Magda's lucky. She's got really good skin.'

I felt the blood draining from my brain as the horrible truth of what Rebecca was saying hit me.

'I mean, she doesn't smile as much as you do. That's probably why she hasn't got so many lines.'

I grasped the table for support, trying to get my breath. I am ageing prematurely, I realized. Like a time-release film of a plum turning into a prune.

'How's your diet going, Rebecca?' said Shazzer.

Aargh. Instead of denying it, Jude and Shazzer were accepting my premature ageing as read, tactfully trying to change the subject to spare my feelings. I sat, in a spiral of terror, grasping my sagging face.

'Just going to the ladies,' I said through clenched teeth like a ventriloquist keeping my face fixed, to reduce the appearance of wrinkles.

'Are you all right, Bridge?' said Jude.

'Fn,' I replied stiffly.

Once in front of the mirror I reeled as the harsh overhead lighting revealed my thick, age-hardened, sagging flesh. I imagined the others back at the table, chiding Rebecca for alerting me to what everyone had long been saying about me but I never needed to know.

Was suddenly overwhelmed by urge to rush out and ask all the diners how old they thought I was: like at school once, when I conceived private conviction that I was mentally subnormal and went round asking everyone in the playground, 'Am I mental?' and twenty-eight of them said, 'Yes.'

Once get on tack of thinking about ageing there is no escape. Life suddenly seems like holiday where, halfway through, everything starts accelerating towards the end. Feel need to do something to stop ageing process, but what? Cannot afford face-lift. Caught in hideous cleft stick as both fatness and dieting are in themselves ageing. Why do I look old? Why? Stare at old ladies in street trying to work out all tiny processes by which faces become old not young. Scour newspapers for ages of everyone, trying to decide if they look old for their age.

11 a.m. Phone just rang. It was Simon, to tell me about the latest girl he has got his eye on. 'How old is she?' I said, suspiciously.

'Twenty-four.'

Aargh aargh. Have reached the age when men of my own age no longer find their contemporaries attractive.

4 p.m. Going out to meet Tom for tea. Decided needed to spend more time on appearance like Hollywood stars and have therefore spent ages putting concealer under eyes, blusher on cheeks and defining fading features.

'Good God,' said Tom when I arrived.

'What?' I said. 'What?'

'Your face. You look like Barbara Cartland.'

I started blinking very rapidly, trying to come to terms with the realization that some hideous time-bomb in my skin had suddenly, irrevocably, shrivelled it up.

'I look really old for my age, don't I?' I said, miserably.

'No, you look like a five-year-old in your mother's make-up,' he said. 'Look.'

I glanced in the mock Victorian pub mirror. I looked like a garish clown with bright pink cheeks, two dead crows for eyes and the bulk of the white cliffs of Dover smeared underneath. Suddenly understood how old women end up wandering around over-made-up with everyone sniggering at them and resolved not to snigger any more.

'What's going on?' he said.

'I'm prematurely ageing,' I muttered.

'Oh, for God's sake. It's that bloody Rebecca, isn't it?' he said. 'Shazzer told me about the Magda conversation. It's ridiculous. You look about sixteen.'

Love Tom. Even though suspected he might have been lying still feel hugely cheered up as even Tom would surely not say looked sixteen if looked forty-five.

Sunday 11 June

8st 13 (v.g., too hot to eat), alcohol units 3, cigarettes 0 (v.g., too hot to smoke), calories 759 (entirely ice-cream).

Another wasted Sunday. It seems the entire summer is doomed to be spent watching the cricket with the curtains drawn. Feel strange sense of unease with the summer and not just because of the drawn curtains on Sundays and mini-break ban. Realize, as the long hot days freakishly repeat themselves, one after the other, that whatever I am doing I really think I ought to be doing something else. It comes from the same feeling *family* as the one which periodically makes you think that just because you live in central London you should be out at the RSC/Albert Hall/Tower of London/Royal Academy/Madame Tussauds, instead of hanging around in bars enjoying yourself.

The more the sun shines the more obvious it seems that others are making fuller, *better* use of it elsewhere: possibly at some giant softball game to which everyone is invited except me; possibly alone with their lover in a rustic glade by waterfalls where Bambis graze, or at some large public celebratory event, probably including the Queen Mother and one or more of the football tenors, to mark the exquisite summer which I am failing to get the best out of. Maybe it is our climatic past that is to blame. Maybe we do not yet have the mentality to deal with a sun and cloudless blue sky, which is anything other than a freak incident. The instinct to panic, run out of the office, take most of your clothes off and lie panting on the fire escape is still too strong.

But there, too, is confusion. It is not the thing to go out courting malignant growths any more so what should you do? A shady barbecue, perhaps? Starve your friends while you tamper with fire for hours then poison them with burnt yet still quivering slices of underdone suckling pig? Or organize picnics in the park and end up with all the women scraping squashed gobbets of mozzarella off tinfoil and yelling at children with ozone asthma attacks; while the men swig warm white wine in the fierce midday sun, staring at the nearby softball games with left-out shame.

Envy summer life on the Continent, where men in smart lightweight suits and designer sunglasses glide around calmly in smart air-conditioned cars, maybe stopping for a *citron pressé* in a shady pavement café in an ancient square, totally cool about the sun and ignoring it because they know for a fact that it will still be shining at the weekend, when they can go and lie quietly on the yacht.

Feel certain this has been factor behind our waning national confidence ever since we started to travel and notice it. I suppose things might change. More and more tables are on pavements. Diners are managing to sit calmly at them, only occasionally remembering the sun and turning their faces to it with closed eyes, breaking into huge excited grins at passer-by – 'Look, look, we're enjoying a refreshing drink in a pavement café, we can do it too' – their expressions of angst merely brief and fleeting which say, 'Ought we to be at an outdoor performance of *A Midsummer Night's Dream*?'

Somewhere at the back of my mind is a new-born, tremulous notion that maybe Daniel is right: what you are supposed to do when it's hot is go to sleep under a tree or watch cricket with the curtains drawn. But to my way of thinking, to actually get to sleep you'd have to know that the next day would be hot as well, and the one after that, and that enough hot days lay in store in your lifetime to do all conceivable hot-day activities in a calm and measured manner with no sense of urgency whatsoever. Fat chance.

Monday 12 June

9st 1, alcohol units 3 (v.g.), cigarettes 13 (g.), minutes spent trying to programme video 210 (poor).

7 p.m. Mum just rang. 'Oh, hello, darling. Guess what? Penny Husbands-Bosworth is on *Newsnight*!!!'

'Who?'

'You know the Husbands-Bosworths, darl*ing*. Ursula was in the year above you at the High School. Herbert died of leukaemia . . .'

'What?'

'Don't say "what", Bridget, say "pardon". The thing is I'm going to be out because Una wants to see a slide show of the Nile so Penny and I wondered if you'd record it . . . Ooh, better dash – there's the butcher!'

8 p.m. Right. Ridiculous to have had video for two years and never to have been able to make it record anything. Also is marvellous FV 67 HV VideoPlus. Simple matter of following operating instructions, locating buttons, etc., certain.

8.15 p.m. Humph. Cannot locate operating instructions.

8.35 p.m. Hah! Found operating instructions under *Hello!*. Right. 'Programming your video is as easy as making a phone call'. Excellent.

8.40 p.m. 'Point the remote control at the video recorder.' V. easy. 'Turn to Index.' Aargh, horror list with 'Timer controlled simultaneous HiFi sound recordings', 'the decoder needed for encoded programmes', etc. Merely wish to record Penny Husbands-Bosworth's rant, not spend all evening reading treatise on spying techniques.

8.50 p.m. Ah. Diagram. 'Buttons for IMC functions'. But what are IMC functions?

8.55 p.m. Decide to ignore that page. Turn to 'Timer-controlled recordings with VideoPlus': '1. Meet the requirements for VideoPlus.' What requirements? Hate the stupid video. Feel exactly the same as feel when trying to follow signposts on roads. Know in heart that signposts and video manual do not make sense but still cannot believe authorities would be so cruel as to deliberately dupe us all. Feel incompetent fool and as if everyone else in world understands something which is being kept from me.

9.10 p.m. 'When you turn your recorder on you must adjust the clock and the calendar for precise TIMER-controlled recording (don't forget to use the quick-adjust options to switch between summer and winter time). Clock menus called with red and digital number 6.'

Press red and nothing happens. Press numbers and nothing happens. Wish stupid video had never been invented.

9.25 p.m. Aargh. Suddenly main menu is on TV saying 'Press 6'. Oh dear. Realize was using telly remote control by mistake. Now news has come on.

Just called Tom and asked him if he could record Penny Husbands-Bosworth but he said he didn't know how to work his video either.

Suddenly there is clicking noise within video and the news is replaced, incomprehensibly, by *Blind Date*.

Just called Jude and she can't work hers either. Aaargh. Aargh. Is 10.15. *Newsnight* in 15 minutes.

10.17 p.m. Cassette will not go in.

10.18 p.m. Ah, *Thelma and Louise* is in there.

10.19 p.m. *Thelma and Louise* will not come out.

10.21 p.m. Frenziedly press all buttons. Cassette comes out and goes back in again.

10.25 p.m. Have got new cassette in now. Right. Turn to 'Recording'.

'Recording will start when in Tuner Mode when any button is pressed (apart from Mem).' What, though, is Tuner Mode? 'When recording from a camcorder or similar press AV prog source 3 x during a bilingual transmission press 1/2 and hold for 3 seconds to make your choice of language.'

Oh God. Stupid manual reminds me of Linguistics professor had at Bangor, who was so immersed in finer points of language that could not speak without veering off into analysis of each individual word: 'This morning I would . . . now "would" you see, in 1570 . . .'

Aargh aargh. *Newsnight* is starting.

10.31 p.m. OK. OK. Calm. Penny Husbands-Bosworth's asbestos leukaemia item is not on yet.

10.33 p.m. Yesss, yesss. RECORDING CURRENT PROGRAMME. Have done it!

Aaargh. All going mad. Cassette has started rewinding and now stopped and ejected. Why? Shit. Shit. Realize in excitement have sat on remote control.

10.35 p.m. Frantic now. Have rung Shazzer, Rebecca, Simon, Magda. Nobody knows how to programme their videos. Only person I know who knows how to do it is Daniel.

10.45 p.m. Oh God. Daniel fell about laughing when said I could not programme video. Said he would do it for me. Still, at least have done best for Mum. It is exciting and historic when one's friends are on TV.

11.15 p.m. Humph. Mum just rang. 'Sorry, darling. It isn't *Newsnight,* it's *Breakfast News* tomorrow. Could you set it for seven o'clock tomorrow morning. BBC1?'

11.30 p.m. Daniel just called. 'Er, sorry, Bridge. I'm not quite sure what went wrong. It's recorded Barry Norman.'

Sunday 18 June

8st 12, alcohol units 3, cigarettes 17.

After sitting in semi-darkness for the third weekend running with Daniel's hand down my bra, fiddling with my nipple as if it were a sort of worry bead and me occasionally feebly saying, 'Was that a run?' I suddenly blurted out, '*Why* can't we go on a mini-break? Why? *Why? Why?*'

'That's a good idea,' said Daniel, mildly, taking his hand out of my dress. 'Why don't you book somewhere for next weekend? Nice country house hotel. I'll pay.'

Wednesday 21 June

8st 11 (v.v.g.), alcohol units 1, cigarettes 2, Instants 2 (v.g.), minutes spent looking at mini-break brochures 237 (bad).

Daniel has refused to discuss the mini-break any more, or look at the brochure, and has forbidden me from mentioning it until we actually set off on Saturday. How can he expect me not to be excited when I have been longing for this for so long? Why is it that men have not yet learnt to fantasize about holidays, choose them from brochures and plan and fantasize about them in the way that they (or some of them) have learnt to cook or sew? The single-handed mini-break responsibility is hideous for me. Wovingham Hall seems ideal – tasteful without being over-formal, with four-poster beds, a lake and even a fitness centre (not to go in), but what if Daniel doesn't like it?

Sunday 25 June

8st 11, alcohol units 7, cigarettes 2, calories 4587 (ooops).

Oh dear. Daniel decided the place was nouveau from the moment we arrived, because there were three Rolls-Royces parked outside, and one of them yellow. I was fighting a sinking realization that it was suddenly freezing cold and I had packed for 90° heat. This was my packing:

Swimsuits 2.
Bikinis 1.
Long floaty white dress 1.

Sundress 1.
Trailer-park-trash pink jelly mules 1 pair.
Tea-rose-pink suede mini dress 1.
Black silk teddy.
Bras, pants, stockings, suspenders (various).

There was a crack of thunder as I teetered, shivering, after Daniel to find the foyer stuffed with bridesmaids and men in cream suits and to discover that we were the only guests staying in the hotel who were not in the wedding party.

'Chuh! Isn't it dreadful what's happening in Srebrenica,' I chattered maniacally to try to put out problems in proportion. 'To be honest, I never feel I've quite *pinned down* what's going on in Bosnia. I thought the Bosnians were the ones in Sarajevo and the Serbians were attacking them, so who are the Bosnian Serbs?'

'Well, if you spent a bit less time reading brochures and more time reading the papers you might know,' smirked Daniel.

'So what *is* going on?'

'God, look at that bridesmaid's tits.'

'And who are the Bosnian Muslims?'

'I cannot believe the size of that man's lapels.'

Suddenly I had the unmistakable feeling that Daniel was trying to change the subject.

'Are the Bosnian Serbs the same lot who were attacking Sarajevo?' I asked.

Silence.

'Whose territory is Srebrenica in, then?'

'Srebrenica is a *safe area,*' said Daniel in deeply patronizing tones.

'So how come the people from the safe area were attacking before?'

'Shut up.'

'Just tell me if the Bosnians in Srebrenica are the same lot as the ones in Sarajevo.'

'Muslims,' said Daniel triumphantly.

'Serbian or Bosnian?'

'Look, will you shut up?'

'You don't know what's going on in Bosnia either.'

'I do.'

'You don't.'

'I do.'

'You *don't.*'

At this point the commissionaire, who was dressed in knickerbockers, white socks, patent leather buckled shoes, a frock coat and a powdered wig, leaned over and said, 'I think you'll find the former inhabitants of Srebrenica and of Sarajevo are Bosnian Muslims, sir.' Adding pointedly, 'Will you be requiring a newspaper in the morning at all, sir?'

I thought Daniel was going to hit him. I found myself stroking his arm murmuring, 'OK now, easy, easy,' as if he were a racehorse that had been frightened by a van.

5.30 p.m. Brrr. Instead of lying side by side with Daniel in hot sun at the side of the lake wearing a long floaty dress, I ended up blue with cold in a rowing boat with one of the hotel bath towels wrapped round me. Eventually we gave up to retire to our room for a hot bath and Codis, discovering en route that another couple were to be sharing the non-wedding party dining room with us that evening, the female half of which was a girl called Eileen whom Daniel had slept with twice, inadvertently bitten dangerously hard on the breast and never spoken to since.

As I emerged from my bath Daniel was lying on the bed giggling. 'I've got a new diet for you,' he said.

'So you *do* think I'm fat.'

'OK, this is it. It's very simple. All you do is not eat any food which you have to pay for. So at the start of the diet you're a bit porky and no one asks you out to dinner. Then you lose weight and get a bit leggy and shag-me hippy and people start taking you out for meals. So then you put a few pounds on, the invitations tail off and you start losing weight again.'

'Daniel!' I exploded. 'That's the most appalling sexist, fattist, cynical thing I've ever heard.'

'Oh, don't be like that, Bridge,' he said. 'It's the logical extension of what you really think. I keep telling you nobody wants legs like a stick insect. They want a bottom they can park a bike in and balance a pint of beer on.'

I was torn between a gross image of myself with a bicycle parked in my bottom and a pint of beer balanced on it, fury at Daniel for his blatantly provocative sexism and suddenly wondering if he might be right about my concept of my body in relation to men, and, in which case, whether I should have something delicious to eat straight away and what that might be.

'I'll just pop the telly on,' said Daniel, taking advantage of my temporary speechlessness to press the remote-control button, and moving towards the curtains, which were those thick hotel ones with blackout lining. Seconds later the room was in complete darkness apart from the flickering light of the cricket. Daniel had lit a fag and was calling down to room service for six cans of Fosters.

'Do you want anything, Bridge?' he said, smirking. 'Cream tea, maybe? I'll pay.'

JULY

Huh

'Oh, hello,' darling, guess what?' Sometimes I think my

Sunday 2 July

8st 10 (continuing good work), alcohol units 0, cigarettes 0, calories 995, Instants 0: perfect.

7.45 a.m. Mum just rang. 'Oh, hello, darling, guess what?'

'I'll just take the phone in the other room. Hang on,' I said, glancing over nervously at Daniel, unplugging the phone, creeping next door and plugging it in again only to find my mother had not noticed my absence for the last two and a half minutes and was still talking.

'. . . So what do you think, darling?'

'Um, I don't know. I was bringing the phone into the other room like I said,' I said.

'Ah. So you didn't hear anything?'

'No.' There was a slight pause.

'Oh, hello, darling, guess what?' Sometimes I think my mother is part of the modern world and sometimes she seems a million miles away. Like when she leaves messages on my answerphone which just say, very loudly and clearly, 'Bridget Jones's mother.'

'Hello? Oh, hello, darling, guess what?' she said, again.

'What?' I said resignedly.

'Una and Geoffrey are having a Tarts and Vicars party in the garden on the twenty-ninth of July. Don't you think that's fun! Tarts and Vicars! Imagine!'

I tried hard not to, fighting off a vision of Una Alconbury in thigh boots, fishnet nights and a peephole bra. For sixty-year-olds to organize such an event seemed unnatural and wrong.

'Anyway, we thought it would be super if you and' – coy, loaded pause – 'Daniel, could come. We're all dying to meet him.'

My heart sank at the thought of my relationship with Daniel being dissected in close and intimate detail amongst the Lifeboat luncheons of Northamptonshire.

'I don't think it's really Daniel's—' Just as I said that the chair I had, for some reason, been balancing on with my knees while I leaned over the table fell over with a crash.

When I retrieved the phone my mother was still talking. 'Yes, super. Mark Darcy's going to be there, apparently, with someone, so . . .'

'What's going on?' Daniel was standing stark naked in the doorway. 'Who are you talking to?'

'My mother,' I said, desperately, out of the corner of my mouth.

'Give it to me,' he said, taking the phone. I like it when he is authoritative without being cross like this.

'Mrs Jones,' he said, in his most charming voice. 'It's Daniel here.'

I could practically hear her going all fluttery.

'This is very bright and early on a Sunday morning for a phone call. Yes, it is an absolutely beautiful day. What can we do for you?'

He looked at me while she chattered for a few seconds then turned back to the receiver.

'Well, that'll be lovely. I shall put that in the diary for the twenty-ninth and look out my dog collar. Now, we'd better get back and catch up on our sleep. You take care of yourself, now. Cheerio. Yes. Cheerio,' he said firmly, and put the phone down.

'You see,' he said smugly, 'a firm hand, that's all it needs.'

Saturday 22 July

8st 11 (hmm must get 1lb off), alcohol units 2, cigarettes 7, calories 1562.

Actually I am really excited about Daniel coming to the Tarts and Vicars party with me next Saturday. It will be so lovely for once not to have to drive up on my own, arrive on my own and face all that barrage of inquisition about why I haven't got a boyfriend. It will be a gorgeous hot day. Maybe we could even make a mini-break of it and stay in a pub (or other hotel without televisions in the bedroom). I'm really looking forward to Daniel meeting my dad. I hope he likes him.

2 a.m. Woke up in floods of tears from a hideous dream I keep having where I'm sitting A-level French and realize as I turn over the paper that I have forgotten to do any revision and I'm wearing nothing except my Domestic Science apron, trying desperately to pull it round me so Miss Chignall won't see that I'm wearing no pants. I expected Daniel to at least be sympathetic. I know it's all to do with my worries about where my career is leading me but he just lit himself a cigarette and asked me to run over the bit about the Domestic Science apron again.

'It's all right for you with your bloody Cambridge First.' I whispered, sniffing. 'I'll never forget the moment when I looked at the notice board and saw a D next to French and knew I couldn't go to Manchester. It altered the course of my whole life.'

'You should thank your lucky stars, Bridge,' he said, lying on his back and blowing smoke at the ceiling. 'You'd probably have married some crashing Geoffrey Boycott character and spent the rest of your life cleaning out the whippet cage. Anyway . . .' he started laughing, '. . . there's nothing wrong with a degree from . . . from . . .' (he was *so* amused now he could hardly speak) '. . . Bangor.'

'Right, that's it. I'm sleeping on the sofa,' I yelled, jumping out of bed.

'Hey, don't be like that, Bridge,' he said, pulling me back. 'You know I think you're a . . . an intellectual *giant*. You just need to learn how to interpret dreams.'

'What's the dream telling me, then?' I said sulkily. 'That I haven't fulfilled my potential intellectually?'

'Not exactly.'

'What, then?'

'Well, I think the pantless apron is a pretty obvious symbol, isn't it?'

'What?'

'It means that the vain pursuit of an intellectual life is getting in the way of your true purpose.'

'Which is what?'

'Well, to cook all my meals for me, of course, darling,'

he said, beside himself at his own amusingness again. 'And walk around my flat with no pants on.'

Friday 28 July

8st 12 (must do diet before tomorrow), alcohol units 1 (v.g.), cigarettes 8, calories 345.

Mmmm. Daniel was really sweet tonight and spent ages helping me choose my outfit for the Tarts and Vicars. He kept suggesting different ensembles for me to try on while he weighed it up. He was quite keen on a dog collar and black T-shirt with black lace-topped hold-ups as a cross between a tart and a vicar but in the end, after I'd walked about for quite a while in both of them, he decided the best one was a black lacy Marks and Spencer body, with stockings and suspenders, a French maid's-style apron which we'd made out of two hankies and a piece of ribbon, a bow-tie, and a cotton-wool rabbit's tail. It was really good of him to give up the time. Sometimes I think he really is quite caring. He seemed particularly keen on sex tonight as well.

Ooh, I am so looking forward to tomorrow.

Saturday 29 July

8st 11 (v.g.), alcohol units 7, cigarettes 8, calories 6245 (sodding Una Alconbury, Mark Darcy, Daniel, Mum, everybody).

2 p.m. Cannot believe what has happened. By 1 p.m. Daniel had still not woken up and I was starting to worry because the party starts at 2.30. Eventually I woke him with a cup of coffee and said, 'I thought you needed to wake up because we're supposed to be there at two-thirty.'

'Where?' he said.

'The Tarts and Vicars.'

'Oh God, love. Listen, I've just realized, I've got so much work to do this weekend. I'm really going to have to stay at home and get down to it.'

I couldn't believe it. He *promised* to come. Everyone knows when you are going out with someone they are supposed to support you at hideous family occasions, and he thinks if he so much as mentions the word 'work' he can get out of anything. Now all the Alconburys' friends will spend the entire time asking me if I've got a boyfriend yet and no one will believe me.

10 p.m. Cannot believe what I have been through. I drove for two hours, parked at the front of the Alconburys' and, hoping I looked OK in the bunny girl outfit, walked round the side to the garden where I could hear voices raised in merriment. As I started to cross the lawn they all went quiet, and I realized to my horror that instead of Tarts and Vicars, the ladies were in Country Casuals-style calf-length floral two-pieces and the men were in slacks and V-necked sweaters. I stood there, frozen, like, well, a rabbit. Then while everyone stared, Una Alconbury came flapping across the lawn in pleated fuchsia holding out a plastic tumbler full of bits of apple and leaves.

'Bridget!! Super to see you. Have a Pimms,' she said.

'I thought it was supposed to be a Tarts and Vicars party,' I hissed.

'Oh dear, didn't Geoff call you?' she said. I couldn't believe this. I mean, did she think I dressed as a bunny girl normally or something? 'Geoff,' she said. 'Didn't you telephone Bridget? We're all looking forward to meeting your new boyfriend,' she said, looking around. 'Where is he?'

'He had to work,' I muttered.

'How's-my-little-Bridget?' said Uncle Geoffrey, lurching over, pissed.

'Geoffrey,' said Una coldly.

'Yup, yup. All present and correct, orders obeyed, Lieutenant,' he said, saluting, then collapsing on to her shoulder giggling. 'But it was one of those ruddy answerphone thingummajigs.'

'Geoffrey,' hissed Una. 'Go-and-see-to-the-barbecue. I'm sorry, darling, you see we decided after all the scandals there've been with vicars around here there'd be no point having a Tarts and Vicars party because . . .' she started to laugh, '. . . because everyone thought vicars *were* tarts anyway. Oh dear,' she said, wiping her eyes. 'Anyway, how's this new chap, then? What's he doing working on a Saturday? Durrrr! That's not a very good excuse, is it? How are we going to get you married off at this rate?'

'At this rate I'm going to end up as a call girl,' I muttered, trying to unpin the bunny tail from my bottom.

I could feel someone's eyes on me and looked up to see Mark Darcy staring fixedly at the bunny tail. Beside him was the tall thin glamorous top family-law barrister clad in a demure lilac dress and coat like Jackie O. with sunglasses on her head.

The smug witch smirked at Mark and blatantly looked

me up and down in a most impolite manner. 'Have you come from another party?' she breathed.

'Actually, I'm just on my way to work,' I said, at which Mark Darcy half smiled and looked away.

'Hello, darling, can't stop. Shooting.' trilled my mother, hurrying towards us in a bright turquoise pleated shirtwaister, waving a clapper board. 'What on earth do you think you're wearing, darling? You look like a common prostitute. Absolute quiet, please, everyone, aaaaand . . .' she yelled in the direction of Julio, who was brandishing a video camera, 'action!'

In alarm I quickly looked round for Dad but couldn't see him anywhere. I saw Mark Darcy talking to Una and gesturing in my direction then Una, looking purposeful, hurried across to me.

'Bridget, I am *so sorry* about the mix-up over the fancy dress,' she said. 'Mark was just saying you must feel dreadfully uncomfortable with all these older chaps around. Would you like to borrow something?'

I spent the rest of the party wearing, over my suspender outfit, a puff-sleeved, floral-sprig Laura Ashley bridesmaid dress of Janine's with Mark Darcy's Natasha smirking and my mother periodically rushing past going, 'That's a pretty dress, darling. Cut!'

'I don't think much of the girlfriend, do you?' said Una Alconbury loudly, nodding in Natasha's direction as soon as she got me alone. 'Very much the Little Madam. Elaine thinks she's desperate to get her feet under the table. Oh, hello, Mark! Another glass of Pimms? What a shame Bridget couldn't bring her boyfriend. He's a lucky chap, isn't he?' All this was said very aggressively as if Una was taking as a personal insult the fact that Mark had chosen a girlfriend who was a) not me and b) had not been introduced to him by Una at a turkey curry buffet. 'What's his name, Bridget? Daniel, is it? Pam says he's one of these sooper-dooper young publishers.'

'Daniel Cleaver?' said Mark Darcy.

'Yes, it is, actually,' I said, jutting my chin out.

'Is he a friend of yours, Mark?' said Una.

'Absolutely not,' he said, abruptly.

'Oooh. I hope he's good enough for our little Bridget,' Una pressed on, winking at me as if this was all hilarious fun instead of hideous.

'I think I could say again, with total confidence, absolutely not,' said Mark.

'Oh, hang on a tick, there's Audrey. Audrey!' said Una, not listening, and tripping off, thank God.

'I suppose you think that's clever,' I said furiously, when she'd gone.

'What?' said Mark, looking surprised.

'Don't you "What?" me, Mark Darcy,' I muttered.

'You sound just like my mother,' he said.

'I suppose you think its all right to slag people's boyfriends off to their parents' friends behind their back when they're not even there for no reason just because you're jealous,' I flailed.

He stared at me, as if distracted by something else. 'Sorry,' he said. 'I was just trying to figure out what you mean. Have I . . .? Are you suggesting that I am jealous of Daniel Cleaver? Over you?'

'No, not over me,' I said, furious because I realized it did sound like that. 'I was just assuming you must have some reason to be so horrible about my boyfriend other than pure malevolence.'

'Mark, darling,' cooed Natasha, tripping prettily across the lawn to join us. She was so tall and thin she hadn't felt the need to put heels on, so could walk easily across the lawn without sinking, as if designed for it, like a camel in the desert. 'Come and tell your mother about the dining furniture we saw in Conran.'

'Just take care of yourself, that's all,' he said quietly, 'and I'd tell your mum to watch out for herself too,' he said, nodding pointedly in the direction of Julio as Natasha dragged him off.

After 45 minutes more horror I thought I could decently leave, pleading work to Una.

'You career girls! Can't put it off forever you know: tick-tock-tick-tock,' she said.

I had to have a cigarette in the car for five minutes before I was calm enough to set off. Then just as I got back to the main road my dad's car drove past. Sitting next to him in the front seat was Penny Husbands-Bosworth, wearing a red lace underwired uplift basque, and two bunny ears.

By the time I got back to London and off the motorway I was feeling pretty shaky and back much earlier than I expected, so I thought, instead of going straight home, I'd go round to Daniel's for a bit of reassurance.

I parked nose to nose with Daniel's car. There was no answer when I rang, so I left it a while and rang again in case it was just in the middle of a really good wicket or something. Still no answer. I knew he must be around because his car was there and he'd said he was going to be working and watching the cricket. I looked up at his window and there was Daniel. I beamed at him, waved and pointed at the door. He disappeared, I assumed to press the buzzer, so I rang the bell again. He took a bit of time to answer: 'Hi, Bridge. Just on the phone to America. Can I meet you in the pub in ten minutes?'

'OK,' I said cheerfully, without thinking, and set off towards the corner. But when I looked round, there he was again, not on the phone, but watching me out of the window.

Cunning as a fox, I pretended not to see and kept walking, but inside I was in turmoil. Why was he watching? Why hadn't he answered the door first time? Why didn't he just press the buzzer and let me come up straight away? Suddenly it hit me like a thunderbolt. He was with a woman.

My heart pounding, I rounded the corner, then, keeping flat against the wall, I peered round to check he had gone from the window. No sign of him. I hurried back and assumed a crouching position in the porch next to his, observing his doorway between the pillars in case a woman came out. I waited, crouched in the position for some time. But then I started to think: if a woman did come out, how would I know it was Daniel's flat she had come out of and not one of the other flats in the building? What would I do? Challenge her? Make a citizen's arrest? Also, what was to stop him leaving the woman in the flat with instructions to stay there until he had had time to get to the pub?

I looked at my watch. 6.30. Hah! The pub wasn't open yet. Perfect excuse. Emboldened, I hurried back towards the door and pushed the buzzer.

'Bridget, is that you again?' he snapped.

'The pub isn't open yet.'

There was silence. Did I hear a voice in the background? In denial, I told myself he was just laundering money or dealing in drugs. He was probably trying to hide polythene bags full of cocaine under the floorboards helped by some smooth South American men with ponytails.

'Let me in,' I said.

'I told you, I'm on the phone.'

'Let me in.'

'What?' He was playing for time, I could tell.

'Press the buzzer, Daniel,' I said.

Isn't it funny how you can detect someone's presence, even though you can't see, hear or otherwise discern them? Oh, of *course* I'd checked the cupboards on the way up the stairs and there was no one in any of them. But I knew there was a woman in Daniel's house. Maybe it was a slight smell . . . something about the way Daniel was behaving. Whatever it was, I just *knew*.

We stood there warily at opposite sides of the sitting room. I was just desperate to start running around opening and closing all the cupboards like my mother and ringing 1471 to see if there was a number stored from America.

'What have you got on?' he said. I had forgotten about Janine's outfit in the excitement.

'A bridesmaid's dress,' I said, haughtily.

'Would you like a drink?' said Daniel. I thought fast. I needed to get him into the kitchen so I could go through all the cupboards.

'A cup of tea, please.'

'Are you all right?' he said.

'Yes! Fine!' I trilled. 'Marvellous time at the party. Only one dressed as a tart, had to put on a bridesmaid dress, Mark Darcy was there with Natasha, that's a nice shirt your wearing . . .' I stopped, out of breath, realizing I had turned (there was no 'was turning' about it) into my mother.

He looked at me for a moment, then set off into the

kitchen at which I quickly leapt across the room to look behind the sofa and the curtains.

'What are you doing?'

Daniel was standing in the doorway.

'Nothing, nothing. Just thought I might have left a skirt of mine behind the sofa,' I said, wildly plumping up the cushions as if I were in a French farce.

He looked suspicious and headed off to the kitchen again.

Deciding there was no time to dial 1471, I quickly checked the cupboard where he keeps the duvet for the sofabed – no human habitation – then followed him to the kitchen, pulling open the door of the hall cupboard as I passed at which the ironing board fell out, followed by a cardboard box full of old 45s which slithered out all over the floor.

'What are you doing?' said Daniel mildly again, coming out of the kitchen.

'Sorry, just caught the door with my sleeve,' I said. 'Just on my way to the loo.'

Daniel was staring at me as if I was mad, so I couldn't go and check the bedroom. Instead I locked the loo door and started frantically looking around for things. I wasn't exactly sure what, but long blonde hairs, tissues with lipstick marks on, alien hairbrushes – any of these would have been a sign. Nothing. Next I quietly unlocked the door, looked both ways, slipped along the corridor, pushed open the door of Daniel's bedroom and nearly jumped out of my skin. There was someone in the room.

'Bridge.' It was Daniel, defensively holding a pair of jeans in front of him. 'What are you doing in here?'

'I heard you come in here so . . . I thought . . . It was a

secret assignation,' I said, approaching him in what would have been a sexy way were it not for the floral sprig dress. I leaned my head on his chest and put my arms around him, trying to smell his shirt for perfume traces and get a good look at the bed, which was unmade as usual.

'Mmmm, you've still got the bunny girl outfit on underneath, haven't you?' he said, starting to unzip the bridesmaid dress and pressing against me in a way which made his intentions very clear. I suddenly thought this might be a trick and he was going to seduce me while the woman slipped out unnoticed.

'Oooh, the kettle must be boiling,' said Daniel suddenly, zipping my dress up again and patting me reassuringly in a way that was most unlike him. Usually once he gets going he will see things through to their logical conclusion come earthquake, tidal wave or naked pictures of Virginia Bottomley on the television.

'Ooh yes, better make that cuppa,' I said, thinking it would give me a chance to get a good look round the bedroom and scout the study.

'After you,' said Daniel, pushing me out and shutting the door so I had to walk ahead of him back into the kitchen. As I did so I suddenly caught sight of the door that led up to the roof terrace.

'Shall we go and sit down?' said Daniel.

That was where she was, she was on the bloody roof.

'What's the matter with you?' he said as I stared at the door suspiciously.

'No-thing,' I sing-songed gaily, flopping into the sitting room. 'Just a little tired from the party.'

I flung myself insouciantly on to the sofa, wondering whether to streak faster than the speed of light down to the study as the final place she might be or just go hell for leather for the roof. I figured if she wasn't on the roof it meant she must be in the study, in the bedroom wardrobe, or under the bed. If we then went up on the roof she would be able to escape. But if that was the case, surely Daniel would have suggested going up on the roof much sooner.

He brought me a cup of tea and sat down at his laptop, which was open and turned on. Only then did I start to think that maybe there was no woman. There was a document up on the screen – maybe he really had been working and on the phone to America. And I was making a complete prat of myself behaving like a madwoman.

'Are you sure everything's all right, Bridge?'

'Fine, yes. Why?'

'Well, coming round unannounced like this dressed as a rabbit disguised as a bridesmaid and burrowing into all the rooms in a strange way. Not meaning to pry or anything, I just wondered if there was an explanation, that's all.'

I felt a complete fool. It was bloody Mark Darcy trying to wreck my relationship by sowing suspicions in my mind. Poor Daniel, it was so unfair to doubt him in this way, because of the word of some arrogant, ill-tempered, top-flight human-rights lawyer. Then I heard a scraping noise on the roof above us.

'I think maybe I'm just a bit hot,' I said, watching Daniel carefully. 'I think maybe I'll go and sit on the roof for a while.'

'For God's sake, will you sit still for two minutes!' he yelled, moving to bar my path, but I was too quick for him. I dodged past, opened the door, ran up the stairs and opened the hatch out into the sunlight.

There, spread out on a sunlounger, was a bronzed, long-limbed, blonde-haired stark-naked woman. I stood there frozen to the spot, feeling like an enormous pudding in the bridesmaid dress. The woman raised her head, lifted her sunglasses and looked at me with one eye closed. I heard Daniel coming up the stairs behind me.

'Honey,' said the woman, in an American accent, looking over my head at him. 'I thought you said she was *thin*.'

AUGUST

Disintegration

Tuesday 1 August

8st 12, alcohol units 3, cigarettes 40 (but have stopped inhaling in order to smoke more), calories 450 (off food), 1471 calls 14, Instants 7.

5 a.m. I'm falling apart. My boyfriend is sleeping with a bronzed giantess. My mother is sleeping with a Portuguese. Jeremy is sleeping with a horrible trollop, Prince Charles is sleeping with Camilla Parker-Bowles. Do not know what to believe in or hold on to any more. Feel like ringing Daniel in hope he could deny everything, come up with plausible explanation for the clothes-free rooftop valkyrie – younger sister, friendly neighbour recovering from flood or similar – which would make everything all right. But Tom has taped a piece of paper to the telephone saying, 'Do not ring Daniel or you will regret it.'

Should have gone to stay with Tom as suggested. Hate being alone in middle of night, smoking and snivelling like mad psychopath. Fear Dan downstairs might hear and ring loony bin. Oh God, what's wrong with me? Why does nothing ever work out? It is because I am too fat. Toy with ringing Tom again but only called him 45 minutes ago. Cannot face going into work.

After rooftop encounter I didn't say a single word to Daniel: just put my nose in the air, slithered past him, marched down to the street into car and drove away. Went immediately to Tom's, who poured vodka straight down my throat from the bottle, adding the tomato juice and Worcester sauce afterwards. Daniel had left three messages when I got back, asking me to call him. Did not, following advice of Tom, who reminded me that the only way to succeed with men is to be really horrible to them. Used to think he was cynical and wrong but I think I was nice to Daniel and look what happened.

Oh God, birds have started singing. Have to go to work in three and a half hours. Can't do it. Help, help. Have suddenly had brainwave: ring Mum.

10 a.m. Mum was *brilliant*. 'Darling,' she said. 'Of course you haven't woken me. I'm just leaving for the studio. I can't believe you've got in a state like this over a stupid *man*. They're all completely self-centred, sexually incontinent and no use to man nor beast. Yes, that *does* include you, Julio. Now come along, darling. Brace up. Back to sleep. Go into work looking drop-dead gorgeous. Leave no one – especially Daniel – in any doubt that you've thrown him over and suddenly discovered how *marvellous* life is without that pompous, dissolute old *fart* bossing you around and you'll be fine.'

'Are *you* all right, Mum?' I said, thinking about Dad arriving at Una's party with asbestos-widow Penny Husbands-Bosworth.

'Darling, you are sweet. I'm under such terrible pressure.'

'Is there anything I can do?'

'Actually, there is something,' she said, brightening. 'Do any of your friends have a number for Lisa Leeson? You know, Nick Leeson's wife? I've been desperate to get her for days. She'd be perfect for "Suddenly Single".'

'I was talking about Dad, not "Suddenly Single,"' I hissed.

'Daddy? I'm not under pressure from Daddy. Don't be silly, darling.'

'But the party . . . and Mrs Husbands-Bosworth.'

'Oh, I know, hilarious. Made a complete silly fool of himself trying to attract my attention. What did she think she looked like, a hamster or something? Anyway, must run, I'm frighteningly busy but will you think who might have a number for Lisa? Let me give you my *direct line*, darling. And let's have no more of this silly whining.'

'Oh, but Mum, I have to work with Daniel, I—'

'Darling – wrong way round. He has to work with you. Give him hell, baby.' (Oh God, I don't know who she's been mixing with.) 'I've been thinking, anyway. It's high time you got out of that silly dead-end job where no one appreciates you. Prepare to hand in your notice, kid. Yes, darling . . . I'm going to get you a job in television.'

Am just off to work looking like Ivana bloody Trump wearing a suit and lip gloss.

Wednesday 2 August

8st 12, thigh circumference 18 inches, alcohol units 3 (but v. pure sort of wine), cigarettes 7 (but did not inhale), calories 1500 (excellent), teas 0, coffees 3 (but made with real coffee beans therefore less cellulite-inducing), total caffeine units 4.

Everything's fine. Am going to get down to 8st 7lb again and free thighs entirely of cellulite. Certain everything will be all right then. Have embarked on intensive detoxification programme involving no tea no coffee no alcohol no white flour no milk and what was it? Oh well. No fish, maybe. What you have to do is dry-skin brushing for five minutes every morning, then a fifteen-minute bath with anti-cellulite essential oils in it, during which one kneads one's cellulite as one would dough, followed by massaging more anti-cellulite oil into the cellulite.

This last bit puzzles me – does the anti-cellulite oil actually soak into the cellulite through the skin? In which case, if you put self-tanning lotion on does that mean you get suntanned cellulite inside? Or suntanned blood? Or a suntanned lymphatic drainage system? Urgh. Anyway . . . (Cigarettes. That was the other thing. No cigarettes. Oh well. Too late now. I'll do that tomorrow.)

Thursday 3 August

8st 11, thigh circumference 18 inches (honestly, what is bloody point), alcohol units 0, cigarettes 25 (excellent, considering), negative thoughts: approx. 445 per hour, positive thoughts 0.

Head state v. bad again. Cannot bear thought of Daniel with someone else. Mind is full of horrid fantasies about them doing things together. The plans to lose weight and change personality kept me aloft for two days, only to collapse around my ears. I realize it was only a complicated form of denial. Was believing could totally reinvent self in space of small number of days, thereby negating impact of Daniel's hurtful and humiliating infidelity, since it had happened to me in a previous incarnation and would never have happened to my new improved self. Unfortunately, I now realize the whole point of the aloof over-made-up ice-queen on anti-cellulite diet palaver was to make Daniel realize the error of his ways. Tom did warn me of this and said 90 per cent of plastic surgery was done on women whose husbands had run off with a younger woman. I said the rooftop giantess was not so much younger as taller but Tom said that wasn't the point. Humph.

Daniel kept sending me computer messages at work. 'We should talk,' etc., which I studiously ignored. But the more he sent the more I got carried away, imagining that the self-reinvention was working, that he realized he had made a terrible, terrible mistake, had only now understood how much he truly loved me, and that the rooftop giantess was history.

Tonight he caught up with me outside the office as I was leaving. 'Darling, please, we really need to talk.'

Like a fool I went for a drink with him to the American Bar at the Savoy, let him soften me up with champagne and 'I feel so terrible I really miss you blar blar blar.' Then the very second he got me to admit, 'Oh, Daniel, I miss you too,' he suddenly went all patronizing and businesslike and said, 'The thing is, Suki and I . . .'

'Suki? Pukey, more like,' I said, thinking he was about to say, 'are brother and sister,' 'cousins,' 'bitter enemies,' or 'history.' Instead he looked rather cross.

'Oh, I can't explain,' he said huffily. 'It's very special.'

I stared at him, astonished at the audacity of his volte-face.

'I'm sorry, love,' he said, taking out his credit card and starting to lean back to get the attention of the waiter, 'but we're getting married.'

Friday 4 August

Thigh circumference 18 inches, negative thoughts 600 per minute, panic attacks 4, crying attacks 12 (but both times only in toilets and remembered to take mascara), Instants 7.

Office. Third-floor toilets. This is just . . . just . . . intolerable. What on earth possessed me to think it was a good idea to have an affair with my boss? Cannot deal with it out there. Daniel has announced his engagement to the giantess. Sales reps who I didn't think even knew about our affair keep ringing up to congratulate me and I have to explain that actually he has got engaged to someone else. I keep remembering how romantic it was when we started and it was all secret computer messages and trysts in the lift. I heard Daniel on the phone arranging to meet Pukey tonight and he said in a flopsy-bunny voice, 'Not too bad . . . so far,' and I knew he was talking about my reaction, as if I were Sara bloody Keays or someone. Am seriously considering face-lift.

Tuesday 8 August

9st, alcohol units 7 (har har), cigarettes 29 (tee hee), calories 5 million, negative thoughts 0, thoughts, general 0.

Just called Jude. I told her a bit about the tragedy with Daniel and she was horrified, immediately declared a state of emergency and said she would call Sharon and fix for us all to meet at nine. She couldn't come till then because she was meeting Vile Richard, who'd at last agreed to come to Relationship Counselling with her.

2 a.m. Gor es wor blurry goofun tonight though. Ooof. Tumbled over.

Wednesday 9 August

9st 2 (but in good cause), thigh circumference 16 inches (either miracle or hangover error), alcohol units 0 (but body still drinking units from last night), cigarettes 0 (ugh).

8 a.m. Ugh. In physically disastrous state but emotionally v. much cheered up by night out. Jude arrived in vixen-from-hell fury because Vile Richard had stood her up for the Relationship Counselling.

'The therapist women obviously just thought he was an imaginary boyfriend and I was a very, very sad person.'

'So what did you do?' I said sympathetically, banishing a rogue disloyal thought from Satan that said, 'She was right.'

'She said I had to talk about the problems I had that were unrelated to Richard.'

'But you don't have any problems that are unrelated to Richard,' said Sharon.

'I know. I told her that, then she said I had a problem with boundaries and charged me fifty-five quid.'

'Why didn't he turn up? I hope the sadistic worm had a decent excuse,' said Sharon.

'He said he got tied up at work,' said Jude. 'I said to him, "Listen, you don't have a monopoly on commitment problems. Actually, I have a commitment problem. If you ever deal with your own commitment problem you might be brought up short by my commitment problem, by which time it'll be *too late*."'

'*Have* you got a commitment problem?' I said, intrigued, immediately thinking maybe I had a commitment problem.

'Of *course* I've got a commitment problem,' snarled Jude. 'It's just that nobody ever sees it because it's so submerged by Richard's commitment problem. Actually, my commitment problem goes much deeper than his.'

'Well, exactly,' said Sharon. 'But you don't go round wearing your commitment problem on your sleeve like every bloody man over the age of twenty does these days.'

'Exactly my point,' spat Jude, trying to light up another Silk Cut but having trouble with the lighter.

'The whole bloody world's got a commitment problem,' growled Sharon in a guttural, almost Clint Eastwood voice. 'It's the three-minute culture. It's a global attention-span deficit. It's typical of men to annex a global trend and turn it into a male device to reject women to make themselves feel clever and us feel stupid. It's nothing but fuckwittage.'

'Bastards!' I shouted happily. 'Shall we have another bottle of wine?'

9 a.m. Blimey. Mum just rang. 'Darling,' she said. 'Guess what? *Good Afternoon!* are looking for researchers. Current affairs, terribly good. I've spoken to Richard Finch, the editor, and told him all about you. I said you had a degree in politics, darling. Don't worry, he'll be far too busy to check. He wants you to come in on Monday for a chat.'

Monday. Oh my God. That only gives me five days to learn Current Affairs.

Saturday 12 August

9st 3 (still in very good cause), alcohol units 3 (v.g.), cigarettes 32 (v.v. bad, particularly since first day of giving up), calories 1800 (g.), Instants 4 (fair), no. of serious current affairs articles read 1.5, 1471 calls 22 (OK), minutes spent having cross imaginary conversations with Daniel 120 (v.g.), minutes spent imagining Daniel begging me to come back 90 (excellent).

Right. Determined to be v. positive about everything. Am going to change life: become well informed re: current affairs, stop smoking entirely and form functional relationship with adult man.

8.30 a.m. Still have not had fag. V.g.

8.35 a.m. No fags all day. Excellent.

8.40 a.m. Wonder if anything nice has come in post?

8.45 a.m. Ugh. Hateful document from Social Security Agency asking for £1452. What? How can this be? Have not got £1452. Oh God, need fag to calm nerves. Mustn't. Mustn't.

8.47 a.m. Just had fag. But no-smoking day does not start officially till have got dressed. Suddenly start thinking of former boyfriend Peter with whom had functional relationship for seven years until finished with him for heartfelt, agonizing reasons can no longer remember. Every so often – usually when he has no one to go on holiday with – he tries to get back together and says he wants us to get married. Before know where am, am carried away with idea of Peter being answer. Why be unhappy and lonely when Peter wants to be with me? Quickly find telephone, ring Peter and leave message on his answerphone – merely asking him to give me call rather than whole plan of spending rest of life together, etc.

1.15 p.m. Peter has not rung back. Am repulsive to all men now, even Peter.

4.45 p.m. No-smoking policy in tatters. Peter finally rang. 'Hi, Bee.' (We always used to call each other Bee and Waspy.) 'I was going to ring you anyway. I've got some good news. I'm getting married.'

Ugh. V. bad feeling in pancreas area. Exes should never, never go out with or marry other people but should remain celibate to the end of their days in order to provide you with a mental fallback position.

'Bee?' said Waspy. 'Bzzzzzzz?'

'Sorry,' I said, slumping dizzily against the wall. 'Just, um, saw a car accident out of the window.'

I was evidently superfluous to the conversation, however, as Waspy gushed on about the cost of marquees for about twenty minutes, then said, 'Have to go. We're cooking Delia Smith venison sausages with juniper berries tonight and watching TV.'

Ugh. Have just smoked entire packet of Silk Cut as act

of self-annihilating existential despair. Hope they both become obese and have to be lifted out of the window by crane.

5.45 p.m. Trying to concentrate hard on memorizing names of Shadow Cabinet to avoid spiral of self-doubt. Have never met Waspy's Intended of course but imagine giant thin blonde rooftop giantess-type who rises at five each morning, goes to gym, rubs herself down with salt then runs international merchant bank all day without smudging mascara.

Realize with sinking humiliation that reason have been feeling smug about Peter all these years was that I finished with him and now he is effectively finishing with me by marrying Mrs Giant Valkyrie bottom. Sink into morbid, cynical reflection on how much romantic heartbreak is to do with ego and miffed pride rather than actual loss, also incorporating sub-thought that reason for Fergie's insane over-confidence may be that Andrew still wants her back (until he marries someone else, har har).

6.45 p.m. Was just starting to watch the 6 o'clock news, notebook poised, when Mum burst in bearing carrier bags.

'Now, darling,' she said sailing past me into the kitchen. 'I've brought you some nice soup, and some smart outfits of mine for Monday!' She was wearing a lime green suit, black tights and high-heeled court shoes. She looked like Cilla Black on *Blind Date*.

'Where *do* you keep your soup ladles?' she said, banging cupboard doors. 'Honestly, darling. What a mess! Now. Have a look through these bags while I heat up the soup.'

Deciding to overlook the fact that it was a) August

b) boiling hot c) 6.15 and d) I didn't want any soup, I peered cautiously into the first carrier bag, where there was something pleated and synthetic in bright yellow with a terracotta leaf design. 'Er, Mum . . .' I began, but then her handbag started ringing.

'Ah, that'll be Julio. Yup, yup.' She was balancing a portable phone under her chin now and scribbling. 'Yup, yup. Put it on, darling,' she hissed. 'Yup, yup. Yup. Yup.'

Now I have missed the news and she has gone off to a Cheese and Wine party, leaving me looking like Teresa Gorman in a bright blue suit with slithery green blouse underneath and blue eyeshadow right up to my eyebrows.

'Don't be silly, darling,' was her parting shot. 'If you don't do *something* about your appearance you'll never get a new job, never mind another boyfriend!'

Midnight. after she'd gone, called Tom, who took me to a party a friend of his from art school was having at the Saatchi Gallery to stop me obsessing.

'Bridget,' he muttered nervously as we walked into the white hole and sea of grunge youths. 'You know it's unhip to laugh at Installation, don't you?'

'OK, OK,' I said sulkily. 'I won't make any dead fish jokes.'

Someone called Gav said 'Hi': twenty-two maybe, sexy, in a shrunken T-shirt revealing a chopping-board-like midriff.

'It's really, really, really, *really* amazing,' Gav was saying. 'It's, like, a sullied Utopia with these really, really, *really* good echoes of, like, lost national identities.'

He led us excitedly across the big white space to a toilet roll: inside out with the cardboard outside the paper.

They looked at me expectantly. Suddenly I knew I was going to cry. Tom was now drooling over a giant bar of soap bearing the imprint of a penis. Gav was staring at me. 'Wow, that is, like, a really, really, *really* wild . . .' he whispered reverently as I blinked back tears, '. . . response.'

'Just going to the loo,' I blurted, rushing away past a configuration of sanitary-towel bags. There was a queue outside a Portaloo, and I joined it, shaking. Suddenly, just when it was almost my turn, I felt a hand on my arm. It was Daniel.

'Bridge, what are you doing here?'

'What does it look like?' I snapped. 'Excuse me, I'm in a hurry.' I burst into the cubicle and was just about to get on with it when I realized the toilet was actually a moulding of the inside of a toilet, vacuum-packed in plastic. Then Daniel put his head round the door.

'Bridge, don't wee on the Installation, will you?' he said, and closed the door again.

When I came out he had vanished. I couldn't see Gav, Tom or anyone I knew. Eventually I found the real toilets, sat down and burst into tears, thinking I wasn't fit to be in society any more, and just needed to get away till I stopped feeling like this. Tom was waiting outside.

'Come and talk to Gav,' he said. 'He's really, like, into you.' Then he took one look at my face and said. 'Oh shit, I'll take you home.'

It's no good. When someone leaves you, apart from missing them, apart from the fact that the whole little world you've created together collapses, and that everything you see or do reminds you of them, the worst is the thought that they tried you out and, in the end, the whole sum of parts which adds up to you got stamped REJECT by the one you love. How can you not be left with the personal confidence of a passed-over British Rail sandwich?

'Gav likes you,' said Tom.

'Gav is ten. Anyway he only liked me because he thought I was crying about a toilet roll.'

'Well you were, in a way,' said Tom. 'Bloody git, Daniel. If that man turns out to be singlehandedly responsible for all the fighting in Bosnia, I wouldn't be in the least surprised.'

Sunday 13 August

V. bad night. On top of everything else, tried to read myself to sleep with new issue of *Tatler*, only to find Mark Bloody Darcy's face smouldering out from feature on London's fifty most eligible bachelors going on about how rich and marvellous he was. Ugh. Made me even more depressed in way cannot quite fathom. Anyway. Am going to stop feeling sorry for myself and spend morning learning newspapers off by heart.

Noon. Rebecca just rang, asking if I was 'all right'. Thinking she meant all right about Daniel I said, 'Chuh, well it's very depressing.'

'Oh, poor you. Yes, I saw Peter last night . . . (Where? What? Why wasn't I invited?) '. . . and he was telling everyone how upset you were about the wedding. As he said, it *is* difficult, single women do tend to get desperate as they get older . . .'

By lunchtime could no longer go on with Sunday, trying to pretend everything was OK. Rang up Jude and told her about Waspy, Rebecca, job interview, Mum, Daniel and general misery and arranged to meet at Jimmy Beez at two for a Bloody Mary.

6 p.m. As luck would have it, Jude had just been reading brilliant book called *Goddesses in Everywoman*. Apparently the book says that at certain times in your life everything goes wrong and you don't know which way to turn and it is as if everywhere around you stainless steel doors are clamping shut like in *Star Trek*. What you have to do is be a heroine and stay brave, without sinking into drink or self-pity and everything will be OK. And that all the Greek myths and many successful movies are all about human beings facing difficult trials and not being wimps but holding hard and thus coming out on top.

The book also says that coping with difficult times is like being in a conical shell-shaped spiral and there is a point at each turn that is very painful and difficult. That is your particular problem or sore spot. When you are at the narrow, pointy end of the spiral you come back to that situation very often as the rotations are quite small. As you go round, you will go through the troubled time less and less frequently but still you must come back to it, so you shouldn't feel when it happens that you are back to square one.

Trouble is now I have sobered up not sure I am 100 per cent sure what she was talking about.

Mum rang up and I tried to talk to her about how difficult it is being a woman and having a sell-by date for reproduction unlike men, but she just said, 'Oh, honestly, darling. You girls are just so picky and romantic these days: you've simply got too much choice. I'm not saying I didn't love Dad but, you know, we were always taught, instead of waiting to be swept off our feet, to "expect little, forgive much". And to be honest, darling, having children isn't all it's built up to be. I mean, no offence, I don't mean this personally but given my chance again I'm not sure I'd have . . .'

Oh God. Even my own mother wishes I'd never been born.

Monday 14 August

9st 5 (great – turned into lard mountain for interview, also have spot), alcohol units 0, cigarettes many, calories 1575 (but threw up so effectively 400, approx.).

Oh God. Terrified about interview. I have told Perpetua I am at the gynaecologist – I know I should have said dentist but opportunities to torture the nosiest woman in the world must not be allowed to slip through the net. I am almost ready and merely need to complete my make-up while practising my opinions on Tony Blair's leadership. Oh my God, who's the Shadow Defence Secretary? Oh fuck, oh fuck. Is it someone with a beard? Shit: telephone. I can't believe it: terrifying telephonic teenager with patronizing South London sing-song going, 'Hel-lo, Bridget, Richard Finch's office here. Richard's in Blackpool this morning so he won't be able to make the meeting.' Rescheduled for Wednesday. Will have to pretend have recurring gynaecological condition. Might as well take rest of morning off anyway.

Wednesday 16 August

Horrible night. Kept waking up bathed in sweat, panicking about the difference between the Ulster Unionists and SDLP and which of them Ian Paisley was involved in.

Instead of being ushered into the office to meet the great Richard Finch, I was left pouring sweat in reception for forty minutes thinking Oh my God who's the Health Secretary? before being picked up by the sing-song personal assistant – Patchouli – who sported Lycra cycle shorts and a nose stud and blanched at my Jigsaw suit, as if, in a hideously misjudged attempt to be formal, I had turned up in a floor-length shot-silk Laura Ashley ballgown.

'Richard says to come to the conference, know what I'm sayin'?' she muttered, powering off down a corridor while I scurried after her. She burst through a pink door into a vast open-plan office strewn with piles of scripts, TV screens suspended from the ceiling, charts all over the walls, and mountain bikes propped against the desks. At the far end was a large oblong table where the meeting was in progress. Everyone turned and stared as we approached.

A plump, middle-aged man with curly blond hair, a denim shirt and red Christopher Biggins spectacles was jigging up and down at the end of the table.

'Come on! Come on!' he was saying, holding up his fists like a boxer. 'I'm thinking Hugh Grant. I'm thinking Elizabeth Hurley. I'm thinking how come two months on they're still together. I'm thinking how come he gets away with it. That's it! How does a man with a girlfriend with looks like Elizabeth Hurley have a blow-job from a prostitute on a public highway and get away with it? What happened to hell hath no fury?'

I couldn't believe this. What about the Shadow Cabinet? What about the Peace Process? He was obviously trying to work out how he could get away with sleeping with a prostitute himself. Suddenly, he was looking straight at me.

'Do *you* know?' The entire table of grunge youths stared. 'You. You must be Bridget!' he shouted impatiently. 'How does a man with a beautiful girlfriend manage to sleep with a prostitute, get found out and get away with it?'

I panicked. My mind went blank.

'Well?' he said. 'Well? Come on, say something!'

'Well, maybe,' I said, because it was the only thing I could think of, 'it was because somebody swallowed the evidence.'

There was a deathly hush, then Richard Finch started to laugh. It was the most repulsive laugh I've ever heard in my life. Then all the grunge youths started to laugh as well.

'Bridget Jones,' said Richard Finch eventually, wiping his eyes. 'Welcome to *Good Afternoon!* Take a seat, my darling,' and then he winked.

Tuesday 22 August

9st 2, alcohol units 4, cigarettes 25, Instants 5.

Still haven't heard anything from the interview. Don't know what to do for Bank Holiday as cannot face remaining alone in London. Shazzer is going to the Edinburgh Festival, as is Tom, I think, also lots of people from the office. Would like to go but not sure can afford it and fear presence of Daniel. Also everyone will be more successful and having a better time than me.

Wednesday 23 August

Definitely going to Edinburgh. Daniel is working in London so no danger of bumping into him on the Royal Mile. It will be good for me to get away instead of obsessing and waiting for *Good Afternoon!* letter.

Thursday 24 August

I'm staying in London. I always think I'm going to enjoy going to Edinburgh then end up only being able to get into the mime acts. Also you dress for summer, then it's freezing cold and you have to teeter shivering for miles up cobble-stone precipices thinking everyone else is at a big party.

Friday 25 August

7 p.m. I *am* going to Edinburgh. Today Perpetua said, 'Bridget, this is *absurdly* short notice, but it's just occurred to me. I've taken a flat up in Edinburgh – I'd adore it if you wanted to stay.' So generous and hospitable of her.

10 p.m. Just called Perpetua and told her I'm not coming. It's all stupid. I can't afford it.

Saturday 26 August

8.30 a.m. Right, I'm going to have a quiet, healthy time at home. Lovely. I might finish *The Famished Road*.

9.00 a.m. Oh God, I'm so depressed. Everybody's gone to Edinburgh except me.

9.15 a.m. I wonder if Perpetua's left yet?

Midnight. Edinburgh. Oh God. I must go to see something tomorrow. Perpetua thinks I'm mad. She spent the entire train journey with the portable phone pressed to her ear, bellowing at the rest of us. 'Arthur Smith's *Hamlet* is completely booked up so we could go to the Coen brothers instead at five but that means we'll be too late for Richard Herring. So shall we not go to Jenny Eclair – Chuh! I frankly don't know why she still *bothers* – and do *Lanark*, then try to get into Harry Hill or Bondages and Julian Clary? Hang on. I'll try the Gilded Balloon. No, Harry Hill's booked up, so shall we skip the Coen brothers?'

I said I'd meet them at the Plaisance at six because I wanted to go to the George Hotel and leave a message for Tom, and I bumped into Tina in the bar. I didn't realize how far it was to the Plaisance, and when I got there it had started and there were no seats left. Secretly relieved, I walked or rather abseiled back to the flat, picked up a lovely jacket potato with a chicken curry and watched *Casualty*. I was supposed to meet Perpetua at the Assembly Rooms at nine. By the time I was ready it was 8.45 but I didn't realize you couldn't ring out on the phone so I couldn't book a taxi and by the time I got there it was too late. I went back to the

George bar to look for Tina and find out where Shazzer was. I'd just got myself a Bloody Mary and was trying to pretend I didn't mind not having any friends when I noticed a flurry of lights and cameras in one corner and nearly screamed. It was my mother, done up like Marianne Faithfull and about to interview Alan Yentob.

'Absolute quiet, everyone!' she trilled in a Una Alconbury flower-arranging voice.

'Aaaaand action!!!! Tell me, Alan,' she said, looking traumatized, 'have you ever had . . . suicidal thoughts?'

The telly's been quite good tonight, actually.

Sunday 27 August, Edinburgh

No. of shows seen 0.

2 a.m. Can't get to sleep. I bet they're all at a really nice party.

3 a.m. Just heard Perpetua come in, giving her verdict on the alternative comedians: 'Puerile . . . completely childish . . . just silly.' I think she might have misunderstood something somewhere along the line.

5 a.m. There is a man in the house. I can just *tell*.

6 a.m. He's in Debby from Marketing's room. Blimey.

9.30 a.m. Woken by Perpetua bellowing, 'Anyone coming to the poetry reading?!' Then it all went quiet and I heard Debby and the man whispering and him going into the kitchen. Then Perpetua's voice boomed out, 'What are you doing here?!! I said NO OVERNIGHT GUESTS.'

2 p.m. Oh my God. I've overslept.

7 p.m. King's Cross train. Oh dear. Met Jude in the George at three. We were going to go to a Question and Answer session but we had a few Bloody Marys and remembered that Question and Answer sessions have a bad effect on us. You get hyper tense trying to think up a question, putting your hand up and down. You finally get to ask it, in a semi-crouching position and odd high-pitched voice, then sit frozen with embarrassment, nodding like a dog in the back of a car whilst a twenty-minute answer in which you had no interest in the first place is directed at you. Anyway, before we knew where we were it was 5.30. Then Perpetua appeared with a whole bunch of people from the office.

'Ah, Bridget,' she bellowed. 'What have you been to see?' There was a big silence.

'Actually, I'm just about to go to . . .' I began confidently '. . . get the train.'

'You haven't been to see anything at all, have you?' she hooted. 'Anyway, you owe me seventy-five pounds for the room.'

'What?' I stammered.

'Yes!' she yelled. 'It would have been fifty pounds, but it's 50 per cent extra if there are two people in the room.'

'But . . . but, there weren't . . .'

'Oh, come *on*, Bridget, we all knew you had a man in there,' she roared. 'Don't worry about it. It isn't love, it's only Edinburgh. I'll make sure it gets back to Daniel and teaches him a lesson.'

Monday 28 August

9st 6 (full of beer and jacket potatoes), alcohol units 6, cigarettes 20, calories 2846.

Got back to message from Mum asking me what I thought about an electric handwhisk for Christmas, and to remember Christmas Day was a Monday this year so was I coming home on the Friday night or the Saturday?

Considerably less annoyingly, there was a letter from Richard Finch, the editor of *Good Afternoon!* offering me a job, I think. This is all it said:

OK, my darling. You're on.

Tuesday 29 August

9st 2, alcohol units 0 (v.g.), cigarettes 3 (g.), calories 1456 (pre-new-job healthy eating).

10.30 a.m. Office. Just called Richard Finch's assistant Patchouli and it is a job offer but must start in a week. I don't know anything about television but sod it, I'm stuck in a dead-end here, and it is just too humiliating working with Daniel now. I had better go and tell him.

11.15 a.m. I can't believe this. Daniel stared at me, ashen-faced. 'You can't do this,' he said. 'Have you any idea how difficult the last few weeks have been for me?' Then Perpetua burst in – she must have been eavesdropping outside the door.

'Daniel,' she exploded. 'You selfish, self-indulgent, manipulative, emotional blackmailer. It was you – for God's sake – who chucked *her*. So you can just bloody well put up with it.'

Suddenly think I might love Perpetua, though not in a lesbian way.

SEPTEMBER

Up The Fireman's Pole

Monday 4 September

9st, alcohol units 0, cigarettes 27, calories 15, minutes spent having imaginary conversations with Daniel telling him what I think of him 145 (good, better).

8 a.m. First day at new job. Must begin as mean to go on, with new calm, authoritative image. And no smoking. Smoking is a sign of weakness and undermines one's personal authority.

8.30 a.m. Mum just rang, I assumed to wish me luck for the new job.

'Guess what, darling?' she began.

'What?'

'Elaine has invited you to their ruby wedding!' she said, pausing breathlessly and expectantly.

My mind went blank. Elaine? Brian - and - Elaine? Colin-and-Elaine? Elaine-married-to-Gordon-who-used-to-be-head-of-Tarmacadam-in-Kettering-Elaine?

'She thought it might be nice to have one or two young 'uns there to keep Mark company.'

Ah. *Malcolm* and Elaine. Begetters of the over-perfect Mark Darcy.

'Apparently he told Elaine he thought you were very attractive.'

'Durr! Don't lie,' I muttered. Pleased though.

'Well, I'm sure that's what he meant, anyway, darling.'

'What did he say?' I hissed, suddenly suspicious.

'He said you were very. . .'

'Mother. . .'

'Well, the word he actually used, darling, was "bizarre". But that's lovely, isn't it – "bizarrre"? Anyway, you can ask him all about it at the ruby wedding.'

'I'm not going all the way to Huntingdon to celebrate the ruby wedding of two people I have spoken to once for eight seconds since I was three, just to throw myself in the path of a rich divorcee who describes me as bizarre.'

'Now, don't be silly, darling.'

'Anyway, I've got to go,' I said, foolishly since she then, as always, began to gabble as if I were on death row and this was our last phone call before I was given a lethal injection.

'He was earning thousands of pounds an hour. Had a clock on his desk, tick-tock-tick-tock. Did I tell you I saw Mavis Enderby in the post office?'

'Mum. It's my first day at work today. I'm really nervous. I don't want to talk about Mavis Enderby.'

'Oh, my godfathers, darling!' What are you going to wear?'

'My short black skirt and a T-shirt.

'Oh, now you're not going to go looking like a *sloppy tramp* in dull colours. Put something smart and bright on. What about that lovely cerise two-piece you used to wear? Oh, by the way, did I tell you Una's gone down the Nile?'

Grrrr. Felt so bad when she put the phone down that smoked five Silk Cut in row. Non-v.g. start to day.

9 p.m. In bed, completely exhausted. I had forgotten how hideous it is starting a new job when nobody knows you, so your entire character becomes defined by every chance remark or slightly peculiar thing you say; and you can't even so much as go to put some make-up on without asking where the ladies' is.

I was late through no fault of my own. It was impossible to get into the TV studios as I had no pass and the door was run by the sort of security guards who think their job is to prevent the staff from entering the building. When I finally reached reception I wasn't allowed upstairs till someone came to get me. By this time it was 9.25 and the conference was at 9.30. Patchouli eventually appeared with two huge barking dogs, one of which started jumping up and licking my face while the other put its head straight up my skirt.

'They're Richard's. Aren't they, like, brilliant?' she said. 'I'll just take them to the car.'

'Won't I be late for the meeting?' I said desperately, holding on to the dog's head between my knees and trying to push it away. She looked me up and down as if to say, 'So?' and then disappeared, dragging the dogs.

By the time I got in to the office, therefore, the meeting had started and everyone stared except Richard, whose portly form was clad in a strange green woollen boilersuit.

'Come on, come on,' he was saying, jigging and beckoning the table towards him with both hands. 'I'm thinking

Nine o'clock Service. I'm thinking dirty vicars. I'm thinking sexual acts in church. I'm thinking, why do women fall for vicars? Come on. I'm not paying you for nothing. Have an idea.'

'Why don't you interview Joanna Trollope?' I said.

'A trollop?' he said, staring at me blankly. 'What trollop?'

'Joanna Trollope. The woman who wrote *The Rector's Wife* that was on the telly. *The Rector's Wife*. She should know.'

A leery smile spread across his face. 'Brilliant,' he said to my breasts. 'Absolutely fucking brilliant. Anyone got a number for Joanna Trollope?'

There was a long pause. 'Er, actually I have,' I said eventually, feeling walls of hate vibes coming from the grunge youths.

When the meeting was over I rushed to the loo to recover my composure where Patchouli was making herself up next to her friend, who was wearing a sprayed-on dress that showed her pants *and* midriff.

'This isn't too tarty, is it?' the girl was saying to Patchouli. 'You should have seen those bitch thirtysomethings' faces when I walked in . . . Oh!'

Both girls looked at me, horrified, with their hands over their mouths.

'We didn't mean you,' they said.

I am not sure if I am going to be able to stand this.

Saturday 9 September

8st 12 (v.g. advantage of new job with attendant nervous tension), alcohol units 4, cigarettes 10, calories 1876, minutes spent having imaginary conversations with Daniel 24 (excellent), minutes spent imagining re-run of conversations with mother in which I come out on top 94.

11.30 a.m. Why oh why did I give my mother a key to my flat? I was just – for the first time in five weeks – starting a weekend without wanting to stare at the wall and burst into tears. I'd got through a week at work. I was starting to think maybe it was all going to be OK, maybe I wasn't *necessarily* going to be eaten by an Alsatian when she burst in carrying a sewing machine.

'What on earth are you doing, silly?' she trilled. I was weighing out 100 grams of cereal for my breakfast using a bar of chocolate (the weights for the scales are in ounces which is no good because the calorie chart is in grams).

'Guess what, darling?' she said, beginning to open and shut all the cupboard doors.

'What?' I said, standing in my socks and nighty trying to wipe the mascara from under my eyes.

'Malcolm and Elaine are having the ruby wedding in London now, on the twenty-third, so you will be able to come and keep Mark company.'

'I don't want to keep Mark company,' I said through clenched teeth.

'Oh, but he's very clever. Been to Cambridge. Apparently he made a fortune in America . . .'

'I'm not going.'

'Now, come along, darling, let's not start,' she said, as if

I were thirteen. 'You see, Mark's completed on the house in Holland Park and he's throwing the whole party for them, six floors, caterers and everything . . . What are you going to wear?'

'Are you going with Julio or Dad?' I said, to shut her up.

'Oh, darling, I don't know. Probably both of them,' she said in the special, breathy voice she reserves for when she thinks she is Diana Dors.

'You can't do that.'

'But Daddy and I are still friends, darling. I'm just friends with Julio as well.'

Grr. Grrr. Grrrrrr. I absolutely cannot deal with her when she's like this.

'Anyway, I'll tell Elaine you'd love to come, shall I?' she said, picking up the inexplicable sewing machine as she headed for the door. 'Must fly. Byee!'

I am not going to spend another evening being danced about in front of Mark Darcy like a spoonful of puréed turnip in front of a baby. I am going to have to leave the country or something.

8 p.m. Off to dinner party. All the Smug Marrieds keep inviting me on Saturday nights now I am alone again, seating me opposite an increasingly horrifying selection of single men. It is very kind of them and I appreciate it v. much but it only seems to highlight my emotional failure and isolation – though Magda says I should remember that being single is better than having an adulterous, sexually incontinent husband.

Midnight. Oh dear. Everyone was trying to cheer up the spare man (thirty-seven, newly divorced by wife, sample view: 'I have to say, I do think Michael Howard is somewhat unfairly maligned.').

'Don't know what you're complaining about,' Jeremy was holding forth to him. 'Men get more attractive when they get older and women get less attractive, so all those twenty-two-year-olds who wouldn't look at you when you were twenty-five will be gagging for it.'

I sat, head down, quivering furiously at their inferences of female sell-by dates and life as game of musical chairs where girls without a chair/man when the music stops/they pass thirty are 'out'. Huh. As if.

'Oh yes, I quite agree it's much the best to go for younger partners,' I burst out, airily. 'Men in their thirties are *such* bores with their hang-ups and obsessive delusions that all women are trying to trap them into marriage. These days I'm only *really* interested in men in their early twenties. They're so much better able to . . . well, you know . . .'

'*Really*?' said Magda, rather too eagerly. 'How . . .?'.

'Yes, *you're* interested,' interjected Jeremy, glaring at Magda. 'But the point is *they're* not interested in *you*.'

'Um. Excuse me. My current boyfriend is twenty-three,' I said, sweetly.

There was a stunned silence.

'Well, in that case,' said Alex, smirking, 'you can bring him to us next Saturday when you come to dinner, can't you?'

Bugger. Where am I going to find a twenty-three-year-old who will come to dinner with Smug Marrieds on a Saturday night instead of taking contaminated Ecstasy tablets?

Friday 15 September

9st, alcohol units 0, cigarettes 4 (v.g.), calories 3222 (British Rail sandwiches hideously impregnated), minutes spent imagining speech will make when resigning from new job 210.

Ugh. Hateful conference with bully-boss Richard Finch going, 'Right. Harrods one pound-a-pee toilets. I'm thinking Fantasy Toilets. I'm thinking studio: Frank Skinner and Sir Richard Rogers on furry seats, armrests with TV screens, quilted loo paper. Bridget, you're Dole Youths Clampdown. I'm thinking the North. I'm thinking Dole Youths, loafing about, live down the line.'

'But . . . but . . .' I stammered.

'Patchouli!' he shouted, at which point the dogs under his desk woke up and started jumping about and barking.

'Wha'?' yelled Patchouli above the din. She was wearing a crocheted midi-dress with a floppy straw hat and an orange Bri-nylon saddle-stitched blouse on top. As if the things I used to wear in my teens were a hilarious joke.

'Where's the Dole Youths OB?'

'Liverpool.'

'Liverpool. OK, Bridget. OB crew outside Boots in the shopping centre, live at five thirty. Get me six Dole Youths.'

Later, as I was leaving to get the train, Patchouli yelled casually, 'Oh yeah, like, Bridget, it's not Liverpool, it's, like, Manchester, right?'

4.15 p.m. Manchester.

Number of Dole Youths approached 44, Number of Dole Youths agreed to be interviewed 0.

Manchester–London train 7 p.m. Ugh. by 4.45 I was running hysterically between the concrete flower tubs, gabbling.

''scuse me, are you employed? Never mind. 'hanks!'

'What are we doing, then?' asked the cameraman with no attempt to feign interest. 'Dole Youths,' I said gaily. 'Back in a mo!' then rushed round the corner and hit myself on the forehead. I could hear Richard over my earpiece going, 'Bridget . . . where the *fuck*. . . ? Dole Youths.' Then I spotted a cashpoint machine on the wall.

By 5.20 six youths claiming to be unemployed were neatly lined up in front of the camera, a crisp £20 note in each of their pockets while I flapped around trying to make oblique amends for being middle-class. At 5.30 I heard the signature tune bonging and crashing then Richard yelling, 'Sorry, Manchester, we're dropping you.'

'Urm . . .' I began, to the expectant faces. The youths clearly thought I had a syndrome that made me want to pretend I worked in TV. Worse, with working like a mad thing all week and coming up to Manchester I had been unable to do anything about the no-date trauma tomorrow. Then suddenly as I glanced across at the divine young whippersnappers, with the cashpoint machine in the background, the germ of an extremely morally suspect idea began to form itself in my mind.

Hmm. Think was right decision not to attempt to lure Dole Youth to Cosmo's dinner party. Would have been exploitative and wrong. Doesn't answer question of what to do about it, though. Think will go have a fag in the smoking carriage.

7.30 p.m. Ugh. 'Smoking Carriage' turned out to be Monstrous Pigsty where smokers were huddled, miserable and defiant. Realize it is no longer possible for smokers to live in dignity, instead being forced to sulk in the slimy underbelly of existence. Would not have been in least surprised if carriage had mysteriously been shunted off into siding never to be seen again. Maybe privatized rail firms will start running Smoking Trains and villagers will shake their fists and throw stones at them as they pass, terrifying their children with tales of fire-breathing freaks within. Anyway, rang Tom from miracle-on-train-phone (How does it work? How? No wires. Weird. Maybe somehow connected through electric contact between wheels and tracks) to moan about the no-twenty-three-year-old-date crisis.

'What about Gav?' he said.

'Gav?'

'You know. The guy you met at the Saatchi Gallery.'

'D'you think he'd mind?'

'No. He was really into you.'

'He wasn't. Shut-urrrrp.'

'He was. Stop obsessing. Leave it to me.'

Sometimes feel without Tom I would sink without trace and disappear.

Tuesday 19 September

8st 12 (v.g.), alcohol units 3 (v.g.), cigarettes 0 (too shameful to smoke in presence of healthy young whippersnappers).

Blimey, must hurry. About to go on date with Diet Coke-esque young whippersnapper. Gav turned out to be completely divine, and behaved exquisitely at Alex's dinner party on Saturday, flirting with all the wives, fawning over me and fending all their trick questions over our 'relationship' with the intellectual dexterity of a Fellow of All Souls. Unfortunately, I was so overcome with gratitude* in the taxi on the way back I was powerless to resist his advances**. I did, however, manage to get a grip of myself*** and not accept his invitation to go in for coffee. Subsequently, however, I felt guilty about being a prick-teaser****, so when Gav rang and asked me round to his house for dinner tonight I accepted graciously*****.

Midnight. Feel like Old Woman of the Hills. Was so long since had been on a date that was completely full of myself and could not resist boasting to taxi driver about my 'boyfriend' and going round to my 'boyfriend's', who was cooking me supper.

Unfortunately, however, when I got there, Number 4 Malden Road was a fruit and vegetable shop.

* lust
** put my hand on his knee
*** my panic
**** could not stop self thinking 'Damn, damn, damn!'
***** could barely contain my excitement

'Do you want to use my phone, love?' said the taxi driver wearily.

Of course I didn't know Gav's number, so I had to pretend to ring Gav and find it engaged and then ring Tom and try to ask him for Gav's address in a way that wouldn't make the taxi driver think I had been lying about having a boyfriend. Turned out it was 44 Malden Villas and had not been concentrating when wrote it down. Conversation between me and the taxi driver had rather dried up as we drove to the new address. I'm sure he thought I was a prostitute or something.

By the time I arrived I was feeling less than assured. It was all very sweet and shy to start with – a bit like going round to a potential Best Friend's house for tea at junior school. Gav had cooked spag bog. The problem came when food preparation and serving were over and activities turned to conversation. We ended up, for some reason, talking about Princess Diana.

'It seemed such a fairytale. I remember sitting on that wall outside St Paul's at the wedding,' I said. 'Were you there?'

Gav looked embarrassed. 'Actually, I was only six at the time.'

Eventually we gave up on conversation and Gav, with tremendous excitement (this, I recall, the fabulous thing about twenty-two-year-olds) began to kiss me and simultaneously try to find entrances to my clothes. Eventually he managed to slide his hand over my stomach at which point he said – it was so humiliating – 'Mmm. You're all squashy.'

I couldn't go on with it after that. Oh God. It's no good. I am too old and will have to give up, teach religious knowledge in a girls' school and move in with the hockey teacher.

Saturday 23 September

9st, alcohol units 0, cigarettes 0 (v.v.g.), draft replies written to Mark Darcy's invitation 14 (but at least has replaced imaginary conversations with Daniel).

10 a.m. Right. I am going to reply to Mark Darcy's invitation and say quite clearly and firmly that I will be unable to attend. There is no reason why I should go. I am not a close friend or relation, and would have to miss both *Blind Date* and *Casualty*.

Oh God, though. It is one of those mad invitations written in the third person, as if everyone is so posh that to acknowledge directly in person that they were having a party and wondered if you would like to come would be like calling the ladies' powder room the toilet. Seem to remember from childhood am supposed to reply in same oblique style as if I am imaginary person employed by self to reply to invitations from imaginary people employed by friends to issue invitations. What to put?

Bridget Jones regrets that she will be unable . . .

Miss Bridget Jones is distraught, that she will be unable . . .

Devastated does not do justice to the feelings of Miss Bridget Jones . . .

It is with great regret that we must announce that so great was Miss Bridget Jones's distress at not being able to accept the kind invitation of Mr Mark Darcy that she has topped herself and will therefore, more certainly than ever, now, be unable to accept Mr Mark Darcy's kind . . .

Ooh: telephone.

It was Dad: 'Bridget, my dear, you are coming to the horror event next Saturday, aren't you?'

'The Darcys' ruby wedding, you mean.'

'What else? It's been the only thing that has distracted your mother from the question of who's getting the mahogany ornament cabinet and nesting coffee tables since she got the Lisa Leeson interview at the beginning of August.'

'I was kind of hoping to get out of it.'

The line went quiet at the other end.

'Dad?'

There was a muffled sob. Dad was crying. I think Dad is having a nervous breakdown. Mind you, if I'd been married to Mum for thirty-nine years I'd have had a nervous breakdown, even without her running off with a Portuguese tour operator.

'What's wrong, Dad?'

'Oh, it's just . . . Sorry. It's just . . . I was hoping to get out of it too.'

'Well, why don't you? Hurray. Let's go to the pictures instead.'

'It's . . .' he broke down again. 'It's the thought of her going with that greasy beperfumed bouffant wop, and all my friends and colleagues of forty years saying "cheers" to the pair of them and writing me off as history.'

'They won't . . .'

'Oh yes, they will. I'm determined to go, Bridget. I'm going to get on my glad rags and hold my head up high and . . . but . . .' Sobs again.

'What?'

'I need some moral support.'

11.30 a.m.

Miss Bridget Jones has great pleasure . . .

Ms Bridget Jones thanks Mr Mark Darcy for his . . .

It is with great pleasure that Miss Bridget Jones accepts . . .

Oh, for God's sake.

Dear Mark,

Thank you for your invitation to your ruby wedding party for Malcolm and Elaine. I would love to come.

Yours,

Bridget Jones

Hmmm.

Yours,

Bridget

or just

Bridget

Bridget (Jones)

Right. Will just copy it out neatly and check spellings then send it.

Tuesday 26 September

8st 13, alcohol units 0, cigarettes 0, calories 1256, Instants 0, obsessive thoughts about Daniel 0, negative thoughts 0. Am perfect saint-style person.

It is great when you start thinking about your career instead of worrying about trivial things – men and relationships. It's going really well on *Good Afternoon!* I think I might have a gift for popular television. The really exciting news is that I am going to be given a try-out in front of the camera.

Richard Finch got this idea into his head at the end of last week that he wanted to do a Live Action Special with reporters attached to emergency services all over the capital. He didn't have much luck to start with. In fact people were going round the office saying he had been turned down by every Accident and Emergency unit, Police and Ambulance force in the Home Counties. But this morning when I arrived he grabbed me by the shoulders yelling, 'Bridget! We're on! Fire. I want you on-camera. I'm thinking mini-skirt. I'm thinking fireman's helmet. I'm thinking pointing the hose.'

Everything has been total mayhem ever since, with the everyday business of the day's news utterly forgotten and everyone gibbering down the phone about links, towers and OBs. Anyway, it is all happening tomorrow and I have to report to Lewisham fire station at 11 o'clock. I'm going to ring round everybody tonight and tell them to watch. Cannot wait to tell Mum.

Wednesday 27 September

8st 11 (shrunk with embarrassment), alcohol units 3, cigarettes 0 (no smoking in fire station) then 12 in 1 hour, calories 1584 (v.g.).

9 p.m. Have never been so humiliated in my life. Spent all day rehearsing and getting everything organized. The idea was that when they cut to Lewisham I was going to slide down the pole into shot and start interviewing a fireman. At five o'clock as we went on air I was perched at the top of the pole ready to slide down on my cue. Then suddenly in my earpiece I heard Richard shouting, 'Go, go, go go, go!' so I let go of the pole and started to slide. Then he continued, 'Go, go, go, Newcastle! Bridget, stand by in Lewisham. Coming to you in thirty seconds'.

I thought about dropping to the bottom of the pole and rushing back up the stairs but I was only a few feet down so I started to pull myself up again instead. Then suddenly there was a great bellow in my ear.

'Bridget! We're on you. What the fuck are you doing? You're meant to be sliding down the pole, not climbing up it. Go, go, go.'

Hysterically I grinned at the camera and dropped myself down, landing, as scheduled, by the feet of the fireman I was supposed to interview.

'Lewisham, we're out of time. Wind it up, wind it up, Bridget.' yelled Richard in my ear.

'And now back to the studio,' I said, and that was it.

Thursday 28 September

8st 12, alcohol units 2 (v.g.), cigarettes 11 (g.), calories 1850, job offers from fire service or rival TV stations 0 (perhaps not altogether surprising).

11 a.m. Am in disgrace and am laughing stock. Richard Finch humiliated me in front of the whole meeting flinging words like 'shambles', 'disgrace', and 'bleedin' bloody idiot' at me randomly.

'And now back to the studio,' seems to have turned into a new catchphrase in the office. Any time anyone gets asked a question they don't know the answer to they go. 'Errrr . . . and now back to the studio,' and burst out laughing. Funny thing is, though, the grunge youths are being much more friendly to me. Patchouli (even!) came up and said, 'Oh, like, don't take any notice of Richard, right? He's, like, you know, really into control, right. You know what I'm sayin'? That fireman's pole thing was really like subversive and brilliant, right. Anyway, like . . . now back to the studio, OK?'

Richard Finch now just either ignores me or shakes his head disbelieving whenever he comes anywhere near me, and I have been given nothing to do all day.

Oh God, I'm so depressed. I thought I'd found something I was good at for once and now it's all ruined, and on top of everything else it is the horrible ruby wedding party on Saturday and I have nothing to wear. I'm no good at anything. Not men. Not social skills. Not work. Nothing.

OCTOBER

Date with Darcy

Sunday 1 October

8st 11, cigarettes 17, alcohol units 0 (v.g., esp for party).

4 a.m. Startling. One of the most startling evenings of life.

After got depressed on Friday Jude came round and talked to me about being more positive about things, bringing with her fantastic black dress for me to borrow for party. Was worried that might split or spill on the dress but she said she had lots of money and dresses because of top job and did not matter so not to worry about it. Love Jude. Girls are so much nicer than men (apart from Tom – but homosexual). Decided to accessorize fantastic dress with black tights with Lycra and Light Shimmer (£6.95) and Pied à terre kitten-heel black suede shoes (have got mashed potato off).

Had shock on arrival at the party as Mark Darcy's house was not a thin white terraced house on Portland Road or similar as had anticipated, but huge, detached wedding cake-style mansion on the other side of Holland Park Avenue (where Harold Pinter, they say, lives) surrounded by greenery.

He had certainly pushed the boat out for his mum and

dad. All the trees were dotted with red fairy lights and strings of shiny red hearts in a really quite endearing manner and there was a red and white canopied walkway leading all the way up the front path.

At the door things began to look even more promising as we were greeted by serving staff who gave us champagne and relieved us of our gifts (I had bought Malcolm and Elaine a copy of Perry Como love songs from the year they were married, plus a Bodyshop Terracotta Essential Oil Burner as an extra present for Elaine as she had been asking me about Essential Oils at the Turkey Curry Buffet). Next we were ushered down a dramatic curved pale wood stairway lit by red heart-shaped candles on each step. Downstairs was one vast room, with a dark wood floor and a conservatory giving on to the garden. The whole room was lit by candles. Dad and I just stood and stared, completely speechless.

Instead of the cocktail fancies you would expect at a parent-generational do – compartmentalized cut-glass dishes full of gherkins; plates sporting savoury doilies and half grapefruits bespined with cheese-and-pineapple-chunk-ladened cocktail sticks – there were large silver trays containing prawn won tons, tomato and mozzarella tartlets and chicken saté. The guests looked as though they couldn't believe their luck, throwing their heads back and roaring with laughter. Una Alconbury looked as though she had just eaten a lemon.

'Oh dear,' said Dad, following my gaze, as Una bore down on us. 'I'm not sure this is going to be Mummy and Una's cup of tea.'

'Bit showy, isn't it?' said Una the second she was within earshot, pulling her stole huffily around her shoulders.

'I think if you take these things too far it gets a bit common.'

Oh, don't be absurd, Una. It's a sensational party,' said my father, helping himself to his nineteenth canapé.

'Mmm. I agree,' I said through a mouthful of tartlet, as my champagne glass was filled as if from nowhere. ''s bloody fantastic.' After psyching myself up for so long for Jaeger two-piece hell, I was euphoric. No one had even asked me why I wasn't married yet.

'Humph,' said Una.

Mum too was now bearing down on us.

'Bridget,' she yelled. 'Have you said hello to Mark?'

I suddenly realized cringing, that both Una and Mum must be coming up to their ruby weddings soon. Knowing Mum, it is highly unlikely she will let a trifling detail like leaving her husband and going off with a tour operator stand in the way of the celebrations and will be determined not to be outdone by Elaine Darcy at whatever price, even the sacrifice of a harmless daughter to an arranged marriage.

'Hold hard there, bigfeller,' said my dad, squeezing my arm.

'What a lovely house. Haven't you got a nice stole to put over your shoulders, Bridget? Dandruff!' trilled Mum, brushing Dad's back. 'Now, darling. Why on *earth* aren't you talking to Mark?'

'Um, well . . .' I mumbled.

'What do you think, Pam?' hissed Una tensely, nodding at the room.

'Showy,' whispered Mum, exaggerating her lip movements like Les Dawson.

'Exactly what I said,' mouthed Una triumphantly. 'Didn't I say so, Colin? Showy.'

I glanced around nervously and jumped in fright. There, looking at us, not three feet away, was Mark Darcy. He must have heard everything. I opened my mouth to say something – I'm not quite sure what – to try to improve matters, but he walked away.

Dinner was served in the 'Drawing Room' on the ground floor and I found myself in the queue on the stairs directly behind Mark Darcy.

'Hi,' I said, hoping to make amends for my mother's rudeness. He looked round, completely ignored me and looked back again.

'Hi,' I said again and poked him.

'Oh, hi, I'm sorry. I didn't see you,' he said.

'It's a great party,' I said. 'Thanks for inviting me.'

He stared at me for a moment. 'Oh, I didn't,' he said. 'My mother invited you. Anyway. Must see to the, er, *placement*. Very much enjoyed your Lewisham fire station report, by the way,' and he turned and strode upstairs, dodging between the diners and excusing himself while I reeled. Humph.

As he reached the top of the stairs Natasha appeared in a stunning gold satin sheath, grabbing his arm possessively and, in her haste, tripping over one of the candles which spilt red wax on the bottom of her dress. 'Fack,' she said. 'Fack.'

As they disappeared ahead I could hear her telling him off. 'I told you it was ridiculous spending all afternoon arranging candles in dangerous places for people to fall over. Your time would have been far better spent ensuring that the placement was . . .'

Funnily enough, the placement turned out to be rather brilliant. Mum was sitting next to neither Dad nor Julio but Brian Enderby, whom she always likes to flirt with. Julio had been put next to Mark Darcy's glamorous fifty-five-year-old aunt, who was beside herself with delight. My dad was pink with pleasure at sitting next to a stunning Shakira Caine look-alike. I was really excited. Maybe I would be sandwiched between two of Mark Darcy's dishy friends, top barristers or Americans from Boston, perhaps. But as I looked for my name on the chart a familiar voice piped up beside me.

'So how's my little Bridget? Aren't I the lucky one? Look, you're right next to me. Una tells me you've split up with your feller. I don't know! Durr! When are we going to get you married off?'

'Well I hope, when we do, I shall be the one to do the deed,' said a voice on my other side. 'I could do with a new vimper. Mmm. Apricot silk. Or maybe a nice thirty-nine-button souterne from Gamirellis.'

Mark had thoughtfully put me between Geoffrey Alconbury and the gay vicar.

Actually, though, once we all got a few drinks down us conversation was by no means stilted. I was asking the vicar what he thought about the miracle of Indian statues of Ganesh the Elephant God taking in milk. The vicar said the word in ecclesiastical circles was that the miracle was due to the effect on terracotta of a hot summer followed by cold weather.

As the meal broke up and people started to make their way downstairs for the dancing, I was thinking about what he said. Overcome with curiosity, and keen, also, to avoid having to do the twist with Geoffrey Alconbury, I excused myself, discreetly taking a teaspoon and milk jug from the table, and nipped into the room where the presents had –

rather proving Una's point about the showy element of things – already been unwrapped and put on display.

It took me a while to locate the terracotta oil burner, as it had been shoved near the back, but when I did I simply poured a little milk on to the teaspoon, tilted it and held it against the edge of the hole where you put the candle in. I couldn't believe it. The Essential Oil Burner was taking in milk. You could actually see the milk disappearing from the teaspoon.

'Oh my God, it's a miracle,' I exclaimed. How was I to know that was when Mark Darcy would be bloody well walking past?

'What are you doing?' he said, standing in the doorway.

I didn't know what to say. He obviously thought I was trying to steal the presents.

'Mmm?' he said.

'The Essential Oil Burner I bought your mother is taking in milk,' I muttered sulkily.

'Oh, don't be ridiculous,' he said, laughing.

'It *is* taking in milk,' I said indignantly. 'Look.'

I put some more milk on the teaspoon, tilted the spoon and sure enough the oil burner slowly started to take it in.

'You see,' I said proudly. 'It's a miracle.'

He was pretty impressed, I can tell you. 'You're right,' he said softly. 'It is a miracle.'

Just then Natasha appeared in the doorway. 'Oh, hi,' she said, seeing me. 'Not in your bunny girl outfit today, then,' and then gave a little laugh to disguise her bitchy comment as an amusing joke.

'Actually we bunnies wear these in the winter for warmth,' I said.

'John Rocha?' she said, staring at Jude's dress. 'Last autumn? I recognize the hem.'

I paused to think up something very witty and cutting to say, but unfortunately couldn't think of anything. So after a bit of a stupid pause I said, 'Anyway, I'm sure you're longing to circulate. Nice to see you again. Byee!'

I decided I needed to go outside for a little fresh air and a fag. It was a wonderful, warm, starry night with the moon lighting up all the rhododendron bushes. Personally, I have never been keen on rhododendrons. They remind me of Victorian country houses up North from D. H. Lawrence where people drown in lakes. I stepped down into the sunken garden. They were playing Viennese waltzes in a rather smart *fin de millennium* sort of way. Then suddenly I heard a noise above. A figure was silhouetted against the French windows. It was a blond adolescent, an attractive public schoolboy-type.

'Hi,' said the youth. He lit a cigarette unsteadily and stared, heading down the stairs towards me. 'Don't suppose you fancy a dance? Oh. Ah. Sorry,' he said, holding out his hand as if we were at the Eton open day and he was a former Home Secretary who had forgotten his manners: 'Simon Dalrymple.'

'Bridget Jones,' I said, holding out my hand stiffly, feeling as if I were a member of a war cabinet.

'Hi. Yah. Really nice to meet you. So *can* we have a dance?' he said, reverting to the public schoolboy again.

'Well, I don't know, I'm sure,' I said, reverting to pissed floozy and giving an involuntary raucous laugh like a prostitute in a Yates Wine Lodge.

'I mean out here. Just for a moment.'

I hesitated. I was flattered, to tell you the truth. What

with this and performing a miracle in front of Mark Darcy it was all starting to go to my head.

'Please,' pressed Simon. 'I've never danced with an older woman before. Oh, gosh, I'm sorry, I didn't mean. . .' he went on, seeing my face. 'I mean, someone who's left school,' he said, seizing my hand passionately. 'Would you mind? I'd be most awfully, awfully grateful.'

Simon Dalrymple had obviously been taught ballroom dancing from birth, so it was rather nice being expertly guided to and fro, but the trouble was, he seemed to have, well, not to put too fine a point on it, the most enormous erection I've ever had the good fortune to come across, and us dancing so close it was not the sort of thing one could pass off as a pencil case.

'I'll take over, now, Simon,' said a voice.

It was Mark Darcy.

'Come along. Back inside. You should be in bed now.'

Simon looked completely crushed. He blushed scarlet and hurried back into the party.

'May I?' said Mark, holding out his hand to me.

'No,' I said, furious.

'What's the matter?'

'Um,' I said, flailing for an excuse for being so angry. 'That was a horrible thing to do to a young whippersnapper, throwing your weight about and humiliating him like that at a sensitive age.' Then, noticing his baffled expression, I gabbled on. 'Though I do appreciate your asking me to your party. Marvellous. Thank you very much. Fantastic party.'

'Yes. I think you've said that,' he said, blinking fast. The truth is, he looked rather agitated and hurt.

'I . . .' He paused, then started pacing around the patio,

sighing and running his hand through his hair. 'How's the . . . Have you read any good books lately?' Unbelievable.

'Mark,' I said. 'If you ask me once more if I've read any good books lately I'm going to eat my head. Why don't you ask me something else? Ring the changes a bit. Ask me if I've got any hobbies, or a view on the single European currency, or if I've had any particularly disturbing experiences with rubber.'

'I . . .' he began again.

'Or if I had to sleep with Douglas Hurd, Michael Howard or Jim Davidson which one I'd choose. Actually, no contest, Douglas Hurd.'

'Douglas Hurd?' said Mark.

'Mmm. Yes. So deliciously strict but fair.'

'Hmmm,' said Mark thoughtfully. 'You say that, but Michael Howard's got an extremely attractive and intelligent wife. He must have some sort of hidden charms.'

'Like what, you mean?' I said, childishly, hoping he would say something about sex.

'Well . . .'

'He might be a good shag, I suppose,' I supplied.

'Or a fantastically skilful potter.'

'Or a qualified aromatherapist.'

'Will you have dinner with me, Bridget?' he said abruptly, and rather crossly, as if he was going to sit me down at a table somewhere and tell me off.

I stopped and stared at him. 'Has my mum put you up to this?' I said, suspiciously.

'No . . . I . . .'

'Una Alconbury?'

'No, no . . .'

Suddenly I realized what was going on. 'It's *your* mum, isn't it?'

'Well, my mother has . . .'

'I don't want to be asked out to dinner just because your mum wants you to. Anyway, what would we talk about? You'd just ask me if I've read any good books lately and then I'd have to make up some pathetic lie and—'

He stared at me in consternation. 'But Una Alconbury told me you were a sort of literary whizz-woman, completely obsessed with books.'

'Did she?' I said, rather pleased by the idea suddenly. 'What else did she tell you?'

'Well, that you're a radical feminist and have an incredibly glamorous life . . .'

'Oooh,' I purred.

'. . .with millions of men taking you out.'

'Huh.'

'I heard about Daniel. I'm sorry.'

'I suppose you did try to warn me,' I muttered sulkily. 'What have you got against him, anyway?'

'He slept with my wife,' he said. 'Two weeks after our wedding.'

I stared at him aghast as a voice above us shouted, 'Markee!' It was Natasha, silhouetted against the lights, peering down to see what was going on.

'Markee!' she called again. 'What are you doing down there?'

'Last Christmas,' Mark went on hurriedly, 'I thought if my mother said the words "Bridget Jones" just once more I would go to the *Sunday People* and accuse her of abusing me as a child with a bicycle pump. Then when I met you . . . and I was wearing that ridiculous diamond-patterned jumper that Una had bought me for Christmas . . . Bridget, all the other girls I know are so lacquered over. I don't know anyone else who would fasten a bunny tail to their pants or . . .'

'Mark!' yelled Natasha, heading down the stairs towards us.

'But you're going out with somebody,' I said, rather pointing out the obvious.

'I'm not any more, actually,' he said. 'Just dinner? Some time?

'OK,' I whispered. 'OK.'

Afterwards I thought I'd better go home: what with Natasha watching my every move as if she were a crocodile and I was getting a bit near to her eggs, and me having given Mark Darcy my address and phone number and having fixed to see him next Tuesday. On my way through the dancing room I saw Mum, Una and Elaine Darcy chatting animatedly to Mark – couldn't help imagining their faces if they knew what had just gone on. I suddenly had a vision of next year's Turkey Curry Buffet with Brian Enderby hitching up the waistband of his trousers going, 'Harumph. Nice to see the young people enjoying themselves, isn't it?' and Mark Darcy and me forced to do tricks for the assembled company, like rubbing noses, or having sex in front of them, like a pair of performing seals.

Tuesday 3 October

8st 12, alcohol units 3 (v.g.), cigarettes 21 (bad), number of times said word 'bastard' in last twenty-four hours 369 (approx.).

7.30 p.m. Complete panic stations. Mark Darcy is coming round to pick me up in half an hour. Just got home from work with mad hair and unfortunate laundry crisis outfit on. Help oh help. Was planning to wear white 501s but suddenly occurs to me he may be the type who will take me to a posh scary restaurant. Oh God, do not have anything posh to wear. Do you think he will expect me to put bunny tail on? Not that I'm interested in him or anything.

7.50 p.m. Oh God oh God. Still have not washed hair. Will quickly get into bath.

8.00 p.m. Drying hair now. V. much hope Mark Darcy is late as do not want him to find me in dressing gown with wet hair.

8.05 p.m. Hair is more or less dry now. Then just have to do make-up, get dressed and put mess behind sofa. Must prioritize. Consider make-up most important, then mess-disposal.

8.15 p.m. Still not here. V.g. Keen on a man who comes round late, in stark contrast to people who come round early, startling and panicking one and finding unsightly items still unhidden in the home.

8.20 p.m. Well, pretty much ready now. Maybe will put something different on.

8.30 p.m. This is weird. Does not seem like him to be more than half an hour late.

9.00 p.m. Cannot quite believe it. Mark Darcy has stood me up. Bastard!

Thursday 5 October

8st 13 (bad), chocolate items 4 (bad), number of times watched video 17 (bad).

11 a.m. In loos at work. Oh no. Oh no. On top of humiliating standing-up débâcle, found self horrible centre of attention at morning meeting today.

'Right, Bridget,' said Richard Finch. 'I'm going to give you another chance. The Isabella Rossellini trial. Verdict expected today. We think she's going to get off. Get yourself down to the High Court. I don't want to see you climbing up any poles or lamp-posts. I want a hard-headed interview. Ask her if this means it's OK for us all to murder people every time we don't fancy having sex with them. What are you waiting for, Bridget? Off you go.'

I had no idea, not even a glimmer of a clue as to what he was talking about.

'You have noticed the Isabella Rossellini trial, haven't you?' said Richard. 'You do read the papers, occasionally?'

The trouble with this job is that people keep flinging names and stories at you and you have a split second to decide whether or not to admit you have no idea what they're talking about, and if you let the moment go then you'll spend the next half hour desperately flailing for clues to what it is you are discussing in depth and at length with a confident air: which is precisely what happened with Isabella Rossellini.

And now I must set off to meet scary camera crew at the law courts in five minutes to cover and report on a story on the television without having the faintest idea what it is about.

11.05 a.m. Thank God for Patchouli. Just came out of the toilets and she was being pulled along by Richard's dogs straining at the leash.

'Are you OK?' she said. 'You look a bit freaked out.'

'No, no, I'm fine,' I said.

'Sure?' she stared at me for a moment. 'Listen, right, you realize he didn't mean Isabella Rossellini at the meeting, didn't you? He's thinking of Elena Rossini, right.'

Oh, thank God and all his angels in heaven above. Elena Rossini is the children's nanny accused of murdering her employer after he allegedly subjected her to repeated rape and effective house arrest for eighteen months. I grabbed a couple of newspapers to gen up and ran for a taxi.

3 p.m. Cannot believe what just happened. Was hanging around outside the High Court for ages with the camera crew and a whole gang of reporters all waiting for the trial to end. Was bloody good fun, actually. Even started to see the funny side of being stood up by Mr Perfect Pants Mark Darcy. Suddenly realized I'd run out of cigarettes. So I whispered to the cameraman, who was really nice, if he thought it would be OK if I nipped to the shop for 5 minutes and he said it would be fine, because you're always given warning when they're about to come out and they'd come and get me if it was about to happen.

When they heard I was going to the shop, a lot of reporters asked me if I'd bring them fags and sweets and so it took quite a while working it all out. I was just standing in the shop trying to keep all the change separate with the shopkeeper when this bloke walked in obviously in a real hurry and said, 'Could you let me have a box of Quality Street?' as if I wasn't there. The poor shopkeeper looked at me as if not sure what to do.

'Excuse me, does the word "queue" mean anything to you?' I said in a hoity-toity voice, turning round to look at him. I made a weird noise. It was Mark Darcy all dressed up in his barrister outfit. He just stared at me, in that way he has.

'Where in the name of arse were you last night?' I said.

'I might ask the same question of you,' he said, icily.

At that moment the camera assistant burst into the shop. 'Bridget!' he yelled. 'We've missed the interview. Elena Rossini's come out and gone. Did you get my Minstrels?'

Speechless, I grabbed the edge of the sweet counter for support.

'Missed it?' I said as soon as I could steady my breathing. 'Missed it? Oh God. This was my last chance after the fireman's pole and I was buying sweets. I'll be sacked. Did the others get interviews?'

'Actually, nobody got any interviews with her,' said Mark Darcy.

'Didn't they?' I said, looking up at him desperately. 'But how do you know?'

'Because I was defending her, and I told her not to give any,' he said casually. 'Look, she's out there in my car.'

As I looked, Elena Rossini put her head out of the car window and shouted in a foreign accent, 'Mark, sorry. You bring me Dairy Box, please, instead of Quality Street?' Just then our camera car drew up.

'Derek!' yelled the cameraman out of the window. 'Get us a Twix and a Lion Bar, will you?'

'So where were you last night?' asked Mark Darcy.

'Waiting for bloody you,' I said between clenched teeth.

'What, at five past eight? When I rang on your doorbell twelve times?'

'Yes, I was . . .' I said, feeling the first twinges of realization, 'drying my hair.'

'Big hairdryer?' he said.

'Yes 1600 volts, Salon Selectives,' I said proudly. 'Why?'

'Maybe you should get a quieter hairdryer or begin your *toilette* a little earlier. Anyway. Come on,' he said laughing. 'Get your cameraman ready, I'll see what I can do for you.'

Oh God. How embarrassing. Am complete berk.

9 p.m. Cannot believe how marvellously everything has turned out. Have just played the *Good Afternoon!* headlines back for the fifth time.

'And a *Good Afternoon!* exclusive,' it says. '*Good Afternoon!*: the only television programme to bring you an exclusive interview with Elena Rossini, just minutes after today's not guilty verdict. Our home news correspondent, Bridget Jones, brings you this exclusive report.'

I *love* that bit: 'Our home news correspondent, Bridget Jones, brings you this exclusive report.'

I'll just play it back once more, then I'll definitely put it away.

Friday 6 October

9st (comfort eating), alcohol units 6 (drink problem), Instants 6 (comfort gambling), 1471 calls to see if Mark Darcy has rung 21 (curiosity only, obviously), number of times watched video 9 (better).

9 p.m. Humph. Left a message for Mum yesterday to tell her all about my scoop so when she rang tonight I assumed it would be to congratulate me, but no, she was just going on about the party. It was Una and Geoffrey this, Brian and Mavis that and how marvellous Mark was and why didn't I talk to him, etc., etc.? Temptation to tell her what happened almost overwhelming but managed to control myself by envisaging consequences: screaming ecstasy at the making of the date and brutal murder of only daughter when she heard the actual outcome.

Keep hoping he might ring me up and ask me for another date after the hairdryer débâcle. Maybe I should write him a note to say thank you for the interview and sorry about the hairdryer. It's not because I fancy him or anything. Simple good manners demands it.

Thursday 12 October

9st 1 (bad), alcohol units 3 (both healthy and normal), cigarettes 13, fat units 17 (wonder if it's possible to calculate fat unit content of entire body? Hope otherwise), Instants 3 (fair), 1471 calls to see if Mark Darcy has rung 12 (better).

Humph. Incensed by patronizing article in the paper by Smug Married journalist. It was headlined, with subtle-as-a-Frankie-Howerd-sexual-innuendo-style irony: 'The Joy of Single Life'.

'They're young, ambitious and rich but their lives hide an aching loneliness . . . When they leave work a gaping emotional hole opens up before them . . . Lonely style-obsessed individuals seek consolation in packeted comfort food of the kind their mother might have made.'

Huh. Bloody nerve. How does Mrs Smug Married-at-twenty-two think she knows, thank you very much?

I'm going to write an article based on 'dozens of conversations' with Smug Marrieds: 'When they leave work, they always burst into tears because, though exhausted, they have to peel potatoes and put all the washing in while their porky bloater husbands slump burping in front of the football demanding plates of chips. On other nights they plop, wearing unstylish pinnies, into big black holes after their husbands have rung to say they're working late again, with the sound of creaking leatherware and sexy Singletons tittering in the background.'

Met Sharon, Jude and Tom after work. Tom, too, was working on a furious imaginary article about the Smug Marrieds' gaping emotional holes.

'Their influence affects everything from the kind of

houses being built to the kind of food that stocks the supermarket shelves,' Tom's appalled article was going to rant. 'Everywhere we see Anne Summers shops catering for housewives trying pathetically to simulate the thrilling sex enjoyed by Singletons and ever-more exotic foodstuffs in Marks & Spencer for exhausted couples trying to pretend they're in a lovely restaurant like the Singletons and don't have to do the washing up.'

'I'm bloody sick of this arrogant hand-wringing about single life!' roared Sharon.

'Yes, yes!' I said.

'You forgot the fuckwittage,' burped Jude. 'We always have fuckwittage.'

'Anyway, we're not lonely. We have extended families in the form of networks of friends connected by telephone,' said Tom.

'Yes! Hurrah! Singletons should not have to explain themselves all the time but should have an accepted status – like geisha girls do,' I shouted happily, slurping on my tumbler of Chilean Chardonnay.

'Geisha girls?' said Sharon, looking at me coldly.

'Shut up, Bridge,' slurred Tom. 'You're drunk. You're just trying to escape from your yawning emotional hole into drunk.'

'Well, so's bloody well Shazzer,' I said sulkily.

'I's not,' said Sharon.

'You's blurr are,' I said.

'Look. Shuddup,' said Jude, burping again. 'Shagernoth-ebol Chardonnay?'

Friday 13 October

9st 3 (but have temporarily turned into wine bag), alcohol units 0 (but feeding off wine bag), calories 0 (v.g.).*
**Actually might as well be honest here. Not really v.g. as only 0 because puked up 5876 calories immediately after eating.*

Oh God, I'm so lonely. An entire weekend stretching ahead with no one to love or have fun with. Anyway, I don't care. I've got a lovely steamed ginger pudding from M&S to put in the microwave.

Sunday 15 October

9st (better), alcohol units 5 (but special occasion), cigarettes 16, calories 2456, minutes spent thinking about Mr Darcy 245.

8.55 a.m. Just nipped out for fags prior to getting changed ready for BBC *Pride and Prejudice*. Hard to believe there are so many cars out on the roads. Shouldn't they be at home getting ready? Love the nation being so addicted. The basis of my own addiction, I know, is my simple human need for Darcy to get off with Elizabeth. Tom says football guru Nick Hornby says in his book that men's obsession with football is not vicarious. The testosterone-crazed fans do not wish themselves on the pitch, claims Hornby, instead seeing their team as their chosen representatives, rather like parliament. That is precisely my feeling about Darcy and Elizabeth. They are my chosen representatives in the field of shagging, or, rather, courtship. I do not, however, wish to see any actual goals. I would hate to see Darcy and Elizabeth in bed, smoking a cigarette afterwards. That would be unnatural and wrong and I would quickly lose interest.

10.30 a.m. Jude just called and we spent twenty minutes growling, 'Fawaw, that Mr Darcy.' I love the way he talks, sort of as if he can't be bothered. *Ding-dong*! Then we had a long discussion about the comparative merits of Mr Darcy and Mark Darcy, both agreeing that Mr Darcy was more attractive because he was ruder but that being imaginary was a disadvantage that could not be overlooked.

Monday 23 October

9st 2, alcohol units 0 (v.g. Have discovered delicious new alcohol substitute drink called Smoothies – v. nice, fruity), cigarettes 0 (Smoothies removes need for cigarettes), Smoothies 22, calories 4265 (4135 of them Smoothies).

Ugh. Just about to watch *Panorama* on 'The trend of well qualified female breadwinners – stealing all the best jobs' (one of which I pray to the Lord in Heaven Above and all his Seraphims I am about to become): 'Does the solution lie in redesigning the educational syllabus?' When I stumbled upon a photograph in the *Standard* of Darcy and Elizabeth, hideous, dressed as modern-day luvvies, draped all over each other in a meadow: she with blonde Sloane hair, and linen trouser suit, he in striped polo neck and leather jacket with Shoestring-style moustache. Apparently they are already sleeping together. That is absolutely disgusting. Feel disorientated and worried, for surely Mr Darcy would never do anything so vain and frivolous as to be an actor and yet Mr Darcy *is* an actor. Hmmm. All v. confusing.

Tuesday 24 October

9st 3 (bloody Smoothies), alcohol units 0, cigarettes 0, Smoothies 32.

On marvellous roll with work. Ever since Elena whatserface interview, seems can do no wrong.

'Come on! Come on! Rosemary West!' Richard Finch was saying, when I got into the office (bit late, actually, sort of thing that could happen to anyone), holding up his fists like a boxer. 'I'm thinking lesbian rape victims, I'm thinking Jeanette Winterson, I'm thinking *Good Afternoon!* doctor, I'm thinking what lesbians actually *do*. That's it! What *do* lesbians actually *do* in bed?' Suddenly, he was looking straight at me.

'Do *you* know?' Everyone stared at me. 'Come on, Bridget-fucking-late-again,' he shouted impatiently. 'What do lesbians actually do in bed?'

I took a deep breath. 'Actually, I think we should be doing the off-screen romance between Darcy and Elizabeth.'

He looked me up and down slowly. 'Brilliant,' he said reverently. 'Absolutely fucking brilliant. OK. The actors who play Darcy and Elizabeth? Come on, come on,' he said, boxing at the meeting.

'Colin Firth and Jennifer Ehle,' I said.

'You, my darling,' he said to one of my breasts, 'are an absolute fucking genius.'

I always hoped I would turn out to be a genius, but I never believed it would actually happen to me – or *my left breast*.

NOVEMBER

A Criminal in the Family

Wednesday 1 November

8st 13lb 8oz (yesss! yesss!), alcohol units 2 (v.g.), cigarettes 4 (but could not smoke at Tom's in case set Alternative Miss World costume alight), calories 1848 (g.), Smoothies 12 (excellent progress).

Just went round to Tom's for top-level summit to discuss the Mark Darcy scenario. Found Tom, however, in a complete lather about the forthcoming Alternative Miss World contest. Having decided ages ago to go as 'Miss Global Warming', he was having a crisis of confidence.

'I haven't got a hope in hell,' he was saying, looking in the mirror, then flouncing to the window. He was wearing a polystyrene sphere painted like map of the globe but with the polar ice-caps melting and a large burn mark on Brazil. In one hand he was holding a piece of tropical hardwood and a Lynx aerosol, and in the other an indeterminate furry item which he claimed was a dead ocelot. 'Do you think I should have a melanoma?' he asked.

'Is it a beauty contest or a fancy dress contest?'

'That's just it, I don't know, no one knows,' said Tom, throwing down his headdress – a miniature tree which he was intending to set alight during the contest. 'It's both. It's everything. Beauty. Originality. Artistry. It's all ridiculously unclear.'

'Do you have to be a pouffe to enter?' I asked, fiddling with a bit of polystyrene.

'No. Anyone can enter: women, animals, anything. That's exactly the problem,' he said, flouncing back to the mirror. 'Sometimes I think I'd stand more chance trying to win with a really confident dog.'

Eventually we agreed that though the global warming theme *in itself* was faultless, the polystyrene sphere was not, perhaps, the most flattering shape for evening wear. In fact in the end we found we were thinking more towards a fluid sheath of shot-silk-effect Yves Klein blue, floating over smoke and earth shades to symbolize the melting of the polar ice-caps.

Deciding I wasn't going to get the best out of Tom over Mark Darcy just at the moment, I excused myself before it got too late, promising to think hard about Swim and Daywear.

When I got back I called Jude but she started telling me about a marvellous new oriental idea in this month's *Cosmopolitan* called Feng Shui, which helps you get everything you want in life. All you have to do, apparently, is clean out all the cupboards in your flat to unblock yourself, then divide the flat up into nine sections (which is called mapping the ba-gua), each of which represents a different area of your life: career, family, relationships, wealth, or offspring, for example. Whatever you have in that area of your house will govern how that area of your life performs. For example, if you keep finding you have no money it could be due to the presence of a wastepaper basket in your Wealth Corner.

V. excited by new theory as could explain a lot. Resolve to buy *Cosmo* at earliest opportunity. Jude says not to tell Sharon as, naturally, she thinks Feng Shui is bollocks. Managed, eventually, to bring conversation round to Mark Darcy.

'*Of course* you don't fancy him, Bridge, the thought never crossed my mind for a second,' said Jude. She said the answer was obvious: I should have a dinner party and invite him.

'It's perfect,' she said. 'It's not like asking him for a date, so it takes away all the pressure and you can show off like mad and get all your friends to pretend to think you're marvellous.'

'Jude,' I said, hurt, 'did you say, "pretend"?'

Friday 3 November

9st 2 (humph), alcohol units 2, cigarettes 8, Smoothies 13, calories 5245.

11 a.m. V. excited about dinner party. Have bought marvellous new recipe book by Marco Pierre White. At last understand the simple difference between home cooking and restaurant food. As Marco says, it is all to do with *concentration* of taste. The secret of sauces, of course, apart from taste concentration, lies in real stock. One must boil up large pans of fish bones, chicken carcasses, etc., then freeze them in form of ice-stockcubes. Then cooking to Michelin star standard becomes as easy as making shepherd's pie: easier, in fact, as do not need to peel potatoes, merely confit them in goose fat. Cannot believe have not realized this before.

This will be the menu:

Velouté of Celery (v. simple and cheap when have made stock).

Char-grilled Tuna on Velouté of Cherry Tomatoes Coulis with Confit of Garlic and Fondant Potatoes.

Confit of Oranges. Grand Marnier Crème Anglaise.

Will be marvellous. Will become known as brilliant but apparently effortless cook.

People will flock to my dinner parties, enthusing, 'It's really great going to Bridget's for dinner, one gets Michelin star-style food in a bohemian setting.' Mark Darcy will be v. impressed and will realize I am not common or incompetent.

Sunday 5 November

9st (disaster), cigarettes 32, alcohol units 6 (shop has run out of Smoothies – careless bastards), calories 2266, Instants 4.

7 p.m. Humph. Bonfire night and not invited to any bonfires. Rockets going off tauntingly left, right and centre. Going round to Tom's.

11 p.m. Bloody good evening at Tom's, who was trying to deal with the fact that the Alternative Miss World title had gone to Joan of Bloody Arc.

'The thing that makes me really angry is that they say it isn't a beauty contest but really it is. I mean, I'm sure if it wasn't for this nose . . .' said Tom, staring at himself furiously in the mirror.

'What?

'My nose.'

'What's wrong with it?'

'What's wrong with it? Chuh! *Look* at it.'

It turned out there was a very, very tiny bump where someone had shoved a glass in his face when he was seventeen. 'Do you see what I mean?'

My feeling was, as I explained, that the bump in itself couldn't be blamed for Joan of Arc snatching the title from directly beneath it, as it were, unless the judges were using a Hubble telescope, but then Tom started saying he was too fat as well and was going on a diet.

'How many calories are you supposed to eat if you're on a diet?' he said.

'About a thousand. Well, I usually aim for a thousand and come in at about fifteen hundred,' I said, realizing as I said it that the last bit wasn't strictly true.

'A thousand?' said Tom, incredulously. 'But I thought you needed two thousand just to survive.'

I looked at him nonplussed. I realized that I have spent so many years being on a diet that the idea that you might actually need calories to survive has been completely wiped out of my consciousness. Have reached point where believe nutritional ideal is to eat nothing at all, and that the only reason people eat is because they are so greedy they cannot stop themselves from breaking out and ruining their diets.

'How many calories in a boiled egg?' said Tom.

'Seventy-five.'

'Banana?'

'Large or small?'

'Small.'

'Peeled?'

'Yes.'

'Eighty,' I said, confidently.

'Olive?'

'Black or green?'

'Black.'

'Nine.'

'Hobnob?'

'Eighty-one.'

'Box of Milk Tray?'

'Ten thousand, eight hundred and ninety-six.'

'How do you know all this?'

I thought about it 'I just do, as one knows one's alphabet or times tables.'

'OK. Nine eights,' said Tom.

'Sixty-four. No, fifty-six. Seventy-two.'

'What letter comes before J? Quick.'

'P. L, I mean.'

Tom says I am sick but I happen to know for a fact that I am normal and no different from everyone else, i.e. Sharon and Jude. Frankly, I am quite worried about Tom. I think taking part in a beauty contest has started to make him crack under the pressures we women have long been subjected to and he is becoming insecure, appearance-obsessed and borderline anorexic.

Evening climaxed with Tom cheering himself up letting off rockets from the roof terrace into the garden of the people below who Tom says are homophobic.

Thursday 9 November

8st 13 (better without Smoothies), alcohol units 5 (better than having huge stomach full of puréed fruit), cigarettes 12, calories 1456 (excellent).

V. excited about the dinner party. Fixed for a week on Tuesday. This is the guest list:

Jude	Vile Richard
Shazzer	
Tom	Pretentious Jerome (unless get v. lucky and it is off between him and Tom by Tuesday)
Magda	Jeremy
Me	Mark Darcy

Mark Darcy seemed very pleased when I rang him up.

'What are you going to cook?' he said. 'Are you good at cooking?'

'Oh, you know . . .' I said. 'Actually, I usually use Marco Pierre White. It's amazing how simple it can be if one goes for a concentration of taste.'

He laughed and then said, 'Well, don't do anything too complicated. Remember everyone's coming to see *you*, not to eat parfaits in sugar cages.'

Daniel would never have said anything nice like that. V. much looking forward to the dinner party.

Saturday 11 November

8st 12, alcohol units 4, cigarettes 35 (crisis), calories 456 (off food).

Tom has disappeared. First began to fear for him this morning when Sharon rang saying wouldn't swear on her mother's life but thought she'd seen him from the window of a taxi on Thursday night wandering along Ladbroke Grove with his hand over his mouth and, she thought, a black eye. By the time she'd got the taxi to go back he'd disappeared. She'd left two messages for him yesterday asking if he was OK but had had no reply.

I suddenly realized, as she spoke, that I had left a message for Tom myself on Wednesday asking if he was around at the weekend and he hadn't replied, which is not like him at all. Frantic phoning ensued. Tom's phone just rang and rang, so I called Jude who said she hadn't heard from him either. I tried Tom's Pretentious Jerome: nothing. Jude said she'd ring Simon, who lives in next street to Tom, and get him to go round. She called back 20 minutes later saying Simon had rung Tom's bell for ages and hammered on the door but no reply. Then Sharon rang again. She'd spoken to Rebecca, who thought Tom was supposed to be going to Michael's for lunch. I called Michael who said Tom had left a weird message talking in an odd distorted voice saying he wasn't going to be able to come and hadn't given a reason.

3 p.m. Starting to feel really panicky, at the same time enjoying sense of being at centre of drama. Am practically Tom's best friend so everyone is ringing me and am adopting calm yet deeply concerned air about whole thing.

Suddenly occurs to me that maybe he's just met someone new and is enjoying honeymoon-style shag hideaway for a few days. Maybe it wasn't him Sharon saw, or black eye is just product of lively enthusiastic young sex or post-modern-style ironic retrospective Rocky Horror Show make-up. Must make more phone calls to test new theory.

3.30 p.m. General opinion quashes new theory, since it is widely agreed to be impossible for Tom to meet new man, let alone start affair, without ringing everyone up to show off. Cannot argue with that. Wild thoughts ranging through head. No denying that Tom has been disturbed lately. Start to wonder whether am really good friend. We are all so selfish and busy in London. Would it be possible for one of my friends to be so unhappy that they . . . ooh, *that's* where I put this month's *Marie Claire*: on top of fridge!

As flicked through *Marie Claire* started fantasizing about Tom's funeral and what I would wear. Aaargh, have suddenly remembered MP who died in a bin liner with tubes round neck and chocolate orange in mouth or something. Wonder if Tom has been doing weird sexual practices without telling us?

5 p.m. Just called Jude again.

'Do you think we should call the police and get them to break in?' I said.

'I already rang them,' said Jude.

'What did they say?' I couldn't help feeling secretly annoyed that Jude had rung the police without clearing it with me first. I am Tom's best friend, not Jude.

'They didn't seem very impressed. They said to call them if we still couldn't find him by Monday. You can see their point. It does seem a bit alarmist to report that a twenty-nine-year-old single man is not in on Saturday morning and has failed to turn up for a lunch party he said he wouldn't be coming to anyway.'

'Something's wrong, though, I just know,' I said in a mysterious, loaded voice, realizing for the first time what an intensely instinctive and intuitive person I am.

'I know what you mean,' said Jude, portentiously. 'I can feel it, too. Something's definitely wrong.'

7 p.m. Extraordinary. After spoke to Jude could not face shopping or similar lighthearted things. Thought this might be the perfect time to do the Feng Shui so went out and bought *Cosmopolitan*. Carefully, using the drawing in *Cosmo*, I mapped the ba-gua of the flat. Had a flash of horrified realization. There was a wastepaper basket in my Helpful Friends Corner. No wonder bloody Tom had disappeared.

Quickly rang Jude to report same. Jude said to move the wastepaper basket.

'Where to, though?' I said. 'I'm not putting it in my Relationship or Offspring Corners.'

Jude said hang on, she'd go have a look at *Cosmo*.

'How about Wealth?' she said, when she came back.

'Hmm, I don't know, what with Christmas coming up and everything,' I said, feeling really mean even as I said it.

'Well, if that's the way you look at things. I mean you're probably going to have one less present to buy anyway . . .' said Jude accusingly.

In the end I decided to put the wastepaper basket in my Knowledge Corner and went out to the greengrocer to get some plants with *round leaves* to put in the Family and

Helpful Friends Corners (spiky-leaved plants, particularly cacti, are counter-productive). Was just getting plant pot out of the cupboard under sink when heard a jangling sound. I suddenly hit myself hard on the forehead. They were Tom's spare keys from when he went to Ibiza.

For a moment I thought about going round there *without Jude*. I mean, she rang the police without telling me, didn't she? But in the end it seemed too mean, so I rang her and we decided we'd get Shazzer to come as well, because she'd raised the alert in the first place.

As we turned into Tom's street, though, I came out of my fantasy about how dignified, tragic and articulate I would be when interviewed by the newspapers, along with a parallel paranoid fear that the police would decide it was me who had murdered Tom. Suddenly it stopped being a game. Maybe something terrible and tragic actually had happened.

None of us spoke or looked at each other as we walked up the front steps.

'Should you ring first?' whispered Sharon as I lifted the key to the lock.

'I'll do it,' said Jude. She looked at us quickly, then pressed the buzzer.

We stood in silence. Nothing. She pressed again. I was just about to slip the key in the lock when a voice on the intercom said, 'Hello?'

'Who's that?' I said tremulously.

'Who'd you think it is, you daft cow.'

'Tom!' I bellowed joyfully. 'Let us in.'

'Who's us?' he said suspiciously.

'Me, Jude and Shazzer.'

'I'd rather you didn't come up, hon, to be honest.'

'Oh, bloody hell,' said Sharon, pushing past me. 'Tom, you silly bloody queen, you've only had half London up in arms ringing the police, combing the metropolis for you because no one knows where you are. Bloody well let us in.'

'I don't want anyone except Bridget,' said Tom petulantly. I beamed beatifically at the others.

'Don't be such a prima bloody donna,' said Shazzer.

Silence.

'Come on, you silly sod. Let us in.'

There was a pause, then the buzzer went. 'Bzzz.'

'Are you ready for this?' came his voice as we reached the top floor and he opened the door.

All three of us cried out. Tom's whole face was distorted, hideous yellow and black, and encased in plaster.

'Tom, what's happened to you?' I cried, clumsily trying to embrace him and ending up kissing his ear. Jude burst into tears and Shazzer kicked the wall.

'Don't worry, Tom,' she growled. 'We'll find the bastards who did this.'

'What happened?' I said again, tears beginning to plop down my cheeks.

'Er, well . . .' said Tom, extracting himself awkwardly from my embrace, 'actually I, er, I had a nose job.'

Turned out Tom had secretly had the operation on Wednesday but was too embarrassed to tell us because we'd all been so dismissive about his minuscule nasal bump. He was supposed to have been looked after by Jerome, henceforth to be known a Creepy Jerome (it was going to be heartless Jerome but we all agreed that sounded too interesting). When, however, Creepy Jerome saw him after the operation he was so repulsed he said he was going away for a few days, buggered off and hasn't been seen or heard of since. Poor Tom was so depressed and traumatized and so weird from the anaesthetic that he just unplugged the phone, hid under the blankets and slept.

'Was it you I saw in Ladbroke Grove on Thursday night, then?' said Shazzer.

It was. Apparently he had waited till dead of night to go out and forage for food under cover of darkness. In spite of our high spirits that he was alive Tom was still very unhappy about Jerome.

'Nobody loves me,' he said.

I told him to ring my answerphone, which held twenty-two frantic messages from his friends, all distraught because he had disappeared for twenty-four hours, which put paid to all our fears about dying alone and being eaten by an Alsatian.

'Or not being found for three months . . . and *bursting* all over the carpet,' said Tom.

Anyway, we told him, how could one moody git with a stupid name make him think nobody loves him?

Two Bloody Marys later he was laughing at Jerome's obsessive use of the term 'self-aware', and his skintight calf-length Calvin-Klein underpants. Meanwhile, Simon, Michael, Rebecca, Magda, Jeremy and a boy claiming to be called Elsie had all rung to see how he was.

'I know we're all psychotic, single and completely dysfunctional and it's all done over the phone,' Tom slurred sentimentally, 'but it's a bit like a family, isn't it?'

I *knew* the Feng Shui would work. Now – its task completed – I am going to quickly move the round-leaved plant to my Relationship Corner. Wish there was a Cookery Corner too. Only nine days to go.

Monday 20 November

8st 12 (v.g.), cigarettes 0 (v. bad to smoke when performing culinary miracles), alcohol units 3, calories 200 (effort of going to supermarket must have burnt off more calories than purchased, let alone ate).

7 p.m. Just returned from hideous middle-class Singleton guilt experience at supermarket, standing at checkout next to functional adults with children buying beans, fish fingers, alphabetti spaghetti, etc., when had the following in my trolley:

20 heads of garlic
tin of goose fat
bottle of Grand Marnier
8 tuna steaks
36 oranges
4 pints of double cream
4 vanilla pods at £1.39 each.

Have to start preparations tonight as working tomorrow.

8 p.m. Ugh, do not feel like cooking. Especially dealing with grotesque bag of chicken carcasses: completely disgusting.

10 p.m. Have got chicken carcasses in pan now. Trouble is, Marco says am supposed to tie flavour-enhancing leek and celery together with string but only string have got is blue. Oh well, expect it will be OK.

11 p.m. God, stock took bloody ages to do but worth it as will end up with over 2 gallons, frozen in ice-cube form and only cost £1.70. Mmm, confit of oranges will be delicious also. Now all have got to do is finely slice thirty-six oranges and grate zest. Shouldn't take too long.

1 a.m. Too tired to stay awake now but stock is supposed to cook for another two hours and oranges need another hour in oven. I know. Will leave the stock on v. low heat overnight, also oranges on lowest oven setting, so will become v. tender in manner of a stew.

Tuesday 21 November

8st 11 (nerves eat fat), alcohol units 9 (v. bad indeed), cigarettes 37 (v.v. bad), calories 3479 (and all disgusting).

9.30 a.m. Just opened pan. Hoped-for 2-gallon stock taste-explosion has turned into burnt chicken carcasses coated in jelly. Orange confit looks fantastic, though, just like in picture only darker. Must go to work. Am going to leave by four, then will think of answer to soup crisis.

5 p.m. Oh God. Entire day has turned into nightmare. Richard Finch gave me a real blowing-up at the morning meeting in front of everyone. 'Bridget, put that recipe book away for God's sake. Fireworks Burns Kids. I'm thinking maiming, I'm thinking happy family celebrations turned into nightmares. I'm thinking twenty years on. What about that kid who had his penis burnt off by bangers in his pockets back in the sixties? Where is he now? Bridget, find me the Fireworks Kid with no Penis. Find me the Sixties Guy Fawkes Bobbit.'

Ugh. I was just grumpily making my forty-eighth phone call to find out if there was a burnt-off-penis victims support group when my phone rang.

'Hello, darling, it's Mummy here.' She sounded unusually high-pitched and hysterical.

'Hi, Mum.'

'Hello, darling, just called to say 'bye before I go, and hope everything goes well.'

'Go? Go where?'

'Oh. Ahahahaha. I told you, Julio and I are popping over to Portugal for a couple of weeks, just to see the family and so on, get a bit of a suntan before Christmas.'

'You didn't tell me.'

'Oh, don't be a silly-willy, darling. Of course I told you. You must learn to listen. Anyway, do take care, won't you?'

'Yes.'

'Oh, darling, just one more thing.'

'What?'

'For some reason I've been so busy I forgot to order my travellers' cheques from the bank.'

'Oh, don't worry, you can get them at the airport.'

'But the thing is, darling, I'm just on my way to the airport now, and I've forgotten my banker's card.'

I blinked at the phone.

'Such a nuisance. I was wondering . . . You couldn't possibly lend me some cash? I mean not much, just a couple of hundred quid or something so I can get some travellers' cheques.'

The way she said it reminded me of the way winos ask for money for a cup of tea.

'I'm in the middle of work, Mum. Can't Julio lend you some money?'

She went all huffy. 'I can't believe you're being so mean, darling. After all I've done for you. I gave you the gift of *life* and you can't even loan your mother a few pounds for some travellers' cheques.'

'But how am I going to get it to you? I'll have to go out to the cashpoint and put it on a motorbike. Then it will be stolen and it'll all be ridiculous. Where are you?'

'Oooh. Well, actually, as luck would have it I'm ever so close, so if you just pop out to the NatWest opposite I'll meet you there in five minutes,' she gabbled. 'Super, darling. Byee!'

'Bridget, where the *fuck* are you off to?' yelled Richard as I tried to sneak out. 'You found the Banger Bobbit Boy yet?'

'Got a hot tip,' I said, tapping my nose, then made a dash for it.

I was waiting for my money to come, freshly baked and piping hot, out of the cashpoint, wondering how my mother was going to manage for two weeks in Portugal on two hundred pounds, when I spotted her scurrying towards me, wearing sunglasses, even though it was pissing with rain, and looking shiftily from side to side.

'Oh, there you are, darling. You are sweet. Thank you very much. Must dash, going to miss the plane. Byee!' she said, grabbing the banknotes from my hand.

'What's going on?' I said. 'What are you doing outside here when it's not on your way to the airport? How are you going to manage without your banker's card? Why can't Julio lend you the money? Why? What are you up to? What?'

For a second she looked frightened, as if she was going to cry, then, her eyes fixed on the middle distance, she adopted her wounded Princess Diana look.

'I'll be fine, darling.' She gave her special brave smile.

'Take care,' she said in a faltering voice, hugged me quickly then was off, waving the traffic to a standstill and tripping across the road.

7 p.m. Just got home. Right. Calm, calm. Inner poise. Soup will be absolutely fine. Will simply cook and purée vegetables as instructed and then – to give concentration of flavour – rinse blue jelly off chicken carcases and boil them up with cream in the soup.

8.30 p.m. All going marvellously. Guests are all in living room. Mark Darcy is being v. nice and brought champagne and a box of Belgian chocolates. Have not done main course yet apart from fondant potatoes but sure will be v. quick. Anyway, soup is first.

8.35 p.m. Oh my God. Just took lid off casserole to remove carcasses. Soup is bright blue.

9 p.m. Love the lovely friends. Were more than sporting about the blue soup, Mark Darcy and Tom even making lengthy argument for less colour prejudice in the world of food. Why, after all, as Mark said – just because one cannot readily think of a blue vegetable – should one object to blue soup? Fish fingers, after all, are not naturally orange. (Truth is, after all the effort, soup just tasted like big bowl of boiled cream which Vile Richard rather unkindly pointed out. At which point Mark Darcy asked him what he did for a living, which was v. amusing because Vile Richard was sacked last week for fiddling his expenses.) Never mind, anyway. Main course will be v. tasty. Right, will start on velouté of cherry tomatoes.

9.15 p.m. Oh dear. Think there must have been something in the blender, e.g. Fairy Liquid, as cherry tomato purée seems to be foaming and three times original volume. Also fondant potatoes were meant to be ready ten minutes ago and are hard as rock. Maybe should put in microwave. . Aargh aargh. Just looked in fridge and tuna is not there. What has become of tuna? What? What?

9.30 p.m. Thank God. Jude and Mark Darcy came in kitchen and helped me make big omelette and mashed up half-done fondant potatoes and fried them in the frying pan in manner of hash browns, and put the recipe book on the table so we could all look at the pictures of what chargrilled tuna would have been like. At least orange confit will be good. Looks fantastic. Tom said not to bother with Grand Marnier Crème Anglaise but merely drink Grand Marnier.

10 p.m. V. sad. Looked expectantly round table as everyone took first mouthful of confit. There was an embarrassed silence.

'What's this, hon?' said Tom eventually. 'Is it marmalade?'

Horror-struck, took mouthful myself. It was, as he said, marmalade. Realize after all effort and expense have served my guests:

Blue soup
Omelette
Marmalade

Am disastrous failure. Michelin-star cookery? Kwik-fit, more like.

Did not think things could get any worse after the marmalade. But no sooner was the horrible meal cleared away than the phone went. Fortunately I took it in the bedroom. It was Dad.

'Are you on your own?' he said.

'No. Everyone's round here. Jude and everyone. Why?'

'I – wanted you to be with someone when . . . I'm sorry, Bridget. I'm afraid there's been some rather bad news.'

'What? What?'

'Your mother and Julio are wanted by the police.'

2 a.m. Northamptonshire in single bed in the Alconburys' spare room. Ugh. Had to sit down and get my breath back while Dad said, 'Bridget? Bridget? Bridget?' over and over again in manner of a parrot.

'What's happened?' I managed to get out eventually.

'I'm afraid they – possibly, and I pray, without your mother's knowledge – have defrauded a large number of people, including myself, and some of our very closest friends, out of a great deal of money. We don't know the scale of the fraud at the moment, but I'm afraid, from what the police are saying, it's possible that your mother may have to go to prison for a considerable period of time.'

'Oh my God. So that's why she's gone off to Portugal with my two hundred quid.'

'She may well be further afield by now.'

I saw the future unfolding before me like a horrible nightmare: Richard Finch dubbing me *Good Afternoon!*'s 'Suddenly Single's Jailbird's Daughter, and forcing me to do a live interview down the line from the Holloway visitors' room before being Suddenly Sacked on air.

'What did they do?'

'Apparently Julio, using your mother as – as it were – 'front man', has relieved Una and Geoffrey, Nigel and Elizabeth and Malcolm and Elaine' (oh my God, Mark Darcy's parents) 'of quite considerable sums of money – many, many thousands of pounds, as down payments on time-share apartments.'

'Didn't you know?'

'No. Presumably because they were unable to overcome some slight vestigial embarrassment about doing business with the greasy beperfumed wop who has cuckolded one of their oldest friends they omitted to mention the whole business to me.'

'So what happened?'

'The time-share apartments never existed. Not a penny of your mother's and my savings or pension fund remains. I also was unwise enough to leave the house in her name, and she has remortgaged it. We are ruined, destitute and homeless, Bridget, and your mother is to be branded a common criminal.'

After that he broke down. Una came to the phone, saying that she was going to give Dad some Ovaltine. I told her I'd be there in two hours but she said not to drive till I'd got over the shock, there was nothing to be done, and to leave it till the morning.

Replacing the receiver, I slumped against the wall cursing myself feebly for leaving my cigarettes in the living room. Immediately though, Jude appeared with a glass of Grand Marnier.

'What happened?' she said.

I told her the whole story, pouring the Grand Marnier straight down my throat as I did. Jude didn't say a word but immediately went and fetched Mark Darcy.

'I blame myself,' he said, running his hands through his hair. 'I should have made myself more clear at the Tarts and Vicars party. I knew there was something dodgy about Julio.'

'What do you mean?'

'I heard him talking on his portable phone by the herbaceous border. He didn't know he was being overheard. If I'd had any idea that my parents were involved I'd . . .' He shook his head. 'Now I think about it, I do remember my mother mentioning something, but I got so aerated at the mere mention of the words "time-share" that I must have terrorized her into shutting up. Where's your mother now?'

'I don't know. Portugal? Rio de Janeiro? Having her hair done?'

He started to pace around the room firing questions like a top barrister.

'What's being done to find her?' 'What are the sums involved?' 'How did the matter come to light?' 'What is the police's involvement?' 'Who knows about it?' 'Where is your father now?' 'Would you like to go to him?' 'Will you allow me to take you?' It was pretty damn sexy, I can tell you.

Jude appeared with coffee. Mark decided the best thing would be if he got his driver to take him and me up to Grafton Underwood and, for a fleeting second, I experienced the totally novel sensation of being grateful to my mother.

It was all very dramatic when we got to Una and Geoffrey's, with Enderbys and Alconburys all over the shop, everyone in tears and Mark Darcy striding around making phone calls. Found myself feeling guilty, since part of self – despite horror – was hugely enjoying the fact of normal business being suspended, everything different from usual and everyone allowed to throw entire glasses of sherry and salmon-paste sandwiches down their throats in manner of Christmas. Was exactly the same feeling as when Granny turned schizophrenic and took all her clothes off, ran off into Penny Husbands-Bosworth's orchard and had to be rounded up by the police.

Wednesday 22 November

8st 10 (hurrah!), alcohol units 3, cigarettes 27 (completely understandable when Mum is common criminal), calories 5671 (oh dear, seem to have regained appetite), Instants 7 (unselfish act to try to win back everyone's money, though maybe would not give them all of it, come to think of it), total winnings £10, total profit £3 (got to start somewhere).

10 a.m. Back in flat, completely exhausted after no sleep. On top of everything else, have to go to work and get bollocking for being late. Dad seemed to be rallying a little when I left: alternating between moments of wild cheerfulness that Julio proved to be a bounder so Mum might come back and start a new life with him and deep depression that the new life in question will be one of prison-visiting using public transport.

Mark Darcy went back to London in small hours. I left a message on his answerphone saying thank you for helping and everything, but he has not rung me back. Cannot blame him. Bet Natasha and similar would not feed him blue soup and turn out to be the daughter of criminal.

Una and Geoffrey said not to worry about Dad as Brian and Mavis are going to stay and help look after him. Find myself wondering why it is always 'Una and Geoffrey' not 'Geoffrey and Una' and yet 'Malcolm and Elaine' and 'Brian and Mavis'. And yet, on the other hand, 'Nigel and Audrey Coles'. Just as one would never, never say 'Geoffrey and Una' so, conversely, one would never say 'Elaine and Malcolm'. Why? Why? Find self, in spite of self, trying out own name imagining Sharon or Jude in years to come, boring their daughters rigid by going 'You know Bridget and *Mark*, darling, who live in the big house in Holland Park and go on lots of holidays to the Caribbean.' That's it. It would be Bridget and Mark. Bridget and Mark Darcy. The Darcys. Not Mark and Bridget Darcy. Heaven forbid. All wrong. Then suddenly feel terrible for thinking about Mark Darcy in these terms, like Maria with Captain Von Trapp in *The Sound of Music*, and that I must run away and go to see Mother Superior, who will sing 'Climb Ev'ry Mountain' to me.

Friday 24 November

8st 13, alcohol units 4 (but drunk in police presence so clearly OK), cigarettes 0, calories 1760, 1471 calls to see if Mark Darcy has rung 11.

10.30 p.m. Everything is going from bad to worse. Had thought only silver lining in cloud of mother's criminality was that it might bring me and Mark Darcy closer together but have not heard a peep from him since he left the Alconburys'. Have just been interviewed in my flat by police officers. Started behaving like people who are interviewed on the television after plane crashes in their front gardens, talking in formulaic phrases borrowed from news broadcasts, courtroom dramas or similar. Found myself describing my mother as being 'Caucasian' and 'of medium build'.

Policemen were incredibly charming and reassuring, though. They stayed quite late, in fact, and one of the detectives said he'd pop round again when he was passing and let me know how everything was going. He was really friendly, actually.

Saturday 25 November

9st, alcohol units 2 (sherry, ugh), cigarettes 3 (smoked out of Alconburys' window), calories 4567 (entirely custard creams and salmon spread sandwiches), 1471 calls to see if Mark Darcy has rung 9 (g.).

Thank God. Dad has had a phone call from Mum. Apparently, she said not to worry, she was safe and everything was going to be all right, then hung up immediately. The police were at Una and Geoffrey's tapping the phone line as in *Thelma and Louise* and said she was definitely calling from Portugal but they didn't manage to get where. So much wish Mark Darcy would ring. Was obviously completely put off by culinary disasters and criminal element in family, but too polite to show it at time. Paddling-pool bonding evidently pales into significance alongside theft of parents' savings by naughty Bridget's nasty mummy. Am going to see Dad this afternoon, in manner of tragic spinster spurned by all men instead of in manner to which have been accustomed: in chauffeur-driven car with top barrister.

1 p.m. Hurrah! Hurrah! Just as I was leaving had phone call, but could not hear anything but beeping sound at the other end. Then the phone rang again. It was Mark, from Portugal. Just incredibly kind and brilliant of him. Apparently he has been talking to the police all week in between being top barrister and flew out to Albufeira yesterday. The police over there have found Mum, and Mark thinks she will get off because it will be pretty obvious she had no idea what Julio was up to. They've managed to track down some of the money, but haven't found Julio yet. Mum is coming back tonight, but will have to go straight to a police station for questioning. He said not to worry, it will probably all be OK, but he's made arrangements for bail if it turns out to be necessary. Then we got cut off before I even had time to say thank you. Desperate to ring Tom to tell him fantastic news but remember no one is supposed to know about Mum and, unfortunately, last time I spoke to Tom about Mark Darcy I think I might have implied he was a creepy mummy's boy.

Sunday 26 November

9st 1, alcohol units 0, cigarettes ½ (fat chance of any more), calories God knows, minutes spent wanting to kill mother 188 (conservative estimate).

Nightmare day. Having first expected Mum back last night, then this morning, then this afternoon and having almost set off to Gatwick a total of three times, it turned out she was arriving this evening at Luton, under police escort. Dad and I were preparing ourselves to comfort a very different person from the one we had last been told off by, naively assuming that Mum would be chastened by what she had gone through.

'Let go of me, you *silly billy*,' a voice rang out through the arrival lounge. 'Now we're on British soil I'm certain to be recognized and I don't want everyone seeing me being *manhandled* by a policeman. Ooh, d'you know? I think I've left my sunhat on the aeroplane under the seat.'

The two policemen rolled their eyes as Mum, dressed in a sixties-style black-and-white checked coat (presumably carefully planned to co-ordinate with the policemen), headscarf and dark glasses, zoomed back towards the baggage hall with the officers of the law wearily tagging after her. Forty-five minutes later they were back. One of the policemen was carrying the sunhat.

There was nearly a stand-up fight when they tried to get her into the police car. Dad was sitting in the front of his Sierra in tears and I was trying to explain to her that she had to go to the station to see whether she was going to be charged with anything, but she just kept going, 'Oh, don't be silly, darling. Come here. What have you got on your face? Haven't you got a tissue?'

'Mum,' I remonstrated as she took a handkerchief out of her pocket and spat on it. 'You might be charged with a criminal offence,' I protested as she started to dab at my face. 'I think you should go quietly to the station with the policemen.'

'We'll see, darling. Maybe tomorrow when I've cleaned out the vegetable basket. I left 2 pounds of King Edwards in there and I bet they've sprouted. Nobody's touched the plants, apparently, the entire time I've been away, and I bet you anything Una's left the heating on.'

It was only when Dad came over and curtly told her the house was about to be repossessed, vegetable basket included, that she shut up and huffily allowed herself to be put in the back of the car next to the policeman.

Monday 27 November

9st 1, alcohol units 0, cigarettes 50 (yesss! yesss!), 1471 calls to see if Mark Darcy has rung 12, hours of sleep 0.

9 a.m. Just having last fag before going to work. Completely shattered. Dad and I were made to wait on a bench in the police station for two hours last night. Eventually we heard a voice approaching along the corridor. 'Yes, that's right it's mee! "Suddenly Single" every morning! Of course you can. Have you got a pen? On here? Who shall I put it to? Oh, you naughty man. Do you know I've been dying to try one of those on . . .'

'Oh, there you are, Daddy,' said Mum, appearing round the corner wearing a policeman's helmet. 'Is the car outside? Oof, d'you know – I'm dying to get home and get the kettle on. Did Una remember to turn on the timer?'

Dad looked rumpled, startled and confused and I didn't feel any less so myself.

'Have you walked free?' I said.

'Oh, don't be silly, darling. Walked free! I don't know!' said Mum rolling her eyes at the senior detective and bustling me out of the door ahead of her. The way the detective was blushing and fussing around her I wouldn't have been in the least surprised if she'd got herself off by giving him sexual favours in the interview room.

'So what happened?' I said, when Dad had finished putting all her suitcases, hats, straw donkey ('Isn't it super?') and castanets in the boot of the Sierra and had started the engine. I was determined she wasn't going to brazen this one out, sweep the whole thing under the carpet and start patronizing us again.

'All sorted out now, darling, just a silly misunderstanding. Has someone been smoking in this car?'

'What happened, Mother?' I said dangerously. 'What about everyone's money and the time-share apartments? Where's my two hundred quid?'

'Durr! It was just some silly problem with the planning permission. They can be very corrupt, you know, the Portuguese authorities. It's all backhanders and baksheesh like Winnie Mandela. So Julio's just paid all the deposits back. We had a super holiday, actually! The weather was very mixed, but . . .'

'Where is Julio?' I said, suspiciously.

'Oh, he's stayed behind in Portugal to sort out all this planning permission palaver.'

'What about my house?' said Dad. 'And the savings?'

'I don't know what you're talking about, Daddy. There's nothing wrong with the house.'

Unfortunately for Mum, however, when we got back to The Gables all the locks had been changed, so we had to go back to Una and Geoffrey's.

'Oof, do you know, Una, I'm so exhausted, I think I'm going to have to go straight to bed,' said Mum after one look at the resentful faces, wilting cold collation and tired beetroot slices.

The phone rang for Dad.

'That was Mark Darcy,' said Dad when he came back. My heart leapt into my mouth as I tried to control my features. 'He's is Albufeira. Apparently some sort of deal's been done with . . . with the filthy wop . . . and they've recovered some of the money. I think The Gables may be saved . . .'

At this a loud cheer went up from us all and Geoffrey launched into 'For He's a Jolly Good Fellow.' I waited for Una to make some remark about me but none was forthcoming. Typical. The minute I decide I like Mark Darcy, everyone immediately stops trying to fix me up with him.

'Is that too milky for you, Colin?' said Una, passing Dad a mug of tea decorated with apricot floral frieze.

'I don't know . . . I don't understand why . . . I don't know what to think,' Dad said worriedly.

'Look, there's absolutely no need to worry,' said Una, with an unusual air of calmness and control, which suddenly made me see her as the mummy I'd never really had. 'It's because I've put a bit too much milk in. I'll just tip a bit out and top it up with hot water.'

When finally got away from scene of mayhem, drove far too fast on way back to London, smoking fags all the way as act of mindless rebellion.

DECEMBER

Oh, Christ

Monday 4 December

9st 2 (hmm, must get weight off before Christmas gorging), alcohol units a modest 3, cigarettes a saintly 7, calories 3876 (oh dear), 1471 calls to see if Mark Darcy has called 6 (g.).

Just went to supermarket and found self unaccountably thinking of Christmas trees, firesides, carols, mince pies, etc. Then I realized why. The air vents by the entrance which usually pump out baking bread smells were pumping out baking mince pies smells instead. Cannot believe cynicism of such behaviour. Reminded of favourite poem by Wendy Cope which goes:

At Christmas little children sing and merry bells jingle.
The cold winter air make our hands and faces tingle.
And happy families go to church and cheerily they mingle,
And the whole business is unbelievably dreadful if you're single.

Still no word from Mark Darcy.

Tuesday 5 December

9st 2 (right, am really going to start dieting today), alcohol units 4 (start of festive season), cigarettes 10, calories 3245 (better), 1471 calls 6 (steady progress).

Repeatedly distracted by 'Stocking Filla' catalogues tumbling out of the newspapers. Particularly keen on the shield-shaped burnished metal 'funfur'-lined Spectacles Holder Stand: 'All too often spectacles are put down flat on a table, inviting an accident.' Couldn't agree more. The sleekly designed 'Black Cat' Key-Chain Light does indeed have a simple flip-down mechanism, as it 'casts a powerful red light on the keyhole of any cat lover.' Bonsai Kits! Hurrah. 'Practise the ancient art of Bonsai with this tub of pre-planted Persian Pink Silk Tree shoots.' Nice, very nice.

Cannot help but feel sad about the brutal trampling on the pink silk shoots of romance burgeoning between me and Mark Darcy by Marco Pierre White and my mother, but trying to be philosophical about it. Maybe Mark Darcy is too perfect, clean and finished off at the edges for me, with his capability, intelligence, lack of smoking, freedom from alcoholism, and his chauffeur-driven cars. Maybe it has been decreed that I should be with someone wilder, earthier and more of a flirt. Like Marco Pierre White, for example, or, just to pick a name totally at random, Daniel. Hmmm. Anyway. Must just get on with life and not feel sorry for self.

Just called Shazzer, who said it has not been decreed that I must go out with Marco Pierre White and certainly not with Daniel. The only thing a woman needs in this day and age is herself. Hurrah!

2 a.m. Why hasn't Mark Darcy rung me? Why? Why? Am going to be eaten by Alsatian despite all efforts to the contrary. Why me, Lord?

Friday 8 December

9st 5 (disaster), alcohol units 4 (g.), cigarettes 12 (excellent), Christmas presents purchased 0 (bad), cards sent 0, 1471 calls 7.

4 p.m. Humph. Jude just rang and just before we said goodbye she said, 'See you at Rebecca's on Sunday.'

'Rebecca's? Sunday? What Rebecca's? What?'

'Oh, hasn't . . .? She's just having a few . . . I think it's just a sort of pre-Christmas dinner party.'

'I'm busy on Sunday, anyway,' I lied. At last – a chance to get into those awkward corners with the duster. I *had* thought that Jude and I were equal friends of Rebecca so why should she invite Jude and not me?

9 p.m. Popped to 192 for refreshing bottle of wine with Sharon and she said, 'What are you wearing for Rebecca's party?'

Party? So it is a *party* party.

Midnight. Anyway. Must not get upset about it. This is just the sort of thing that is not important in life any more. People should be allowed to invite who they want to *their* parties without others pettily getting upset.

5.30 a.m. Why hasn't Rebecca invited me to her party?

Why? Why? How many more parties are going on that everyone has been invited to except me? I bet everyone is at one now, laughing and sipping expensive champagne. No one likes me. Christmas is going to be a total party-desert, apart from a three-party pile-up on December 20th, when I am booked into an editing session all evening.

Saturday 9 December

Christmas parties to look forward to 0.

7.45 a.m. Woken by Mum.

'Hello, darling. Just rang quickly because Una and Geoffrey were asking what you wanted for Christmas and I wondered about a Facial Sauna.'

How, after being totally disgraced and narrowly escaping several years in custody, can my mother just plop back into being exactly like she was before, flirting openly with policemen and torturing me.

'By the way, are you coming to . . .' for a moment my heart leapt with the thought that she was going to say 'turkey curry buffet' and bring up, in a manner of speaking, Mark Darcy, but no '. . .the Vibrant TV party on Tuesday?' she continued brightly.

I shuddered with humiliation. I *work* for Vibrant TV, for God's sake.

'I haven't been invited,' I mumbled. There is nothing worse than having to admit to your mum that you are not very popular.

'Oh, darling, of course you've been invited. *Everyone*'s going.'

'I haven't been.'

'Well, maybe you haven't worked there long enough. Anyway—'

'But, Mum,' I interrupted, 'you don't work there at all.'

'Well, that's different, darling. Anyway, Must run. Byeee!'

9 a.m. Brief moment of party oasis when an invitation arrived in the post but turned out to be party mirage: invitation to a sale of designer eyewear.

11.30 a.m. Called Tom in paranoid desperation to see if he wanted to go out tonight.

'Sorry,' he chirped, 'I'm taking Jerome to the PACT party at the Groucho Club.'

Oh God, I hate it when Tom is happy, confident and getting on well with Jerome, much preferring it when he is miserable, insecure and neurotic. As he himself never tires of saying, 'It's always so nice when things go badly for other people.'

'I'll see you tomorrow, anyway,' he gushed on, 'at Rebecca's.'

Tom has only ever met Rebecca twice, both times at my house, and I've known her for nine years. Decided to go shopping and stop obsessing.

2 p.m. Bumped into Rebecca in Graham and Greene buying a scarf for £169. (What is going on with scarves? One minute they were stocking filler-type items which cost £9.99; next minute they have to be fancy velvet and cost as much as a television. Next year it will probably happen to socks or pants and we will feel left out if we are not wearing £145 English Eccentrics knickers in textured black velvet.)

'Hi,' I said excitedly, thinking at last the party nightmare would be over and she too would say, 'See you on Sunday.'

'Oh, hello,' she said coldly, not meeting my eye. 'Can't stop. I'm in a real rush.'

As she left the shop they were playing 'Chestnuts roasting on an open fire' and I stared hard at a £185 Phillipe Starck colander, blinking back tears. I hate Christmas. Everything is designed for families, romance, warmth, emotion and presents, and if you have no boyfriend, no money, your mother is going out with a missing Portuguese criminal, and your friends don't want to be your friend any more, it makes you want to emigrate to a vicious Muslim regime, where at least *all* the women are treated like social outcasts. Anyway, I don't care. I am going to quietly read a book all weekend and listen to classical music. Maybe will read *The Famished Road*.

8.30 p.m. *Blind Date* was v.g. Just going for another bottle of wine.

Monday 11 December

Returned from work to icy answerphone message.

'Bridget. This is Rebecca. I know you work in TV now. I know you have much more glamorous parties to go to every night, but I would have thought you could at least have the courtesy to reply to an invitation from a friend, even if you are too grand to deign to come to her party.'

Frantically called Rebecca but no reply or answerphone. Decided to go round and leave a note and bumped into Dan on the stairs, the Australian guy from downstairs who I snogged in April.

'Hi. Merry Christmas,' he said leerily, standing too close. 'Did you get your mail?' I looked at him blankly. 'I've been putting it under your door so you don't have to get cold in your nighty in the mornings.'

I shot back upstairs, grabbed back the doormat and there, nestling underneath like a Christmas miracle, was a little pile of cards, letters and invitations all addressed to me. Me. Me. Me.

Thursday 14 December

9st 3, alcohol units 2 (bad, as did not drink any units yesterday – must make up extra tomorrow to avoid heart attack), cigarettes 14 (bad? or maybe good? Yes: a sensible level of nicotine units is probably good for you as long as do not binge-smoke), calories 1500 (excellent), Instants 4 (bad but would have been good if Richard Branson had won non-profit-making lottery bid), cards sent 0, presents purchased 0, 1471 calls 5 (excellent).

Parties, parties, parties! Plus Matt from the office just rang asking if I'm going to the Christmas lunch on Tuesday. He *can't* fancy me – I'm old enough to be his great-aunt – but then why did he ring me in the evening? And why did he ask me what I was wearing? Must not get over-excited and allow party casbah and phone call from feller-me-lad to go to self's head. Should remember old saying 'once bitten twice shy' as regards dipping pen in office ink. Also must remember what happened last time snogged whipper-snapper: ghastly 'Ooh, you're all squashy' humiliation with Gav. Hmmm. Sexually tantalizing Christmas lunch followed bizarrely by disco dancing in the afternoon (such being editor's idea of a good time) involves severe outfit choice complexity. Best ring Jude, I think.

Tuesday 19 December

9st 7 (but still nearly one week to lose half-stone before Christmas), alcohol units 9 (poor), cigarettes 30, calories 4240, Instants 1 (excellent), cards sent 0, cards received 11, but include 2 from paper boy, 1 from dustman, 1 from Peugeot garage and 1 from hotel spent night in for work four years ago. Am unpopular, or maybe everyone sending cards later this year.

9 a.m. Oh God, feel awful: horrible sick acidic hangover and today is office disco lunch. Cannot go on. Am going to burst with pressure of unperformed Christmas tasks, like revision for finals. Have failed to do cards or Christmas shopping apart from doomed panic-buy yesterday lunchtime as realized was going to see girls for last time before Christmas at Magda and Jeremy's last night.

Dread the exchange of presents with friends as, unlike with the family, there is no way of knowing who is and isn't going to give and whether gifts should be tokens of affection or proper presents, so all becomes like hideous exchange of sealed bids. Two years ago I bought Magda lovely Dinny Hall earrings, rendering her embarrassed and miserable because she hadn't bought me anything. Last year, therefore, I didn't get her anything and she bought me an expensive bottle of Coco Chanel. This year I bought her a big bottle of Saffron Oil with Champagne and a distressed wire soapdish, and she went into a complete grump muttering obvious lies about not having done her Christmas shopping yet. Last year Sharon give me bubble bath shaped like Santa, so last night I just gave her Body Shop Algae and Polyp Oil shower gel at which point she presented me with a handbag. I had wrapped up a spare bottle of posh olive oil as a generalized emergency gift which fell out of my coat and broke on Magda's Conran Shop rug.

Ugh. Would that Christmas could just *be*, without presents. It is just so stupid, everyone exhausting themselves, miserably haemorrhaging money on pointless items nobody wants: no longer tokens of love but angst-ridden solutions to problems. (Hmmm. Though must admit, pretty bloody pleased to have new handbag.) What is the point of entire nation rushing round for six weeks in a bad mood preparing for utterly pointless Taste-of-Others exam which entire nation then fails and gets stuck with hideous unwanted merchandise as fallout? If gifts and cards were completely eradicated, then Christmas as pagan-style twinkly festival to distract from lengthy winter gloom would be lovely. But if government, religious bodies, parents, tradition, etc. insist on Christmas Gift Tax to ruin everything why not make it that everyone must go out and spend £500 on themselves then distribute the items among their relatives and friends to wrap up and give to them instead of this psychic-failure torment?

9.45 a.m. Just had Mum on the phone. 'Darling, I've just rung to say I've decided I'm not doing presents this year. You and Jamie know there isn't a Santa now, and we're all far too busy. We can just appreciate each other's company.'

But we always get presents from Santa in sacks at the bottom of our beds. World seems bleak and grey. Won't seem like Christmas any more.

Oh God, better go to work – but will not have anything to drink at disco-lunch, just be friendly and professional to Matt, stay till about 3.30 p.m., then leave and do my Christmas cards.

2 a.m. *Course* is OK – everyone drunks office Christmas parties. Is a good fun. Must gust sleep – doen mattr about clothesoff.

Wed 20 December

5.30 a.m. Oh my God. *Oh my God*. Where am I?

Thursday 21 December

9st 3 (actually, in funny sort of way there is no reason why should not actually lose weight over Christmas since am so full that – certainly any time after Christmas dinner it is perfectly acceptable to refuse all food on grounds of being too full. In fact it is probably the one time of year when it is OK not to eat).

For ten days now have been living in state of permanent hangover and foraging sub-existence without proper meals or hot food.

Christmas is like war. Going down to Oxford Street is hanging over me like going over the top. Would that the Red Cross or Germans would come and find me. Aaargh. It's 10 a.m. Have not done Christmas shopping. Have not sent Christmas cards. Got to go to work. Right, am never, never going to drink again for the rest of life. Aargh – field telephone.

Humph. It was Mum but might as well have been Goebbels trying to rush me into invading Poland.

'Darling, I was just ringing to check what time you're arriving on Friday night.'

Mum, with dazzling bravado, has planned schmaltzy family Christmas, with her and Dad pretending the whole of last year never happened 'for the sake of the children' (i.e. me and Jamie, who is thirty-seven).

'Mum, as I *think* we've discussed, I'm not coming home on Friday, I'm coming home on Christmas Eve. Remember all those conversations we've had on the subject? That first one . . . back in August—'

'Oh, don't be *silly*, darling. You can't sit in the flat on your own all weekend when it's Christmas. What are you going to eat?'

Grrr. I hate this. It's as if, just because you're single, you don't have a home or any friends or responsibilities and the only possible reason you might have for not being at everyone else's beck and call for the entire Christmas period and happy to sleep bent at odd angles in sleeping bags on teenagers' bedroom floors, peel sprouts all day for fifty, and 'talk nicely' to perverts with the word 'Uncle' before their name while they stare freely at your breasts is complete selfishness.

My brother, on the other hand, can come and go as he likes with everyone's respect and blessing just because he happens to be able to stomach living with a vegan Tai Chi enthusiast. Frankly, I would rather set fire to my flat all on my own than sit in it with Becca.

Cannot believe my mother is not more grateful to Mark Darcy for sorting everything out for her. Instead of which he has become part of That Which Must Not Be Mentioned, i.e. the Great Time-Share Rip-Off, and she behaves as if he never existed. Cannot help but think he must have coughed up a bit to get everyone their money back. V. nice good person. Too good for me, evidently.

Oh God. Must put sheets on bed. Disgusting to sleep on uncomfortable button-studded mattress. Where are sheets, though? Wish had some food.

Friday 22 December

Now it is nearly Christmas, find self feeling sentimental about Daniel. Cannot believe have not had Christmas card from him (though come to think of it have not managed to send any cards yet myself). Seems weird to have been so close during the year and now be completely out of touch. V. sad. Maybe Daniel is unexpectedly Orthodox Jew. Maybe Mark Darcy will ring tomorrow to wish me Happy Christmas.

Saturday 23 December

9st 4, alcohol units 12, cigarettes 38, calories 2976, friends and loved ones who care about self this festive tide 0.

6 p.m. So glad decided to be festive Home Alone Singleton like Princess Diana.

6.05 p.m. Wonder where everybody is? I suppose they are all with their boyfriends or have gone home to their families. Anyway, chance to get things done . . . or they have families of own. Babies. Tiny fluffy children in pyjamas with pink cheeks looking at the Christmas tree excitedly. Or maybe they are all at a big party except me. Anyway. Lots to do.

6.15 p.m. Anyway. Only an hour till *Blind Date*.

6.45 p.m. *Oh God, I'm so lonely*. Even Jude has forgotten about me. She has been ringing all week panicking about what to buy Vile Richard. Mustn't be too expensive: suggests getting too serious or an attempt to emasculate him (v.g. idea if ask self); nor anything to wear as taste-gaffe minefield and might remind Vile Richard of last girlfriend Vile Jilly (whom he does not want to get back with but pretends still to love in order to avoid having to be in love with Jude – creep). Latest idea was whisky but combined with other small gift so as not to seem cheapskate or anonymous – possibly combined with tangerines and chocolate coins, depending on whether Jude decided Christmas Stocking concept over-cute to point of nausea or terrifyingly smart in its Post-Modernity.

7 p.m Emergency: Jude on phone in tears. Is coming round. Vile Richard has gone back to Vile Jilly. Jude blames gift. Thank God stayed home. Am clearly Emissary of Baby Jesus here to help those persecuted at Christmas by Herod-Wannabees, e.g. Vile Richard. Jude will be here at 7.30.

7.15 p.m. Damn. Missed start of *Blind Date* as Tom rang and is coming round. Jerome, having taken him back, has chucked him again and gone back with former boyfriend who is member of chorus in *Cats*.

7.17 p.m. Simon is coming round. His girlfriend has gone back to her husband. Thank God stayed at home to receive chucked friends in manner of Queen of Hearts or Soup Kitchen. But that's just the kind of person I am: liking to love others.

8 p.m. Hurrah! A magic-of-Christmas miracle. Daniel just called 'Jonesh' he slurred. 'I love you, Jonesh. I made tebble mishtake. Stupid Suki made of plastic. Breast point north at all times. I love you, Jonesh. I comin' round to check how your skirts is.' Daniel. Gorgeous, messy, sexy, exciting, hilarious Daniel.

Midnight. Humph. None of them turned up. Vile Richard changed his mind and came back to Jude, as did Jerome, and Simon's girlfriend. It was just over-emotional Spirit-of-Christmas-Past making everyone wobbly about ex-partners. And Daniel! He rang up at 10 o'clock.

'Listen, Bridge. You know I always watch the match on Saturday nights? Shall I come round tomorrow before the football?' Exciting? Wild? Hilarious? Huh.

1 a.m. Totally alone. Entire year has been failure.

5 a.m. Oh, never bloody mind. Maybe Christmas itself will not be awful. Maybe Mum and Dad will emerge radiantly shag-drunk in the morning, holding hands shyly and saying, 'Children, we've got something to tell you,' and I could be a bridesmaid at the reaffirming of vows ceremony.

Sunday 24 December: Christmas Eve

9st 4, alcohol units 1 measly glass of sherry, cigarettes 2 but no fun as out of window, calories 1 million, probably, number of warm festive thoughts 0.

Midnight. V. confused about what is and is not reality. There is a pillowcase at the bottom of my bed which Mum put there at bedtime, cooing, 'Let's see if Santa comes,' which is now full of presents. Mum and Dad, who are separated and planning to divorce, are sleeping in the same bed. In sharp contrast, my brother and his girlfriend, who have been living together for four years, are sleeping in separate rooms. The reason for all this is unclear, except that it may be to avoid upsetting Granny who is a) insane and b) not here yet. The only thing that connects me to the real world is that once again I am humiliatingly spending Christmas Eve alone in my parents' house in a single bed. Maybe Dad is at this moment attempting to mount Mum. Ugh, ugh. No, no. Why did brain think such thought?

Monday 25 December

9st 5 (oh God, have turned into Santa Claus, Christmas pudding or similar), alcohol units 2 (total triumph), cigarettes 3 (ditto), calories 2657 (almost entirely gravy), totally insane Christmas gifts 12, number of Christmas gifts with any point to them whatsoever 0, philosophical reflections on the meaning of the Virgin Birth 0, number of years since self was Virgin, hmmm.

Staggered downstairs hoping hair did not smell of fags to find Mum and Una exchanging political views while putting crosses in the end of sprouts.

'Oh yes, I think what's-his-name is *very* good.'

'Well, he is, I mean, he got through his what-do-you-mer-call-it clause that nobody thought he would, didn't he?'

'Ah, but then, you see, you've got to watch it because we could easily end up with a nutcase like what-do-you-mer-call-him that used to run the miners. Do you know? The problem I find with smoked salmon is that it repeats on me, especially when I've had a lot of chocolate brazils. Oh, hello, darling,' said Mum, noticing me. 'Now, what are you going to put on for Christmas Day?'

'This,' I muttered sulkily.

'Oh, don't be silly, Bridget, you can't wear that on *Christmas Day*. Now, are you going to come into the lounge and say hello to Auntie Una and Uncle Geoffrey before you change?' she said in the special bright, breathy isn't-everything-super? voice that means, 'Do what I say or I'll Magimix your face.'

'So, come on, then, Bridget! How's yer love-life!'

quipped Geoffrey, giving me one of his special hugs, then going all pink and adjusting his slacks.

'Fine.'

'So you still haven't got a chap. Durr! What are we going to do with you!'

'Is that a chocolate biscuit?' said Granny, looking straight at me.

'Stand up straight, darling,' hissed Mum.

Dear God, please help me. I want go home. I want my own life again. I don't feel like an adult, I feel like a teenage boy who everyone's annoyed with.

'So what *are* you going to do about babies, Bridget?' said Una.

'Oh look, a penis,' said Granny, holding up a giant tube of Smarties.

'Just going to change!' I said, smiling smarmily at Mum, rushed up to the bedroom, opened the window and lit up a Silk Cut. Then I noticed Jamie's head sticking out of window one floor below, also having fag. Two minutes later the bathroom window opened and an auburn-coiffed head stuck out and lit up. It was bloody Mum.

12.30 p.m. Gift exchange was nightmare. Always overcompensate for bad presents, yelping with delight, which means I get more and more horrid gifts each year. Thus Becca – who, when I worked in publishing, gave me a worsening series of book-shaped clothes-brushes, shoehorns and hair ornaments – this year gave me a clapperboard fridge magnet. Una, for whom no household task must remain ungadgeted, gave me a series of mini-spanners to fit different jar or bottle lids in the kitchen. While my mum, who gives me presents to try and make my life more like hers, gave me a slo-cooker for one person: 'All you have to do is brown the meat before you go to work and stick a bit of veg in.' (Has she any idea how hard it is some mornings to make a glass of water without vomiting?)

'Oh look. It isn't a penis, it's a biscuit,' said Granny.

'I think this gravy's going to need sieving, Pam,' called Una, coming out of the kitchen holding a pan.

Oh no. Not this. Please not this.

'I don't think it will, dear,' Mum said already spitting, murderously through clenched teeth. 'Have you tried stirring it?'

'Don't patronize me, Pam,' said Una, smiling dangerously. They circled each other like fighters. This happens every year with the gravy. Mercifully there was a distraction: a great crash and scream as a figure burst through the French windows. Julio.

Everyone froze, and Una let out a scream.

He was unshaven and clutching a bottle of sherry. He stumbled over to Dad and drew himself up to his full height.

'You sleep with my woman.'

'Ah,' replied Dad. 'Merry Christmas, er . . . Can I get you a sherry – ah, got one already. Jolly good. Mince pie?'

'You sleep,' said Julio dangerously, 'with my woman.'

'Oh, he's so Latin, hahaha,' said Mum coquettishly while everyone else stared in horror. Every time I've met Julio he has been clean and coiffed beyond all sense and carrying a gentleman's handbag. Now he was wild, drunk, unkempt and, frankly, just the type I fall for. No wonder Mum seemed more aroused than embarrassed.

'Julio, you naughty person,' she cooed. Oh God. She was still in love with him.

'You sleep,' said Julio, 'with him.' He spat on the Chinese carpet and bounded upstairs, pursued by Mum, who trilled back at us, 'Could you carve, Daddy, please, and get everyone sitting down?'

Nobody moved.

'OK, everybody,' said Dad, in a tense, serious, manly sort of voice. 'There is a dangerous criminal upstairs using Pam as a hostage.'

'Oh, she didn't seem to mind, if you ask me,' piped up Granny in a rare and most untimely moment of clarity. 'Oh look, there's a biscuit in the dahlias.'

I looked out of the window and nearly jumped out of my skin. There was Mark Darcy slipping, lithe as a whipper-snapper, across the lawn and in through the French windows. He was sweating, dirty, his hair was unkempt, his shirt unbuttoned. *Ding-dong*!

'Everyone keep completely still and quiet, as if everything is normal,' he said softly. We were all so stunned, and he so thrillingly authoritative, that we started doing as he said as if hypnotized zombies.

'Mark,' I whispered as I walked past him with the gravy. 'What are you saying? There is no normal.'

'I'm not sure whether Julio's violent. The police are outside. If we can get your mum to come downstairs and leave him up there they can go in and get him.'

'OK. Leave it to me,' I said, and walked to the bottom of the stairs.

'Mum!' I yelled. 'I can't find any savoury doilies.'

Everyone held their breath. There was no response.

'Try again,' whispered Mark, looking at me admiringly.

'Get Una to take the gravy back into the kitchen,' I hissed. He did what I said, then gave me a thumbs-up. I gave him a thumbs-up back and cleared my throat.

'Mum?' I shouted up the stairs again. 'Do you know where the sieve is? Una's a bit worried about the gravy.'

Ten seconds later there was a pounding down the stairs and Mum burst in, looking flushed.

'The savoury doilies are in the savoury doily holder on the wall, you silly willy. Now. What's Una done with this gravy. Durr! We're going to have to use the Magimix!'

Even as she spoke there were footsteps running up the stairs and a scuffle broke out above us.

'Julio!' shrieked Mum and started to run for the door.

The detective I recognized from the police station was standing in the living room doorway. 'All right, everyone, keep calm. It's all under control,' he said.

Mum let out a scream as Julio, handcuffed to a young policeman, appeared in the hallway and was bundled out of the front door behind the detective.

I watched her as she collected herself and looked round the room, appraising the situation.

'Well, thank goodness I managed to calm Julio down,' she said gaily after a pause. 'What a to do! Are you all right, Daddy?'

'Your top – Mummy – is inside out,' said Dad.

I stared at the hideous scene, feeling as though my whole world was collapsing around my ears. Then I felt a strong hand on my arm.

'Come on,' said Mark Darcy.

'What?' I said.

'Don't say "what", Bridget, say "pardon",' hissed Mum.

'Mrs Jones,' said Mark firmly. 'I am taking Bridget away to celebrate what is left of the Baby Jesus's birthday.'

I took a big breath and grasped Mark Darcy's proffered hand.

'Merry Christmas, everyone,' I said with a gracious smile. 'I expect we'll see you all at the Turkey Curry Buffet.'

This is what happened next:

Mark Darcy took me to Hintlesham Hall for champagne and late Christmas lunch, which was v.g. Particularly enjoyed freedom to pour gravy on to Christmas turkey for first time in life without having to take sides about it. Christmas without Mum and Una was a strange and wonderful thing. Was unexpectedly easy to talk to Mark Darcy, especially with Festive Julio Police Siege Scene to dissect.

It turns out Mark has spent quite lot of time in Portugal over the last month, in manner of heartwarming private detective. He told me he tracked Julio down to Funchal and found out quite a bit about where the funds were, but couldn't cajole, or threaten, Julio into returning anything.

'Think he might now, though,' he said, grinning. He's really v. sweet, Mark Darcy, as well as being rocky smart.

'How come he came back to England?'

'Well, sorry to use a cliché, but I discovered his Achilles' heel.'

'What?'

'Don't say "what", Bridget, say "pardon",' he said, and I giggled. 'I realized that, although your mother is the most impossible woman in the world, Julio loves her. He really loves her.'

Bloody Mum, I thought. How come she gets to be the irresistible sex goddess? Maybe I should go to Colour Me Beautiful after all.

'So what did you do?' I said, sitting on my hands to stop myself shouting *'What about me? Me? Why doesn't anyone love me?'*

'I simply told him that she was spending Christmas with your dad, and, I'm afraid, that they'd be sleeping in the same bed. I just had a feeling he was crazy enough, and stupid enough, to attempt to er, *undermine* those plans.'

'How did you know?'

'A hunch. It kind of goes with the job.' God, he's cool.

'But it was so kind of you, taking time off work and everything. 'Why did you bother doing all this?'

'Bridget,' he said. 'Isn't it rather obvious?'

Oh my God.

When we got upstairs it turned out he had taken a suite. It was fantastic, v. posh and bloody good fun and we played with all the guest features and had more champagne and he told me all this stuff about how he loved me: the sort of stuff, to be honest, Daniel was always coming out with.

'Why didn't you ring me up before Christmas, then?' I said suspiciously. 'I left you *two* messages.'

'I didn't want to talk to you till I'd finished the job. And I didn't think you liked me much.'

'*What?*'

'Well, you know. You stood me up because you were drying your *hair*? And the first time I met you I was wearing that stupid jumper and bumblebee socks from my aunt and behaved like a complete clod. I thought you thought I was the most frightful stiff.'

'Well, I did, a bit,' I said. 'But . . .'

'But what . . .?'

'Don't you mean but pardon?'

Then he took the champagne glass out of my hand, kissed me, and said, 'Right, Bridget Jones, I'm going to give you pardon for,' picked me up in his arms, carried me off into the bedroom (which had a fourposter bed!) and did all manner of things which mean whenever I see a diamond-patterned V-neck sweater in future, I am going to spontaneously combust with shame.

Tuesday 26 December

4 a.m. Have finally realized the secret of happiness with men, and it is with deep regret, rage and an overwhelming sense of defeat that I have to put it in the words of an adulteress, criminal's accomplice and G-list celebrity:

'Don't say "what", say "pardon", darling, and do as your mother tells you.'

January–December: A Summary

Alcohol units 3836 (poor)

Cigarettes 5277

Calories 11,090,265 (repulsive)

Fat units 3457 (approx.) (hideous idea in every way)

Weight gained 5st 2lb

Weight lost 5st 3lb (excellent)

Correct lottery numbers 42 (v.g.)

Incorrect lottery numbers 387

Total Instants purchased 98

Total Instants winnings £110

Total Instants profit £12 (Yessss! Yessss! Have beaten system while supporting worthwhile causes in manner of benefactor)

1471 calls (quite a lot)

Valentines 1 (v.g.)

Christmas cards 33 (v.g.)

Hangover-free days 114 (v.g.)

Boyfriends 2 (but one only for six days so far)

Nice boyfriends 1

Number of New Year Resolutions kept 1 (v.g.)

An *excellent* year's progress.

Bridget Jones:
The Edge of Reason

To the other Bridgets

Acknowledgements

With thanks to Gillon Aitken, Sunetra Atkinson, Peter Bennet-Jones, Frankie Bridgewood, Richard Coles, Richard Curtis, Scarlett Curtis, Pam Dorman, Ursula Doyle, Breene Farrington, Nellie Fielding, the Fielding family, First Circle Films, Andrew Forbes, Colin Firth, Paula Fletcher, Piers Fletcher, Henrietta Perkins, Tracey MacLeod, Sharon Maguire, Tina Jenkins, Sara Jones, Emma Parry, Harry Ritchie, Sarah Sands, Tom Shone, Peter Straus, Russ Warner, Working Title Films, for inspiration, feedback and support.

And special thanks to Kevin Curran.

Research by Sara Jones

Contents

1. HAPPILY EVER AFTER 1

2. JELLYFISH AT LARGE 27

3. DOOOOM! 65

4. PERSUASION 109

5. MR DARCY, MR DARCY 137

6. ITALIAN JOB 161

7. MOOD-SWINGING SINGLETONS 179

8. OH BABY 201

9. SOCIAL HELL 233

10. MARS AND VENUS IN THE DUSTBIN 261

11. THAI TAKEAWAY 289

12. STRANGE TIMES 331

13. GAAAH! 361

14. FOR BETTER OR WORSE? 389

15. EXCESS CHRISTMAS SPIRIT 407

1

Happily Ever After

Monday 27 January

9st 3 (total fat groove), boyfriends 1 (hurrah!), shags 3 (hurrah!), calories 2,100, calories used up by shags 600, so total calories 1,500 (exemplary).

7.15 a.m. Hurrah! The wilderness years are over. For four weeks and five days now have been in functional relationship with adult male thereby proving am not love pariah as previously feared. Feel marvellous, rather like Jemima Goldsmith or similar radiant newlywed opening cancer hospital in veil while everyone imagines her in bed with Imran Khan. Ooh. Mark Darcy just moved. Maybe he will wake up and talk to me about my opinions.

7.30 a.m. Mark Darcy has not woken up. I know, will get up and make him fantastic fried breakfast with sausages, scrambled eggs and mushrooms or maybe Eggs Benedict or Florentine.

7.31 a.m. Depending what Eggs Benedict or Florentine actually are.

7.32 a.m. Except do not have any mushrooms or sausages.

7.33 a.m. Or eggs.

7.34 a.m. Or – come to think of it – milk.

7.35 a.m. Still has not woken up. Mmmm. He is lovely. Love looking at Him asleep. V. sexy broad shoulders and hairy chest. Not that sex object or anything. Interested in brain. Mmmm.

7.37 a.m. Still has not woken up. Must not make noise, realize, but maybe could wake Him subtly by thought vibes.

7.40 a.m. Maybe will put . . . GAAAAAH!

7.50 a.m. Was Mark Darcy sitting bolt upright yelling, 'Bridget, will you stop. Bloody. Staring at me when I am asleep. Go find something to do.'

8.45 a.m. In Coins Café having cappuccino, chocolate croissant, and cigarette. Is relief to have fag in open and not to be on best behaviour. V. complicated actually having man in house as cannot freely spend requisite amount of time in bathroom or turn into gas chamber as conscious of other person late for work, desperate for pee etc.; also disturbed by Mark folding up underpants at night, rendering it strangely embarrassing now simply to keep all own clothes in pile on floor. Also he is coming round again tonight so have to go to supermarket either before or after work. Well, do not *have to* but horrifying truth is want to, in bizarre possibly genetic-throwback-style way such as could not admit to Sharon.

8.50 a.m. Mmm. Wonder what Mark Darcy would be like as father (father to own offspring, mean. Not self. That would indeed be sick in manner of Oedipus)?

8.55 a.m. Anyway, must not obsess or fantasize.

9 a.m. Wonder if Una and Geoffrey Alconbury would let us put marquee on their lawn for the recept— Gaaah!

Was my mother, walking into my café bold as brass in a Country Casuals pleated skirt and apple-green blazer with shiny gold buttons, like a spaceman turning up in the House of Commons squirting slime and sitting itself down calmly on the front bench.

'Hello, darling,' she trilled. 'Just on my way to Debenhams and I know you always come in here for your breakfast. Thought I'd pop in and see when you want your colours done. Ooh I fancy a cup of coffee. Do you think they'll warm up the milk?'

'Mum, I've told you I don't want my colours done,' I muttered, scarlet, as people stared and a sulky, rushed-off-her-feet waitress bustled up.

'Oh don't be such a stick-in-the-mud, darling. You need to make a statement about yourself! Not sitting on the fence all the time in all these fudges and slurries. Oh, hello, dear.'

Mum went into her slow, kindly 'Let's try to make best friends with the waiting staff and be the most special person in the café for no fathomable reason' voice.

'Now. Let. Me. See. D'you know? I think I'll have a

coffee. I've had so many cups of tea this morning up in Grafton Underwood with my husband Colin that I'm sick to death of tea. But could you warm me up some milk? I can't drink cold milk in coffee. It gives me indigestion. And then my daughter Bridget will have . . .'

Grrr. Why do parents do this. Why? Is it desperate mature person's plea for attention and importance, or is it that our urban generation are too busy and suspicious of each other to be open and friendly? I remember when I first came to London I used to smile at everyone until a man on the tube escalator masturbated into the back of my coat.

'Espresso? Filter? Latte? Cap: half fat or de-caf?' snapped the waitress, sweeping all the plates off the table next to her and looking at me accusingly as if Mum was my fault.

'Half fat de-caf cap and a latte,' I whispered apologetically.

'What a surly girl, doesn't she speak English?' huffed Mum at her retreating back. 'This is a funny place to live, isn't it? Don't they know what they want to put on in the morning?'

I followed her gaze to the fashionable Trustafarian girls at the next table. One was tapping at her laptop and wearing Timberlands, a petticoat, a Rastafarian bonnet and a fleece, while the other, in Prada stilettos, hiking socks, surfing shorts, a floor-length llamaskin coat and a Bhutanese herdsman's woolly hat with earflaps, was yelling into her mobile headset, 'I mean, he said if he found me smoking skunk again he'd take away the flat. And I'm like, "Fucking, Daddy"' – while her six-year-old child picked miserably at a plate of chips.

'Is that girl talking to herself with that language?' said Mum. 'It's a funny world you live in, isn't it? Wouldn't you do better living near normal people?'

'They are normal people,' I said furiously, nodding in illustration out at the street where unfortunately a nun in a brown habit was pushing two babies along in a pram.

'You see this is why you get yourself all mixed up.'

'I don't get myself mixed up.'

'Yes you do,' she said. 'Anyway. How's it going with Mark?'

'Lovely,' I said moonily, at which she gave me a hard stare.

'You're not going to you-know-what with him, are you? He won't marry you, you know.'

Grrr. Grrrr. No sooner have I started going out with the man she'd been trying to force me onto for eighteen months ('Malcolm and Elaine's son, darling, divorced, terribly lonely and rich') than I feel like I'm running some kind of Territorial Army obstacle course, scrambling over walls and nets to bring her home a big silver cup with a bow on.

'You know what they say afterwards,' she was going on. '"Oh, she was easy meat." I mean when Merle Robertshaw started going out with Percival her mother said, "Make sure he keeps that thing just for weeing with."'

'Mother—' I protested. I mean it was a bit rich coming from her. Not six months ago she was running around with a Portuguese tour operator with a gentleman's handbag.

'Oh, did I tell you,' she interrupted, smoothly changing the subject, 'Una and I are going to Kenya.'

'What!' I yelled.

'We're going to Kenya! Imagine, darling! To darkest Africa!'

My mind started to whirl round and round searching through possible explanations like a fruit machine before it comes to a standstill: Mother turned missionary? Mother rented *Out of Africa* again on video? Mother suddenly remembered about *Born Free* and decided to keep lions?

'Yes, darling. We want to go on safari and meet the Masai tribesmen, then stay in a beach hotel!'

The fruit machine clunked to a halt on a series of lurid images of elderly German ladies having sex on the beach with local youths. I stared levelly at Mum.

'You're not going to start messing around again, are you?' I said. 'Dad's only just got over all that stuff with Julio.'

'Honestly, darling! I don't know what all the fuss was about! Julio was just a friend – a penfriend! We all need friends, darling. I mean even in the best of marriages one person just isn't enough: friends of all ages, races, creeds and tribes. One has to expand one's consciousness at every . . .'

'When are you going?'

'Oh, I don't know, darling. It's just an idea. Anyway must whizz. Byee!'

Bugger. It's 9.15. Am going to be late for morning meeting.

11 a.m. Sit Up Britain office. Was luckily only two minutes late for meeting, also managed to conceal coat by rolling it into ball to create pleasing sense of having been in for hours and merely detained on urgent trans-departmental business elsewhere in building. Made my way in composed manner through hideous open-plan office littered with the tell-tale remnants of bad daytime TV – here an inflatable sheep with a hole in its bottom, there a blow-up of Claudia Schiffer wearing Madeleine Albright's head, there a large cardboard sign saying: 'LESBIANS! Out! Out! Out!' – towards where Richard Finch, sporting sideburns and black Jarvis Cocker spectacles, his portly frame squeezed hideously into a 70s retro safari suit was bellowing at the assembled twenty-something research team.

'Come on, Bridget Droopy-Drawers Late Again,' he yelled, spotting my approach. 'I'm not paying you to roll coats into a ball and try to look innocent, I'm paying you to turn up on time and come up with ideas.'

Honestly. The lack of respect day after day is beyond human endurance.

'Right, Bridget!' he roared. 'I'm thinking New Labour Women. I'm thinking image and roles. I want Barbara Follett in the studio. Get her to give Margaret Beckett a make-over. Highlights. Little black dress. Stockings. I want to see Margaret looking like sex on legs.'

Sometimes there seems no limit to the absurdity of what Richard Finch will ask me to do. One day, I will find myself persuading Harriet Harman and Tessa Jowell to stand in a supermarket while I ask passing shoppers if they can tell which one is which, or trying to persuade a Master of the Hunt to be chased naked through the countryside by a pack of vicious foxes. Must find more worthwhile fulfilling job of some kind. Nurse, perhaps?

11.03 a.m. At desk. Right, had better ring Labour press office. Mmmm. Keep getting shag flashbacks. Hope Mark Darcy was not really annoyed this morning. Wonder if it is too early to ring him at work?

11.05 a.m. Yes. As it says in *How to Get the Love You Want* – or maybe it was *Keeping the Love You Find?* – the blending together of man and woman is a delicate thing. Man must pursue. Will wait for him to ring me. Maybe had better read papers to brief self about New Labour policy in case actually get Margaret Beckett on end of . . . Gaaah!

11.15 a.m. Was Richard Finch yelling again. Have been put on the fox-hunting item instead of Labour Women and have got to do live insert from Leicestershire. Must not panic. Am assured, receptive, responsive woman of substance. My sense of self comes not from my worldly achievements but from within. Am assured, receptive . . . Oh God. Is pissing it down. Do not want to go out in fridge-crossed-with-swimming pool-like world.

11.17 a.m. Actually is v.g. to get interview to do. Big responsibility – relatively speaking, obviously, not like having to decide whether to send cruise missiles to Iraq, or holding clamp on main arterial valve during surgery – but chance to grill Fox-Murderer on camera and actually make a point rather like Jeremy Paxman with Iranian – or Iraqi – Ambassador.

11.20 a.m. Might even be asked to do trial item for *Newsnight*.

11.21 a.m. Or series of short specialized reports. Hurrah! Right, better get out cuts . . . Oh. Telephone.

11.30 a.m. Was going to ignore it but thought it might be interviewee: Sir Hugo Rt Hon. Boynton-Fox-Murderer with directions about silos, pig-huts on the left etc. so picked up: was Magda.

'Bridget, hi! I was just ringing to say in the potty! In the potty! Do it in the potty!'

There was a loud crashing noise followed by the sound of running water and screaming in manner of Muslims being massacred by Serbs with 'Mummy will smack! She will smack!' as if on a loop in the background.

'Magda!' I yelled. 'Come back!'

'Sorry, hon,' she said, eventually returning. 'I was just ringing to say . . . tuck your willy inside the potty! If you let it hang out it'll go on the floor!'

'I'm in the middle of work,' I said pleadingly. 'I've got to set off to Leicestershire in two minutes . . .'

'Great, fine, rub it in, you're all very glamorous and important and I'm stuck at home with two people who haven't learned to speak the English language yet. Anyway, I was just ringing to say that I've fixed for my builder to come round and do your shelves tomorrow. Sorry to have bothered you with my boring domesticity. He's called Gary Wilshaw. Bye.'

Phone rang again before had time to call back. Was Jude, sobbing in a sheep's voice.

'It's OK, Jude, it's OK,' I said, tucking the phone under my chin and trying to shove the cuttings into my handbag.

'It's Vile Richard hegggggggg.'

Oh dear. After Christmas Shaz and I convinced Jude that if she had *just one more* mad conversation with Vile Richard about the shifting sands of his Commitment Problem she would have to be put into a mental hospital; and therefore they would not be able to have any mini-breaks, relationship counselling, or future together *anyway* for years and years until she was released into Care in the Community.

In a magnificent feat of self-love she ditched him, cut her hair and started turning up to her staid job in the City wearing leather jackets and hipster jeans. Every striped-shirted Hugo, Johnny or Jerrers who had ever idly wondered what was under Jude's suit was catapulted into a state of priapic frenzy and she seems to have a different one on the phone every night. But somehow, the whole subject of Vile Richard still makes her sad.

'I was just going through all the stuff he left, ready to chuck it out, and I found this self-help book . . . book called . . . called . . .'

'It's OK. It's OK. You can tell me.'

'Called *How to Date Young Women: A Guide For Men Over Thirty-Five*.'

Jesus.

'I just feel terrible, terrible . . .' she was saying '. . . I can't stand being out in dating hell again . . . It's an impenetrable sea . . . I'm going to be on my own for ever . . .'

Working towards balance between importance of friendship and impossibility of getting to Leicestershire in negative amount of time, gave merely preliminary first-aid advice in manner of holding on to sense of self: probably left it there on purpose; no you're not; etc.

'Oh, thanks, Bridge,' said Jude, after a while seeming a bit calmer. 'Can I see you tonight?'

'Um, well, Mark's coming round.'

There was a silence.

'Fine,' she said coolly. 'Fine. No, you have a good time.'

Oh God, feel guilty with Jude and Sharon now I have boyfriend, almost like traitorous double-crossing side-switching guerrilla. Have arranged to see Jude tomorrow night instead, with Shaz, and merely talk through everything again on phone tonight, which seemed to go down OK. Now, had better quickly ring Magda and make sure she doesn't feel boring and realizes how opposite-of-glamorous job is.

'Thanks, Bridge,' said Magda after we'd talked for a bit. 'I'm just feeling really low and lonely since the baby. Jeremy's working again tomorrow night. Don't suppose you'd like to come round?'

'Um, well, I'm supposed to be seeing Jude in 192.'

There was a loaded pause.

'And I suppose I'm too much of a dull Smug Married to come along?'

'No, no, come. Come, that would be great!!' I overcompensated. Knew Jude would be cross as would take focus away from Vile Richard but resolved to sort out later. So now am really late and have got to go to Leicestershire without actually having read fox-hunting cuts. Maybe could read in car when at traffic lights. Wonder if should quickly ring Mark Darcy to tell him where am going?

Hmmm. No. Bad move. But then what if I'm late? Had better ring.

11.35 a.m. Humph. Conversation went like this:

Mark: Yes? Darcy here.

Me: It's Bridget.

Mark: (pause) Right. Er. Everything OK?

Me: Yes. It was nice last night, wasn't it? I mean – you know, when we . . .

Mark: I do know, yes. Exquisite. (Pause) I'm actually with the Indonesian Ambassador, the Head of Amnesty International and the Under-Secretary of State for Trade and Industry just at the moment.

Me: Oh. Sorry. I'm just going to Leicestershire. I thought I'd let you know in case anything happens to me.

Mark: In case anything . . . ? What?

Me: I mean in case I'm . . . late. (I finished lamely.)

Mark: Right. Well, why not ring with an ETA when you're through? Jolly good. Bye now.

Hmmm. Don't think I should have done that. It says specifically in *Loving Your Separated Man Without Losing Your Mind* that the one thing they really do not like is being called up for no real reason when they are busy.

7 p.m. Back in flat. Nightmare rest of day. After challenging traffic and rain-blocked journey, found self in rain-swept Leicestershire, knocking on the door of a big square house surrounded by horseboxes, with only thirty minutes to go till transmission. Suddenly the door burst open, and a tall man was standing in corduroy trousers and a quite sexy baggy jumper.

'Humph,' he said, eyeing me up and down. 'Better

bloody well come in. Your chaps are out the back. Where have you bloody well been?'

'I have been suddenly diverted from a top political story,' I said hoity-toitily, as he led me into a big kitchen full of dogs and bits of saddle. Suddenly he turned and stared at me furiously, then biffed the table.

'It's supposed to be a free country. Once they start telling us we can't even bloody hunt on a Sunday where will it end? Baaaah!'

'Well, you could say that about people keeping slaves, couldn't you?' I muttered. 'Or cutting the ears off cats. It just doesn't seem very gentlemanly to me, a crowd of people and dogs careering after one frightened little creature for fun.'

'Have you ever bloody seen what a fox does to a chicken?' Sir Hugo bellowed, turning red in the face. 'If we don't hunt 'em the countryside will be overrun.'

'Shoot them then,' I said, staring at him murderously. 'Humanely. And chase something else on Sundays, like in greyhound racing. Fasten a little fluffy animal impregnated with fox smell on to a wire.'

'Shoot them? Have you ever tried to shoot a bloody fox? There'll be your little frightened foxes left wounded in agony all over the bloody shop. Fluffy animal. Grrrrr!'

Suddenly he grabbed the phone and dialled. 'Finch, you total arse!' he bellowed. 'What have you sent me . . . some bloody little pinko? If you think you're coming out with the Quorn next Sunday . . .' At which moment the cameraman put his head round the door and said huffily, 'Oh you're here, are you?' Then looked at his watch. 'Don't feel you have to let us know or anything.'

'Finch wants to talk to you,' said Sir Hugo.

Twenty minutes later, under pain of sacking, I was on a horse preparing to trot into shot and interview the Rt Hon. Bossybottom, also on a horse.

'OK, Bridget, we're coming to you in fifteen, go, go, go,' yelled Richard Finch in my earpiece from London, at which I squeezed my knees into the horse, as instructed. Unfortunately, however, the horse would not set off.

'Go, go, go, go, go!' yelled Richard. 'I thought you said you could bloody ride.'

'I said I had a natural seat,' I hissed, digging frantically with my knees.

'OK, Leicester, tighter on Sir Hugo till fucking Bridget gets it together five, four, three, two . . . go.'

At this the Hon. Purpleface launched into a bellowing pro-hunting advertisement as I dug frantically with my heels until the horse reared up neurotically, cantering sideways into the shot as I clung to its neck.

'Oh my fuck, wind it up, wind it up!' yelled Richard.

'Well, that's all we've got time for. Now back to the studio!' I trilled as the horse wheeled round again and started reversing at the cameraman.

After the sniggering crew had gone I went – mortified – into the house for my things, only to practically bump into the Rt Hon. Biffing Giant.

'Hah!' he growled. 'Thought that stallion might teach you what's what. Fancy a bloody one?'

'What?' I said.

'Bloody Mary?'

Fighting instinctive urge to glug at the vodka I drew myself up to my full height. 'Are you saying you sabotaged my report on purpose?'

'Maybe.' He smirked.

'That's absolutely disgraceful,' I said. 'And not worthy of a member of the aristocracy.'

'Hah! Spirit. I like that in a woman,' he said throatily, then lunged towards me.

'Get off!' I said, dodging out of his way. I mean honestly. What was he thinking of? Am professional woman, not there to be made passes at. In any sense. Though, actually, just goes to prove how much men like it if they think you are not after them. Must remember for more useful occasion.

Now have just got in, having trailed round Tesco Metro and staggered up stairs with eight carrier bags. Am really tired. Humph. How come is always me who goes to supermarket? Is like having to be career woman and wife at same time. Is like living in seventeenth . . . Oooh. Answerphone light is flashing.

'Bridget,' – Richard Finch – 'I want to see you in my office at 9 o'clock tomorrow. Before the meeting. That's 9 a.m. not 9 p.m. Morning. Daylight. I don't know how else to put it, really. Just bloody well make sure you're there.'

He sounded really pissed off. Hope am not about to discover impossibility of having a nice flat, a nice job and a nice boyfriend. Anyway, am going to give Richard Finch what for about journalistic integrity. Right. Better start getting everything ready. Am so tired.

8.30 p.m. Have managed to get energy back using Chardonnay, shoved all mess away, lit fire and candles, had bath, washed hair and put on make-up and v. sexy black jeans and spaghetti-strap top. Not exactly comfortable, in fact crotch of trousers and spaghetti straps really digging into self, but look nice, which is important. For as Jerry Hall said, a woman must be a cook in the kitchen and a whore in the sitting room. Or some room anyway.

8.35 p.m. Hurrah! Will be lovely cosy, sexy evening with delicious pasta – light yet nourishing – and firelight. Am marvellous career woman/girlfriend hybrid.

8.40 p.m. Where the bloody hell is he?

8.45 p.m. Grrr. What is point of self rushing round like scalded flea if he is just going to swan in whenever he feels like it?

8.50 p.m. Bloody Mark Darcy, am really . . . Doorbell. Hurrah!

He looked gorgeous in his work suit with the top buttons of his shirt undone. As soon as he came in he dropped his briefcase, took me in his arms and turned me round in a little sexy dance. 'So good to see you,' he murmured into my hair. 'I really enjoyed your report, fantastic horsewomanship.'

'Don't,' I said, pulling away. 'It was awful.'

'It was brilliant,' he said. 'For centuries people have been riding horses forwards and then, with one seminal report, a lone woman changes the face – or arse – of British horsemanship for ever. It was ground-breaking, a triumph.' He sat down on the sofa wearily. 'I'm wrecked. Bloody Indonesians. Their idea of a breakthrough in human rights is to tell a person he's under arrest while they're shooting the back of his head off.'

I poured him a glass of Chardonnay and brought it to him in manner of James Bond-style hostess saying, with a calming smile, 'Supper won't be long.'

'Oh my God,' he said, looking around terrified as if there might be Far Eastern militia hiding in the microwave. 'Have you cooked?'

'Yes,' I said indignantly. I mean you would have thought he would have been pleased! Also he had not so much as mentioned the whore outfit.

'Come here,' he said, patting the sofa, 'I'm only teasing you. I've always wanted to go out with Martha Stewart.'

Was nice having cuddle but, thing was, pasta had already been on for six minutes and was going to go floury.

'I'll just do the pasta,' I said, extracting myself. Just then, the phone rang and I lunged at it out of pure habit, thinking it might be him.

'Hi. It's Sharon. How's it going with Mark?'

'He's here,' I whispered keeping my teeth and mouth clenched in the same position so Mark would not lip-read.

'What?'

' 'E's 'ere,' I hissed clenched-teethedly.

'It's all right,' said Mark, nodding reassuringly. 'I realize I'm here. I don't think it's the sort of thing we should be keeping from each other.'

'OK. Listen to this,' said Shaz excitedly. '"We are not saying that all men cheat. But all men do think about it. Men have these desires eating at them all the time. We try to contain our sexual urges . . ."'

'Actually, Shaz, I'm just cooking pasta.'

'Oooh, "just cooking pasta", are we? I hope you're not turning into a Smug Going-Out-With-Someone. Just listen to this and you'll want to put it on his head.'

'Hang on,' I said, glancing nervously at Mark. I took the pasta off the heat and went back to the phone.

'OK,' said Shaz excitedly. '"Sometimes instincts override higher-level thinking. A man will stare at, approach or bed a woman with small breasts if he is involved with a woman with large breasts. You may not think variety is the spice of life, but believe us, your boyfriend thinks so."'

Mark was starting to drum his fingers on the arm of the sofa.

'Shaz . . .'

'Wait . . . wait. It's this book called *What Men Want*. Right . . . "If you have a beautiful sister, or friend, rest assured that your boyfriend is HAVING THOUGHTS ABOUT SEX WITH HER."'

There was an expectant pause. Mark had started miming throat slitting and toilet chain flushing motions.

'I mean isn't that revolting? Aren't they just . . . ?'

'Shaz, can I call you back later?'

Next thing Shaz was accusing me of being obsessed with men when I was supposed to be a feminist. So I said, if she was supposed to be so uninterested in them, why was she reading a book called *What Men Want*? It was all turning into a hideously unfeminist man-based row when we realized it was ridiculous and said we'd see each other tomorrow.

'So!' I said brightly, sitting down next to Mark on the sofa. Unfortunately had to get up again as had sat on something that turned out to be an empty Müller Lite yoghurt carton.

'Yeees?' he said, brushing the yoghurt off my bottom. Sure there cannot have been that much on or needing quite such hard brushing but was very nice. Mmm.

'Shall we have supper?' I said, trying to keep my mind on the task in hand.

Had just put pasta in bowl and poured jar of sauce on it when the phone rang again. Decided to leave it till had eaten but answerphone clicked on and Jude sheep-voiced out, 'Bridge, are you there? Pick up, pick up. Come on, Bridge, pleeeeeease.'

I picked up the phone, as Mark hit himself hard on the forehead. The thing is, Jude and Shaz have been kind to me for years before I even met Mark so obviously it would not be right to leave the answerphone on now.

'Hi, Jude.'

Jude had been to the gym where she ended up reading some article calling single girls over thirty 're-treads'.

'The guy was arguing that the sort of girls who wouldn't go out with him in their twenties would go out with him now but he didn't want them any more,' she said sadly. 'He said they were all obsessed with settling down and babies and his rule with girls now was "Nothing over twenty-five".'

'Oh honestly!' I laughed gaily trying to fight a lurch of insecurity in my own stomach. 'That's just complete bollocks. No one thinks you're a re-tread. Think of all those merchant bankers who've been ringing you up. What about Stacey and Johnny?'

'Huh,' said Jude, though she was starting to sound more cheerful. 'I went out with Johnny and his friends from Credit Suisse last night. Someone told a joke about this guy who drank too much in an Indian restaurant and passed out in a korma and Johnny is so literal that he went, "Christ! How bloody awful. I knew a bloke who ate a lot of Indian food once, and he ended up with a stomach ulcer!"'

She was laughing. The crisis had clearly passed. You see there is nothing seriously wrong, she just gets a bit paranoid sometimes. Chatted a bit more and, once her confidence seemed firmly back in residence, I rejoined Mark at the table only to discover the pasta was not quite as had planned: slopping about wetly in white-coloured water.

'I like it,' said Mark supportively, 'I like string, I like milk. Mmmm.'

'Do you think we'd better call out for a pizza?' I said, feeling a failure and a re-tread.

We ordered pizzas and ate them in front of the fire. Mark told me all about the Indonesians. I listened carefully and gave him my opinions and advice, which he said were very interesting and very 'fresh', and I told him about horrid sacking meeting with Richard Finch. He gave me very good advice about working out what I wanted from the meeting and giving Richard plenty of places to go other than sacking me. As I explained to him, it was rather like the win-win mentality as advocated in *The Seven Habits of Highly Effective People* when the phone rang again.

'Leave it,' said Mark.

'Bridget. Jude. Pick up. I think I've done the wrong thing. I just called Stacey and he hasn't called back.'

I picked up. 'Well, maybe he's out.'

'Of his mind just like you,' said Mark.

'Shut up,' I hissed, while Jude ran through the scenario. 'Look, I'm sure he'll ring tomorrow. But if he doesn't, just move back one of the *Mars and Venus* Stages of Dating. He's pulling away like a Martian rubber band and you have to let him feel his attraction and spring back.'

When I got off the phone, Mark was watching the football.

'Rubber bands and win-win Martians,' he said, smirking at me. 'It's like war command in the land of gibberish here.'

'Don't you talk to your friends about emotional matters?'

'Nope,' he said, flicking the remote control from one football match to the other. I stared at him in fascination.

'Do you want to have sex with Shazzer?'

'I'm sorry?'

'Do you want to have sex with Shazzer and Jude?'

'I'd be delighted! Did you mean individually? Or both at the same time?'

Trying to ignore his superficial tone, I pressed on. 'When you met Shazzer after Christmas did you want to sleep with her?'

'Well. The thing is, you see, I was sleeping with you.'

'But has it crossed your mind ever?'

'Well, of course it's crossed my *mind*.'

'What?' I exploded.

'She's a very attractive girl. It would have been odd, surely, if it hadn't?' He grinned wickedly.

'And Jude,' I said indignantly. 'Sleeping with Jude. Has that ever "crossed your mind"?'

'Well, from time to time, fleetingly, I suppose it has. It's just human nature, isn't it?'

'Human nature? I've never imagined sleeping with Giles or Nigel from your office.'

'No,' he murmured. 'I'm not sure that anyone else has either. Tragically. Except possibly Jose in the post room.'

Just as we'd cleared away the plates and started snogging on the rug, the phone rang again.

'Leave it,' said Mark. 'Please – in the name of God and all his cherubim, seraphim, saints, archangels, cloud attendants and beard trimmers – leave it.'

The answerphone was already clicking on. Mark crashed his head down on to the floor as a man's voice boomed out.

'Ah, hi. Giles Benwick here, friend of Mark's. Don't suppose he's there, is he? It's just . . .' Suddenly his voice cracked. 'It's just my wife just told me she wants a separation and . . .'

'Good God,' said Mark and grabbed the phone. An expression of pure panic spread across his face. 'Giles. Christ. Steady on . . . um . . . ah . . . um, Giles, I think I'd better give you to Bridget.'

Mmm. Did not know Giles but think advice was quite good. Managed to calm him down and point him in direction of one or two useful volumes. Had lovely shag with Mark afterwards and felt v. safe and cosy lying on his chest, made all the worrying theories seem irrelevant. 'Am I a re-tread?' I said sleepily as he leaned over to blow out the candle.

'A retard? No, darling,' he said, patting my bottom reassuringly. 'A little strange, perhaps, but not a retard.'

2

Jellyfish at Large

Tuesday 28 January

9st 2, cigarettes smoked in front of Mark 0 (v.g.), cigarettes smoked in secret 7, cigarettes not smoked 47 (v.g.).*

** i.e. nearly smoked but remembered had given up so specifically did not smoke those particular 47. Number is not therefore number of cigarettes in entire world not smoked (would be ridiculous, over-large-type number).*

8 a.m. Flat. Mark has gone off to his flat to change before work so can have little cigarette and develop inner growth and win-win mentality ready for sacking meeting. So what I am working towards is creating a feeling of calm equilibrium and . . . Gaaah! Doorbell.

8.30 a.m. It was Magda's builder, Gary. Fuck, fuck, fucketty fuck. Forgot he was supposed to be coming round.

'Ah! Super! Hello! Could you come back in ten minutes? I'm just in the middle of something,' I trilled, then doubled up, cringing in nightie. What would I be in the middle of? Sex? A soufflé? Making a vase on a potter's wheel that absolutely couldn't be left in case it dried in an incomplete form?

Still had wet hair when doorbell rang again but at least had clothes on. Felt surge of middle-class guilt as Gary smirked at decadence of those who loll idly in bed while a whole different world of genuine hardworking folk have been up for so long is practically time for their lunch.

'Would you care for some tea or coffee?' I said graciously.

'Yeah. Cup of tea. Four sugars but don't stir it.'

I looked at him hard wondering if this was a joke or a bit like smoking cigarettes but not inhaling. 'Right,' I said, 'right,' and started making the tea at which Gary sat down at kitchen table and lit up a fag. Unfortunately, however, when came to pour out tea realized did not have any milk or sugar.

He looked at me incredulously, surveying the array of empty wine bottles. 'No milk or sugar?'

'The milk's, er, just run out and actually I don't know anybody who takes sugar in tea . . . though of course it's great to . . . er . . . to take sugar,' I tailed off. 'I'll just pop to the shop.'

When I came back, I thought somehow he might have got his tools out of the van, but he was still sitting there, and started telling a long complicated story about carp fishing on reservoir near Hendon. Was like business lunch where everyone chats away from the subject for so long, it becomes too embarrassing to destroy fantasy of delightful purely social occasion and you never actually get to the point.

Eventually, I crashed into seamlessly incomprehensible fish anecdote with, 'Right! Shall I show you what I want doing?' and instantly realized had made crass, hurtful gaff suggesting that I was not interested in Gary as person but merely as workman so had to re-enter fish anecdote to make amends.

9.15 a.m. Office. Rushed into work, hysterical at being five minutes late, to find bloody Richard Finch nowhere to be seen. Though actually is good as have time to further plan my defence. Weird thing is: office is completely empty! So, clearly most days, when I am panicking about being late and thinking everyone else is already here reading the papers they are all being late as well, though just not quite as late as me.

Right, am going to write down my key points for meeting. Get it clear in my head like Mark says.

'Richard, to compromise my journalistic integrity by . . .'

'Richard, as you know, I take my profession as a TV journalist very seriously . . .'

'Why don't you just go fucking fuck yourself, you fat . . .'

No, no. As Mark says, think what you want, and what he wants, and also think win-win as instructed in *The Seven Habits of Highly Effective People*. Gaaaaah!

11.15 a.m. Was Richard Finch clad in a crushed raspberry Galliano suit with an aquamarine lining, galloping backwards into the office as if on a horse.

'Bridget! Right. You're crap but you're off the hook. They loved it upstairs. Loved it. Loved it. We have a proposition. I'm thinking bunny girl, I'm thinking Gladiator, I'm thinking canvassing MP. I'm thinking Chris Serle meets Jerry Springer meets Anneka Rice meets Zoe Ball meets Mike Smith off the *Late, Late Breakfast Show*.'

'What?' I said indignantly.

Turned out they had cooked up some demeaning scheme where every week I had to try out a different profession then fuck it up in an outfit. Naturally I told him I am a serious professional journalist and will not consider prostituting myself in such a way with the result that he went into a foul sulk and said he was going to consider what my value was to the programme, if any.

8 p.m. Had completely stupid day at work. Richard Finch was trying to order me to appear on the programme wearing tiny shorts next to blow-up of Fergie in gym wear. Was trying to be very win-win about the whole thing, saying was flattered but thought they might do better with a real model, when sex-god Matt from graphics came in carrying the blow-up and said, 'Do you want us to put up an animated ring round the cellulite?'

'Yeah, yeah, if you can do the same over Fergie,' said Richard Finch.

That was it. That was just about enough. Told Richard was not in the terms of my contract to be humiliated on screen and was no way going to do it.

Got home, late and exhausted, to find Gary the Builder still there and house completely taken over with burnt toast under the grill, washing up and copies of the *Angler's Mail* and *Coarse Fisherman* all over the shop.

'What do you think?' said Gary, proudly nodding at his handiwork.

'They're great! They're great!' I gushed, feeling mouth

going into funny tight shape. 'There's just one little thing. Do you think you could make it so the supports are all in line with each other?'

Shelves, in fact were put up in mad asymmetrical manner with supports here, there and everywhere, different on each layer.

'Yeah, well, you see, the problem is it's your electric cable, because if I plug the wall here it'll short-circuit the lot,' Gary began, at which point the phone rang.

'Hello?'

'Hi, is that dating war command?' Was Mark on the mobile.

'The only thing I could do is take them out and put rivets under the awlings,' gibberished Gary.

'Have you got someone there?' crackled Mark above the traffic.

'No, it's just the . . .' I was about to say builder but did not want to insult Gary so changed it to 'Gary – a friend of Magda's.'

'What's he doing there?'

'Course you'll need a new raw-gidge,' continued Gary.

'Listen, I'm in the car. Do you want to come out for supper tonight with Giles?'

'I've said I'll see the girls.'

'Oh Christ. I suppose I'll be dismembered and dissected and thoroughly analysed.'

'No you won't . . .'

'Hang on. Just going under the Westway.' Crackle, crackle, crackle. 'I met your friend Rebecca the other day. She seemed very nice.'

'I didn't know you knew Rebecca,' I said, breathing very quickly.

Rebecca is not exactly a friend, except that she's always turning up in 192 with me and Jude and Shaz. But the thing about Rebecca is, she's a jellyfisher. You have a conversation with her that seems all nice and friendly, then you suddenly feel like you've been stung and you don't know where it came from. You'll be talking about jeans and she'll say 'Yes, well, if you've got cellulite jodhpurs, you're best in something really well cut like Dolce & Gabbana,' – she herself having thighs like a baby giraffe – then smoothly move on to DKNY chinos as if nothing has happened.

'Bridge, are you still there?'

'Where . . . where did you see Rebecca?' I said, in a high, strangled voice.

'She was at Barky Thompson's drinks last night and introduced herself.'

'Last night?'

'Yes, I dropped in on my way back because you were running late.'

'What did you talk about?' I said, conscious of Gary smirking at me, with a fag hanging out of his mouth.

'Oh. You know, she asked about my work and said nice things about you,' said Mark casually.

'What did she say?' I hissed.

'She said you were a free spirit . . .' The line broke up for a moment.

Free spirit? Free spirit in Rebecca-speak is tantamount to saying, 'Bridget sleeps around and takes hallucinatory drugs.'

'I suppose I could put up an RSJ and suspend them,' Gary started up again, as if the phone conversation were not going on.

'Well. I'd better let you go, hadn't I, if you've got someone there,' said Mark. 'Have a good time. Shall I call you later?'

'Yes, yes, talk to you later.'

I put the phone down, mind reeling.

'After someone else is he?' said Gary in a rare and extremely unwelcome moment of lucidity.

I glared at him. 'What about these shelves . . . ?'

'Well. If you want them all in line, I'll have to move your leads, and that'll mean stripping the plaster off unless we rawl in a 3 by 4 of MDF. I mean if you'd told me you wanted them symmetrical before I'd have known, wouldn't I? I suppose I could do it now.' He looked round the kitchen. 'Have you got any food in?'

'They're fine, absolutely lovely just like that,' I gabbled.

'If you want to cook me a bowl of that pasta I'll . . .'

Have just paid Gary £120 in cash for insane shelves to get him out of the house. Oh God, am so late. Fuck, fuck, telephone again.

9.05 p.m. Was Dad – which was strange since normally he leaves telephonic communication to Mum.

'Just called to see how you're doing.' He sounded very odd.

'I'm fine,' I said worriedly. 'How are you?'

'Jolly good, jolly good. Very busy in the garden, you know, very busy though not much to do out there in the winter of course . . . So, how's everything?'

'Fine,' I said. 'And everything's fine with you?'

'Oh, yes, yes, perfectly fine. Um, and work? How's work?'

'Work's fine. Well, I mean disastrous obviously. But are you all right?'

'Me? Oh yes, fine. Of course the snowdrops will be pop, plop, ploppeeddee plopping through soon. And everything's all right with you, is it?'

'Yes, fine. How's things with you?'

After several more minutes of the impenetrable conversational loop I had a breakthrough: 'How's Mum?'

'Ah. Well, she's, she's ah . . .'

There was a long, painful pause.

'She's going to Kenya. With Una.'

The worst of it was, the business with Julio the Portuguese tour operator started last time she went on holiday with Una.

'Are you going too?'

'No, no,' blustered Dad. 'I've no desire to sit getting skin cancer in some appalling enclave sipping pina colada and watching topless tribal dancers prostitute themselves to lascivious crusties in front of tomorrow's breakfast buffet.'

'Did she ask you to?'

'Ah. Well. You see, no. Your mother would argue that she is a person in her own right, that our money is her money, and she should be allowed to freely explore the world and her own personality at a whim.'

'Well, I suppose as long as she keeps it to those two,' I said. 'She does love you, Dad. You saw that' – nearly said 'last time' and changed it to – 'at Christmas. She just needs a bit of excitement.'

'I know but, Bridget, there's something else. Something quite dreadful. Can you hold on?'

I glanced up at the clock. I was supposed to be in 192

already and hadn't got round to telling Jude and Shaz yet that Magda was coming. I mean it is delicate at the best of times, trying to combine friends from opposite sides of the marriage divide, but Magda has just had a baby. And I feared that wouldn't be good for Jude's mindset.

'Sorry about that: just closing the door.' Dad was back. 'Anyway,' he went on conspiratorially. 'I overheard your mother talking on the phone earlier today. I think it was to the hotel in Kenya. And she said, she said . . .'

'It's all right, it's all right. What did she say?'

'She said, "We don't want twins and we don't want anything under five foot. We're coming here to enjoy ourselves."'

Christ alive.

'I mean,' – poor Dad, he was practically sobbing – 'am I actually to stand by and allow my own wife to hire herself a gigolo on arrival?'

For a moment was at a loss. Advising one's own father on the suspected gigolo-hiring habits of one's own mother is not a subject had ever seen covered in any of my books.

In the end I plumped for trying to help Dad boost his own self-esteem, whilst suggesting a period of calm distance before discussing things with Mum in the morning: advice I realized I would be completely incapable of following myself.

By this time I was beyond late. Explained to Dad that Jude was having a bit of a crisis.

'Off you go, off you go! When you've got time. Not to worry!' he said overcheerily. 'Better get out in the garden while the rain's holding off.' His voice sounded odd and thick.

'Dad,' I said, 'it's 9 o'clock at night. It's midwinter.'

'Ah, right,' he said. 'Jolly good. Better have a whisky, then.'

Hope he is going to be OK.

Wednesday 29 January

9st 5 (gaah! But possibly due to wine-bag inside self), cigarettes 1 (v.g.), jobs 1, flats 1, boyfriends 1 (continuing good work).

5 a.m. Am never, never going to drink again as long as live.

5.15 a.m. Evening keeps coming back to me disturbingly in lumps.

After panting rush through rain, arrived at 192 to find Magda not arrived yet, thank God, and Jude already in a state, allowing her thinking to get into a Snowball Effect, extrapolating huge dooms from small incidents as specifically warned against in *Don't Sweat the Small Stuff*.

'I'm never going to have any children,' she was monotoning, staring straight ahead. 'I'm a re-tread. That guy said women over thirty are just walking pulsating ovaries.'

'Oh for God's sake!' snorted Shaz, reaching for the Chardonnay. 'Haven't you read *Backlash*? He's just a moral-free hack, recycling woman-bashing, Middle-England propaganda to keep women down like *slaves*. I hope he goes prematurely bald.'

'But how likely is it I am going to meet someone new, now, and have time to form a relationship and persuade them they want to have children? Because they never do before they get them.'

Wish Jude would not talk about biological clock in public. Obviously one worries about such things in private and tries to pretend whole undignified situation isn't happening. Bringing it up in 192 merely makes one panic and feel like a walking cliché.

Happily, Shazzer was off on a rant. 'Far too many women are wasting their young lives having children in their twenties, thirties and early forties when they should be concentrating on their careers,' she growled. 'Look at that woman in Brazil who had one at sixty.'

'Hurrah!' I said. 'Nobody wants never to have any children but it's the sort of thing you always want to do in two or three years' time!'

'Fat chance,' said Jude darkly. 'Magda said even after she and Jeremy were married, whenever she mentioned children he went all funny and said she was getting too serious.'

'What, even after they were married?' said Shaz.

'Yes,' said Jude, picked up her handbag and went off to the loo in a huff.

'I've had a great idea for Jude's birthday,' said Shaz. 'Why don't we get her one of her eggs frozen?'

'Shhh.' I giggled. 'Wouldn't it be a bit difficult to do as a surprise?'

Just then, Magda walked in, which was all very unfortunate as (a) had still not got round to warning the girls and (b) got shock of life as had only seen Magda once since the birth of her third baby and her stomach had not gone down yet. She was sporting a gold shirt and velvet headband, in unignorable contrast to everyone else's urban combat/sportswear outfits.

Was just pouring Magda a glass of Chardonnay when Jude reappeared, looked from Magda's stomach to me, and gave me a filthy look. 'Hi, Magda,' she said gruffly. 'When's it due?'

'I had her five weeks ago,' said Magda, chin wobbling.

Knew it was a mistake to combine different species of friends, knew it.

'Do I look that fat?' Magda whispered to me, as if Jude and Shaz were the enemy.

'No, you look great,' I said. 'Glowing.'

'Do I?' Magda said, brightening. 'It just takes a bit of time to . . . you know . . . deflate. Also, you know I had mastitis . . .'

Jude and Shaz flinched. Why do Smug Married girls do this, why? Casually launching into anecdotes about slashings, stitchings and effusions of blood, poison, newts and God knows what as if making light and delightful social chit-chat.

'Anyway,' Magda was going on, glugging at the Chardonnay and beaming happily at the friends like someone let out of prison, 'Woney said to put a couple of cabbage leaves in your bra – it has to be savoy – and after about five hours it draws out the infection. Obviously it gets a bit manky, with the sweat and milk and discharge. And Jeremy got a bit annoyed about me getting into bed with all the bleeding Down There and a bra full of damp leaves but I feel so much better! I've practically used up a whole cabbage!'

There was a stunned pause. I glanced worriedly around the table but Jude seemed to have suddenly cheered up, sleeking down her Donna Karan crop top, which revealed a beguiling glimpse of pierced navel and perfectly honed flat midriff while Shazzie adjusted her Wonderbra.

'Anyway. Enough of me. How are things going with *you*?' said Magda as if she had been reading one of those books advertised in the newspapers with a drawing of a strange 50s-looking man and a headline *Does Good Conversation Elude You*? 'How's Mark?'

'He's *lovely*,' I said happily. 'He makes me feel so . . .' Jude and Shazzer were exchanging glances. Realized I was probably sounding a bit too smug. 'The only thing is . . .' I tack-changed.

'What?' said Jude, leaning forward.

'It's probably nothing. But he called me tonight, and said he'd met Rebecca.'

'WHATTTT?' exploded Shazzer. 'How the fuck dare he? Where?'

'At a party last night.'

'What was he doing at a party last night?' yelled Jude. 'With Rebecca, without you?'

Hurrah! Was suddenly just like old times again. Carefully dissected whole tone of phone call, feelings about, and possible significance of, fact that Mark must have come straight to my flat *from the party*, yet did not mention either the party or Rebecca till a full *24 hours* later.

'It's Mentionitis,' Jude was saying.

'What's that?' said Magda.

'Oh, you know, when someone's name keeps coming up all the time, when it's not strictly relevant: "Rebecca says this" or "Rebecca's got a car like that".'

Magda went quiet. I knew exactly why. Last year she

kept telling me she thought something was up with Jeremy. Then eventually she found out he'd been having an affair with a girl in the City. I handed her a Silk Cut.

'I know exactly what you mean,' she said, putting it into her mouth and nodding at me appreciatively. 'How come he always comes round to your place anyway? I thought he had some great big mansion in Holland Park.'

'Well, he does, but he seems to prefer to . . .'

'Hmm,' said Jude. 'Have you read *Beyond Co-dependency With a Man Who Can't Commit?*'

'No.'

'Come back to my place after. I'll show you.'

Magda looked up at Jude like Piglet hoping to be included on an outing with Pooh and Tigger. 'He's probably just trying to get out of the shopping and clearing up,' she said eagerly. 'I've never met a man who didn't secretly think he should be looked after like his father was by his mother no matter how evolved they pretend to be.'

'Exactly,' snarled Shazzer, at which Magda beamed with pride. Unfortunately things immediately swung back to the fact that Jude's American hadn't returned her call, at which Magda immediately undid all her good work.

'Honestly, Jude!' said Magda. 'I can't understand how you can deal with the collapse of the rouble to a standing ovation from the entire trading floor and then get into a state like this over a stupid man.'

'Well, the thing is, Mag,' I explained, trying to smooth things over, 'the rouble is much easier to deal with than a man. There are clear and precise rules governing its behaviour.'

'I think you should leave it a couple of days,' said Shaz thoughtfully. 'Try not to obsess and then when he does ring just be light and really busy and say you haven't got time to talk.'

'Wait a minute,' Magda bludgeoned in. 'If you want to talk to him, what's the point of waiting three days, then saying you haven't got time to talk to him? Why don't *you* call *him*?'

Jude and Shazzer gaped at her, incredulous at the insane Smug Married suggestion. Everyone knows that Anjelica Huston never, ever rang Jack Nicholson, and that men cannot bear not to be the pursuer.

Whole scenario went from bad to worse, with Magda talking wide-eyedly about how when Jude met the right man it would be 'as easy as leaves falling off a tree'. At 10.30 Magda jumped to her feet and said, 'Well, better go! Jeremy's back at 11!'

'What did you have to ask Magda for?' said Jude the second she was out of earshot.

'She was lonely,' I said lamely.

'Yeah, right. Because she had to spend two hours on her own without Jeremy,' said Shazzer.

'She can't have it both ways. She can't be in a Smug Married Family then moan because she isn't in a Singleton Urban Family,' said Jude.

'Honestly, if that girl were thrown out into the cut and thrust of the modern dating world she'd be eaten alive,' muttered Shaz.

'ALERT, ALERT, REBECCA ALERT,' nuclear-sirened Jude.

We followed her gaze out of the window to where a Mitsubishi urban jeep was pulling up containing Rebecca with one hand on the wheel and the other holding the phone to her ear.

Rebecca eased her long legs out, rolling her eyes at someone who had the nerve to be walking past when she was on the phone, crossed the road without paying any attention to cars so they had to screech to a halt, did a little pirouette as if to say 'Fuck off, everyone, this is my personal space,' then walked smack into a tramp lady with a shopping trolley and completely ignored her.

She burst into the bar, swishing her long hair over her head from her face so it immediately swished back again in a swingy, shiny curtain. 'OK, must run. Love you! Byeee!' she was saying into her mobile. 'Hi, hi,' she said, kissing us all, sitting down and gesturing to the waiter for a glass. 'How's it going? Bridge, how's it going with Mark? You must be really pleased to get a boyfriend at last.'

'At last'. Grrr. First jellyfish of the evening. 'Are you in heaven?' she cooed. 'Is he taking you to the Law Society dinner on Friday?'

Mark hadn't said anything about any Law Society dinner.

'Oh sorry, have I put my big foot in it?' said Rebecca. 'I'm sure he's just forgotten. Or maybe he thinks it isn't fair on *you*. But I think you'll cope fine. They'll probably think you're really sweet.'

As Shazzer said afterwards, it wasn't so much a jellyfish as a Portuguese man-of-war. The fishermen were surrounding it in their boats trying to drag it back to the beach.

Rebecca flounced off to some do or other, so the three of us ended up lurching back to Jude's flat.

'"The Man Who Can't Commit will not want you in

his own domain,"' Jude was reading out as Shaz fiddled with the *Pride and Prejudice* video to try to find the bit where Colin Firth dives into the lake.

'"He likes to come to your tower, like a knight errant with no responsibilities. And then he goes back to his castle. He can take and make whatever phone calls he likes without you knowing about it. He can keep his place – and himself – to himself."'

'Too right,' muttered Shaz. 'OK, come on, he's going to dive in.'

We all fell silent then, watching Colin Firth emerging from the lake dripping wet, in the see-through white shirt. Mmm. Mmmm.

'Anyway,' I said defensively, 'Mark isn't a Man Who Can't Commit – he's already been married.'

'Well, then it might mean he thinks you're a "Just For Now Girl",' hiccuped Jude.

'Bastard!' slurred Shazzer. 'Blurry bastards. Fwaw, look at that!'

Eventually staggered home, lunged expectantly towards answerphone then stopped in dismay. No red light. Mark hadn't called. Oh God, is 6 a.m. already and have got to get some more sleep.

8.30 a.m. Why hasn't he rung me? Why? Humph. Am assured, receptive, responsive woman of substance. My sense of self depends on myself and not on . . . Wait a minute. Maybe phone is not working.

8.32 a.m. Dialling tone seems normal, but will ring from mobile to check. If not working might mean everything is fine.

8.35 a.m. Humph. Phone is working. I mean he definitely said he was going to call last . . . Oh goody, telephone!

'Oh hello, m'dear. Didn't wake you up, did I?'

Was my dad. Instantly felt guilty for being horrible, selfish daughter, more interested in own four-week-old relationship than threat to parents' three-decade-long marriage from higher than five foot, non-twin Kenyan gigolos.

'What's happened?'

'It's fine.' Dad laughed. 'I brought the phone call up with her and – oops-a-daisy – here she comes.'

'Honestly, darling!' said Mum, grabbing the phone. 'I don't know where Daddy gets these silly ideas from. We were talking about the beds!'

I smiled to myself. Obviously Dad and I have minds like sewers.

'Anyway,' she went on, 'it's all going ahead. We're off on the eighth of Feb! Kenya! Imagine! The only nigger in the woodpile is . . .'

'Mother!' I exploded.

'What, darling?'

'You can't say "nigger in the woodpile". It's racist.'

'We're not going to put anyone in a *woodpile*, silly! Daddy and I have got central heating.'

'If expressions like that are allowed to linger in the vocabulary it poisons attitudes and . . .'

'Durrrr! You do miss the wood for the trees sometimes. Ooh did I tell you? Julie Enderbury's preggy again.'

'Listen, I really do have to go, I . . .'

What is it about mothers and the phone which, immediately you say you have to go, makes them think of nineteen completely irrelevant things they have to tell you that minute?

'Yes. It's her third,' she said accusingly. 'Oh and the other thing is, Una and I have decided we're going to ski the net.'

'I think the expression is "surf" but I've . . .'

'Ski, surf, snowboard – doesn't matter, darling! Merle and Percival are on it. You know: used to be head of the burns unit at Northampton Infirmary. Anyway, the other thing is, are you and Mark coming home for Easter?'

'Mum, I've got to go now, I'm late for work!' I said. Finally, after about ten more minutes of irrelevance I managed to get rid of her and sank gratefully back on the pillow. Does make me feel a bit feeble though, if mother is online and I'm not. I was on it but a company called GBH sent me 677 identical junkmails by mistake and have not been able to get any sense out of it since.

Thursday 30 January

9st 5, (emergency: lacy pants have begun to leave patterns on self), items of lovely sexy slippy underwear tried on 17, items of giant incontinence-wear-style scary unsightly underwear purchased 1, boyfriends 1 (but entirely dependent on concealing scary new underwear from same).

9 a.m. Coins Café. Having coffee. Hurrah! Everything is lovely. He just rang! Apparently he did call me last night but didn't leave a message as he was going to ring back later, but then fell asleep. Slightly suspicious, but he asked me to come to the law thing tomorrow. Also Giles from his office said how nice I'd been on the phone.

9.05 a.m. Bit scary, though, law do. Is black tie. Asked Mark about what was expected of me and he said, 'Oh nothing. Don't worry about it. We'll just sit at a table and eat a meal with some people from work. They're just my friends. They'll love you.'

9.11 a.m. 'They'll love you'. You see that, already, is tacit admission that am up on trial. So is very important to make a good impression.

9.15 a.m. Right, am going to be positive about this. Am going to be marvellous: elegant, vivacious, beautifully dressed. Oh, though. Do not have long dress. Maybe Jude or Magda will lend me one.

Right:

Pre-Law Society Dinner Countdown

Day 1. (today)

Projected food intake:

1. Breakfast: fruit shake, comprising oranges, banana, pears, melons or other fruit in season. (NB pre-breakfast cappuccino and chocolate croissant already consumed.)
2. Snack: fruit but not too near lunch as takes one hour to get enzymes down.
3. Lunch: salad with protein.
4. Snack: celery or broccoli. Will go to gym after work.
5. After-gym snack: celery.
6. Dinner: grilled chicken and steamed vegetables.

6 p.m. Just leaving office. Am going late-night underwear shopping tonight with Magda to solve figure problems in short term. Magda is going to lend me jewels and v. elegant long, dark-blue dress which, she says, needs a bit of 'help' and apparently all film stars etc. wear controlling undergarments at premieres. Means cannot go to gym but sturdy undergarment much more effective in short term than gym visit.

Also, just in general, have decided against random daily gym visits in favour of whole new programme beginning with fitness assessment tomorrow. Obviously cannot expect body to be significantly transformed in time for dinner, which is precisely point of underwear shopping, but at least will be invigorated. Oh, telephone.

6.15 p.m. Was Shazzer. Quickly told her about pre-law party programme (including unfortunate pizza-for-lunch debacle), but when told her about fitness assessment she seemed to spit down the telephone:

'Don't do it,' she warned in a sepulchral whisper.

Turns out Shaz previously endured similar assessment with enormous *Gladiators*-style woman with fierce red hair called 'Carborundum' who stood her in front of a mirror in the middle of the gym and bellowed, 'The fat on your bottom has slipped down, pushing the fat on your thighs round to the sides in the form of saddlebags.'

Hate the idea of the *Gladiators*-style woman. Always suspect one day *Gladiators* programme will get out of control, Gladiators will turn flesh-eating and producers will start tossing Christians to Carborundum and her ilk. Shaz says I should definitely cancel, but my point is if, as Carborundum suggests, fat is able to behave in this slippage-style way then clearly it ought to be possible to mould and squeeze existing fat into nicer shape – or even different shapes as occasion demands. Cannot help but wonder if was free to arrange own fat according to choice would I still wish to reduce amount? Think would have huge big breasts and hips and tiny waist. But would there be too much fat to dispose of in this way? And where could one put the excess? Would it be bad to have fat feet or ears if the rest of one's body was perfect?

'Fat lips would be all right,' Shazzer said, 'but not . . .' lowering her voice to a disgusted whisper '. . . fat labia.'

Ugh. Sometimes Shazzer is completely disgusting. Right. Got to go. Am meeting Magda in Marks & Sparks at 6.30.

9 p.m. Back home. Shopping experience was perhaps best described as educational. Magda insisted on waving ghastly huge scary pants at me. 'Come on, Bridget: the New Corsetry! Think 70s, think Cross Your Heart, think girdle,' she said, holding up a sort of Cyclist Serial Killer's outfit in black Lycra with shorts, boning and a sturdy bra.

'I'm not wearing that,' I hissed out of the corner of my mouth. 'Put it back.'

'Why not?'

'What if someone, you know, feels it?'

'Honestly, Bridget. Underwear is there to do a job. If you're wearing a sleek little dress or a pair of trousers – for work, say – you want to create a smooth line. Nobody's going to feel you at work, are they?'

'Well, they might,' I said defensively, thinking about what used to happen in the lift at work when I was 'going out' – if one can describe that commitment-phobicity nightmare as such – with Daniel Cleaver.

'What about these?' I said hopefully, holding up a gorgeous set that was made out of the same material as sheer black stockings only bra and pants shaped.

'No! No! Totally 1980s. This is what you want,' she said, waving something that looked like one of Mum's roll-ons crossed with her long johns.

'But what if someone puts their hand up your skirt?'

'Bridget, you are unbelievable,' she said loudly. 'Do you get up every morning with the idea that some man might randomly put his hand up your skirt during the course of the day? Don't you have any control over your sexual destiny?'

'Yes I do actually,' I said defiantly, marching towards the changing room with a whole handful of sturdy pants. Ended up trying to squeeze myself into a black rubber-like sheath, which came up to just below my breasts and kept unravelling itself from both ends like an unruly condom. 'What if Mark sees me in it or feels it?'

'You're not going to smooch in a club. You're going to a formal dinner where he'll be making an impression on his colleagues. He'll be concentrating on that – not trying to grope you.'

Not sure Mark ever concentrates on making an impression on anyone actually, as is confident in self. But Magda is right about the underwear. One must move with the times, not becoming entrenched in narrow underwear concepts.

Right, must get early night. Gym appointment is at 8 in morning. Actually really think whole personality is undergoing seismic change.

9st 4, alcohol units 6 (2), cigarettes 12 (0), calories 4,284 (1,500), lies told to fitness assessor (14).*

** Figures in brackets denote data given to fitness assessor.*

9.30 a.m. It is typical of the new louche health club culture that personal trainers are allowed to behave like doctors without any sort of Hippocratic oath.

'How many alcohol units do you drink a week?' said 'Rebel': Brad Pitt-style whippersnapper fitness assessor as I sat trying to hold in stomach in bra and pants.

'Fourteen to twenty-one,' I lied smoothly, at which he had the nerve to flinch.

'And do you smoke?'

'I've given up,' I purred.

At this, Rebel glanced pointedly into my bag where, OK, there was a packet of Silk Cut Ultra, but so?

'When did you give up?' he said primly, typing something into the computer that would obviously go straight to Conservative Central Office and ensure I am sent to a boot camp next time I get a parking fine.

'Today,' I said firmly.

Ended up standing having fat measured with pinchers by Rebel.

'Now I'm just making these marks so I can see what I'm measuring,' he said bossily, putting circles and crosses all over me with a felt tip. 'They'll come off if you rub them with a bit of white spirit.'

Next had to go into gym and do exercises with all sorts of unexplained eye contact and touching with Rebel –

e.g. standing opposite with hands on each other's shoulders with Rebel doing squats, bouncing bottom robustly on mat and me making awkward attempts to bend knees slightly. At end of whole thing felt as though had had long and intimate sex session with Rebel and we were practically going out. Afterwards got dressed and had shower then was unsure what to do – seemed ought at least to go back in and ask what time he'd be home for dinner. But of course am having dinner with Mark Darcy.

V. excited about dinner. Have been practising in outfit and really it looks excellent, sleek smooth lines, all thanks to scary pants, which there is no reason he should find out about. Also really no reason why should not be v.g. escort. Am woman of world with career etc.

Midnight. When finally arrived at Guildhall, Mark was pacing up and down outside in black tie and big overcoat. Fwaw. Love when you are going out with someone and they suddenly seem like an extremely attractive stranger and all you want to do is rush home and shag them senseless as if you have only just met. (Not, of course, that that is what normally do with people have only just met.) When he saw me he looked really shocked, laughed, then composed his features and gestured me towards the doors in polite, public-school fashion.

'Sorry I'm late,' I said breathlessly.

'You're not,' he said, 'I lied about the kick-off.' He looked at me again in a strange way.

'What?' I said.

'Nothing, nothing,' he said over-calmly and pleasantly, as if I were a lunatic standing on a car holding an axe in one hand and his wife's head in the other. He ushered me through the door, as a uniformed footman held it open for us.

Inside was high, dark-panelled entrance hall with many black-tied old people murmuring around. Saw woman in sequinned crusty top thing looking at me in odd way. Mark nodded pleasantly at her and whispered in my ear, 'Why don't you just slip into the cloakroom and look at your face.'

I shot off into loo. Unfortunately, in the dark of taxi, I had applied dark grey Mac eyeshadow to my cheeks instead of blusher: the sort of thing that could happen to anyone, obviously, as packaging identical. When came out of toilets, neatly scrubbed with coat handed in, stopped dead in tracks. Mark was talking to Rebecca.

She was wearing a coffee-coloured plunging, backless satin number that clung to her every fleshless bone with clearly no corset. Felt like my dad did when he put a cake into the Grafton Underwood fête and when he returned to it after the judging it had a note on saying, 'Not up to Competition Standard.'

'I mean it was just too funny,' Rebecca was saying and laughing full in Mark's face affectionately. 'Oh Bridget,' Rebecca said, as I joined them. 'How are you, lovely girl!' She kissed me at which could not stop self pulling face. 'Feeling nervous?'

'Nervous?' said Mark. 'Why would she be nervous? She's the embodiment of inner poise, aren't you, Bridge.'

For just a split second saw a look of annoyance cross Rebecca's face before she composed it again and said, 'Ahhh, isn't that sweet? I'm so happy for you!' Then she glided off with a coy little backwards look at Mark.

'She seems very nice,' said Mark. 'Always seems extremely nice and intelligent.'

Always?? I was thinking. Always? I thought he'd only met her twice. He slid his arm dangerously close to my corset so had to jump away. A couple of huffer-puffers came up to us and started congratulating Mark about something he'd done with a Mexican. He chatted pleasantly for a minute or two then skilfully extracted us, and led us through to the dining room.

Was v. glamorous: dark wood, round tables, candlelight and shimmering crystal. Trouble was, kept having to jump away from Mark every time he put his hand on my waist.

Our table was already filling up with an array of brittly confident thirty-something lawyers, bellowing with laughter and trying to outdo each other with the sort of flippant conversational sallies that are obviously tips of huge icebergs of legal and Zeitgeisty knowledge:

'How do you know if you're addicted to the Internet?'

'You realize you don't know the gender of your three best friends.' Haaar Waagh. Harharhar.

'You can't write full stops any more without adding co.uk.' BAAAAAAAAAAA!

'You do all your work assignments in HMTL Protocol.' Blaaaaagh harhar. Braaaah. Hahah.

As the room started to settle into the meal, a woman called Louise Barton-Foster (incredibly opinionated lawyer and the sort of woman you can imagine forcing you to eat liver) started holding forth for what seemed like 3 months with complete bollocks.

'But in a sense,' she was saying, staring ferociously at

the menu, 'one could argue the entire ER Emeuro Proto is a Gerbilisshew.'

Was perfectly OK – just sat quietly and ate and drank things – until Mark suddenly said, 'I think you're absolutely right, Louise. If I'm going to vote Tory again I want to know my views are being (a) researched and (b) represented.'

I stared at him in horror. Felt like my friend Simon did once when he was playing with some children at a party when their grandfather turned up and he was Robert Maxwell – and suddenly Simon looked at toddlers and saw they were all mini-Robert Maxwells with beetling brows and huge chins.

Realize when start a relationship with a new person there will be differences between you, differences that have to be adapted to and smoothed down like rough corners, but had never, ever in a million years suspected I might have been sleeping with a man who voted Tory. Suddenly felt I didn't know Mark Darcy at all, and for all I knew, all the weeks we had been going out he had been secretly collecting limited edition miniature pottery animals wearing bonnets from the back pages of Sunday supplements, or slipping off to rugby matches on a coach and mooning at other motorists out of the back window.

Conversation was getting snootier and snootier and more and more showy-offy.

'Well, how do you know it's 4.5 to 7?' Louise was barking at a man who looked like Prince Andrew in a stripy shirt.

'Well, I did read economics at Cambridge.'

'Who taught you?' snapped another girl, as if this were going to win the argument.

'Are you all right?' whispered Mark out of the corner of his mouth.

'Yes,' I muttered, head down.

'You're . . . *quivering.* Come on. What is it?'

Eventually I had to tell him.

'So I vote Tory, what's wrong with that?' he said, staring at me incredulously.

'Shhhhhh,' I whispered, looking nervously round the table.

'What's the problem?'

'It's just,' I began, wishing Shazzer were here, 'I mean, if I voted Tory I'd be a social outcast. It would be like turning up at Café Rouge on a horse with a pack of beagles in tow, or having dinner parties on shiny tables with side plates.'

'Rather like this, you mean?' He laughed.

'Well, yes,' I muttered.

'So what do you vote, then?'

'Labour, of course,' I hissed. 'Everybody votes Labour.'

'Well, I think that's patently been proved not to be the case, *so far,*' he said. 'Why, as a matter of interest?'

'What?'

'Why do you vote Labour?'

'Well,' I paused thoughtfully, 'because voting Labour stands for being left wing.'

'Ah.' He seemed to think this was somehow hugely amusing. Everyone was listening now.

'And socialist,' I added.

'Socialist. I see. Socialist meaning . . . ?'

'The workers standing together.'

'Well, Blair isn't exactly going to shore up the powers of the unions, is he?' he said. 'Look what he's saying about Clause Four.'

'Well, the Tories are rubbish.'

'Rubbish?' he said. 'The economy's in better shape now than it's been in for seven years.'

'No it's not,' I said emphatically. 'Anyway, they've probably just put it up because there's an election coming.'

'Put what up?' he said. 'Put the economy up?'

'How does Blair's stand on Europe compare to Major's?' Louise joined in.

'Yar. And why hasn't he matched the Tory promise to increase spending on health year by year in real terms?' said Prince Andrew.

Honestly. Off they went again all showing off to each other. Eventually could stand it no longer.

'The point is you are supposed to vote for the principle of the thing, not the itsy-bitsy detail about this per cent and that per cent. And it is perfectly obvious that Labour stands for the principle of sharing, kindness, gays, single mothers and Nelson Mandela as opposed to braying bossy men having affairs with everyone shag-shag-shag left, right and centre and going to the Ritz in Paris then telling all the presenters off on the *Today* programme.'

There was a cavernous silence round the table.

'Well, I think you've got it in a nutshell there,' said Mark, laughing and rubbing my knee. 'We can't argue with that.'

Everyone was looking at us. But then, instead of someone taking the piss – such as would have happened in the normal world – they pretended nothing had happened and went back to the clinking and braying, completely ignoring me.

Could not gauge how bad or otherwise incident was. Was like being amongst a Papua New Guinea tribe, and treading on the chief's dog and not knowing whether the murmur of conversation meant it didn't matter or that they were discussing how to make your head into a frittata.

Someone rapped on the table for the speeches, which were just really, really, crashingly, fist-eatingly boring. As soon as they were over Mark whispered,. 'Let's get out, shall we?'

We said our goodbyes, and set off across the room. 'Er . . . Bridget,' he said, 'I don't want to worry you. But you've got something slightly odd-looking round your waist.'

Shot my hand down to check. Scary corset had somehow unravelled itself from both ends turning into bulging roll round my waist like giant spare tyre.

'What is it?' said Mark, nodding and smiling to people as we made our way through the tables.

'Nothing,' I muttered. As soon as we got out of the room I made a bolt for the loo. Was really difficult getting the dress off and unravelling the scary pants then putting the whole nightmare ensemble back again. Really wished I was at home wearing a pair of baggy trousers and a sweater.

When I emerged into the hallway I nearly turned straight back into the loos. Mark was talking to Rebecca. Again. She whispered something in his ear, then burst out into a horrid hooting laugh.

I walked up to them and stood there awkwardly.

'Here she is!' said Mark. 'All sorted out?'

'Bridget!' said Rebecca, pretending to be pleased to see me. 'I hear you've been impressing everyone with your political views!'

Wished could think of something v. amusing to say, but instead just stood there looking out under lowered eyebrows.

'Actually, it was great,' said Mark. 'She made the whole lot of us look like pompous arses. Anyway, must be off, nice to see you again.'

Rebecca kissed us both effusively in a cloud of Gucci Envy then sashayed back into the dining room in a way that was really obvious she hoped Mark was watching.

Couldn't think what to say as we walked to the car. He and Rebecca had obviously been laughing at me behind my back and then he'd tried to cover up for it. Wished could ring up Jude and Shaz for advice.

Mark was behaving as if nothing had happened. As soon as we set off he started trying to slide his hand up my thigh. Why is it that the less you appear to want sex with men the more they do?

'Don't you want to keep your hands on the wheel?' I said, desperately trying to shrink back, to keep the edge of the rubber roll-on thing away from his fingers.

'No. I want to ravish you,' he said, lunging at a bollard.

Managed to remain intact by feigning road safety obsession.

'Oh. Rebecca said did we want to go round for dinner sometime?' he said.

I couldn't believe this. I've known Rebecca for four years and she has never once asked me round for dinner.

'She looked nice, didn't she? Nice dress thing.'

It was Mentionitis. It was Mentionitis happening before my very ears.

We'd reached Notting Hill. At the lights, without asking me, he just turned in the direction of my house, and away from his. He was keeping his castle intact. It was probably full of messages from Rebecca. I was a Just For Now Girl.

'Where are we going?' I burst out.

'Your flat. Why?' he said, looking round in alarm.

'Exactly. Why?' I said furiously. 'We've been going out for four weeks and six days. And we've never stayed at your house. Not once. Not ever! Why?'

Mark went completely silent. He indicated, turned left, then swung back towards Holland Park Avenue without saying a word.

'What's the matter?' I said eventually.

He stared straight ahead and flicked on the indicator. 'I don't like shouting.'

When we got back to his house it was awful. Walked up the steps together in silence. He opened the door, picked up the mail and flicked the lights on in the kitchen.

Kitchen is the height of a double-decker bus and one of those seamless stainless steel ones where you cannot tell which one is the fridge. Was a strange absence of things lying around and three pools of cold light in the middle of the floor.

He strode off to the other end of the room, footsteps echoing hollowly as if in underground cavern on school trip, stared worriedly at the stainless steel doors and said, 'Would you like a glass of wine?'

'Yes please, thank you,' I said politely. There were some modern-looking high stools at a stainless steel breakfast bar. I climbed awkwardly on to one, feeling like Des O'Connor preparing to do a duet with Anita Harris.

'Right,' said Mark. He opened one of the stainless steel cupboard doors, noticed it had a bin attached to it, then closed it again, opened another door and gazed down in surprise at a washing machine. I looked down, wanting to laugh.

'Red or white wine?' he said abruptly.

'White, please.' Suddenly I felt really tired, my shoes hurt, my scary pants were digging into me. I just wanted to go home.

'Ah.' He had located the fridge.

Glanced across and saw the answerphone on one of the counters. Stomach lurched. The red light was flashing. Looked up to find Mark standing right in front of me holding a wine bottle in Conran-esque ,distressed iron decanter. He looked really miserable too.

'Look, Bridget, I . . .'

I got off the stool to put my arms round him, but then immediately his hands went to my waist. I pulled away. I had to get rid of the bloody thing.

'I'm just going to go upstairs for a minute,' I said.

'Why?'

'To the loo,' I said wildly, then teetered off in the now agonizing shoes towards the stairs. Went into the first room I came to, which seemed to be Mark's dressing room, a whole room full of suits and shirts and lines of shoes. Got myself out of the dress and, with huge relief, started peeling off the scary pants, thinking could put on a dressing gown and maybe we could get all cosy and sort things out but suddenly Mark appeared in the doorway. I stood frozen in full scary undergarment exposure then started to frantically pull it off while he stared, aghast.

'Wait, wait,' he said, as I reached for the dressing gown, looking intently at my stomach. 'Have you been drawing noughts and crosses on yourself?'

Tried to explain to Mark about Rebel and not being able to buy white spirit on a Friday night but he just looked very tired and confused.

'I'm sorry, I have no idea what you're talking about,' he said. 'I've got to get some sleep. Shall we just go to bed?'

He pushed open another door, turned on the light. I took one look then let out a big noise. There, in the huge white bed, was a lithe oriental boy, stark naked, smiling weirdly, and holding out two wooden balls on a string, and a baby rabbit.

3

Doooom!

Saturday 1 February

9st 3, alcohol units 6 (but mixed with tomato juice, v. nutritious), cigarettes 400 (entirely understandable), rabbits, deer, pheasants or other wildlife found in bed 0 (massive improvement on yesterday), boyfriends 0, boyfriends of ex-boyfriend 1, no. of normal potential boyfriends remaining in world 0.

12.15 a.m. Why do these things keep happening to me? Why? WHY? The one time someone seems a nice sensible person such as approved of by mother and not married, mad, alcoholic or fuckwit, they turn out to be gay bestial pervert. No wonder he didn't want me to go to his house. Was not that he is commitment phobic or fancies Rebecca or I am Just For Now Girl. Is because he was keeping oriental boys in bedroom together with wildlife.

Was hideous shock. Hideous. Stared at the oriental boy for about two seconds then shot back into the dressing room, flung my dress on, ran down the stairs hearing shouting in the bedroom behind me in manner of American troops being massacred by Vietcong, teetered into the street and started waving frantically at taxis like call girl who has stumbled on a client who wanted to do a dump on her head.

Maybe is true what Smug Marrieds say that only men left single are single because they have massive flaw. That is why everything is such a fucking, fucking, fucking . . . I mean not that being gay is itself a flaw, but definitely is if are girlfriend of one who pretended was not. Am going to be on own on Valentine's Day for fourth year running, spend next Christmas in single bed in parents' house. Again. Doom. Doooom!

Wish could ring up Tom. Typical of him to go to San Francisco just when need advice from gay perspective, typical. He is always asking me to give him advice for hours on end about his crises with other homosexuals then when I need advice about a crisis with a homosexual, what does he do? He goes to BLOODY SAN FRANCISCO.

Calm, calm. Realize is wrong to blame entire incident on Tom, especially in view of fact that incident has nothing to do with Tom, but must not medicate by blaming. Am assured, receptive, responsive woman of substance, totally complete within myself . . . Gaah! Telephone.

'Bridget. It's Mark. I'm so sorry. I'm so sorry. That was an awful thing to happen.'

He sounded terrible.

'Bridget?'

'What?' I said, trying to stop my hands shaking so I could light a Silk Cut.

'I know what it must have looked like. I got as much of a shock as you. I've never seen him before in my life.'

'Well, who was he then?' I burst out.

'It turns out he's my housekeeper's son. I didn't even know she had a son. Apparently he's schizophrenic.'

There was shouting in the background.

'I'm coming, I'm coming. Oh God. Look, I'm going to have to go sort this out. It sounds like he's trying to strangle her. Can I call you later?' – more shouting – 'Hang on, just . . . Bridget, I'll call you in the morning.'

Very confused. Wish could ring Jude or Shaz to find out if excuse is valid but is middle of night. Maybe will try to sleep.

9 a.m. Gaah! Gaah! Telephone. Hurrah! No! Doom! Have just remembered what happened.

9.30 a.m. Was not Mark but my mother.

'D'you know, darling, I'm absolutely livid.'

'Mum,' I interrupted resolutely. 'Do you mind if I ring you back on the mobile?'

It was all coming back to me in waves. I had to get her off the phone in case Mark was trying to call.

'Mobile, darling? Don't be silly – you haven't had one of those since you were two. Do you remember? With little fishes on? Oh. Daddy wants a word but . . . Anyway, here he is.'

I waited, looking frantically between the mobile and the clock.

'Hello, my dear,' said Dad wearily. 'She's not going to Kenya.'

'Great, well done,' I said, glad that at least one of us not in crisis. 'What did you do?'

'Nothing. Her passport's expired.'

'Hah! Brilliant. Don't tell her you can get new ones.'

'Oh, she knows, she knows,' he said. 'The thing is, if you have a new one, you have to have a new photo. So it's not out of any respect for me, it's purely a matter of flirting with customs officials.'

Mum grabbed the phone. 'It's just completely ridiculous, darling. I had my photo taken and I look as old as the hills. Una said try it in a booth but it's worse. I'm keeping the old passport and that's an end of the matter. Anyway, how's Mark?'

'He's fine,' I said, in a high, strangled voice, narrowly avoiding adding: he likes to sleep with oriental youths and fiddle with rabbits, isn't that fun?

'Well! Daddy and I thought you and Mark would like to come to lunch tomorrow. We haven't seen you both together. I thought I'd just stick a lasagne in the oven with some beans.'

'Can I ring you back later? I'm late for . . . yoga!' I said, inspired.

Managed to get free of her after a freakishly short fifteen-minute wind-down during which it became increasingly clear that the entire might of the British Passport Office was not going to be much of a match for Mum and the old photo, then fumbled for another Silk Cut, desolate and confused. Housekeeper? I mean I know he does have a housekeeper but . . . And then all this stuff with Rebecca. And he votes Tory. Maybe will eat some cheese. Gaah! Telephone.

Was Shazzer.

'Oh Shaz,' I said miserably, and started to blurt out the story.

'Stop right there,' she said, before I'd even got as far as

the oriental boy. 'Stop. I'm going to say this once and I want you to listen.'

'What?' I said, thinking if there was one person in the world incapable of just saying something once – apart from my mother – it was Sharon.

'Get out.'

'But . . .'

'Get out. You've had the warning sign, he votes Tory. Now get out before you get too involved.'

'But wait, that's not . . .'

'Oh for God's sake,' she growled. 'He's got it every which way, hasn't he? He comes to your house, he has everything done for him. You turn up all dressed up to the nines for his ghastly Tory friends and what does he do? Flirts with Rebecca. Patronizes you. And votes Tory. It's all just manipulative, paternalistic . . .'

I glanced nervously at the clock. 'Um, Shaz, can I ring you back on the mobile?'

'What! In case he rings you? No!' she exploded.

Just then the mobile actually started ringing.

'Shaz, I'm going to have to go. I'll call you later.'

Pressed OK eagerly on the mobile.

Was Jude. 'Oh, oh I feel so hungover. I think I'm going to throw up.' She started launching into great long story about party at the Met Bar but had to stop her as really felt whole oriental youth issue was more pressing. Really felt was right about this. Was not being selfish.

'Oh God, Bridge,' said Jude when I'd finished. 'You poor thing. I think you've handled it really, really well. I really do. You've really come on.'

Felt huge glow of pride, followed by puzzlement.

'What did I do?' I said, looking round the room alternating between self-satisfied smiling and confused blinking.

'You've done exactly what it says in *Women Who Love Too Much*. You've done nothing. Just detached. We cannot solve their problems for them. We simply detach.'

'Right, right,' I said, nodding earnestly.

'We don't wish them ill. We don't wish them well. We do not call them. We do not see them. We simply detach. Housekeeper's son my arse. If he's got a housekeeper how come he's always round your place getting you to wash up?'

'But what if it *was* the housekeeper's son?'

'Now, Bridget,' said Jude sternly, 'this is what's called Denial.'

11.15 a.m. Have arranged to meet Jude and Shazzer in 192 for lunch. Right. Am not going to be in Denial.

11.16 a.m. Yes. Am completely detached. You see!

11.18 a.m. Cannot believe he still hasn't fucking, fucking, fucking well rung. Hate passive-aggressive behaviour of telephone in modern dating world, using non-communication as means of communication. Is terrible, terrible: with simple ring or non-ring meaning difference between love and friendliness and happiness and being cast out into ruthless dating trench war again, exactly the same but feeling even more of a fuck up than last time.

Noon. Could not believe it. Phone actually started ringing while I was staring at it, as if I had made it ring through thought-vibe energy and this time it was Mark.

'How are you?' he said wearily.

'I'm fine,' I said, trying to be detached.

'Shall I pick you up and we'll go for lunch and talk?'

'Um, I'm having lunch with the girls,' I said really quite detachedly indeed.

'Oh *God*.'

'*What*?'

'Bridget. Do you have any idea what sort of night I've had? I had this boy trying to strangle his mother in the kitchen, the police and ambulance round, tranquillizer darts, drives to the hospital, hysterical Filipinos all over the house. I mean I'm really, really sorry you had to go through all that, but so did I and it was hardly my fault.'

'Why didn't you call before?'

'Because every time I got a second to call, either on the phone or the mobile, you were bloody well engaged!'

Hmmm. Detachment did not go particularly well. He really has had an awful time. Have arranged to meet him for dinner and he says he's going to sleep this afternoon. Alone, I do so deeply and sincerely hope.

Sunday 2 February

9st 2 (excellent: am turning into Oriental Boy), cigarettes 3 (v.g.), calories 2,100 (v. modest), boyfriends 1 again (hurrah!), self-help books counted out loud in dismissive incredulous manner by newly re-instated boyfriend 37 (only sensible in this day and age).

10 p.m. In flat. Everything is good again. Dinner was a bit awkward to start with but got better when decided I did believe him about story, especially as he said I should come and see the housekeeper today.

But then, when we were having our chocolate mousses, he said, 'Bridge? Last night even before this happened I'd started to feel as though things weren't right.'

Felt cold clunk of dread in stomach. Which was ironic really considering had been thinking things weren't right myself. But really, it is all very well you yourself thinking things aren't right in a relationship, but if the other person starts doing it is like someone else criticizing your mother. Also it starts you thinking you are about to be chucked, which, apart from pain, loss, heartbreak etc. is very humiliating.

'Bridge? Are you in a hypnotic state?'

'No. Why did you think things weren't right?' I whispered.

'Well, every time I tried to touch you, you shrank away as if I were some elderly lech.'

Huge sense of relief. Explained to him about the scary pants at which he started really laughing. Ordered some dessert wine, both got a bit squiffy and ended up going back to my flat and having fantastic shag.

This morning, when we were lying around reading the papers in front of the fire, started wondering whether should bring up the Rebecca business, and why he always stays at my house. But then Jude said I shouldn't because jealousy is v. unattractive trait to opposite sex.

'Bridget,' said Mark, 'you seem to have gone into a trance. I was asking what was the meaning of the new shelving system. Are you meditating? Or is the shelf support system in some way Buddhist?'

'It's because of the electric wire,' I said vaguely.

'What are all these books?' he said, getting up and looking at them. *'How to Date Young Women: A Guide For Men Over Thirty-Five? If the Buddha Dated? Going For It* by Victor Kyam?'

'They're my self-help books!' I said protectively.

'What Men Want? Beyond Co-dependency With a Man Who Can't Commit? How to Love Your Separated Man Without Losing Your Mind? You do realize you're building up the largest body of theoretical knowledge about the behaviour of the opposite sex in the known universe. I'm starting to feel like a laboratory animal!'

'Um . . .'

He was grinning at me. 'Are you supposed to read them in pairs?' he said, pulling a book off the shelves. 'Cover yourself both ways? *Happy to Be Single* with *How to Find Your Perfect Partner in Thirty Days? Buddhism Made Simple* with *Going For It* by Victor Kyam?'

'No,' I said indignantly. 'You read them individually.'

'Why on earth do you buy this stuff?'

'Well, actually I have a theory about this,' I began excitedly (because actually I do have a theory about it). 'If you consider other world religions such as . . .'

'Other world religions? Other than what?'

Grrr. Sometimes wish Mark was not so bloody legally trained.

'Other than self-help books.'

'Yes, I thought you might be about to say that. Bridget, self-help books are not a religion.'

'But they are! They are a new *form* of religion. It's almost as if human beings are like streams of water so when an obstacle is put in their way, they bubble up and surge around it to find another path.'

'Bubble up and surge around, Bridge?'

'What I mean is if the organized religion collapses then people start trying to find another set of rules. And actually, as I was *saying*, if you look at self-help books they have a lot of ideas in common with other religions.'

'Such as . . . ?' he said, waving his hand in an encouraging circle.

'Well, Buddhism and . . .'

'No. Such as what ideas?'

'Well,' I began, panicking slightly as unfortunately the theory is not all that well developed as yet, 'positive thinking. It says in *Emotional Intelligence* that optimism, that everything will turn out all right, is the most important thing. Then, of course, there is belief in yourself, like in *Emotional Confidence*. And if you look at Christianity . . .'

'Yeees . . . ?'

'Well, that bit they read at weddings, it's the same: "These three things remain: faith, *hope* and love." Then there's living in the moment – that's *The Road Less Travelled* and also Buddhist.'

Mark was looking me as if I were mad.

'. . . And forgiveness: it says in *You Can Heal Your Life* that holding on to resentment is bad for you and you have to forgive people.'

'So what's that then? Not Muslim, I hope. I don't think you find much forgiveness in a faith that lops people's hands off for stealing bread buns.'

Mark was shaking his head and staring at me. It did not seem to me that he really understood the theory. But maybe that was because Mark's spiritual soul is not very advanced, which could actually prove to be another problem in our relationship.

'"Forgive us our trespasses as we forgive those who trespass against us"!!' I said indignantly. Just then the phone rang.

'That'll be dating war command,' said Mark. 'Or maybe the Archbishop of Canterbury!'

Was my mum. 'What are you doing still there? Chop, chop. I thought you and Mark were coming to lunch.'

'But Mum . . .' Was sure had not said we were coming to lunch, was sure of it. Mark was rolling his eyes and turning on the football.

'Honestly, Bridget. I've made three pavlovas – though actually it's just as easy to make three pavlovas as one, and I've taken a lasagne out and . . .'

Could hear Dad going, 'Leave her alone, Pam,' in the background as she went on and on huffily about the dangers of refreezing meat, then he came on the phone.

'Don't worry, m'dear. I'm sure you didn't tell her you were coming. It just turned into that in her head. I'll try to calm things down. Anyway, the bad news is, she's going to Kenya.'

Mum grabbed the phone. 'It's all sorted out with the passport. We got a lovely photo done in that wedding shop in Kettering, you know, where Ursula Collingwood had Karen's pictures done.'

'Was it air-brushed?'

'No!' she said, indignantly. 'At least they may have done something with the computer but it was nothing to do with brushes. Anyway, Una and I are going next Saturday. Just for ten days. Africa! Imagine!'

'What about Dad?'

'Honestly, Bridget! Life is for living! If Daddy wants to live between golf and the potting shed, that's up to him!'

Eventually managed to get away, encouraged by Mark standing over me holding a rolled newspaper in one hand and tapping his watch with the other. Went round to his house and definitely do believe him now, because the housekeeper was there cleaning the kitchen with fifteen members of her family who all seemed to want to worship Mark as a god. Then we stayed at his house and had all candles in the bedroom. Hurrah! Think it is all right. Yes. Is definitely all right. Love Mark Darcy. Sometimes he seems a bit scary but underneath he is very kind and sweet. Which is good. I think.

Particularly as is Valentine's Day in twelve days' time.

Monday 3 February

9st 1 (v.g.), alcohol units 3, cigarettes 12, no. of days to Valentine's Day 11, no. of minutes spent obsessing about feminist wrongness of obsessing re: Valentine's Day 162 approx.(bad).

8.30 a.m. Hope Dad is going to be OK. If Mum is going on Saturday that means she will be leaving him on his own for Valentine's Day, which is not very nice. Maybe I will send him a card, as if from a mystery admirer.

Wonder what Mark will do? Sure he will send a card, at least.

I mean definitely, he will.

And maybe we will go out for dinner or other treat. Mmmm. V. nice to have boyfriend on Valentine's Day for once. Ah, telephone.

8.45 a.m. Was Mark. He is going to New York tomorrow for two weeks. He sounded a bit unfriendly actually, and said he was too busy to meet up tonight because he had to get all his papers and everything together.

Managed to be nice about it and just said, 'Oh that's nice,' waiting till had put phone down to yell 'But it's Valentine's Day a week on Friday, it's Valentine's Day. Baaaaaaah!'

Anyway. That is just immature. Thing that matters is the relationship, not cynical marketing ploys.

Tuesday 4 February

8 a.m. In café having cappuccino and chocolate croissant. There, you see! Have got self out of negative thought-bog, and actually is probably very good that Mark is going away. Will give him chance to spring away like a Martian rubber band, as it says in *Mars and Venus on a Date*, and really feel his attraction. Also will give me chance to work on myself and catch up with own life.

Plan For When Mark is Away

1. Go to gym every day.
2. Have lots of lovely evenings with Jude and Shazzer.
3. Do continuing good work sorting out flat.
4. Spend time with Dad when Mum is away.
5. Really work hard at work to improve position.

Oh. Lose half stone, also, obviously.

Noon. Office. Peaceful morning. Was given an item to do on green cars. 'That's environmentally green, Bridget,' said Richard Finch, 'not green coloured.'

Became clear early on green car item would never make it, leaving self free to fantasize re: Mark Darcy and design new headed stationery for self using different fonts and hues while thinking up new item ideas that would really bring me to the forefront of . . . Gaaah!

12.15 p.m. Was bloody Richard Finch yelling: 'Bridget. This isn't arseing Care in the Community. It is a television production office meeting. If you must stare out of the window, at least try to do it without sliding that pen in and out of your mouth. So can you do that?'

'Yes,' I said sulkily, putting the pen down on the table.

'No, not can you take the pen out of your mouth, can you find me a Middle-England, middle-class voter, fifty plus, own home, who is in favour?'

'Yes, no problem,' I breathed airily, thinking I could ask Patchouli in favour of what later.

'In favour of what?' said Richard Finch.

I gave him a really quite enigmatic smile. 'I think you might find you've answered your own question there,' I said. 'Male or female?'

'Both,' said Richard sadistically, 'one of each.'

'Straight or gay?' I exoceted back.

'I said Middle England,' he snarled witheringly. 'Now get on the bloody phone, and try to remember to put a skirt on in future, you're distracting my team.'

Honestly, as if they would take any bloody notice as

they are all obsessed with their careers and it is not that short, it had just ridden up.

Patchouli says it is in favour of the European or single currency. Which she thinks means either. Oh fuck, oh fuck. Right. Ah, telephone. That'll be the Shadow Treasury press office.

12.25 p.m. 'Oh, hello, darling.' Grrr. Was my mother. 'Listen, have you got a "boob tube"?'

'Mum, I've told you not to ring me at work unless it's an emergency,' I hissed.

'Oh I know, but you see the problem is we're going on Saturday and the shops are still full of their winter things.'

Suddenly, I had an idea. It took a while to get it through.

'Honestly, Bridget,' she said after I explained. 'We don't want lorries coming from Germany taking all our gold away in the night.'

'But Mum, as you say, life is for living! You've got to try everything.'

Silence.

'It will help the currency of the African people.' Not sure if this was strictly true but never mind.

'Well, that may well be, but I haven't got time for TV appearances when I'm trying to pack.'

'Listen,' I hissed, 'do you want the boob tube or not?'

12.40 p.m. Hurrah! Have managed to get not one, not two but three Middle-England voters. Una wants to come up with Mum so they can go through my wardrobe and pop into Dickens and Jones, and Geoffrey wants to be on the television. Am top-flight researcher.

'So! Busy, are we?' Richard Finch was looking all post-luncheon sweaty and swaggery. 'Planning the Jones version of the really effective single currency plan, are we?'

'Well, not quite,' I murmured with a cool self-deprecating smile. 'But I have got you your Middle-England voters who are pro. Three of them, actually,' I added casually while rifling through my 'notes'.

'Oh, didn't anyone tell you?' he said, smirking evilly. 'We've dropped it. We're doing bomb scares now. Can you get me a couple of Tory commuters from Middle England who can see the IRA's argument?'

8 p.m. Ugh. Spent three hours in wind-whipped Victoria trying to manipulate commuters' opinions in direction of IRA to point where began to fear immediate arrest and transfer to Maze Prison. Got back to office, worrying what Mum and Una would find in my wardrobe, to guffawing conversation with Richard Finch along lines of 'You didn't really think you were going to find anyone, did you? Sucker!'

Have got to, got to find another job. Ooh goody, telephone.

Was Tom. Hurrah! He is back!

'Bridget! You've lost so much weight!'

'Have I?' I said delighted, before remembering observation was being made down telephonic line.

Tom then went into great long enthuse about his trip to San Francisco.

'The boy on customs was completely divine. He said, "Anything to declare?" I said, "Only this outrageous tan!" Anyway, he gave me his number and I shagged him in a bathhouse!'

Felt familiar flash of envy at ease of gay sex, where people seem to shag each other immediately just because they both feel like it and nobody worries about having three dates first or how long to leave it before phoning afterwards.

After forty-five minutes outlining increasingly outrageous escapades he went, 'Anyway, you know how I hate talking about me. How are *you*? How's that Mark guy, with his firm little buttocks?'

Told him Mark was in New York but decided to leave Rabbitboy till later for fear of over-arousing him. Chose instead to bore on about work.

'I've got to find another job, it's really undermining my sense of personal dignity and self-esteem. I need something that will allow me to make serious use of my talents and abilities.'

'Hmmm. I see what you mean. Have you thought about going on the game?'

'Oh very funny.'

'Why don't you do some journalism on the side? Do some interviews in your spare time?'

Was really brilliant idea. Tom said he was going to talk to his friend Adam on the *Independent* about giving me an interview or a review to do or something!

Am going to be top-flight journalist and gradually build up more and more work and extra money so can give up job and merely sit on sofa with laptop on knee. Hurrah!

Wednesday 5 February

Just called Dad to see how he was and if he would like to do something nice on Valentine's Day.

'Oh you are good, m'dear. But your mother said I need to expand my consciousness.'

'So?'

'I'm going up to Scarborough to play golf with Geoffrey.'

Goody. Glad he's feeling OK.

Thursday 13 February

9st 3, alcohol units 4, cigarettes 19, gym visits 0, early Valentines 0, mentions of Valentine's Day by boyfriend 0, point of Valentine's Day if boyfriend does not even mention it 0.

V. fed up. Is Valentine's Day tomorrow and Mark has not even mentioned it. Do not understand why he has to stay in New York all weekend anyway. Surely the legal offices are closed.

Goals achieved in Mark's absence:

No. of gym visits 0.

Evenings spent with Jude and Shazzer 6 (and another one tomorrow night, looks like).

Minutes spent with Dad 0. Minutes spent talking to Dad about his feelings 0. Minutes spent talking to Dad about golf with Geoffrey bellowing in the background 287.

Journalistic articles written 0.

Pounds lost 0.

Pounds gained 2.

Have sent Mark Valentine anyway. Chocolate heart. Sent it to hotel before he went saying 'not to open till Feb 14th'. Think he will know it is from me.

Friday 14 February

9st 4, gym visits 0, Valentines 0, flowers, trinkets, Valentine's gifts 0, point of Valentine's Day 0, difference between Valentines Day and any other day 0, point of living: uncertain, possibility of overreaction to disaster of Non-Valentine's Day: slight

8 a.m. Really beyond caring about things like Valentine's Day. Is just so not important in general scheme of things.

8.20 a.m. Will just go downstairs and see if post has come.

8.22 a.m. Post has not come.

8.27 a.m. Post has still not come.

8.30 a.m. Post has come! Hurrah!

8.35 a.m. Was bank statement. Nothing from Mark, nothing, nothing, nothing, nothing, nothing. Nothing.

8.40 a.m. Cannot believe am spending Valentine's Day alone again. Worst was two years ago when went to Gambia with Jude and Shaz and had to go one day early because of flights. When went down to dinner was all hearts in trees. Every single table contained couple holding hands and had to sit there on own reading *Learning to Love Yourself*.

Feel v. sad. He can't have not known. He just doesn't care. It must mean I am a Just For Now Girl because, as it says in *Mars and Venus on a Date*, I think if a man is seriously interested in you he always buys you presents like lingerie and jewels and not books or vacuums. Maybe is his way of saying it is all over and is going to tell me when he gets back.

8.43 a.m. Maybe Jude and Shaz were right and should have just got out when warning signs came. You see with Daniel last year if first time he stood me up on our first date with a pathetic excuse I had got out and detached, instead of going into Denial, would never have ended up finding a naked woman on a sun lounger on his roof terrace. Actually come to think of it, Daniel is anagram of Denial!

Is a pattern. Keep on finding naked people in boyfriends' houses. Am repeating patterns.

8.45 a.m. Oh my God. Am £200 overdrawn. How? How? How?

8.50 a.m. You see. Something good comes out of everything. Have found weird cheque on statement for £149, which do not recognize. Convinced it is cheque that wrote out to dry-cleaner's for £14.90 or similar.

9 a.m. Rang up bank to see who it was to, and it was a 'Monsieur S. F. S.' Dry-cleaners are fraudsters. Will ring

Jude, Shazzer, Rebecca, Tom and Simon telling them not to go to Duraclean any more.

9.30 a.m. Hah. Just went into Duraclean to check out 'Monsieur S. F. S.' under guise of taking little black silk nightie in to be cleaned. Could not help remarking that staff of dry-cleaner's seemed to be not so much French but Indian. Maybe Indo-French, though.

'Could you tell me your name, please?' I said to the man as I handed in my nightie.

'Salwani,' he said smiling suspiciously nicely.

S. Hah!

'And your name?' he asked.

'Bridget.'

'Bridget. You write your address here, please, Bridget.'

You see that was very suspicious. Decided to put Mark Darcy's address as he has staff and burglar alarms.

'Do you know a Monsieur S. F. S.?' I said, at which the man became almost playful.

'No, but I think I am knowing you from somewhere,' he said.

'Don't think I don't know what's going on,' I said, then shot out of the shop. You see. Am taking things into own hands.

10 p.m. Cannot believe what has happened. At half past eleven, youth came into office bearing enormous bunch of red roses and brought them to my desk. Me! You should have seen the faces of Patchouli and Horrible Harold. Even Richard Finch was stunned into silence, only managing a pathetic 'Sent them to ourself, did we?'

Opened the card and this is what it said:

> Happy Valentine's Day to the light of my dreary old life. Be at Heathrow, Terminal 1, at 8.30 a.m. tomorrow to pick up ticket from British Airways desk (ref: P23/R55) for magical mystery mini-break. Return Monday a.m. in time for work. Will meet you at the other end.
>
> (Try to borrow a ski suit and some sensible shoes.)

Cannot believe it. Just cannot believe it. Mark is taking me on Valentine ski surprise. Is a miracle. Hurrah! Will be v. romantic in Christmas-card village amongst twinkling lights etc. sashaying down slopes hand in hand like Snow King and Queen.

Feel awful for getting into negative thought-bog obsession, but was sort of thing that could happen to anyone. Definitely.

Just called Jude, has lent me ski outfit: black all-in-one in manner of Michelle Pfeiffer as Catwoman or similar. Only slight problem have only been skiing once when at school and sprained ankle on first day. Never mind. Sure it will be easy.

Saturday 15 February

12st (feels like – giant inflatable ball full of fondue, hot dogs, hot chocolate etc.), grappas 5, cigarettes 32, hot chocolates 6, calories 8,257, feet 3, near-death experiences 8.

1 p.m. Edge of precipice. Cannot believe situation am in. When got to top of mountain felt paralysed by fear so encouraged Mark Darcy to go ahead, while I put skis on watching him going 'whoosh, fzzzzzz, fzzzz' down slope in manner of exocet missile, banned killer firework or similar. Whilst v. much grateful for being brought skiing, could not believe nightmare of getting up on to hill in first place, baffled by what was point of clunking through giant concrete edifices full of grills and chains like something out of concentration camp, with half bent knees and equivalent of plaster casts on each foot, carrying unwieldy skis, which kept separating, being shoved through automated turnstile in manner of sheep heading for sheep dip when could have been all cosy in bed. Worst of it is hair has gone mad in altitude, forming itself into weird peaks and horns like bag of Cadbury's Misshapes, and Catwoman-suit is designed exclusively for long thin people like Jude with result that look like golliwog, or pantomime aunt. Also three-year-olds keep whizzing by without using any poles, standing on one leg performing somersaults etc.

Skiing really is v. dangerous sport, am not imagining it. People get paralysed, buried by avalanches etc., etc. Shazzer told me about when friend of hers had gone on very scary off-piste skiing mission and lost nerve so pisteurs had to come and take him down on a stretcher then *let go of the stretcher*.

2.30 p.m. Mountain café. Mark came whizzing up 'whooosh fzzzzzzz' and asked me if I was ready to come down now.

Explained in whisper, had made mistake by coming on slope as skiing actually is v. dangerous sport – so much so that holiday insurance won't even insure it. Is one thing having accident that you could not foresee; quite another willingly putting yourself in an extremely dangerous situation, knowingly dicing with death or maiming, like doing bungee jumping, climbing Everest, letting people shoot apples off head etc.

Mark listened quietly and thoughtfully. 'I take your point, Bridget,' he said. 'But this is the nursery slope. It's practically horizontal.'

Told Mark I wanted to go back down on the lift thing but he said it was a button lift and you can't go downhill on a button. Forty-five minutes later Mark had got me down slope by pushing me along a bit then running round to catch me. When got to bottom thought fit to broach question of perhaps popping down cable car back to village again in order to have a little rest and a cappuccino.

'The thing is, Bridget,' he said, 'skiing is like everything else in life. It's just a question of confidence. Come on. I think you need a grappa.'

2.45 p.m. Mmm. Love the delicious grappa.

3 p.m. Grappa is really v.g. top beverage. Mark is right. Am probably marvellous natural at skiing. Only thing need to get blurry confidence up.

3.15 p.m. Top of nursery slope. Argor. This blurry easy-peasy. Off go. Wheeeee!

4 p.m. Am marvellous, am fantastic skier. Just came down slope perfect with Mark: 'whoosh fzzzzzz', whole body swaying, moving in perfect harmony as if instinctive. Wild elation! Have discovered whole new lease of life.

Am sportswoman in manner of Princess Anne! Filled with new vigour and positive thought! Confidence! Hurrah! New confident life ahead! Grappa! Hurrah!

5 p.m. Went for rest to mountain café and Mark was suddenly greeted by a whole bunch of lawyery-banker-type people amongst whom tall, thin, blonde girl standing with back to me in white ski suit, fluffy ear muffs and Versace shades. She was hooting with laughter. As if in slow motion, she flicked her hair back off her face, and as it swooshed forward in a soft curtain, I began to realize I recognized her laugh then watched her turn her face towards us. It was Rebecca.

'Bridget!' she said, clinking over and kissing me. 'Gorgeous girl! How fantastic to see you! What a coincidence!'

I looked at Mark, who was all perplexed, running his hand through his hair.

'Um, it's not really a coincidence, is it?' he said awkwardly. 'You did suggest that I bring Bridget here. I mean, delightful to see you all of course, but I'd no idea you were all going to be here too.'

One thing that is really good about Mark is that I do always believe him, but when did she suggest it? When?

Rebecca looked flustered for a moment, then smiled winningly. 'I know, it just reminded me how gorgeous it is in Courcheval, and all the others were coming so . . . Oooh!' Conveniently, she 'wobbled over' and had to be 'caught' by one of the waiting admirers.

'Hmmm,' said Mark. He didn't look very happy at all. I stood head down trying to work out what was going on.

Eventually could stand the strain of trying to be normal no longer, so whispered to Mark that was just going to have another little go on the nursery slope. Got self in queue for button lift much more easily than usual, just so grateful to be away from weird scenario. Missed first couple of buttons through inaccurate grabbing but managed to get next one.

Trouble was once set off, nothing seemed to be quite right, all bumpy and non-smooth almost as if was scampering. Suddenly was aware of child waving at me from sidelines and yelling something in French. Looked across in horror to café balcony to see all Mark's friends shouting and waving as well. What going on? Next thing saw Mark running towards me frantically from direction of café. 'Bridget,' he yelled as he got within earshot, 'you've forgotten to put your skis on.'

'Bloody fool,' roared Nigel as we returned to the café. 'Stupidest thing I've seen for years.'

'Do you want me to stay with her?' said Rebecca to Mark, all wide-eyed concern – as if I were a troublesome toddler. 'Then you can have a good ski before dinner.'

'No, no, we're fine,' he said, but I could see from his face he wanted to go off and have a ski, and I really wanted him to because he loves skiing. But simply could not face the thought of a skiing lesson from bloody Rebecca.

'Actually, I think I need a rest,' I said. 'I'll just have a hot chocolate and recover my composure.'

Drinking chocolate in the café was fantastic, like drinking huge cup of chocolate sauce, which was good because distracted me from sight of Mark and Rebecca travelling up on the chair lift together. Could see her being all gay and tinkly touching his arm.

Eventually they reappeared whizzing down like the

Snow King and Queen – him in black and her in white – looking like a couple out of an upmarket Chalet brochure in the picture that implies that – as well as eight black runs, 400 lifts and half board – you can have great sex like these two are just about to have.

'Oh, it's so exhilarating,' said Rebecca, putting her goggles on her head and laughing into Mark's face. 'Listen, do you both want to have supper with us tonight? We're going to have a fondue up the mountain, then a torchlight ski down – oh sorry, Bridget, but you could come down in the cable car.'

'No,' Mark said abruptly. 'I missed Valentine's Day so I'm taking Bridget for a Valentine's dinner.'

The good thing about Rebecca is there is always a split second when she gives herself away by looking really pissed off.

'Okey-dokey, whatever, have a fun time,' she said, flashed the toothpaste advert smile, then put her goggles on and skied off with a flourish towards the town.

'When did you see her?' I said. 'When did she suggest Courcheval?'

He frowned. 'She was in New York.'

I reeled, dropping one of my ski poles. Mark burst out laughing, picked it up and gave me a big hug.

'Don't look like that,' he said against my cheek. 'She was there with a crowd, I had one ten-minute conversation with her. I said I wanted to do something nice to make up for missing Valentine's Day and she suggested here.'

A small indeterminate noise came out of me.

'Bridget,' he said, 'I love you.'

Sunday 16 February

Weight: do not care (actually, no scales), number of times replayed sublime L-word moment in head: exorbitant black-hole-type number.

Am just so happy. Do not feel angry about Rebecca but generous and accepting. She is a perfectly pleasant, posey stick insect/cow. Me and Mark had lovely v. good fun dinner with lots of laughing and said how much we had missed each other. Gave him a present, which was a little key chain with Newcastle United on it, and Newcastle United boxer shorts, which he really, really liked. He gave me a Valentine gift of a red silk nightie, which was a bit on the small side but he didn't seem to mind, rather the opposite if perfectly honest about it. Also afterwards he told me about all the work things that had happened in New York and I gave him my opinions about it all, which he said were very reassuring and 'unique'!

P.S. No one must read this bit as is shameful. Was so excited about him saying the L-word so early on in the relationship that accidentally rang up Jude and Shaz and left messages telling them. But realize now this was shallow and wrong.

Monday 17 February

9st 6 (gaah! Gaah! Bloody hot chocolate), alcohol units 4 (but including aeroplane flight so v.g.), cigarettes 12, embarrasing neo-colonialist acts committed by mother 1 extremely large one.

Mini-break was fantastic, apart from Rebecca, but had a bit of a shock at Heathrow this morning. Were just standing in the arrivals hall looking for the taxi sign when voice said: 'Darling! You shouldn't have come to meet me, you silly billy. Geoffrey and Daddy are waiting for us outside. We've just come to get Daddy a present. Come and meet Wellington!'

Was my mother, tanned bright orange, with her hair in Bo Derek braids with beads on the ends and wearing a voluminous orange batik outfit like Winnie Mandela.

'I know you're going to think he's a Masai but he's a Kikuyu! A Kikuyu! Imagine!'

I followed her gaze to where Una Alconbury, also orange and dressed in head to toe batik but wearing her reading glasses and carrying a green leather handbag with a big gold clasp was standing at the counter in Sock Shop with her purse open. She was gazing up delightedly at an enormous black youth with a loop of flesh hanging from each ear with a film canister in one of them and dressed in a bright blue checked cloak.

'*Hakuna Matata*. Don't worry, be happy! Swahili. Isn't it smashing? Una and I have had the most super time and Wellington's come back to stay! Hello, Mark,' she said, perfunctorily acknowledging his presence. 'Come along, darling, why don't you say *Jambo* to Wellington!'

'Shut up, Mother, shut up,' I hissed out of the corner of my mouth, looking from side to side nervously. 'You can't have an African tribesman to stay. It's neo-colonialist and Daddy's only just got over Julio.'

'Wellington is not,' said my mum, drawing herself up to her full height, 'a tribesman. Well, at least he is, darling, a proper tribesman! I mean he lives in a dung hut! But he wanted to come! He wants to do worldwide travel just like Una and I!'

Mark was a bit uncommunicative in taxi home. Bloody Mother. Wish I had a normal round mum like other people, with grey hair, who would just make lovely stews.

Right, am going to call Dad.

9 p.m. Dad has retreated into his worst suppressed Middle-English emotional state and sounded completely plastered again.

'How's things?' I ventured when I eventually got an excitable Mum off the phone and him on.

'Oh fine, fine, you know. Zulu warriors in the rockery. Primroses coming through. Everything fine with you?'

Oh God. I don't know if he can cope with all the craziness again. Have said to call me any time but is v. hard when he is being all stiff upper lip.

Tuesday 18 February

9st 6 (serious emergency now), cigarettes 13, masochistic fantasies about Mark being in love with Rebecca 42.

7 p.m. In turmoil. Got back from another nightmare day at work in a rush (Shaz has inexplicably decided she is into football, so me and Jude are going round there to watch Germans beat Turks, Belgians, or similar) to two answerphone messages, neither from Dad.

First was from Tom saying his friend Adam on the *Independent* says he wouldn't mind giving me a go at interviewing someone as long as I find somebody really famous to interview and I don't expect to be paid.

I mean surely that is not what happens in newspapers? How does everybody pay for their mortgages and drink problems?

Second was from Mark. Said he was out with Amnesty and the Indonesians tonight and could he ring me at Shazzer's to see what happened in the match. Then there was a sort of pause and he said, 'Oh and, er, Rebecca has invited us and all the "gang" to her parents' house in Gloucestershire for a house party next weekend. What do you think? I'll call you later.'

Know exactly what I think. Think I would rather sit in a little hole in Mum and Dad's rockery making friends with all the worms all weekend than go to Rebecca's house party and watch her flirting with Mark. I mean why didn't she ring me up to invite us?

It's Mentionitis. It's just complete Mentionitis. There's no question about it. Telephone. Bet it's Mark. What shall I say?

'Bridget, pick up, put it down, put it down. PUT IT DOWN.'

I picked up confusedly. 'Magda?'

'Oh Bridget! Hi! How was the skiing?'

'It was great but . . .' Told her the whole story about Rebecca and New York and the house party. 'I don't know whether I should go or not.'

'Of course you've got to go, Bridge,' said Magda. 'If Mark wanted to go out with Rebecca he'd be going out with Rebecca, just say – get off, get off, Harry get off the back of that chair now or Mummy will smack. You're two very different kinds of people.'

'Hmmm. You see, I *think* Jude and Shazzer would argue . . .'

Jeremy grabbed the phone. 'Listen, Bridge, taking advice on dating from Jude and Shazzer is like taking advice from a diet consultant who weighs twenty stone.'

'Jeremy!' bellowed Magda. 'He's just playing devil's advocate, Bridge. Ignore him. Every woman has her aura. He's chosen you. Just go along, be gorgeous, and keep an eye on her. Nooo! Not on the floor!'

She's right. Am going to be assured, receptive, responsive woman of substance and have a lovely time emanating aura. Hurrah! Will just call Dad then go to football.

Midnight. Back in flat. Once out in freezing cold assured woman of substance evaporated into insecurity. Had to walk past workmen working under bright lights on gas main. Was wearing v. short coat and boots so braced myself to deal with lewd catcalls and embarrassing remarks then felt complete arse when none came.

Reminded me of when was fifteen and walking along lonely backstreet into town and man started following me then grabbed my arm. Turned to look at attacker in alarm. At time was v. thin in tight jeans. Also, however, had winged spectacles and brace on teeth. Man took one look at my face and ran off.

On arrival confided feelings re: workmen to Jude and Sharon. 'That's the whole point, Bridget,' Shazzer exploded. 'These men are treating women as objects, as if our only function is physical attractiveness.'

'But they weren't,' said Jude.

'That's exactly why the whole thing is so objectionable. Now come on, we're supposed to be watching the match.'

'Mmm. They've got lovely big thighs, haven't they?' said Jude.

'Mmmm,' I agreed, distractedly wondering if Shaz would go mad if brought up Rebecca during the match.

'I knew someone who slept with a Turk once,' said Jude. 'And he had a penis that was so enormous he couldn't sleep with anyone.'

'What? I thought you said she slept with him,' said Shazzer, keeping one eye on the television.

'She slept with him but she didn't do it,' explained Jude.

'Because she couldn't because his thing was too big,' I said supportively of Jude's anecdote. 'What a terrible thing. Do you think it goes by nationality? I mean do you think the Turks . . . ?'

'Look, shut up,' said Shazzer.

For a while we all fell silent, imagining the many penises tucked neatly into shorts and thinking of all the games of many different nationalities in the past. Was just about to open my mouth, but then Jude, who seemed to have become rather fixated for some reason, piped up, 'It must be very weird having a penis.'

'Yes,' I agreed, 'very weird to have an active appendage. If I had one I would think about it all the time.'

'Well, yes, you'd worry about what it would do next,' said Jude.

'Well, exactly,' I agreed. 'You might suddenly get a gigantic erection in the middle of a football match.'

'Oh for God's sake!' yelled Sharon.

'OK, keep your hair on,' said Jude. 'Bridge? Are you all right? You seem a bit down about something.'

I looked nervously at Shaz then decided this was too

important to let lie. I cleared my throat for attention and announced: 'Rebecca rang Mark up and asked us on a mini-break this weekend.'

'WHAT?' Jude and Shaz exploded simultaneously.

Was really glad the seriousness of the situation was fully appreciated. Jude got up for the Milk Tray and Shaz fetched another bottle from the fridge.

'The thing is,' Sharon was summing up, 'we've known Rebecca for four years. Has she ever once in all that time invited you, me or Jude on one of her posh house-party weekends?'

'No.' I shook my head solemnly.

'But the thing is,' said Jude, 'if you don't go then what if he goes on his own? You can't let Rebecca get him in her clutches. And also it's obviously important to someone in his position to have someone who's a good social partner.'

'Hgumph,' snorted Shazzer. 'That's just retrospective bollocks. If Bridget says she doesn't want to go and he goes without her and he gets off with Rebecca then he's a second-rate charlatan and not worth having. Social partner – pah. We're not in the 1950s now. She's not cleaning the house all day in a pointy bra then entertaining his colleagues like some trophy Stepford wife. Tell him you know Rebecca's after him and that's why you don't want to go.'

'But then he'll be flattered,' said Jude. 'There's nothing a man finds more attractive than a woman who is in love with him.'

'Says who?' said Shaz.

'The baroness in *The Sound of Music,*' said Jude, sheepishly.

Unfortunately, by the time we turned our attention back to it the game appeared to be over.

Next thing Mark rang.

'What happened?' he said excitedly.

'Um . . .' I said, gesturing wildly at Jude and Shazzer who looked completely blank.

'You did watch it, didn't you?'

'Yes, of course, *football's coming home, it's coming* . . .' I sang, vaguely remembering this was something to do with Germany.

'So why don't you know what happened then? I don't believe you.'

'We did. But we were . . .'

'What?'

'Talking,' I finished lamely.

'Oh God.' There was a long silence. 'Listen, do you want to go to Rebecca's?'

I looked from Jude to Shaz, frantically. One yes. One no. And a yes from Magda.

'Yes,' I said.

'Oh great. It'll be fun, I think. She said to bring a swimsuit.'

A swimsuit! Doom. Dooooooooom.

On way home, discovered same lot of workmen tumbling pissed out of pub. Put nose in air and decided did not care whether they whistled or not but just as walked past was huge cacophony of appreciative noises. Turned round, pleased to give them a filthy look only to find they were all looking the other way and one of them had just thrown a brick through the window of a Volkswagen.

Saturday 22 February

9st 5 (horrifying), alcohol units 3 (best behaviour), cigarettes 2 (huh), calories 10,000 (probably: suspected Rebecca sabotage), dogs up skirt 1 (constantly).

Gloucestershire. Turns out Rebecca's parents' 'country cottage' has stable blocks, outbuildings, pool, full staff and its own church in the 'garden'. As we scrunched across the gravel, Rebecca – snooker-ball-bottomed in jeans in manner of Ralph Lauren ad – was playing with a dog, sunlight dappling her hair, amongst an array of Saab and BMW convertibles.

'Emma! Get down! Hiiiii!' she cried, at which dog broke free and put its nose straight up my coat.

'Mwah, come and have a drink,' she said welcoming Mark as I wrestled with the dog's head.

Mark rescued me, shouting, 'Emma! Here!' and chucking the stick, so the dog brought it back, tail wagging.

'Oh, she adores you, don't you, darling, don't you, don't you, don't you?' Rebecca cooed, fussing the dog's head like it was her and Mark's first-born baby.

My mobile rang. Tried to ignore it.

'I think that's yours, Bridget,' said Mark.

I took it out and pressed the button.

'Oh, hello, darling, guess what?'

'Mother, what are you ringing me on my mobile for?' I hissed, watching Rebecca leading Mark away.

'We're all going to *Miss Saigon* next Friday! Una and Geoffrey and Daddy and I and Wellington. He's never been to a musical before. A Kikuyu at *Miss Saigon*. Isn't that fun? And we've got tickets for you and Mark to join us!'

Gaah! Musicals! Strange men standing with their legs apart bellowing songs straight ahead.

By the time I got into house Mark and Rebecca had disappeared and was nobody around except the dog, which put its nose up my coat again.

4 p.m. Just back from walk round 'garden'. Rebecca kept installing me in conversations with men, then dragging Mark off miles ahead of everyone else. Ended up walking along with Rebecca's nephew: sub-Leonardo DiCaprio lookalike, hunted-looking in an Oxfam overcoat, whom everyone referred to as 'Johnny's boy'.

'I mean, like, I do have a name,' he muttered.

'Oh don't be absuuuuuuuuuurd!' I said, pretending to be Rebecca. 'What is it?'

He paused, looking embarrassed. 'St John.'

'Oh.' I sympathized.

He laughed and offered me a fag.

'Better not,' I said, nodding in Mark's direction.

'Is he your boyfriend or your father?'

He steered me off the path towards a mini lake and lit me a cigarette.

Was v. nice smoking and giggling naughtily. 'We'd better go back,' I said, stubbing cigarette out under my welly.

Others were miles ahead, so we had to run: young and wild and free, in manner of Calvin Klein adverts. When we caught up Mark put his arms round me. 'What have you been doing?' he said into my hair. 'Smoking like a naughty schoolgirl?'

'I haven't had a cigarette for five years!' tinkled Rebecca.

7 p.m. Mmm. Mmm. Mark just got all horny before supper. Mmmmm.

Midnight. Rebecca made a great fuss of putting me next to 'Johnny's boy' at dinner – 'You two are getting on sooooooo well!!' – and herself next to Mark.

They looked perfect together in their black tie. Black tie! As Jude said, was only because Rebecca wanted to show off her figure in Country Casuals gear and evening wear like Miss World entrant. Right on cue she went, 'Shall we change into our swimwear now?' and tripped off to change, reappearing minutes later in an immaculately cut black swimsuit, legs up to the chandelier.

'Mark,' she said, 'would you give me a hand? I need to take the cover off the pool.'

Mark looked from her to me worriedly.

'Of course. Yes,' he said awkwardly and disappeared after her.

'Are you going to swim?' said the whippersnapper.

'Well,' I began, 'I wouldn't want you to think I'm not a determined and keenly motivated sportswoman, but eleven o'clock at night after a five-course dinner is not my most swimmy time.'

We chatted for a while, then I noticed the last of our fellow diners were leaving the room.

'Shall we go and have coffee?' I said, getting up.

'Bridget.' Suddenly, he lurched drunkenly forward, and started trying to kiss me. The door burst open. Was Rebecca and Mark.

'Oops! Sorry!' said Rebecca, and shut the door.

'What do you think you're doing!' I hissed, horrified, at the whippersnapper.

'But . . . Rebecca said you told her you really fancied me, and, and . . .'

'And what?'

'She said you and Mark were in the process of splitting up.'

I grabbed the table for support. 'Who told her that?'

'She said' – he looked so mortified I felt really sorry for him – 'she said Mark did.'

Sunday 23 February

12st 4 (probably), alcohol units 3 (since midnight and is only 7 a.m.), cigarettes 100,000 (feels like), calories 3,275, positive thoughts 0, boyfriends: extremely uncertain figure.

When I got back to room, Mark was in the bath so I sat in nightie, planning my defence.

'It was not what you think,' I said with tremendous originality, as he emerged.

'No?' he said, whisky in hand. He started striding around in his barrister mode, clad only in a towel. Was unnerving, but unbelievably sexy. 'Had you a marble stuck in your throat, perhaps?' he said. 'Was "Sinjun" being, rather than the trust-funded teenage layabout he appears, actually a top ear, nose and throat surgeon attempting to extract it with his tongue?'

'No,' I said, carefully and thoughtfully. 'That is not what it was either.'

'Then were you hyperventilating? Was "Sinjun" – having garnered the rudiments of first aid into his marijuana-addled brain, perhaps from a poster on the wall of the many drug rehab units he has visited in his short and otherwise uneventful life – trying to administer the kiss of life? Or did he simply mistake you for a choice morsel of "skunk" and find himself unable to . . .'

I started to laugh. Then he started laughing too, then we started kissing and one thing led to another and afterwards we fell asleep in each other's arms.

In the morning, woke up all rosy thinking everything was OK but then looked around and saw him already dressed, and knew was not anywhere near OK.

'I can explain,' I said, dramatically sitting bolt upright. For a moment we looked at each other and started laughing. But then he turned serious.

'Go on, then.'

'It was Rebecca,' I said. 'St John told me Rebecca told him that I told her I fancied him and . . .'

'And you believed this bewildering catalogue of Chinese whispers?'

'And that you told her we were . . .'

'Yes?'

'Splitting up,' I said.

Mark sat down and started rubbing his fingers very slowly across his forehead.

'Did you?' I whispered. 'Did you say that to Rebecca?'

'No,' he said eventually. 'I didn't say that to Rebecca, but . . .'

I daren't look at him.

'But maybe we . . .' he began.

The room started to go blotchy. Hate this about dating.

One minute you're closer to someone than anyone in the whole world, next minute they only need to say the words 'time apart', 'serious talk' or 'maybe you . . .' and you're never going to see them again and will have to spend the next six months having imaginary conversations in which they beg to come back, and bursting into tears at the sight of their toothbrush.

'Do you want to split up . . . ?'

There was a knock at the door. Was Rebecca radiant in dusky pink cashmere. 'Last call for breakfast, folks!' she cooed and didn't go.

Ended up breakfasting with mad unwashed hair, while Rebecca swung her shiny mane and served kedgeree.

On the way home we drove in silence while I struggled not to show how I felt or say anything wet. Know from experience how awful it is trying to persuade someone you shouldn't split up when they have already made up their mind, and then you think back over what you said. And feel such an idiot.

'Don't do this!' I wanted to yell when we stopped outside my house. 'She's trying to pinch you and it's all a plot. I didn't kiss St John. I love you.'

'Well, bye then,' I said dignifiedly, and forced myself to get out of the car.

'Bye,' he muttered, not looking at me.

Watched him turn the car round really fast and screechily. As he drove off, I saw him angrily brush his cheek as if he was wiping something away.

4

Persuasion

Monday 24 February

15st (combined weight of self and unhappiness), alcohol units 1 – i.e. me, cigarettes 200,000, calories 8,477 (not counting chocolate), theories as to what's going on 447, no. of times changed mind about what to do 448.

3 a.m. Don't know what I would have done without the girls yesterday. Called them instantly after Mark drove off, and they were round within fifteen minutes, never once saying 'I told you so.'

When Shazzer bustled in with armfuls of bottles and carrier bags, barking, 'Has he rung?' was like being in *ER* when Dr Greene arrives.

'No,' said Jude, popping a cigarette in my mouth as if it were a thermometer.

'Only a matter of time,' said Shaz brightly, unpacking a bottle of Chardonnay, three pizzas, two tubs of Häagen-Daaz Pralines and Cream and a packet of fun-sized Twixes.

'Yup,' said Jude, putting the *Pride and Prejudice* tape on top of the video, together with *Through Love and Loss to Self-Esteem, The Five Stages of Dating Workbook*, and *How to Heal the Hurt by Hating*. 'He'll be back.'

'Do you think I should call him?' I said.

'No!' yelled Shaz.

'Have you gone out of your mind?' bellowed Jude. 'He's being a Martian rubber band. The *last* thing you must do is call him.'

'I know,' I said huffily. I mean surely she didn't think I was *that* badly read.

'You *let* him go back to his cave and feel his attraction, and you move back from Exclusivity to Uncertainty.'

'But what if he . . . ?'

'You'd better unplug it, Shaz,' sighed Jude. 'Otherwise she'll spend the whole night waiting for him to ring instead of working on her self-esteem.'

'Noooo!' I cried, feeling like they were going to cut my ear off.

'Anyway,' said Shaz brightly, pulling the phone out of the wall with a click, 'it'll do him good.'

Two hours later was feeling quite confused.

'"The more a man likes a woman the more he will avoid getting involved"!' said Jude triumphantly, reading from *Mars and Venus on a Date*.

'Sounds like masculine logic to me!' said Shaz.

'So chucking me could actually be a sign that he's really serious about the relationship?' I said excitedly.

'Wait, wait.' Jude was staring hard at *Emotional Intelligence*. 'Was his wife unfaithful to him?'

'Yes,' I mumbled through a mouthful of Twix. 'A week after their wedding. With Daniel.'

'Hmmm. You see it sounds to me that he was *also* having an Emotional Hijacking, probably because of an earlier emotional "bruise" that you have inadvertently hit. Of course! Of course! That's it! That's why he overreacted to you snogging the boy. So don't worry, once the bruise has stopped sending his whole nervous system into disarray he'll realize his mistake.'

'And realize he ought to go out with someone else because he likes you so much!' said Sharon, merrily lighting up a Silk Cut.

'Shut up, Shaz,' hissed Jude. 'Shut up.'

It was too late. The spectre of Rebecca loomed up, filling the room like an inflatable monster.

'Oh, oh, oh,' I said, screwing up my eyes.

'Quick, get her a drink, get her a drink,' yelled Jude.

'I'm sorry, I'm sorry. Put *Pride and Prejudice* on,' gabbled Shaz, pouring neat brandy into my mouth. 'Find the wet shirt. Shall we have the pizzas?'

Was a bit like Christmas, or more like when somebody dies and with funeral and all the fuss nothing is normal so people do not notice the loss because they are so distracted. It is when life goes back to what it was without the person that the trouble starts. Like now for example.

7 p.m. Wild joy! Got home to find answerphone light flashing.

'Bridget, hi, it's Mark. I don't know where you were last night but anyway, just checking in. I'll try you again later.'

Try me again later. Hmmm. So presumably that means not to ring him.

7.13 p.m. He hasn't rung. Unsure what is correct procedure now. Better ring Shaz.

On top of everything else, hair has gone mad as if in sympathy. Bizarre the way that hair is normal for weeks on end then suddenly in space of five minutes goes berserk, announcing it is time to cut in manner of baby starting yelling to be fed.

7.30 p.m. Played the message over the phone to Shaz and said, 'Should I call him back?'

'No! Let him suffer. If he's chucked you and changed his mind he's got to prove he bloody well deserves you.'

Shaz is right. Yes. Am in v. assertive mood re: Mark Darcy.

8.35 p.m. Oh, though. Maybe he is sad. Hate thinking of him sitting in his Newcastle United tee-shirt being sad. Maybe I should just ring him and get to the bottom of it.

8.50 p.m. Was just about to ring Mark and blurt out how much I liked him and it was all just misunderstandings but fortunately Jude rang before I had time to pick up the phone. Told her about the brief but worryingly positive mood.

'So you mean you're in Denial again?'

'Yes,' I said uncertainly. 'Should I ring him tomorrow maybe?'

'No, if you want to get back together, you've got to leave it unsullied by scenes. So wait four or five days till you've recovered your composure, then, yes, there's nothing wrong with giving him a light, friendly call just to let him know everything's OK.'

11 p.m. He hasn't rung. Oh fuck. Am so confused. Whole dating world is like hideous game of bluff and double bluff with men and women firing at each other from opposite lines of sandbags. Is as if there is a set of rules that you are supposed to be sticking to, but no one knows what they are so everyone just makes up their own. Then you end up getting chucked because you didn't follow the rules correctly, but how could you be expected to, when you didn't know what they were in the first place?

Tuesday 25 February

No. of times driven past Mark Darcy's house to see if there are any lights on 2 (or 4 if count both ways). No. of times dialled 141 (so cannot trace my number if he 1471s) then rang his answerphone just to hear his voice 5 (bad) (v.g. for not leaving message though). No. of times looked Mark Darcy's number up in phone book just to prove to self he still exists 2 (v. restrained), percentage of outgoing calls made from mobile to keep line clear in case he rings 100. Percentage of incoming callers creating angry resentment for not being Mark Darcy – unless ringing to talk about Mark Darcy – and urged to get off the phone as quickly as possible in case blocking call from Mark Darcy 100.

8 p.m. Magda just called to ask how the weekend went. Ended up blurting out the whole story.

'Listen, if you take it from him one more time you're going in the naughty chair! Harry! Sorry, Bridge. So what does he say about it?'

'I haven't spoken to him.'

'What? Why not?'

Explained about the answerphone message and the whole rubber band/emotional bruise/liking me too much theory.

'Bridget, you are literally unbelievable. There's nothing in the entire story to suggest he's chucked you at all. He just got in a bad mood because he caught you snogging someone.'

'I wasn't snogging someone. I was being happened upon against my will!'

'But he's not a mind-reader. How's he supposed to know what you feel? You have to communicate. Take that out of his mouth now! You're coming with me. You're coming upstairs with me to the naughty chair.'

8.45 p.m. Maybe Magda is right. Maybe I just assumed that he was chucking me and he didn't mean that at all. Maybe in the car he was just upset about the whole snogging thing and wanted *me* to say something and now he thinks I am avoiding him!! Am going to ring. That is the trouble with modern (or ex) relationships, there just isn't enough *communication*.

9 p.m. Right, am going to do it.

9.01 p.m. Here goes.

9.10 p.m. Mark Darcy answered by barking 'Yesssss?' in incredibly impatient voice with all noise in background.

Crestfallen, I whispered, 'It's me, it's Bridget.'

'Bridget! Are you mad? Don't you know what's going

on? You haven't called me for two days and now you ring me in the middle of the most important, the most crucial – Noooooo! Nooooo! You stupid, bloody . . . Jesus Christ. You stupid – right beside the ref. That was a foul! You'll be . . . he's booking him. He's going off. Oh Jesus – look, I'll call you back when it's over.'

9.15 p.m. Of course knew it was some kind of Trans-Universe final or whatever it is, had just forgotten owing to emotional thought-bog. Sort of thing that could happen to anyone.

9.30 p.m. How could I be so stupid? How? How?

9.35 p.m. Oh goody – telephone! Mark Darcy!

Was Jude. 'What?' she said. 'He didn't talk to you because he was in the middle of a *football match*? Go out. Go out immediately. Don't be in when he calls back. How dare he!'

Immediately realized Jude was right and if Mark really cared about me football would not have been more important. Shaz was even more emphatic.

'The only reason men are so obsessed with football is that they're bone idle,' she exploded. 'They think by supporting some team or other and making a lot of noise they've actually won the match themselves and deserve to have cheering and clapping and a great fuss made of them.'

'Yes. So are you coming round to Jude's?'

'Er, no . . .'

'Why not?'

'I'm watching the match with Simon.'

Simon? Shazzer and Simon? But Simon is just one of our mates.

'But I thought you just said . . . ?'

'That's different. The reason I like football is it's a very interesting game.'

Hmm. Was just leaving the house when phone rang again.

'Oh, hello, darling. It's Mum. We're having the most marvellous time. Everyone adores Wellington! We took him to the Rotary and . . .'

'Mother,' I hissed. 'You can't parade Wellington around like some sort of exhibit.'

'Do you know, darling,' she said icily, 'if there's one thing I really don't like it's racism and bigotry.'

'What?'

'Well. When the Robertsons were up from Amersham we took them to the Rotary and you didn't say anything about that, did you?'

I gawped, trying to untangle the web of warped logic.

'Always putting everyone in little boxes, aren't you, with your "Smug Marrieds" and "Singletons" and coloured people and homos. Anyway, I was just ringing about *Miss Saigon* on Friday. It starts at seven thirty.'

Oh Christ. 'Er . . . !' I said wildly. Sure I didn't say yes, sure of it.

'Now come along, Bridget. We've bought the tickets.'

Resignedly agreed to bizarre jaunt, making gabbling excuse about Mark working, which completely set her off.

'Working, durrr! What's he doing working on a Friday

night? Are you sure he's not working too hard? I really don't think working . . .'

'Mum, I've really got to go, I'm late for Jude,' I said firmly.

'Oh, always rushing about. Jude, Sharon, yoga. I'm surprised you and Mark have got any time to see each other at all!'

Once round at Jude's flat, the conversation moved naturally to Shazzer and Simon.

'But, actually' – Jude leaned forward confidentially, even though no one else was there – 'I bumped into them in the Conran Shop on Saturday. And they were giggling together over cutlery like a pair of Smug Marrieds.'

What is it about modern Singletons that only way they can have a normal relationship is if it isn't supposed to be a relationship? There's Shaz who isn't going out with Simon doing what couples are supposed to do, and me and Mark who are supposed to be going out not seeing each other at all.

'If you ask me people should not say "just good friends" but "just going out with each other",' I said darkly.

'Yup,' said Jude. 'Maybe the answer is platonic friends combined with a vibrator.'

Got back to remorseful message from Mark saying he had tried to ring straight after the match but phone was permanently engaged and now I was out. Was just wondering whether to call him back when he rang.

'Sorry about earlier,' he said. 'I'm just really down about it, aren't you?'

'I know,' I said tenderly, 'I feel exactly the same.'

'I just keep thinking: why?'

'Exactly!' I beamed, huge rush of love and relief washing over me.

'So stupid and unnecessary,' he said, anguished. 'A pointless outburst with devastating consequences.'

'I know,' I nodded, thinking, blimey, he's taking it even more dramatically than me.

'How can a man live with that?'

'Well, everyone's only human,' I said thoughtfully. 'People have to forgive each other and . . . themselves.'

'Chuh! It's easy to say that,' he said. 'But if he hadn't been sent off we'd never have been subjected to the tyranny of the penalty shoot-out. We fought like kings amongst lions, but it cost us the game!'

I gave a strangled cry, mind reeling. Surely it cannot be true that men have football instead of emotions? Realize football is exciting and binds nations together with common goals and hatreds but surely wholesale anguish, depression and mourning hours later is taking . . .

'Bridget, what's the matter? It's only a game. Even I can see that. When you called me during the match I was so caught up in my own feelings that . . . But it's only a game.'

'Right, right,' I said, staring around the room crazily.

'Anyway, what's going on? I haven't heard a peep from you for days. Hope you haven't been snogging any more teenage . . . Oh hang on, hang on, they're playing it back. Shall I come round tomorrow, no, wait, I'm playing five-a-side – Thursday?'

'Er . . . yes,' I said.

'Great, see you about eight o clock.'

Wednesday 26 February

9st 4, alcohol units 2 (v.g.), cigarettes 3 (v.g.), calories 3,845 (poor), minutes not spent obsessing re: Mark Darcy 24 (excellent progress), variations on twin-horned sculpture dreamed up by hair 13 (alarming).

8.30 a.m. Right. Everything is probably fine (apart, obviously, from hair) though it is possible that Mark was avoiding issue as did not want to talk about emotions on the phone. So tomorrow night is crucial.

Important thing is to be assured, receptive, responsive, not complain about anything, move back a Stage and . . . er, look really sexy. Will see if can get hair cut in lunch hour. And will go to gym before work. Maybe have a steam bath so will be all glowing.

8.45 a.m. Letter has come for me! Hurrah! Maybe late Valentine card from secret admirer, which has been misdirected owing to incorrect postcode.

9 a.m. Was letter from bank about overdraft. Also enclosing cheque to 'M. S. F. S.' Hah! Had forgotten about that. Dry-cleaner fraud is about to be exposed and I will get £149 back. Ooh, note just fluttered out.

Note said: 'This cheque is to Marks & Spencer's Financial Services.'

Was for Christmas payment on M&S card. Oh. Oh dear. Feel bit bad now for mentally accusing innocent dry-cleaner's and being all funny with the boy. Hmm. Too late to go to gym now, also too generally upset. Will go after work.

2 p.m. Office. In loos. Total, total disaster. Just got back from hairdresser's. Told Paolo about just wanting tiny trim to turn hair from mad chaos into that of Rachel from *Friends*. He started running his hands through it and I instantly felt in care of genius who understood self's inner beauty. Paolo seemed marvellously in control, throwing the hair this way and that, then blowing it about into huge bouff, giving me knowing looks as if to say 'I'm gonna make you into one *hot* chick.'

Then suddenly he stopped. Hair looked totally insane – like schoolteacher who has had perm followed by pudding-basin cut. He looked at me with an expectant, confident smirk and his assistant came up and started gushing 'Oh it's *heaven*.' Panicked, staring at self in horror but had established such a bond of mutual admiration with Paolo that to say I hated hair would make whole thing collapse like impossibly embarrassing house of cards. Ended up joining in mad gushing about monster hair and giving Paolo £5 tip. When got back to work, Richard Finch said I looked like Ruth Madoc from *Hi-de-Hi*.

7 p.m. Back home. Hair is complete fright wig with hideous short fringe. Just spent forty-five minutes staring in mirror with brows raised trying to make fringe look longer but cannot spend whole of tomorrow night looking like Roger Moore when the baddy with the cat has threatened to blow up him, the world, and the tiny box full of MI5 vital computers.

7.15 p.m. Attempt to mimic early Linda Evangelista by arranging fringe into diagonal line using gel has turned self into Paul Daniels.

Incensed with rage at stupid Paolo. Why would someone do that to another person? Why? Hate sadistic megalomaniac hairdressers. Am going to sue Paolo. Am going to report Paolo to Amnesty International, Esther Rantzen, Penny Junor or similar and expose him on national television.

Far too depressed to go to gym.

7.30 p.m. Called Tom to tell him of trauma who said I should not be so superficial but to think of Mo Mowlam and bald head. V. ashamed. Not going to obsess any more. Also Tom said had I thought up anyone to interview yet.

'Well, I've been a bit busy,' I said guiltily.

'You know what? You gotta get your ass in gear' – oh God, don't know what has come over him in California – 'Who are you really interested in?' he went on. 'Isn't there a celebrity you'd really like to interview?'

Thought about this then suddenly realized. 'Mr Darcy!' I said.

'What? Colin Firth?'

'Yes! Yes! Mr Darcy! Mr Darcy!'

So now have got project. Hurrah! Am going to get to work and set up interview using his agent. Will be marvellous, can get out all cuttings and really bring out unique perspective on . . . Oh, though. Had better wait till fringe has grown. Gaaah! Doorbell. Had better not be Mark. But he definitely said tomorrow! Calm, calm.

'It's Gary,' went the entryphone.

'Oh hi, hi. Gareeeee!' I overcompensated without a blind idea who he was. 'How are you?' I said, thinking, and come to mention it, who?

'Cold. Are you gonna let me in?'

Suddenly recognized the voice – 'Oh *Gary*,' I gushed even more crazily overcompensatorly. 'Come on up!!!'

Hit self hard on head. What was he doing here?

He came in wearing paint-smeared, builder-type jeans, an orange tee-shirt and strange checked jacket with pretend sheepskin collar.

'Hi,' he said, sitting down at the kitchen table as if he were my husband. Was unsure how to deal with – two-people-in-room-with-totally-different-concept-of-reality-scenario.

'Now, Gary,' I said. 'I'm in a bit of a rush!'

He said nothing and started rolling a cigarette. Suddenly started to feel scared. Maybe he was a mad rapist. But he never tried to rape Magda, at least as far as I know.

'Was there something you'd forgotten?' I said nervously.

'Nope,' he said, still rolling the cigarette. I glanced at the door wondering if I should make a run for it. 'Where's your soil pipe?'

'Gareeeeeeeee!' I wanted to yell. 'Go away. Just go away. I'm seeing Mark tomorrow night, and I've got to do something with my fringe and work out on the floor.'

He put the cigarette in his mouth and stood up. 'Let's have a look in the bathroom.'

'Noooo!' I yelled, remembering there was an open tub of Jolene bleach and a copy of *What Men Want* on the side of the washbasin. 'Look, can you come back another . . . ?'

But he was already poking about, opening the door and peering down the stairs and heading towards the bedroom.

'Have you got a back window in here?'

'Yes.'

'Let's have a look.'

I stood nervously in the bedroom doorway, while he opened the window and looked out. He did seem more interested in pipes than actually attacking me.

'Thought so!' he said triumphantly, bringing his head back in and closing the window. 'You've got room for an infill extension out there.'

'I'm afraid you're going to have to go away,' I said, drawing myself up to my full height and moving back into the living room. 'I've got to go somewhere.'

But he was already heading past me to the stairs again.

'Yup, you've got room for an infill. Mind you, you'll have to move the soil pipe.'

'Gary . . .'

'You could have a second bedroom – little roof terrace on top. Sweet.'

Roof terrace? Second bedroom? I could make it into an office and start my new career.

'How much would it cost?'

'Oooh.' He started shaking his head sorrowfully. 'Tell you what, let's go down to the pub and have a think.'

'I can't,' I said firmly. 'I'm going out.'

'All right. Well, I'll have a think and give you a ring.'

'Jolly good. Well! Best get going!'

He picked up his coat, tobacco and Rizlas, opened his bag and laid a magazine down reverentially on the kitchen table.

As he reached the door, he turned and gave me a knowing look. 'Page seventy-one,' he said. 'Ciao.'

Picked up the magazine, thinking it was going to be

Architectural Digest and found myself looking at *Coarse Fisherman*, with a man holding a gigantic slimy grey fish on the front. Leafed through an enormous number of pages all containing many pictures of men holding up gigantic slimy grey fish. Reached page 71 and there opposite an article on 'BAC Predator Lures', sporting a denim hat with badges on and a proud, beaming smile was Gary, holding up a gigantic slimy grey fish.

Thursday 27 February

9st 3 (lost 1lb was hair), cigarettes 17 (due to hair), calories 625 (off food due to hair), imaginary letters to solicitors, consumer programmes, Dept of Health etc. complaining about Paolo's massacring of hair 22, visits to mirror to check growth of hair 72, millimetres grown by hair in spite of all hard work 0.

7.45 p.m. Fifteen minutes to go. Just checked fringe again. Hair has gone from fright wig to horrified, screaming, full-blown terror wig.

7.47 p.m. Still Ruth Madoc. Why did this have to happen on most important night of relationship-so-far with Mark Darcy? Why? At least, though, makes change from checking thighs in mirror to see if they have shrunk.

Midnight. When Mark Darcy appeared at door lungs got in throat.

He walked in purposefully without saying hello, took a card-shaped envelope out of his pocket and handed it to me. It had my name on it but Mark's address. It had already been opened.

'It's been in the in-tray since I got back,' he said, slumping down on the sofa. 'I opened it this morning by mistake. Sorry. But it's probably all for the best.'

Trembling I took the card from the envelope.

It depicted two cartoon hedgehogs watching a bra entwined with a pair of underpants going round in a washing machine.

'Who's it from?' he said pleasantly.

'I don't know.'

'Yes you do,' he said, in the sort of calm, smiley way that suggests someone is about to pull out a meat hatchet and cut your nose off. 'Who is it from?'

'I told you,' I muttered. 'I don't know.'

'Read what it says.'

I opened it up. Inside, in spidery red writing it said: 'Be Mine Valentine – I'll see you when you come to pick up your nightie – love – Sxxxxxxxx'

I stared at it in shock. Just then the phone rang.

Baaah! I thought, it'll be Jude or Shazzer with some hideous advice about Mark. I started to spring towards it but Mark put his hand on my arm.

'Hi, doll, Gary here.' Oh God. How dare he be so overfamiliar? 'Right, what we were talking about in the bedroom – I've got some ideas so give me a ring and I'll come round.'

Mark looked down blinking very fast. Then he sniffed, and rubbed the back of his hand across his face as if to pull himself together. 'OK?' he said. 'Do you want to explain?'

'It's the builder.' I wanted to put my arms round him.

'Magda's builder, Gary. The one that put the crap shelves up. He wants to put an infill extension between the bedroom and the stairs.'

'I see,' he said. 'And is the card from Gary as well? Or is it St John? Or some other . . .'

Just then the fax started grunting. Something was coming through.

While I was staring Mark pulled the piece of paper off the fax, looked at it and handed it over. It was a scrawled note from Jude saying 'Who needs Mark Darcy when £9.99 plus P&P will buy you one of these', on top of an advert for a vibrator with a tongue.

Friday 28 February

9st 2 (only bright spot on horizon), reasons why people like going to musicals: mysterious unfathomable number, reasons Rebecca allowed to be alive 0, reasons for Mark, Rebecca, Mum, Una and Geoffrey Alconbury and Andrew Lloyd Webber or similar to ruin life: unclear.

Must keep calm. Must be positive. Was very bad luck all those things happening at once, no question about it. Completely understandable that Mark would just leave after all that and he did say he was going to call when he calmed down and . . . Hah! I've just realized who that bloody card was from. It must have been the dry-cleaner. When I was trying to get it out of him about the fraud and saying 'Don't think I don't know what's going on,' I was dropping off my nightie. And I gave him Mark's address in case he was dodgy. The world is full of lunatics and madmen and I've got to go see *Miss Sai*fucking*gon* tonight.

Midnight. Initially, it wasn't too bad. It was a relief to get away from the prison of my own thoughts and the hell of dialling 1471 every time I went to the loo.

Wellington, far from being a tragic victim of cultural imperialism, looked coolly at home in one of Dad's 1950s suits as if he might have been one of the waiters from the Met Bar on his night off, responding with dignified graciousness while Mum and Una twittered around him like groupies. I turned up late so managed to exchange only the briefest of apologetic words with him at the interval.

'Is it strange being in England?' I said, then felt stupid because obviously it would be strange.

'It is interesting,' he said, looking at me searchingly. 'Do you find it strange?'

'So!' burst in Una. 'Where's Mark? I thought he was supposed to be coming too!'

'He's working,' I muttered as Uncle Geoffrey lurched up, pissed, with Dad.

'That's what the last one said, didn't he!' roared Geoffrey. 'Always the same with my little Bridget,' he said, patting me dangerously near my bottom. 'Off they go. Weeeeeeeh!'

'Geoffrey!' said Una, adding as if making light conversation, 'Do you have older women who can't get married off in your tribe, Wellington?'

'I am not an older woman,' I hissed.

'That is the responsibility of the elders of the tribe,' said Wellington.

'Well, I've always said that was the best way, haven't

I, Colin?' said Mum smugly. 'I mean didn't I tell Bridget she should go out with Mark?'

'But when she is older, with or without husband, a woman has the respect of the tribe,' said Wellington with a twinkle in my direction.

'Can I move there?' I said glumly.

'I am not sure you would be liking the smell of the walls.' He laughed.

Managed to get Dad on one side and whisper, 'How's it going?'

'Oh, not so bad, you know,' he said. 'Seems a nice enough feller. Can we take our drinks in with us?'

Second half was a nightmare. Whole hideous jamboree on stage passed in a blur as mind went into a horrifying snowball-effect roll with images of Rebecca, Gary, vibrators and nighties getting more and more lurid as they spun past.

Fortunately the crush of people spewing out of the foyer and yelling with – presumably – joy prevented conversation till we all piled into Geoffrey and Una's Range Rover. We were going along with Una driving, Geoffrey in the front, Dad giggling merrily in the boot and me sandwiched between Mum and Wellington in the back when incident happened, horrifying and incredible.

Mum had just plonked a pair of enormous, gold-rimmed glasses on her nose.

'I didn't know you'd started wearing glasses,' I was saying, startled by this uncharacteristic nod in the direction of acknowledging the ageing process.

'I haven't started wearing glasses,' she said gaily. 'Mind that belisha beacon, Una.'

'But' I said, 'you are.'

'No, no, no! I only wear them for driving.'

'But you're not.'

'Yes she is.' Dad grinned ruefully as Mum yelled, 'Mind that Fiesta, Una! He's indicating!'

'Isn't that Mark?' said Una suddenly. 'I thought he was working.'

'Where!' said Mum bossily.

'Over there,' said Una. 'Ooh, by the way, did I tell you Olive and Roger have gone to the Himalayas? Littered with toilet paper, apparently. The whole of Mount Everest.'

I followed Una's pointing finger to where Mark, dressed in his dark blue overcoat and a very white, semi-undone shirt, was getting out of a taxi. As if in slow motion, I saw a figure emerging from the back of the cab: tall, slim, with long blonde hair, laughing up into his face. It was Rebecca.

The level of torture unleashed in the Range Rover was unbelievable: Mum and Una crazed with indignation on my behalf – 'Well, I think it's absolutely disgusting! With another woman on a Friday night when he said he was working! I've a good mind to ring Elaine and give her what for; Geoffrey drunkenly saying 'Off they go! Weeh!' and Dad trying to quieten the whole thing down. The only silent people were me and Wellington, who took my hand and held it, very still and strong, without saying a word.

When we reached my flat he climbed out of the Range Rover to let me out, with the babble of 'Well! I mean his first wife left him, didn't she?' 'Well exactly. No smoke without fire,' in the background.

'In darkness the stone becomes the buffalo,' Wellington said. 'In sunlight all is as it is.'

'Thanks,' I said gratefully, then stumbled back to the

flat wondering if I could turn Rebecca into a buffalo and set her on fire without creating enough smoke to alert Scotland Yard.

Saturday 1 March

10 p.m. My flat. Very black day. Jude, Shaz and I went emergency shopping and have all come back here to get ready for night on town, designed by the girls to keep my mind off things. By 8 p.m. things were already getting squiffy. 'Mark Darcy's gay,' Jude was declaring.

'Of course he's gay,' snarled Shazzer, pouring out more Bloody Marys.

'Do you really think so?' I said, momentarily relieved by the depressing yet ego-comforting theory.

'Well, you did find a boy in his bed, didn't you?' said Shaz.

'Why else would he go off with someone freakishly tall like Rebecca, with no sense of girlfriend-hood, no tits and no bottom – i.e. a virtual man?' said Jude.

'Bridge,' said Shaz, looking up at me drunkenly, 'God, d'you know? When I look at you from this angle, you've got a real double chin.'

'Thanks,' I said wryly, pouring myself another glass of wine and pressing ANSWER PLAY again, at which Jude and Shazzer put their hands over their ears.

'Hi, Bridget. It's Mark. You don't seem to be returning my calls. I really think, whatever, I . . . I'm really . . . We – at least I feel – I owe it to you to be friends, so I hope you'll . . . we'll. Oh God, anyway, give me a ring sometime soon. If you want to.'

'Seems to have totally lost touch,' grumbled Jude. 'As if it's nothing to do with him when he's run off with Rebecca. You've really got to detach now. Look, are we going to this party or not?'

'Yurrr. Who's 'e bloody think he is?' said Shaz. 'Owe it to you! Hggnah! You shoulssay, "Honey, I don't need anyone in my life becauseey *owe* it to me."'

At that moment the phone rang.

'Hi.' It was Mark. Heart was inconveniently overtaken with great wave of love.

'Hi,' I said eagerly, mouthing 'It's him', at the others.

'Did you get your message? I mean my message?' said Mark.

Shazzer was jabbing my leg, frantically hissing, 'Give it to him, go on.'

'Yes,' I said, hoity-toitily. 'But as I got it minutes after I saw you emerging from the taxi with Rebecca at 11 o'clock at night, I wasn't in the most amenable of humours.'

Shaz stuck her fist in the air going 'Yesss!!!' and Jude put her hand over Shazzer's mouth, gave me a thumbs up and reached for the Chardonnay.

There was silence on the end of the phone.

'Bridge, why do you always have to jump to conclusions?'

I paused, hand over mouthpiece. 'He says I'm jumping to conclusions,' I hissed, at which Shaz, furious, made a lunge for it.

'Jump to conclusions?' I said. 'Rebecca's been making a play for you for a month, you chuck me for things I haven't done, then next thing I see you getting out of a taxi with Rebecca . . .'

'But it wasn't my fault, I can explain, and I had just called you.'

'Yes – to say you owed it to me to be my friend.'

'But . . .'

'Go on!' hissed Shaz.

I took a big breath. 'Owed it to me? Honey . . .' At this Jude and Shaz collapsed on each other in ecstasy. Honey! Was practically being Linda Fiorentino in *The Last Seduction*. 'I don't need anyone in my life because they owe it to me,' I went on determinedly. 'I have got the best, most loyal, wise, witty, caring, supportive friends in the world. And if I *were* to be your friend after the way you've treated me . . .'

'But . . . What way?' He sounded anguished.

'If I was still to be your friend . . .' I was flagging.

'Go on,' hissed Shaz.

'. . . You would be *really* lucky.'

'All right, you've said enough,' said Mark. 'If you don't want me to explain, I won't pester you with phone calls. Goodbye, Bridget.'

I replaced the handset, stunned, and looked round at the friends. Sharon was lying on the rug, waving a fag triumphantly in the air and Jude was swigging straight out of the bottle of Chardonnay. Suddenly I had an awful feeling I had made the most terrible mistake.

Ten minutes later the doorbell rang. I ran at it.

'Can I come in?' said a muffled man's voice. Mark!

'Of course,' I said, relieved, turning to Jude and Shaz saying, 'Do you think you could, like, go in the bedroom?'

They were just disgruntledly picking themselves up from the floor when the door to the flat opened, only it wasn't Mark but Tom.

'Bridget! You're looking so thin!' he said. 'Oh God.' He slumped at the kitchen table. 'Oh God. Life is shite, life is a tale told by a cynical . . .'

'Tom,' said Shazzer. 'We were having a conversation.'

'And none of us 'ave seen you for blurry weeks,' slurred Jude resentfully.

'A conversation? Not about me? Whatever can it have been about? Oh God – fucking Jerome, fucking, fucking Jerome.'

'Jerome?' I said, horrified. 'Pretentious Jerome? I thought you'd banished him from your life for ever.'

'He left all these messages when I went to San Francisco,' said Tom sheepishly. 'So we started seeing each other and then tonight I just hinted at us getting back together, well, tried to snog him, and Jerome said, he said . . .' Tom brushed angrily at one eye. 'He just didn't fancy me.'

There was a stunned silence. Pretentious Jerome had committed a vicious, selfish, unforgivable, ego-destroying crime against all the laws of dating decency.

'I'm not attractive,' said Tom despairingly. 'I'm a confirmed love pariah.'

Instantly we swung into action, Jude grabbing Chardonnay while Shaz put her arm round him and I brought a chair gabbling, 'You're not, you're not!'

'Then why did he say that? Why? WHYYYYYYYYY?'

'It'ss perfickly obvious,' said Jude, handing him a glass. 'Iss because Pretentious Jerome is straight.'

'Straight as a die,' said Shaz. 'I've known that boy wasn't gay since first time I blurry sawim.'

'Straight.' Jude giggled in agreement. 'Straight as a very straight, straight . . . penis.'

5

Mr Darcy, Mr Darcy

Sunday 2 March

5 a.m. Aaargh. Have just remembered what happened.

5.03 a.m. Why did I do that? Why? Why? Wish could get back to sleep or up.

5.30 a.m. Weird how quickly time goes when you have a hangover. Is because you have so few thoughts: exactly opposite to when people are drowning, entire life flashes past and moment seems to last for ever because they are having so many thoughts.

6 a.m. You see half an hour just went like that, because I did not have any thoughts. Oof. Actually head hurts quite a lot. Oh God. Hope was not sick on coat.

7 a.m. Trouble is, they never tell you what will happen if you drink more than two units a day or, more to point, entire week's worth of alcohol units in one night. Does it mean you will get a magenta face and gnarled nose in manner of gnome, or that you are an alcoholic? But in that case everybody at the party we went on to last night must have been an alcoholic. Except that the only people who weren't drinking were the alcoholics. Hmm.

7.30 a.m. Maybe am pregnant and will have harmed child with alcohol. Oh, though. Cannot be pregnant as just finished period and will never have sex with Mark again. Never. Never.

8 a.m. Worst of it is, being alone in middle of night without anyone to talk to or ask how drunk I was. Keep remembering increasingly hideous things that I said. Oh no. Have just remembered giving beggar 50p who, instead of 'Thank you', said, 'You look really pissed.'

Suddenly also remember childhood mother saying: 'There is nothing worse than a woman drunk.' Am Yates Wine Lodge-style easy meat gutter floozy. Must go back to sleep.

10.15 a.m. Feel bit better for sleep. Maybe hangover has gone. Think will open curtains. GAAAAAAAAAAAAH! Surely is not natural for sun to be that bloody bright in the morning.

10.30 a.m. Anyway. Am going to gym in a minute and am never going to drink again, therefore is perfect moment to start Scarsdale diet. So actually what happened last night was v.g. because this is start of totally new life. Hurrah! People will say . . . Oooh, telephone.

11.15 a.m. Was Shazzer. 'Bridge, was I really pissed and awful last night?'

For a moment could not remember her at all. 'No, of course not,' I said nicely to cheer Shazzer up, as sure if she had been really drunk I would have remembered. I gathered all my courage together and asked, 'Was I?' There was silence.

'No, you were lovely, you were really sweet.'

There, you see, was just hungover paranoia. Ooh, telephone. Maybe him.

Was my mother.

'Bridget, what on earth are you doing still at home? You're supposed to be here in an hour. Daddy's whizzing the baked Alaska!'

11.30 a.m. Fuck, oh fuck. She asked me for lunch on Friday night and was too weak to argue, then too pissed to remember. I can't not go again. Can I? Right. The thing to do is stay calm and eat fruit because the enzymes clear the toxicity and it will be fine. I'll just eat a tiny bit and try not to vomit and then I'll ring Mum back when I've emerged from Land of Indecision.

Pros of Going

Will be able to check that Wellington is being treated in a manner that would not offend Commission for Racial Equality.

Will be able to talk to Dad.

Will be good daughter.

Will not have to take on Mum.

Cons of Going

Will have to face torture and torment over Mark/Rebecca incident.

May be sick on table.

Phone again. Had better not be her.

'So how's your head today?' It was Tom.

'Fine,' I trilled gaily, blushing. 'Why?'

'Well, you were pretty far gone last night.'

'Shazzer said I wasn't.'

'Bridget,' said Tom, 'Shazzer wasn't there. She went to the Met Bar to meet Simon and from what I gather she was in much the same state as you.'

Monday 3 March

9st 5 (hideous instant fat production after lard-smeared parental Sunday lunch), cigarettes 17 (emergency), incidents during parental lunch suggesting there is any sanity or reality remaining in life 0.

8 a.m. Hangover is at last beginning to clear. Massive relief to be back in own home where am adult lord of castle instead of pawn in other people's games. Decided was no real way out of Mum's lunch yesterday, but all the way up the motorway to Grafton Underwood could feel sick coming up in my throat. Village looked surreally idyllic, trimmed with daffodils, conservatories, ducks etc. and people clipping hedges for all the world as if life were easy and peaceful, disaster had not happened, and there was such a thing as God.

'Oh hello, darling! *Hakuna Matata*. Just back from the Co-op,' mum said bustling me through into the kitchen. 'Short of peas! I'm just going to play this answering-phone back.'

Sat down nauseously while the answerphone boomed

out, and Mum crashed around turning on gadgets, which ground and screamed in already-painful head.

'Pam,' went the answerphone. 'Penny here. You know that chap who lives up round the corner from the garage? Well, he's committed suicide because of the noise from the clay-pigeon shooting. It's in the *Kettering Examiner*. Oh and I meant to say, can Merle put a couple of dozen mince pies in your freezer while they've got the gas board in?'

'Hello, Pam! Margo! On the scrounge! Have you got a six-inch Swiss roll tin I can borrow for Alison's twenty-first?'

I stared wildly round the kitchen, crazed at the thought of the different worlds that would be revealed by playing back people's answerphone tapes. Maybe someone should do it as an installation at the Saatchi Gallery. Mum was clattering about in the cupboards then dialled a number. 'Margo. Pam. I've got a sponge *ring* tin if that's any good? Well, why don't you use a Yorkshire pudding tin and just line the bottom with a bit of greaseproof paper?'

'Hello, hello, bomdibombom,' said Dad, pottering into the kitchen. 'Does anybody know the postcode for Barton Seagrave? Do you think it's KT4 HS or L? Ah, Bridget, welcome to the trenches, World War Three in the kitchen, Mau Mau in the garden.'

'Colin, will you tip that oil out of the chip pan?' said Mum. 'Geoffrey says when you've brought it up to a high temperature ten times it should be thrown away. By the way, Bridget, I've bought you some talc.' She handed me a lilac Yardley's bottle with a gold top.

'Er, why?' I said, taking hold of it gingerly.

'Well! It keeps you nice and fresh, doesn't it?'

Grrr. Grrrr. The whole thought-groove was just so transparent. Mark had gone out with Rebecca because . . .

'Are you saying I smell?' I said.

'No, darling.' She paused. 'It's always nice to keep nice and fresh, though, isn't it?'

'Afternoon, Bridget!' It was Una appearing as if from nowhere with a plate of boiled eggs. 'Pam! I forgot to tell you, Bill's trying to get the council to skim his drive because they didn't grate the top off it and that's why they've got potholes, so Eileen said will you tell them the water used to run down from your drive until they put a grate in?'

Was all gibberish. Gibberish. Felt like a patient in a coma whom nobody thought could hear anything.

'Come on, Colin, where's that Spam? They're going to be here in a moment.'

'Who?' I said suspiciously.

'The Darcys. Una, pop some salad cream and paprika on those eggs, will you?'

'The Darcys? Mark's parents? Now? Why?'

Just then, the doorbell – which plays the entire tune of a town-hall clock – started chiming out.

'We are the elders of the tribe!' twinkled Mum, taking off her pinny. 'Come on, everyone, galvanize!'

'Where's Wellington?' I hissed at Mum.

'Oh, he's out in the garden practising his football! He doesn't like these sit-down lunches having to yaketty yak to us all.'

Mum and Una dashed off and Dad patted my arm. 'Forward to the breach,' he said.

Followed him into the swirly-carpet-and-ornament-land of the lounge, wondering whether I had the strength and control of my limbs to bolt and deciding I didn't. Mark's mum and dad and Una and Geoffrey were standing in an awkward circle each holding a glass of sherry. 'OK, love,' said Dad. 'Let's get you a drink.'

'Have you met . . . ?' He gestured to Elaine. 'Do you know, my dear, I am sorry, I've known you for thirty years and I've completely forgotten your name.'

'So how's that son of yours?' Una bludgeoned in.

'My son! Well, he's getting married, you know!' said Admiral Darcy, a genial bellower. The room suddenly went blotchy. Getting married?

'Getting married?' said Dad, holding my arm, as I tried to control my breathing.

'Oh I know, I know,' said Admiral Darcy cheerily. 'There's no keeping up with any of these young ones any more: married to someone one minute, off with someone else the next! Isn't that right, m'dear?' he said, patting Mark's mother on the bottom.

'I think Una was asking about Mark, not Peter, darling,' she said, with a flash of understanding in my direction. 'Peter is our other son out in Hong Kong. He's getting married in June. Now come along, can't one of you chaps find Bridget a drink? They're all mouth and no trousers, aren't they?' she said, with a sympathetic look.

Somebody get me out of here, I thought. I don't want to be tortured. I want to lie on the bathroom floor with my head near the toilet bowl like normal people.

'Would you like one of these?' said Elaine, holding out a silver case full of Black Sobranies. 'I'm sure they're death on a stick but I'm still here at sixty-five.'

'Right, come along and sit down, everyone!' said Mum, swirling in with a plate of liver sausage. 'Oof.' She made a great show of coughing and fanning the air and said icily, 'No smoking at table, Elaine.'

I followed her into the dining room where beyond the French windows Wellington was playing an astonishingly accomplished game of keepy-uppy in a sweatshirt and a pair of blue silky shorts.

'There he goes. Keep it up, lad,' chortled Geoffrey, looking out of the window, jiggling his hands up and down in his pockets. 'Keep it up.'

We all sat down and stared at each other awkwardly. It was like a pre-wedding get-together for the happy couple and both sets of parents except that the groom had run off with someone else two nights before.

'So!' said Mum. 'Salmon, Elaine?'

'Thank you,' said Elaine.

'We went to *Miss Saigon* the other night!' Mum began with dangerous brightness.

'Baah! Musicals. Can't bloody stand 'em, load of bloody ponces,' muttered Admiral Darcy as Elaine served him a piece of salmon.

'Well, we enjoyed it!' said Mum. 'Anyway . . .'

I looked frantically out of the window for some sort of inspiration and saw Wellington looking at me. 'Help,' I mouthed. He nodded towards the kitchen and disappeared.

'Standing around with their legs apart bellowing,' roared the Admiral, a man after my own heart. 'Now Gilbert and Sullivan. *HMS Pinafore*, that's a different thing.'

'Excuse me a moment,' I said, and slipped out, ignoring Mum's furious stare.

Dashed into the kitchen to find Wellington already there. I slumped against the fridge freezer.

'What?' he said, looking at my eyes intently. 'What is wrong?'

'She thinks she's one of the elders of the tribe,' I whispered. 'She's taking on Mark's parents, you know Mark, who we saw . . .'

He nodded. 'I know all about this.'

'What have you been saying to her? She's trying to engineer some powwow about him seeing Rebecca as if . . .'

Just then the kitchen door burst open.

'Bridget! What are you doing in here? Oh.' Spotting Wellington, Mum rather stopped in her tracks.

'Pamela?' said Wellington. 'What is happening?'

'Well, I just thought after what you said, we adults could . . . could sort something out!' she said, recovering her confidence and almost managing a beam.

'You were adopting the behaviours of our tribe?' said Wellington.

'Well . . . I . . .'

'Pamela. Your culture has evolved over many centuries. When outside influence appears you must not allow it to infect and dilute your birthright. As we discussed, world-wide travel brings a responsibility to observe, not to destroy.' Could not help wondering how Wellington's brand new CD Walkman fitted into all this, but Mum was nodding penitently. Had never seen her so under anyone's spell before.

'Now. Return to your guests and leave Bridget's court-ship be, as is the time-old tradition of your tribe.'

'Well I suppose you're right,' she said, patting her hair.

'Enjoy your lunch,' said Wellington, giving me the slightest of winks.

Back in the dining room, it seemed that Mark's mother had already deftly deflected the showdown. 'It's a total mystery to me how anyone gets married to anyone these days,' she was saying. 'If I hadn't married so young I'd never have done it.'

'Oh, I quite agree!' said Dad, rather too heartily.

'What I don't understand,' said Uncle Geoffrey, 'is how a woman manages to get to Bridget's age without hooking anyone. New York, Outer Space, off they go! Wheee!'

'Oh, just shut up! Shut up!' I felt like yelling.

'It's very hard for young people now,' Elaine interrupted again, looking hard at me. 'One can marry anyone when one is eighteen. But when one's character is formed, taking on the reality of a man must seem insufferable. Present company excepted of course.'

'I should hope so,' roared Mark's father merrily, patting her arm. 'Otherwise, I'm going to have to swap you for two thirty-somethings. Why should my son have all the fun!' He gave a gallant nod in my direction at which my heart lurched again. Did he think we were still together? Or did he know about Rebecca and think Mark was going out with us both?

Thankfully the conversation then steamed back to *HMS Pinafore*, bounced on to Wellington's football skills, swung out on to Geoffrey and Dad's golfing holiday, fluttered over herbaceous borders, skimmed Bill's drive and then it was 3.45 and the whole nightmare was over.

Elaine pressed a couple of Sobranies into my hand as they left – 'I think you might need these for the drive back. I do hope we see you again' – which seemed encouraging but not enough to build one's life on. It was Mark I wanted to go out with again not, unfortunately, his parents.

'Right, darling,' said Mum, bustling out of the kitchen with a Tupperware box. 'Where've you put your bag?'

'Mum,' I said through clenched teeth. 'I don't want any food.'

'Are you all right, darling?'

'As all right as I can be under the circumstances,' I muttered.

She gave me a hug. Which was nice but startling. 'I know it's hard,' she said. 'But don't take any nonsense from Mark. It'll all work out for you. I know it will.' Just as I was enjoying the unaccustomed mummy-comfort she said, 'So you see! *Hakuna Matata!* Don't worry. Be happy! Now. D'you want to take a couple of packets of minestrone back with you when you go? How about some Primula and some Tuc biscuits? Can I just get past you into that drawer? Ooh, I'll tell you what. I've got a couple of pieces of fillet steak.'

Why does she think food is better than love? If I'd stayed in the kitchen a minute longer I swear I would have thrown up.

'Where's Dad?'

'Oh, he'll be out in his shed.'

'What?'

'His shed. He spends hours in there and then comes out smelling of . . .'

'Of what?'

'Nothing, darling. Off you go and say goodbye if you want to.'

Outside, Wellington was reading the *Sunday Telegraph* on the bench.

'Thanks,' I said.

'No problem,' he said, then added, 'She is a good woman. A woman of strong mind, good heart and enthusiasm, but maybe . . .'

'. . . about 400 times too much, sometimes?'

'Yeah,' he said, laughing. Oh my God, I hope it was just enthusiasm for life he was on about.

As I approached the shed, Dad came out looking rather red in the face and shifty. His Nat King Cole tape was playing inside.

'Ah, off back to the big, big, smokeedeesmoke of London?' he said, stumbling slightly and grabbing hold of the shed. 'You a bit down, old love?' he slurred gently.

I nodded. 'You too?' I said.

He folded me up in his arms and gave me a big squeeze like he used to do when I was little. It was nice: my dad.

'How have you managed to stay married so long to Mum?' I whispered, wondering what that vaguely sweet smell was. Whisky?

'Sssnot so complicated really,' he said, lurching against the shed again. He cocked his head on one side, listening to Nat King Cole.

'*The greatest thing,*' he started to croon, '*you'll ever learn is how to love and be loved in return*. Just hope she still loves me not the Mau Mau.'

Then he leaned over and gave me a kiss.

Wednesday 5 March

9st 2 (good), alcohol units 0 (excellent), cigarettes 5 (a pleasant, healthy number), number of times driven past Mark Darcy's house 2 (v.g.), no. of times looked up Mark Darcy's name in phone book to prove still exists 18 (v.g.), 1471 calls 12 (better), no. of phone calls from Mark 0 (tragic).

8.30 a.m. My flat. Very sad. I miss Mark. Heard nothing all day Sunday and Monday then got back from work last night to message saying he was going to New York for a few weeks. 'So I guess it really is goodbye.'

Am trying best to keep spirits up. Have found that if when wake up in morning, immediately before feeling first stab of pain, put on Radio 4 *Today* programme – even if programme does appear to consist of hours and hours of *Just a Minute*-type game with politicians trying not to say 'Yes' or 'No' or answer any of the questions – then I can actually avoid getting caught in obsessive 'if only' thought cycles and imaginary Mark Darcy conversational loops that only increase sadness and inability to get out of bed.

Must say Gordon Brown was v.g. on programme this morning, managing to go on about European currency without hesitating, pausing or actually saying anything, but all the time talking calmly and fluently with John Humphreys shouting, 'Yes or No? Yes or No?' like Leslie Crowther in the background. So . . . well, could be worse. I suppose.

Wonder if European currency is the same as single currency? In some ways am in favour of this as presumably we would have different coins, which might be quite European and chic. Also they could get rid of the brown ones, which are too heavy and the 5ps and 20ps, which are too tiny and insignificant to be pleasurable. Hmm. We should hang on to the £1s though, which are fantastic, like sovereigns, and you suddenly find you have £8 in your purse when you thought you had run out. But then they would have to alter all the slot machines and . . . Gaaaaaah! Doorbell. Maybe Mark coming to say goodbye.

Was just bloody Gary. Eventually managed to get out of him that he had come to tell me that the infill extension would 'only' cost £7,000.

'Where am I going to get £7,000?'

'You could get a second mortgage,' he said. 'It would only cost you another hundred a month.'

Fortunately even he could see I was late for work so managed to get him out of the house. £7,000. Honestly.

7 p.m. Back home. Surely it is not normal to be treating my answerphone like an old-fashioned human partner: rushing home to it from work to see what mood it is in, whether it will tinklingly confirm that I am loveable and an acceptable member of society or be empty and distant, like now for example. Not only is there no message from Mark for the 42nd day running, but also no message from anyone else. Maybe should read a bit of *The Road Less Travelled*.

7.06 p.m. Yes, you see love is not something that happens to you but something you do. So what didn't I do?

7.08 p.m. Am assured, receptive, responsive woman of substance. My sense of self comes not from other people but from . . . from . . . myself? That can't be right.

7.09 p.m. Anyway. Good thing is am not obsessing about Mark Darcy. Am starting to detach.

7.15 p.m. Goody, telephone! Maybe Mark Darcy!

'Bridget, you're looking so thin!' Tom. 'How are you doing, my baby?'

'Crap,' I said, taking my Nicorette gum out of my mouth and starting to mould it into a sculpture. 'Obviously.'

'Oh come on, Bridgelene! Men! Ten a penny. How's the new interviewing career?'

'Well, I rang Colin Firth's agent and got out all the cuts. I really thought he might do it because *Fever Pitch* is coming out soon and I thought they might want the publicity.'

'And?'

'They rang back and said he was too busy.'

'Hah! Well, actually that's exactly what I'm ringing about. Jerome says he knows . . .'

'Tom,' I said dangerously, 'would this be Mentionitis by any chance?'

'No, no . . . I'm not going to go back with him,' he lied transparently. 'But anyway, Jerome knows this guy who worked on the last film with Colin Firth and he said do you want him to put in a good word for you?'

'Yes!' I said excitedly.

Realize is just another excuse for Tom to keep in touch with Pretentious Jerome but then all kind acts are a mixture of altruism and self-interest, and maybe Colin Firth will say yes!

Hurrah! Will be perfect job for me! Can go all over the world interviewing famous celebrities. Also with all the extra money could get the second mortgage for the office and roof terrace then give up hateful Sit Up Britain job and work at home. Yes! Everything is falling into place! Am going to ring up Gary. You cannot expect anything to change unless you change. Am taking things into my own hands!

Right, am not going to lie in bed being sad. Am going to get up and do something useful. Like. Um. Have a fag? Oh God. Cannot bear the thought of Mark calling up Rebecca, going through all the little details of the day like he used to do with me. Mustn't, mustn't be negative. Maybe Mark is not going out with Rebecca and will come back and be with me! You see? Hurrah!

Wednesday 12 March

9st 2, alcohol units 4 (but am journalist now so obviously must be drunk), cigarettes 5, calories 1,845 (g.), lights at end of tunnel 1 (v. tiny).

4 p.m. Tom just called me at work.

'It's on!'

'What?'

'The Colin Firth thing!'

I sat straight up in my chair, quivering.

'Yes! Jerome's friend called up and Colin Firth was really nice and said if you can place it in the *Independent* he'll do it. And I'm going out for dinner with Pretentious Jerome!'

'Tom, you're a saint, a God and an archangel. So what do I have to do?'

'Just ring up Colin Firth's agent and then call Adam at the *Independent*. Oh, by the way, I told them you'd done loads of stuff before.'

'But I haven't.'

'Oh, don't be so bloody *literal*, Bridgelene, just tell him you have.'

Tuesday 18 March

9st 3 (v. unfair crimeless punishment), calories 1,200 (rest my case), mortgages 2 (hurrah!), number of bedrooms in flat: about to be 2 (hurrah!).

Have rung up bank and is fine about the second mortgage! All I have to do is fill in a few forms and stuff and then I can have £7,000 and it is only £120 a month! Cannot believe have not thought of this before. Could have been answer to all my overdraft problems!

Wednesday 2 April

9st 4, calories 998 (bizarre calorie/fat inverse relationship seems to render food-restraint pointless), miracles: multiple, new-found joy: infinite.

5 p.m. Something strange is going on. Not only is Colin Firth interview happening but it is going to be in Rome! Next thing they will say interview is to take place naked in sea off Caribbean island in manner of *Blind Date*. Can understand God granting one favour to make up for everything but this, surely, is beyond all normal religious reason. Suggests life is peaking in some terrifying final way followed by rapid rush downhill towards untimely death. Maybe is belated April Fool.

Just called Tom who said stop always thinking there is a trick to everything and reason interview is taking place in Rome is that Colin Firth lives there – he is right – and to try to concentrate on fact that there are other things about Colin Firth apart from playing Mr Darcy. Like his new film *Fever Pitch* for example.

'Yup, yup, yup,' I said, then told Tom was v. grateful for all his help in setting this up. 'You see this is exactly what I needed!' I said excitedly. 'I feel so much better now I'm concentrating on my career instead of obsessing about men.'

'Er, Bridget,' said Tom. 'You do realize Colin Firth has a girlfriend, don't you?'

Humph.

Friday 11 April

9st 2, alcohol units 5 (journalism training), cigarettes 22, calories 3,844 (you see? You see? Am never going to diet again).

6 p.m. A wonderful thing has happened! Just spoke to

PR lady and Colin Firth is going to call me at home over the weekend to arrange things! Cannot believe it. Obviously will not be able to go out of house all weekend but that is good as will be able to do research by watching *Pride and Prejudice* video, though obviously realize must talk about other projects as well. Yes. Actually this could be real turning point in career. You see ironically enough, in a spooky sixth sense meant-to-be-type way, Mr Darcy has made me forget obsession with Mark Darcy . . . Telephone! Maybe Mr or Mark Darcy, must quickly put impressive jazz or classical record on.

Huh. Was bloody bossy man called Michael from *Independent*. 'Now listen. We haven't used you before. I don't want any messing about with this. You come back on the plane we have booked for you on Monday night, you sit down with it on Tuesday morning and you hand it in by 4 o'clock or it won't go in. And you're asking him about the film *Fever Pitch*. *Fever Pitch*, in which, as you know, he plays a character who is not Mr Darcy.'

Actually that is quite right. Ooh, telephone.

Was Jude. She and Shazzer are coming round. Fear they will make me laugh when Mr Darcy rings but on other hand need something to take mind off it or will burst.

Saturday 12 April

9st 3 (but can definitely lose 3lbs before tomorrow using Hospital Frankfurter diet), alcohol units 3 (v. g.), cigarettes 2 (perfect saint-style person), Frankfurters 12, 1471 calls to see if not heard Colin Firth ring owing to sudden unnoticed deafness 7, sq. ft of floor space not covered in pizza boxes, outfit choices, ashtrays etc. 2 (under sofa), no. of times watched Pride and Prejudice *video where Colin Firth dives into lake 15 (top-flight researcher), calls from Colin Firth 0 (so far).*

10 a.m. Colin Firth hasn't rung.

10.03 a.m. Still hasn't rung.

10.07 a.m. Still hasn't rung. Wonder if is too early to wake Jude and Shazzer up? Maybe he is waiting till his girlfriend has gone out shopping to ring me.

5 p.m. Flat looks like bomb has hit it, due to Mr Darcy stakeout: all sprawled all over sitting room like in *Thelma and Louise* when Thelma's house is taken over by police and Harvey Keitel is waiting for them to ring with tape recorders whirring in background. Really appreciate Jude and Shazzer's support and everything, but means have not been able to get on with preparation, apart from physical.

6 p.m. Mr Darcy still has not rung.

6.05 p.m. Still has not rung. What am I supposed to do? Do not even know where am meeting him.

6.15 p.m. Still has not rung. Maybe girlfriend has just *refused* to go out shopping. Maybe they have just been having sex all weekend and sending out for Italian ice cream and just laughing at me behind my back.

6.30 p.m. Jude suddenly woke up and put her fingertips on her forehead.

'We must go out,' she said in a strange, Mystic Meg-style voice.

'Are you mad?' hissed Sharon. 'Go out? Have you gone out of your *mind*?'

'No,' said Jude coldly. 'The reason the phone isn't ringing is there is too much energy focused on it.'

'Phwnaw,' snorted Sharon.

'Apart from anything else it has started to stink in here. We need to clean up, let the energy flow, then go out and have a Bloody Mary,' she said, looking at me temptingly.

Minutes later we were outside, blinking in the unexpectedly spring-like not-dark-yet air. I made a sudden bolt back towards the door but Shazzer grabbed me.

'We are going. For. A. Bloody. Mary,' she hissed, marching me along the road like a big policeman.

Fourteen minutes later we were back. I flung myself across the room and froze. The light was flashing on the answerphone.

'You see,' said Jude in a horrible smug voice. 'You see.'

Tremulously, as if it were an unexploded bomb, Shazzer reached forward and pressed ANSWER PLAY.

'Hello, Bridget, this is Colin Firth.' We all jumped a foot backwards. It was Mr Darcy. The same posh, deep, can't-be-bothered voice that he proposed to Elizabeth Bennet in on the BBC. Bridget. Me. Mr Darcy said Bridget. On my answerphone.

'I gather you're coming to Rome to interview me on Monday,' he went on. 'I was calling to arrange somewhere to meet. There's a square called the Piazza Navona, sort of easy place to find in a taxi. I'll meet you about 4.30 by the fountain. Have a safe journey.'

'1471, 1471,' gabbled Jude, '1471, quick, quick. No, get the tape out, get the tape out!'

'Call him back,' screamed Sharon like an SS torturer. 'Call him back and ask him to meet you *in* the fountain. OhmyGod.'

The phone had rung again, we stood there rigid, mouths open. Then Tom's voice boomed out, 'Hello, you pretty little things, it's Mr Darcy here just calling to see if anyone could help me out of this wet shirt.'

Shazzer suddenly de-tranced. 'Stop him, stop him,' she screamed, flinging herself at the receiver. 'Shut up, Tom, shut up, shut up, shut up.'

But it was too late. My answerphone recording of Mr Darcy saying the word Bridget and asking me to meet him in Rome by a fountain has been lost for ever. And there is nothing anyone in the world will ever be able to do about it. Nothing. Nothing.

6

Italian Job

Monday 21 April

8st 13 (fat consumed by excitement and fear), alcohol units 0: excellent (but is only 7.30 in morning), cigarettes 4 (v.g.).

7.30 a.m. Really it is a marvellous step forward to be setting off on journey with so much time to spare. It just goes to show, as it says in *The Road Less Travelled,* that human beings have capacity to change and grow. Tom came round last night and went through questions with me. So am pretty much all prepared with clear brief though was tiny bit on pissed side, to be perfectly honest.

9.15 a.m. Actually have loads of time. Everyone knows when businessmen whizz between European airports they turn up forty minutes before lift-off, with just a brief-case with nylon shirts in. Plane is at 11.45. Must be at Gatwick at 11, so 10.30 train from Victoria and tube at 10. Perfect.

9.30 a.m. What if it all gets too much and I just, like, burst out and kiss him? Also trousers are too tight and will show stomach. Think will just change into something else. Also maybe need to take sponge bag to freshen up before interview.

9.40 a.m. Cannot believe have wasted time on packing sponge bag, when most important thing, surely, is to look nice on arrival. Hair is completely mad. Will have to wet it again. Where is passport?

9.45 a.m. Have got passport, and hair is calm, so better go.

9.49 a.m. Only problem being: cannot lift bag. Maybe had better reduce sponge bag contents to toothbrush, paste, mouthwash, cleanser and moisturiser. Oh and must take £3,500 out of microwave and leave for Gary so he can start getting materials and stuff for new office and roof terrace! Hurrah!

9.50 a.m. Goody. Have ordered mini-cab. Will be here in two mins.

10 a.m. Where is mini-cab?

10.05 a.m. Where the fuck is mini-cab?

10.06 a.m. Have just rung up mini-cab firm who say silver Cavalier is outside.

10.07 a.m. Silver Cavalier is not outside or anywhere in street.

10.08 a.m. Mini-cab man says silver Cavalier is definitely turning into my street at this moment.

10.10 a.m. Still no mini-cab. Fucking fucking mini-cab and all it's . . . Gaah. Is here. Oh fuck, where are keys?

10.15 a.m. In mini-cab now. Have definitely done journey in fifteen mins before.

10.18 a.m. Aargh. Mini-cab is suddenly on Marylebone Road – inexplicably deciding on scenic tour of London instead of route to Victoria. Fight instinct to attack, kill and eat mini-cab driver.

10.20 a.m. Back on course now i.e. no longer heading for Newcastle, but traffic is solid. There is no occasion now in London when is not rush hour.

10.27 a.m. Wonder if is possible to get from Marble Arch to Gatwick Express in one minute?

10.35 a.m. Victoria. OK. Calm, calm. Train has gone without self. Still if get 10.45 will have clear thirty minutes before plane goes. Also plane will probably be delayed.

10.40 a.m. Wonder if there will be time to get new trousers at airport? Actually am not going to be neurotic about this. Marvellous thing about travelling alone is you can really start to develop a new character, and be quite elegant and Zen-like and no one knows you.

10.50 a.m. Wish did not keep thinking passport has jumped out of bag and gone back home.

11.10 a.m. Train has inexplicably stopped. Suddenly all extra things did e.g. putting extra polish coat on toenails, seem unimportant alongside not actually turning up.

11.45 a.m. Cannot believe it. Plane has gone without me.

Noon. Thank God, Mr Darcy, and all angels in heaven. Turns out can go on another plane in one hour forty minutes. Just called publicist who said no problem, she would get him to meet me two hours later. Goody, can do airport shopping.

1 p.m. V. keen on floaty-chiffon-with-roses-on-style fashions for spring but do not think they should design them so they will not fit over people's arses. Love the lovely airport shopping area. Sir Richard Rogers, Terence Conran and similar are always complaining that airports have turned into great big shopping malls but I consider that to be good. Possibly will incorporate that into next major profile possibly with Sir Richard himself if not Bill Clinton. Maybe will just try bikini on.

1.30 p.m. Right. Will just post letters and get Body Shop necessities, then go through.

1.31 p.m. Was announcement: 'Will Passenger Jones, the last remaining passenger for flight BA 175 to Rome, please make her way immediately to Gate 12 where the plane is waiting to depart.'

Tuesday 22 April

9st 2, alcohol units 2, cigarettes 22, calls from bossy Michael at Independent *to 'see how we're getting along': about 30, no. of times listened to tape of interview 17, words of interview written 0.*

9 a.m. Back in flat in London after heaven-sent trip. Right, am going to write up interview. You see is amazing way that concentrating on work and career completely takes mind off romantic sadness. Was just so fantastic. Taxi dropped me off in Roman square and thought was going to faint: just fantastic – golden sunshine and huge massive square full of high up ruins and in the middle of it all Mr . . . Ooh, telephone.

It was Michael from the *Independent.*

'So did you do it, then?'

'Yes,' I said hoity-toitily.

'And you remembered to take your tape recorder, not your Sony Walkman?'

Honestly. Do not know what Tom has told him about me but something in his tone suggests may not have been particularly respectful.

'Well, you've got till 4 o'clock. So get on with it.'

Lala. That is ages. Will just relive day for a bit. Mmm. He looked exactly like Mr Darcy: all smouldery and lean. And he even took me round a church with a hole in and some Adrian's tomb or other and a statue of Moses and was incredibly masterful preventing me from being knocked over by cars and kept talking Italian. Mmm.

Noon. Morning has not gone particularly well, though obviously needed some time to absorb what happened, and discuss impressions with peers so probably has been highly productive.

2 p.m. Telephone again. You see this is what it is like when you are major profile writer: phones ringing incessantly.

Was bloody bossy Michael again: 'How are we coming along?'

Bloody nerve. Is not even my deadline till 4 p.m., which obviously means the end of the day. Actually really pleased with tape. Did really good thing of starting him off with easy questions before going into Tom's meaty questions, which I had written down night before despite being a little on squiffy side. Think he was really quite impressed with my line of questioning, actually.

2.30 p.m. Will just have quick cup of coffee and fag.

3 p.m. Better just listen to tape again.

Ding dong! Will just ring Shaz and play her this last bit.

Aargh, aargh. Is 3.30 and have not started. Anyway, no need to panic. They are not going to be back from lunch for ages and then will be drunk as, as . . . as journalists. Wait till they see my scoops.

How to start? Obviously interview must include my impressions of Mr Darcy as well as skilfully weaving in stuff about new film *Fever Pitch*, theatre, film etc. They will probably give me a regular interview spot every week: the Bridget Jones Profile. Jones meets Darcy. Jones meets Blair. Jones meets Marcos except dead.

4 p.m. How can I be expected to create if bloody Michael keeps ringing up all the time saying what I must and must not put in? Grrr. If that is him again . . . They have no respect for journalists in that office. None whatsoever.

5.15 p.m. Harhar. 'I. Am. Do. Ing. It,' I said. That has shut him up.

6 p.m. Anyway is OK. All top journalists have deadline crises.

7 p.m. Oh fuck, oh fuck. Oh fuck, oh fuck.

Wednesday 23 April

9st 3 (really seem to be stuck in some kind of fat-groove), congratulatory calls from friends, relatives and colleagues about Colin Firth interview 0, congratulatory calls from Independent *staff about Colin Firth interview 0, congratulatory calls from Colin Firth about Colin Firth interview 0 (odd, surely?).*

8 a.m. Article is coming out today. Was a bit rushed but probably not that bad. Might be quite good actually. Wish paper would hurry up and come.

8.10 a.m. Paper has still not come.

8.20 a.m. Hurrah! Paper is here.

Have just seen interview. *Independent* have completely ignored what wrote. Realize was bit on late side but this is intolerable. Here is what was published:

Due to insuperable technical difficulties it has been necessary to print Bridget Jones's interview with Colin Firth as a direct transcript of the recording.

BJ: Right. I'm going to start the interview now.
CF: (*Slightly hysterical sounding*) Good, good.
(*Very long pause*)
BJ: What is your favourite colour?
CF: I'm sorry?
BJ: What is your favourite colour?
CF: Blue.
(*Long pause*)
BJ: What is your favourite pudding?
CF: Er. Crème brûlée.
BJ: You know the oncoming film *Fever Pitch* by Nick Hornby?
CF: I do know it, yes.
BJ: (*Pause. Rustling paper*) Do . . . Oh. (*More rustling paper*) Do you think the book of *Fever Pitch* has spored a confessional gender?
CF: Excuse me?
BJ: Has. Spored. A. Confessional. Gender.
CF: *Spored* a confessional gender?
BJ: Yes.
CF: Well. Certainly Nick Hornby's style has been very much imitated and I think it's a very appealing, er, gender whether or not he actually, um . . . *spored* it.

BJ: You know in the BBC *Pride and Prejudice*?

CF: I do know it, yes.

BJ: When you had to dive into the lake?

CF: Yes.

BJ: When they had to do another take, did you have to take the wet shirt off and then put a dry one on?

CF: Yes, I, I probably did have to, yes. *Scusi. Ha vinto. É troppo forte. Si grazie.*

BJ: (*Breathing unsteadily*) How many takes diving into the lake did you have to do?

CF: (*Coughs*) Well. The underwater shots were a tank in Ealing Studios.

BJ: Oh no.

CF: I'm afraid so. The, um, *moment* of being airborne – *extremely* brief – was a stuntman.

BJ: But it looked like Mr Darcy.

CF: That was because he had stuck on sideburns and a Mr Darcy outfit on top of a wet suit, which actually made him look like Elvis as you last saw him. He could only do it once for insurance reasons and then he had to be checked for abrasions for about six weeks afterwards. All the other wet-shirt shots were me.

BJ: And did the shirt have to keep being re-wet?

CF: Yes. They'd spray it down. They'd spray it down and then . . .

BJ: What with?

CF: I'm sorry?

BJ: What with?

CF: A squirter thing. Look can we . . . ?

BJ: Yes, but what I mean is did you ever have to take the shirt off and . . . and put another one on?

CF: Yes.

BJ: To be wet again?

CF: Yes.

BJ: (*Pause*) You know the oncoming film *Fever Pitch*?

CF: Yes.

BJ: What do you see as the main differences and similarities between the character Paul from *Fever Pitch* and . . . ?

CF: And?

BJ: (*Sheepishly*) Mr Darcy.

CF: No one's ever asked me that.

BJ: Haven't they?

CF: No. I think the main differences are . . .

BJ: Do you mean it's a really obvious question?

CF: No. I mean no one's ever asked me that.

BJ: Don't people ask you that all the time?

CF: No, no. I can assure you.

BJ: So it's a . . .

CF: It's a totally brand new, new-born question, yes.

BJ: Oh goody.

CF: Shall we get on now?

BJ: Yes.

CF: Mr Darcy's not an Arsenal supporter.

BJ: No.

CF: He's not a schoolteacher.

BJ: No.

CF: He lived nearly two hundred years ago.

BJ: Yes.

CF: Paul in *Fever Pitch* loves being in a football crowd.

BJ: Yes.

CF: Whereas Mr Darcy can't even tolerate a country dance. Now. Can we talk about something that isn't to do with Mr Darcy?

BJ: Yes.

(*Pause. Rustling papers*)

BJ: Are you still going out with your girlfriend?

CF: Yes.

BJ: Oh.

(*Long pause*)

CF: Is everything all right?

BJ: (*Almost inaudible*) Do you think small British movies are the way forward?

CF: I can't hear.

BJ: (*Miserably*) Do you think small British movies are the way forward?

CF: The way forward to . . . (*Encouragingly*) . . . to what?

BJ: (*Very long thoughtful pause*) The future.

CF: Right. They seem to be getting us along step by step, I think. I quite like small movies but I do also like big movies and it would be nice if we made more of those as well.

BJ: But don't you find it a problem her being Italian and everything?

CF: No.

(*Very long silence*)

BJ: (*Sulkily*) Do you think that Mr Darcy has a political dimension?

CF: I did speculate on what his politics might be, if he had any. And I don't think that they would be very appealing to a reader of the *Independent*. It's that pre-Victorian or Victorian idea of being the rich social benefactor, which would be very Thatcherite probably. I mean the thought of socialism obviously hadn't entered the . . .

BJ: No.

CF: . . . entered his sphere. And it is clearly stated by way of showing what a good chap he is that he is very nice towards his tenants. But I think that he'd be closer to a sort of Nietzschean figure, a . . .

BJ: What is neacher?

CF: You know, the idea of the, er, human being as superman.

BJ: Superman?

CF: Not Superman himself, no. No. (*Slight groaning noise*) I don't think he wore his underpants over his breeches, no. Look, I'd *really* like to get off this subject now.

BJ: What will be your next project?

CF: It's called *The World of Moss*.

BJ: Is it a nature programme?

CF: No. No, no. No. It's um, it's, er, about an eccentric family in the 30s, the father of which owns a moss factory.

BJ: Doesn't moss grow naturally?

CF: Well, no, he makes something called Sphagnum moss, which was used to dress World War One wounds and, er, it's, er, quite a light, er, comic . . .

BJ: (*Very unconvincingly*) It sounds very good.

CF: I very much hope it will be.

BJ: Could I just check something about the shirt?

CF: Yes.

BJ: How many times altogether exactly did you have to take it off and put it on again?

CF: Precisely . . . I don't know. Um. Let me see . . . there was the bit where I was walking towards Pemberley. That was shot once. One take. Then there was the bit where I give my horse to somebody . . . I think there was a change.

BJ: (*Brightening*) There was a change?

CF: (*Strictly*) There was. One change.

BJ: So it was mainly just the one wet shirt, though?

CF: The one wet shirt, which they kept respraying, yes. All right?

BJ: Yes. What is your favourite colour?

CF: We've had that.

BJ: Um. (*Paper rustling*) Do you think the film *Fever Pitch* was in reality all about emotional fuckwittage?

CF: Emotional what?

BJ: Fuckwittage. You know: men being mad alcoholic commitment phobics and just being interested in football all the time.

CF: No, I don't really. I think in some ways Paul is much more at ease with his emotions and has much more liberty with them than his girlfriend. I think that, in fact, in the final analysis, is what's so appealing about what Nick Hornby's trying to say on his behalf: that, in a rather mundane, everyday world he has found something where you have access to emotional experiences that . . .

BJ: Excuse me.

CF: (*Sighs*) Yes?

BJ: Don't you find the language barrier a problem with your girlfriend?

CF: Well, she speaks very good English.

BJ: But don't you think you'd be better off with someone who *was* English and more your own age?

CF: We seem to be doing all right.

BJ: Humph. (*Darkly*) So far. Do you ever prefer doing the theatre?

CF: Um. I don't subscribe to the view that the theatre's where the real acting is, that film's not really acting. But I find I do prefer the theatre when I'm doing it, yes.

BJ: But don't you think the theatre's a bit unrealistic and embarrassing and also you have to sit through the acting for hours before you have anything to eat and you can't talk or . . .

CF: Unrealistic? Embarrassing and unrealistic?

BJ: Yes.

CF: Do you mean unrealistic in the sense that it . . . ?

BJ: You can tell it isn't real.

CF: That sort of unrealistic, yes. (*Slight moaning sound*) Um. I think it shouldn't be if it's good. It's much more . . . It feels more artificial to make a film.

BJ: Does it? I suppose it doesn't go all the way through, does it?

CF: Well, no. It doesn't. No. Yes. A film doesn't go all the way through. It's shot in little bits and pieces. (*Louder groaning noise*) Little bits and pieces.

BJ: I see. Do you think Mr Darcy would have slept with Elizabeth Bennet before the wedding?

CF: Yes, I do think he might have.

BJ: *Do* you?

CF: Yes. I think it's entirely possible. Yes.

BJ: (*Breathlessly*) Really?

CF: I think it's possible, yes.

BJ: *How* would it be possible?

CF: Don't know if Jane Austen would agree with me on this but . . .

BJ: We can't know because she's dead.

CF: No, we can't . . . but I think Andrew Davies's Mr Darcy would have done.

BJ: *Why* do you think that, though. Why? Why?

CF: Because I think it was very important to Andrew Davies that Mr Darcy had the most enormous sex drive.

BJ: (*Gasps*)

CF: And, um . . .

BJ: I think that came across really, really well with the acting. I really think it did.

CF: Thank you. At one point Andrew even wrote as a stage direction: 'Imagine that Darcy has an erection.'

(*V. large crashing noise*)

BJ: Which bit was that?

CF: It's when Elizabeth's been walking across the country and bumps into him in the grounds in the early stages.

BJ: The bit where she's all muddy?

CF: And dishevelled.

BJ: And sweaty?

CF: Exactly.

BJ: Was that a difficult bit to act?

CF: You mean the erection?

BJ: (*Awed whisper*) Yes.

CF: Um, well, Andrew also wrote that I don't propose that we should focus on it, and therefore no acting required in that department at least.

BJ: Mmm.

(*Long pause*)

CF: Yes.

(*More pause*)

BJ: Mmm.

CF: Is that it, then?

BJ: No. What was it like with your friends when you started being Mr Darcy?

CF: There were a lot of jokes about it: growling, 'Mr Darcy' over breakfast and so on. There was a brief period when they had to work quite hard to hide their knowledge of who I really was and . . .

BJ: Hide it from who?

CF: Well, from anyone who suspected that perhaps I was like Mr Darcy.

BJ: But do you think you're not like Mr Darcy?

CF: I do think I'm not like Mr Darcy, yes.

BJ: I think you're exactly like Mr Darcy.

CF: In what way?

BJ: You talk the same way as him.

CF: Oh, do I?

BJ: You look exactly like him, and I, oh, oh . . .

(*Protracted crashing noises followed by sounds of struggle*)

7

Mood-Swinging Singletons

Friday 25 April

9st (yesss! yesss!), alcohol units 4, cigarettes 4, spiritual realizations as joint result of Road Less Travelled *and alcohol units 4, flats without holes in 0, no. of pounds in bank 0, boyfriends 0, people to go out with tonight 0, election parties invited to 0.*

5.30 p.m. Office. Challenging two days at work with Richard Finch reading out bits of the interview then bellowing with deep, gurgling laughter in manner of Dracula, but at least has got me out of myself. Also Jude said the interview was quite good and really gave an excellent sense of the atmosphere of the whole thing. Hurrah! Have not heard anything back from Adam or Michael at *Independent* but sure they will ring soon and maybe ask me to do another one, then can be freelance in home office, typing on roof terrace with herbs in terracotta pots! Also is only one week to election when everything is going to change! Will stop smoking, and Mark will come back and find new professional me with large indoor/outdoor living flat.

5.45 p.m. Humph. Just rang in for messages. One only, from Tom saying he had spoken to Adam and everyone at the *Independent* is really annoyed. Left him urgent message to call me back and explain.

5.50 p.m. Oh dear. Worried about arranging second mortgage now. Will not have any extra money and what if lose job? Maybe had better tell Gary do not want the infill extension and get the £3,500 back. Lucky thing is, Gary was supposed to start yesterday but he just came and left all his tools then went away again. Seemed annoying at the time, but maybe, as it turns out, was message from God. Yes. Will call him when get home then go to gym.

6.30 p.m. Back home. Gaaah! Gaaah! Gaaah! Is bloody great hole in side of flat! Is left open to outside world in manner of gaping precipice and all the houses at the other side can see in. Is entire weekend stretching ahead with giant hole in wall, all bricks everywhere and nothing to do! Nothing! Nothing!

6.45 p.m. Ooh, telephone – maybe someone inviting me to an election party! Or Mark!

'Oh, hello, darling, guess what?' My mother. Obviously I had to get a cigarette.

'Oh, hello, darling, guess what?' she said again. Sometimes I wonder how long she would carry on like this, in manner of a parrot. It is one thing to say 'Hello? Hello?' if there is silence on the other end, but 'Oh, hello, darling, guess what? Oh, hello, darling, guess what?' is surely not normal.

'What?' I said, sulkily.

'Don't speak to me in that tone of voice.'

'What?' I said again in a lovely appreciative daughter voice.

'Don't say "What?" Bridget, say "Pardon?"'

I took a puff on my kind normal friend the Silk Cut Ultra.

'Bridget, are you smoking?'

'No, no,' I said, panicking, stubbing out the cigarette and hiding the ashtray.

'Anyway, guess what? Una and I are holding a Kikuyu election party for Wellington behind the rockery!'

I breathed deeply through my nose and thought about Inner Poise.

'Don't you think that's super? Wellington's going to leap over a bonfire as a full warrior! Imagine! Right over! Dress is tribal. And we're all going to drink red wine and pretend it's cow's blood! Cow's blood! That's why Wellington's got such strong thighs.'

'Er, does Wellington know about this?'

'Not yet, darling, but he's bound to want to celebrate the election. Wellington's very keen on the free market and we don't want the Thin Red Wedge back under the bed. I mean we'll end up with what's-his-name and the miners back. You won't remember the power cuts when you were at school, but Una was giving the speech at the Ladies' Luncheon and she couldn't plug her tongs in.'

7.15 p.m. Eventually managed to get Mum off the phone, at which it rang again immediately on Ringback. Was Shaz. Told her how fed up I was feeling, and she was really sweet: 'Come on, Bridge. We simply can't define ourselves in terms of being with another person! We should celebrate how fantastic it is being free! And there'll be the election soon and the whole mood of the nation is going to change!'

'Hurrah!' I said. 'Singletons! Tony Blair! Hurrah!'

'Yes!' enthused Shazzer. 'Many people in relationships have a terrible time at weekends, forced to slave for ungrateful children and being beaten by their own spouses.'

'You're right! You're right!' I said. 'We can go out whenever we like and have fun. Shall we go out tonight?'

Humph. Sharon is going to a dinner party with Simon in manner of Smug Married.

7.40 p.m. Jude just rang in a spirit of highly-charged over sexual confidence. 'It's on again with Stacey!' she said. 'I saw him last night and he was talking about his family!'

There was an expectant pause.

'Talking about his family!' she said again. 'Which means he's thinking seriously about me. And we snogged. And I'm seeing him tonight and it's the fourth date so . . . doobeedoobeedoo. Bridge? Are you still there?'

'Yes,' I said in a small voice.

'What's the matter?'

Mumbled something about the hole in the wall and Mark.

'The thing is, Bridge. You've got to Attain Closure on that one and move on,' she said, seemingly not noticing that her last lot of advice had completely failed, which might just invalidate this.

'You've got to start working on Loving Yourself. Come on, Bridge! It's fantastic. We can shag whoever we want.'

'Singletons hurrah!' I said. So why am I depressed?

Am going to call Tom again.

8 p.m. Out. Everyone is out enjoying themselves except me.

9 p.m. Just read a bit of *You Can Heal Your Life* and now see exactly where have been going wrong. As Sondra Ray, the great re-birther, said, or maybe it wasn't her. Anyway, this is it: 'Love is never outside ourselves, love is within us.'

Yes!

'What may be keeping love away? . . . Unreasonable standards? Movie Star Images? Feelings of unworthiness? A belief that you are unloveable?'

Huh. Is not belief is fact. Am going to open bottle of Chardonnay and watch *Friends*.

11 p.m. Argor. *Road Less Travelled* blurry good. Is Cathexis or similar. 'Unitary division of loveinclud self love if love for another.' Sblurry good. Ooof. Tumbled over.

Saturday 26 April

9st 4, alcohol units 7 (hurrah!), cigarettes 27 (hurrah!), calories 4,248 (hurrah!), gym visits 0 (hurrah!).

7 a.m. Aargh. Who set that bloody thing off?

7.05 a.m. Today I will take responsibility for my own life and start loving myself. I am lovely. I am marvellous. Oh God. Where's the Silk Cut?

7.10 a.m. Right. Going to get up and go to gym.

7.15 a.m. Actually, though, it is probably quite dangerous to work out before you have properly woken up. Will jar joints. Will go tonight before *Blind Date*. Is stupid to go in the daytime on Saturday when there is so much to do e.g. shopping. Must not mind that Jude and Shaz are both probably in bed shagging wildly, shag, shag, shag.

7.30 a.m. Shag.

7.45 a.m. Obviously it is too early for anyone to ring. Just because I am awake does not mean anyone else is. Must learn to have more empathy with others.

8 a.m. Jude just rang but practically impossible to tell as total sheep-voice sobbing, gulping experience.

'Jude, what's wrong?' I said, devastated.

'I'm having a breakdown,' she sobbed. 'Everything seems black, black. I can't see any way out I can't . . .'

'It's all right. It's going to be all right,' I said, staring wildly out of the window to see if there was a psychiatrist passing. 'Does it feel serious or is it just PMT?'

'It's very, very bad,' she said in a zombie-like voice. 'It's been building up in me for about eleven years.' She broke down again. 'The whole weekend stretching ahead alone, alone. I just don't want to carry on living.'

'Good, that's good,' I said reassuringly, wondering whether I should ring the police or the Samaritans.

Turned out Stacey had inexplicably just dropped her off after dinner last night and not mentioned seeing her again. So now she felt she'd failed at Thursday's snog.

'I'm so depressed. The whole weekend stretching ahead. Alone alone, I could die and . . .'

'Do you want to come round tonight?'

'Oooh, yes please!! Shall we go to 192? I can wear my new Voyage cardi.'

Next thing Tom rang.

'Why didn't you call me back last night?' I said.

'What?' he said in a strange, dull monotone.

'You didn't call me back.'

'Oh,' he said wearily. 'I didn't think it was fair to talk to anyone.'

'Why?' I said, puzzled.

'Oh. Because I have lost my former personality and become a manic-depressive.'

It turned out Tom has been working alone at home all week, obsessing about Jerome. Eventually helped Tom to realize that the phantom madness was quite funny, given that if he hadn't informed me he was clinically insane I wouldn't have noticed any difference.

I reminded Tom of when Sharon once didn't come out of the house for three days because she thought her face was collapsing from sun damage like a movie ageing special effect and didn't want to face anyone or expose herself to UVP rays till she'd privately come to terms with it. Then when she came to Café Rouge she looked exactly like she did the week before. Managed, finally, to get off the subject of Tom and on to my career as a major celebrity interviewer which unfortunately seems to be over, for the time being at least.

'Don't worry, babe,' said Tom. 'They'll have forgotten all about it in ten minutes, you'll see. You can make a comeback.'

2.45 p.m. Feeling much better now. Have realized answer is not to obsess about own problems but help others. Have just spent an hour and fifteen minutes on phone cheering up Simon who was clearly not in bed with Shazzer. Turns out he was supposed to see this girl called Georgie tonight, who he has been intermittently secretly shagging on Saturday nights, but now Georgie says she doesn't think Saturday night is a good idea because it seems too much like they are an 'item'.

'I'm a love pariah doomed by the gods always to be alone,' Simon raged. 'Always, always. The whole of Sunday stretching ahead.'

As I told him, it is great being single because we are free! Free! (Somehow hope Shaz does not find out exactly how free Simon is, though.)

3 p.m. Am marvellous: have been almost like therapist all day. As I said to Jude and Tom, any time day or night they can call me, not just be sad on their own. So you see I am very wise and well-balanced almost in manner of the Mother Superior in *The Sound of Music*. In fact can easily imagine self singing 'Climb Every Mountain' at wall in middle of 192 with Jude kneeling appreciatively behind.

4 p.m. Phone just rang. Was Shazzer on verge of tears but trying to pretend she wasn't. Turns out Simon just called her with the Georgie scenario (v. annoying as obviously own Mother Superior act was not sufficient for the, now realize, emotionally greedy Simon).

'But I thought you were "just good friends"?' I said.

'So did I,' she said. 'But I now realize I was just secretly fantasizing that we were in a higher form of love. It's just awful being single,' she burst out. 'No one to put their arm round you at the end of the day, no one to help you mend the boiler. The whole weekend stretching ahead! Alone! Completely alone!'

4.30 p.m. Hurrah! Everyone is coming round, Shaz, Jude and Tom (though not Simon as in disgrace for Mixed Messages), and we are going to get an Indian takeaway and watch videos of *ER*. Love being single as you can have fun with all different people and life is full of freedom and potential.

6 p.m. A terrible thing has happened. Magda just called.

'Put it back in the potty. Put it back in! Listen, I don't know if I should tell you this, Bridge, but put it back. Put the ploppy BACK IN!'

'Magda . . .' I said dangerously.

'Sorry, hon. Look, I just rang to tell you that Rebecca . . . now look that's really nasty, isn't it? Yakky! Yakky! Say yakky.'

'WHAT?'

'Mark's coming home next week. She's invited us to a post-election welcome back dinner for him and . . . NOOOOOOO! OK, OK, put it in my hand.'

I slumped dizzily at the kitchen table fumbling for a cigarette.

'All right. Put it in Daddy's hand, then. The thing is, Bridge, would you rather we said yes or are you doing another one? Well, do it in the potty, then. In the potty!'

'Oh God,' I said. 'Oh God.'

6.30 p.m. Am going out for fags.

7 p.m. Whole of London is full of couples holding hands in spring, shagging each other shag, shag, shag, and planning lovely mini-breaks. Am going to be alone for rest of life. Alone!

8 p.m. Everything is turning out fantastic. Jude and Tom came round first with wine and magazines and were taking piss out of me for not knowing what a pashmina was. Jude decided Stacey had a big bum and also kept putting his hand on hers and saying 'Happy', which she had not revealed before and definitely meant he was out of the window.

Also, everyone agreed it was good that Magda should go to the hateful Rebecca's dinner party as a spy, and that if Mark really *is* going out with Rebecca then he is definitely gay, which is good – especially for Tom, who was really cheered up. Also, Jude is going to have election party and not ask Rebecca. HA!

AHAHAHAHAHAHHAHAHAHAHAHAHHA-HAHAHAHHAHAHAHAHAHA!

Next thing, Shaz turned up in tears, which was really nice in a way because usually she does not show that she minds about anything.

'Bloodybloodys,' she got out eventually. 'It's just been an entire year of emotional fuck-ups, and I'm so confused.'

All rushed to first aid with *Vogue*, sparkling wine, cigarettes etc. and Tom announced there was no such thing as platonic friendship.

'Of course there blurry is,' slurred Jude. 'You jus obsessed with sex.'

'No, no,' said Tom. 'It's just a fin-de-millennium way of dealing with the nightmare of relationships. All friendships between men and women are based on the sexual dynamic. The mistake people make is ignoring this, then getting upset when their friend doesn't shag them.'

'I'm not getting upset,' muttered Shazzer.

'What about friends when neither fancies the other?' said Jude.

'Doesn't happen. Sex is what drives it. "Friends" is a bad definition.'

'Pashminas,' I slurred, slurping on my Chardonnay.

'That's it!' said Tom excitedly. 'It's fin-de-millennium pashmina-ism. Shazzer is Simon's "pashmina" because she wants to shag him most so he diminishes her and Simon is Shazzer's "pashmaster".'

At this, Sharon burst into tears, which took twenty minutes to sort out with another bottle of Chardonnay and packet of fags until we could come up with a list of further definitions, as follows:

Pashmincer A friend who you really fancy who's actually gay. ('Me, me, me,' Tom said.)

Pashmarried A friend who you used to go out with and is now married with children who likes having you around as memory of old life but makes you feel like mad barren pod-womb imagining vicar is in love with self.

Ex-pashspurt An ex-partner who wants to get back with you but pretends just to want to be friends then keeps making passes and getting cross.

'What about "pash-hurts"?' said Shaz sulkily. 'Friends who turn your own private emotional disaster into a sociological study at the expense of your feelings.'

At this point I decided I'd better go out for cigarettes. Was just standing in sordid pub on corner, waiting for change for cigarette machine when nearly jumped out of skin. Across the bar was a man who looked exactly like Geoffrey Alconbury, only instead of a yellow diamond-patterned sweater and golfing slacks, he was wearing pale blue jeans, ironed with a crease down the front and a leather jacket over a black nylon string vest. Tried to compose self by staring furiously at a bottle of Malibu. It couldn't be Uncle Geoffrey. Glanced up and realized he was talking to a boy who looked about seventeen. It was Uncle Geoffrey. It definitely was!

Hesitated, unsure what to do. Briefly considered abandoning cigarettes and departing to spare Geoffrey's feelings. But then some Gazza-esque inner angriness reminded me of all the times Geoffrey has totally humiliated me in his environment, bellowing at the top of his voice. Ha! Ahahahaha! Uncle Geoffrey was on my territory now.

Was just about to go over and bellow 'Who's this then? Durr! Got yourself a young whippersnapper!' at the top of my voice, when felt a tap on my shoulder. Turned round to see no one there and felt a tap on my other shoulder. This was Uncle Geoffrey's favourite trick.

'Ahahahaha, what's my little Bridget doing in here, looking for a fellah?' he roared.

I couldn't believe it. He'd put a yellow sweater with a cougar on over the vest, the boy was nowhere to be seen, and he was trying to brazen it out.

'You're not going to find one in here, Bridget, they all look like Julian Clarys to me. Bent as a 10-bob note! Ahahaha. I've just come in for a packet of slim panatellas.'

At that moment the boy reappeared holding the leather jacket and looking all twitchy and disturbed.

'Bridget,' said Geoffrey as if with the full weight of Kettering Rotary behind him, then ran out of steam, and turned to the barman. 'Come on, lad! Have you got those slim panatellas I asked you for? I've been waiting twenty minutes.'

'What are you doing in London?' I said suspiciously.

'London? I've been up at the AGM for the Rotarians. It doesn't belong to you, you know, London.'

'Hi, I'm Bridget,' I said pointedly to the boy.

'Oh yes. This is, er, Steven. He's wanting to put himself up for Treasurer, aren't you, Steven? Just giving him a spot of advice. Right. Better be off. Be good! And if you can't be good be careful!! Ahahaha!' And he shot out of the pub, followed by the boy, looking back at me resentfully.

Back at the flat Jude and Shazzer could not believe I had let such an opportunity for revenge go by.

'Think what you could have said,' said Shaz, screwing her eyes up with disbelieving regret.

'Well! Glad to see you've got yourself a feller at last, Uncle GeoffrEEEEEY! We'll see how long this one lasts, won't we? Off they go – weeeeh!'

Tom, though, had a really annoying expression of pompous concern on his face.

'It's tragic, tragic,' he burst out. 'So many men up and down the country living a lie! Imagine all the secret thoughts, shames and desires eating away within the walls of suburbia, between the sofa and the French window of Lies! He probably goes to Hampstead Heath. He's probably taking terrible, terrible risks. You should talk to him, Bridget.'

'Look,' said Shaz. 'Shut up. You're drunk.'

'I feel sort of justified,' I said thoughtfully and carefully. Started to explain that have long suspected Smug Married world of Geoffrey and Una was not all it seemed and that therefore am not freak and that living together in normal heterosexual couple is not God-instructed only way.

'Bridge, shut up. You're drunk as well,' said Shaz.

'Hurrah! Let's bring it back to ourselves. There's nothing more annoying than being distracted from our own self-obsession by others,' said Tom.

All got really plastered after that. Was completely fantastic evening. As Tom said, if Miss Havisham had had some jolly flatmates to take the piss out of her she would never have stayed so long in her wedding dress.

Monday 28 April

9st 2, alcohol units 0, cigarettes 0, boyfriends 0, calls from Gary the Builder 0, possibilities of new job 0 (promising), gym visits 0, no. of gym visits so far this year 1, cost of gym membership per year £370; cost of single gym visit £123 (v. bad economy).

Right. Am definitely going to start gym programme today so can go round saying smugly 'Yes it hurt. Yes it worked,' in manner of Conservative Party, and – in sharp contrast to them – everyone will believe me and think I am marvellous. Oh dear, though, is 9 o'clock. Will go tonight instead. Where the fuck is Gary?

Later. In office. Haha! Aahahahaha! Was marvellous at work today.

'So,' said Richard Finch, when we were all assembled round the table. 'Bridget. Tony Blair. Women's committees. New policies with Women in Mind, any suggestions? Nothing to do with Colin Firth if you can possibly manage it.'

I smiled beatifically, glancing down at my notes, then looked up with poise and confidence.

'Tony Blair should introduce a code of Dating Practice for Singletons,' I said eventually.

There was a jealous pause from all the other researchers round the table.

'That's it, is it?' said Richard Finch.

'Yup,' I said confidently.

'You don't think,' he said, 'that our potential new

Prime Minister might have better things to do with his time?'

'Just think of the number of working hours lost through distraction, sulks, discussions to interpret situations and waiting for the phone to ring,' I said. 'It must be easily on a par with back pain. Also, all other cultures have specific dating rituals, but we are operating in an ill-defined sea with men and women increasingly alienated from each other.'

At this, Horrid Harold let out a snort of derision.

'Oh God,' drawled Patchouli, lounging with her Lycra cycle-shorted legs all over the table. 'You can't proscribe people's emotional behaviour. That's fascism.'

'No, no, Patchouli, you haven't been listening,' I said strictly. 'These would be just guidelines for sexual good manners. Since a quarter of all households are single, it would significantly help the nation's mental wellbeing.'

'I really think, in the run up to the election . . .' Horrid Harold sneerily began.

'No, wait,' said Richard Finch chewing, twitching his leg up and down and looking at us oddly. 'How many of you are married?'

Everyone stared foolishly at the table.

'So it's just me, is it?' he said. 'Just me who's holding together the tattered shreds of the fabric of British society?'

Everyone tried not to look at Saskia, the researcher Richard had been shagging all summer till he abruptly lost interest and started on the sandwich girl.

'Mind you, I'm not surprised,' he went on. 'Who'd marry any of you? You're incapable of committing to fetching the cappuccinos let alone to one person for the rest of your lives.' At this Saskia let out a strange noise and shot out of the office.

Did a great deal of research all morning, making phone calls and talking to people. Was actually quite interesting that even those researchers who had pooh-poohed whole thing kept on coming out with suggestions.

'OK, Bridget,' said Richard Finch just before lunch. 'Let's hear this ground-breaking, great *oeuvre*.'

Explained that Rome was not built in a day, and obviously had not completed whole work yet but these were lines was working along. I cleared my throat and began:

'***Code of Dating Practice***

1) If citizens know they do not want to go out with someone else they must not egg them on in the first place.
2) When a man and woman decide they would like to sleep together, if either party knows they just want a "fling" this should be clearly stated beforehand.
3) If citizens snog or shag other citizens they must not pretend nothing is going on.
4) Citizens must not go out with other citizens for years and years but keep on saying they don't want to get too serious.
5) After sexual relations it is definitely bad manners not to stay the night.'

'But what if . . .' rudely interrupted Patchouli.

'*Could* I just finish?' I said graciously and authoritatively as if I were Michael Heseltine and Patchouli were Jeremy Paxman. I then ran through the rest of the list adding, 'Also, if governments are going to go on about family values then they have to do something more positive for Singletons than slagging them off.' I paused, shuffling my papers pleasantly. 'Here are my proposals:

Smug Marriage Promotional Suggestions

1) Teach *Men are from Mars, Women are from Venus* in schools so both sides of opposing armies understand each other.
2) Teach all boy children that sharing the housework does not mean twiddling one fork under the tap.
3) Form giant Government Matchmaking Agency for Singletons, with strict Code of Dating Practice, Mate-Seekers Allowance for drinks, phone calls, cosmetics etc., penalties for Emotional Fuckwittage and rule that you have to go on at least 12 government-arranged dates before you can declare yourself a Singleton; and only then if have reasonable grounds for rejecting all 12.
4) If grounds are deemed unreasonable, then you have to declare yourself a Fuckwit.'

'Oh Christ,' said Horrid Harold. 'I mean I really do think the issue is the Euro.'

'No, this is good, this is ver-y good,' said Richard, staring fixedly at me, at which Harold looked as though he'd eaten a pigeon. 'I'm thinking live studio discussion. I'm thinking Harriet Harman, I'm thinking Robin Cook. I'm maybe even thinking Blair. Right, Bridget. Move. Set this up. Get Harman's office on the phone and get her in tomorrow, then try Blair.'

Hurrah. Am head researcher on lead item. Everything is going to change for me and for the nation!

7 p.m. Humph. Harriet Harman has never rung back. And neither has Tony Blair. Item is cancelled.

Tuesday 29 April

Cannot believe Gary the Builder. Have left him a message every day this week and nothing. No reply. Maybe he's sick or something. Also keep getting whiff of really horrible smell on stairs.

Wednesday 30 April

Hmm. Just got home from work and hole has been covered up with big sheet of polythene but no note, no message, nothing about giving me the £3,500 back. Nothing. Wish Mark would ring.

8

Oh Baby

Thursday 1 May

9st 2, alcohol units 5 (but celebrating New Labour victory), contribution to New Labour victory – other than alcohol units – 0.

6.30 p.m. Hurrah! Really there is a fantastic atmosphere today: election days are one of the few occasions when you realize it is we, the people, who are in charge and the government are just our mutatedly bloated, arrogant pawns and now our time has come to stand together and wield our power.

7.30 p.m. Just got back from shop. Is amazing out there. Everyone spilling out of the pubs completely drunk. Really feel part of something. It is not just that people want a change. No. It is a great rising up of we, the nation, against all the greed, lack of principles and of respect for real people and their problems and . . . Oh goody, telephone.

7.45 p.m. Humph. Was Tom.

'Have you voted yet?'

'Actually I was just on my way,' I said.

'Oh yes. To which voting station?'

'The one round the corner.'

Hate it when Tom gets like this. Just because he used to be a member of Red Wedge and go round singing 'Sing If You're Glad to be Gay' in a morbid voice, there is no need for him to behave like the Spanish Inquisition.

'And which candidate will you be voting for?'

'Um,' I said, looking frantically out of the window for red signs on the lamp-posts. 'Buck!'

'Go on then,' he said. 'Remember Mrs Pankhurst.'

Honestly, who does he think he is – the three line whip or something? Obviously I am going to vote. Better get changed, though. I do not look very lefty in this.

8.45 p.m. Just back from polling station. 'Do you have your voting card?' bossy whippersnapper asked. What voting card? That's what I want to know. Turned out I was not registered on any of their lists even though I have been paying poll tax for bloody years so have to go to another voting station. Just come back for *A–Z*.

9.30 p.m. Humph. Was not bloody well registered there either. Have to go to some library or other miles away. Mind you, is great being out on the streets tonight. We, the people, uniting for change. Yesssss! Wish had not worn platforms though. Wish, also, did not keep getting whiff of horrible smell on stairs every time I go out.

10.30 p.m. Cannot believe what has happened. I have let down Tony Blair and my country through no fault of my own. Turned out, although flat was on list, am not registered to vote, even though I had Community Charge book with me. Honestly, all that fuss about not having the vote if you don't pay your poll tax and turns out you do not have vote even if you do.

'Did you fill the form in last October?' said self-important baggage in ruffly-collared shirt and brooch, enjoying crazed moment of glory just because she happened to be in charge of table in voting station.

'Yes!' I lied. Obviously people who live in flats cannot be expected to open every boring brown envelope addressed 'To The Occupant' which plops through the door. What if Buck loses by one vote then entire election lost by one seat? Will be my fault, my fault. Walk to Shazzer's from polling station was hideous walk of shame. Also cannot wear platforms now as feet too crippled so will look short.

2.30 a.m. Argor was blurbrill party. DaviMellor. Out! Out! Out! Oops.

Friday 2 May

9st 3 (hurrah! New-born New Labour pound first of new era).

8 a.m. Hurrah! Could not be more pleased about landslide. That will be one in eye for shaming Tory-Party-Member mother and ex-boyfriend. Har har. Cannot wait to gloat. Cherie Blair is fantastic. You see, she too would probably not fit into tiny bikinis in communal changing rooms. She too has not got snooker-ball bottom yet somehow is able to obtain clothes that encompass bottom and still make her look like role model. Maybe Cherie will now use her influence over new Prime Minister, who will order all clothes shops to start producing clothes that will fit attractively over everyone's arses.

Worry, though, that New Labour will be like having a crush on someone, finally being able to go out with them and then when you have your first row it is cataclysmically awful. But then Tony Blair is the first Prime Minister I can completely imagine having voluntary sex with. Actually Shaz had a theory last night that the reason he and Cherie were always touching each other was not the spin doctors but that Cherie was becoming increasingly aroused as the landslides came in – the aphrodisiac of power or . . . Ooh, telephone.

'Oh, hello, darling, guess what?' My mother.

'What?' I said smugly, preparing to gloat.

'We've won, darling. Isn't that marvellous! A landslide! Imagine!'

A cold shudder suddenly went over me. When we went to bed Peter Snow was striding marvellously but incomprehensibly about and it seemed pretty clear the swingometer was to Labour but . . . Oh-oh. Maybe we misunderstood. We were a bit squiffy and nothing made any particular sense other than all the blue Tory buildings on the map of Britain being blown up. Or maybe something happened in the night and turned it back Tory.

'And guess what?'

Is all my fault. Labour has lost and is all my fault. I and people like me who, as Tony Blair warned, had become complacent. Am not fit to call myself British citizen or woman. Doom. Dooooom.

'Bridget, are you listening to me?'

'Yes,' I whispered, mortified.

'We're having a Tony and Gordon Ladies' Night at the Rotary! Everyone's going to call each other by their first names and wear casual wear instead of ties. Merle Robertshaw's trying to put the kybosh on it because she says no one wants to come in slacks except the vicar, but actually Una and I think it's just because Percival's furious about the handguns. Then Wellington's going to give a speech. A black man speaking at the Rotary! Imagine! But you see that's the whole spirit of Labour, darling. Colours and ethical like Nelson Mandela. Geoffrey's been taking Wellington on little drives and showing him the pubs in Kettering. The other day they got stuck behind a Nelson Myers lorry full of scaffolding planks and we thought they'd had an accident!'

Trying not to think about the possible motivation behind Uncle Geoffrey's 'little drives' with Wellington, I said, 'I thought you'd just had an election party with Wellington?'

'Oh no, actually, darling, Wellington decided he didn't want to do that. He said he didn't want to pollute our culture and have Una and I jumping over fires at parties instead of handing out vol-au-vents.' I burst out laughing. 'So anyway he wants to do this speech and raise some money for his jet-ski bike.'

'What?'

'A jet-ski, darling, you know? He wants to set up a little business on the beach instead of selling shells. He says the Rotary are bound to go for it because they're supporters of business. Anyway, must whizz! Una and I are taking him to get his colours done!'

Am assured, receptive, responsive woman of substance who does not take responsibility for others' behaviour. Only for own. Yes.

Saturday 3 May

9st 2, alcohol units 2 (standard health issue to avoid heart attacks), cigarettes 5 (v.g.), calories 1,800 (v.g.), positive thoughts 4 (excellent).

8 p.m. Whole new positive mood. Sure everyone is being more courteous and giving under new Blair regime. Is surely clean sweep with broom sweeping out evils of Tory rule. Even feel different about Mark and Rebecca. Just because she is having a dinner party does not mean they are going out, does it? She is just being manipulative. Really, it is marvellous when one feels one has reached a plateau and everything just seems lovely. All things I used to think about not being attractive beyond a certain age are not true. Look at Helen Mirren and Francesca Annis.

8.30 p.m. Hmm, though. Is not very nice thought that dinner party is actually tonight. Think will read a bit of *Buddhism: The Drama of the Moneyed Monk.* Is good to calm down. Cannot expect life always to turn out well and everyone needs to nourish their soul.

8.45 p.m. Yes! You see problem is have been living in fantasy world, constantly turning to past or future instead of enjoying present moment. Am just going to sit here and enjoy present moment.

9 p.m. Not enjoying present moment at all. Is hole in wall, stink on stairs, growing overdraft in bank and Mark is at dinner party with Rebecca. Maybe will open bottle of wine and watch *ER*.

10 p.m. Wonder if Magda is back yet. She promised to call me the second she got in with full report. Sure she will say Mark is not going out with Rebecca and he was asking about me.

11.30 p.m. Have just rung Magda's babysitter. They are not back yet. Have left message to remind her to ring.

11.35 p.m. Still hasn't rung. Maybe Rebecca's dinner party is fantastic triumph and they are all still there having riotous time climaxing with Mark Darcy standing on table announcing engagement to Rebecca . . . Ooh, telephone.

'Hi, Bridge, it's Magda.'

'So how was it?' I said, too quickly.

'Oh, it was quite nice actually.'

I flinched. Totally wrong thing to say, totally.

'She'd done grilled crottin on a green salad and then *penne carbonara* only with asparagus instead of *pancetta*, which was lovely and then peaches baked in Marsala with mascarpone.'

This was terrible.

'It was obviously Delia Smith but she denied it.'

'Did she?' I said eagerly. This at least was good. He does not like people being pretentious. 'And how was Mark?'

'Oh fine. He's a really nice chap, isn't he? Terribly attractive.' Magda has no idea. No idea, none. Not to praise ex-boyfriends who have chucked one. 'Oh and then she did orange peel coated in chocolate.'

'Right,' I said patiently. I mean honestly, if this were Jude or Shazzer they would have every nuance, ready and deconstructed. 'And do you think he's going out with Rebecca?'

'Hmmm, I'm not sure. She was very flirty with him.'

Tried to remember about Buddhism and that at least have own spirit.

'Was he already there when you got there?' I said slowly and understandingly as if talking to a very confused two-year-old.

'Yes.'

'And did he leave when everyone else did?'

'Jeremy!' she suddenly yelled at the top of her voice. 'Was Mark Darcy still there when we left?'

Oh *God*.

'Mark Darcy what?' I heard Jeremy bellow, and then something else.

'Has he done it in the bed?' Magda yelled. 'A wee or a poo? IS IT A WEE OR A POO? Sorry, Bridge, I'm going to have to go.'

'Just one more thing,' I gabbled. 'Did he mention me?'

'Take it out of the bed – with your hands! Well, you can wash them, can't you? Oh for God's sake grow up. Sorry, Bridge, what was that?'

'Did he mention me?'

'Um. Um. Oh fuck off, Jeremy.'

'Well?'

'To be honest, Bridge, I don't think he did.'

Sunday 4 May

9st 2, alcohol units 5, cigarettes 9 (must stop slide into decadence), hatred poison plans to kill Rebecca 14, Buddhist shame at homicidal thoughts: extensive, Catholic guilt (even though not Catholic): growing.

My flat. Very bad day. Went round to Jude's earlier in zomboid state. She and Shaz were going on and on saying I had to get back on some kind of horse and started – frankly insultingly – leafing through the *Time Out* Lonely Hearts.

'I don't want to look at Lonely Hearts,' I said indignantly. 'It's not that bad.'

'Er, Bridget,' said Sharon coldly. 'Weren't you the one that wanted Tony Blair to set up dating agencies for Singletons? I thought we agreed that political integrity was important.'

'Oh my God, this is outrageous.' Jude was reading out loud, shoving large pieces of a leftover Crunchie Easter Egg into her mouth. '"Genuine tall attractive male 57, GSOH, WLTM civilized, married luscious lady 20–25 for discreet uninhibited no-commitment relationship." Who do they think they are, these creeps?'

'What's GSOH and WLTM?' I said.

'Giant sore on head. Willy limp, thin mollusc?' suggested Sharon.

'Great sex on horse with little tiny mouse?' I wondered.

'It means: Good Sense of Humour, Would Like to Meet,' said Jude, suspiciously suggesting she might have done this before.

'I suppose you'd have to have a sense of humour to be too mean to fork out enough to say so in genuine words,' sniggered Sharon.

Talking Hearts turned out to be v. entertaining. You can actually ring up and *hear* the people advertising themselves like contestants on *Blind Date*.

'Right. My name's Barret and if you'll be my sugar and spice, I'll give *you* champers on ice.'

Is not very cool to start message saying 'Right' thereby giving impression of huge build-up to scary message-leaving, even though obviously is scary.

'My work is thoughtful, fulfilling and rewarding and I'm interested in all the usual kind of things – magic, occult, paganism.'

'I'm handsome, I'm very passionate. I'm a writer and I'm looking for a very special leading laydee. She'll take pleasure in having a good body, I'll be at least ten years older than her and she'll like that.'

'Pah!' said Shazzer. 'I'm going to ring some of these sexist bastards up.'

Shazzer was in seventh heaven putting them on speaker phone then murmuring sexily, 'Hello, is that "First Time Advertised" on the line? Well, get off it quickly there's a train coming.' Not very mature admittedly, but seemed amusing with all Chardonnay in selves.

'"Hi, I'm Wild Boy. I'm tall, I'm Spanish with long

black hair, dark eyes, long black lashes and a lean, wild body . . ."' I read out in a stupid voice.

'Ooh!' said Jude brightly. 'He sounds rather nice.'

'Well, why don't you call him then?' I said.

'No!' said Jude.

'So why are you trying to get me to ring someone?'

Jude went all coy then. Turned out whole Stacey, Singleton Depression weekend thing had catapulted her into returning one of Vile Richard's calls.

'Oh God,' said Shazzer and I simultaneously.

'I'm not going back out with him or anything. It's just . . . nice,' she finished lamely, trying to avoid my and Shazzer's accusing stares.

Got back home to hear answerphone clicking on. 'Hello, Bridget,' said deep, sexy, foreign *young-sounding* voice. 'This is Wild Boy . . .'

Bloody girls must have given him my number. Horrified by sense of danger implied by total stranger having phone number, did not pick up but merely listened while Wild Boy explained he will be in 192 tomorrow night holding a red rose.

Then immediately called Shazzer and gave her bollocking.

'Oh come on,' said Shaz. 'Let's all go. It'll be a laugh.'

So plan is, we are all going tomorrow night. Ho hum. What am I going to do about hole in wall and stench on stairs? Bloody Gary! He's got £3,500 of mine. Right. Am going to bloody well ring him up.

Monday 5 May

9st 1 (hurrah!), progress on hole in wall by Gary: none, progress on getting over Mark Darcy by fantasizing about Wild Boy: medium (hampered by eyelashes).

Got back to message from Gary. Said he got caught up on another job and as I was having second thoughts he thought there was no hurry. Claims he is going to sort everything out and come round tomorrow night. So you see, was worrying unnecessarily. Mmmm. Wild Boy. Maybe Jude and Shazzer are right. Have just to move on, not keep imagining Mark and Rebecca in different loving scenarios. Worry about lashes, though. How long, exactly? Fantasies of Wild Boy's lean, wild, devil body slightly spoilt by image of Wild Boy blinking under the weight of lengthy lashes like Walt Disney Bambi.

9 p.m. Got to 192 at 8.05, with Jude and Shaz in tow to sit at other table and keep eye on self. No sign of Wild Boy. Only man on own was horrible old creep in denim shirt, ponytail and sunglasses who kept staring at me. Where was Wild Boy? Gave creep filthy look. Eventually creep was staring so much decided to move. Started to get up then nearly jumped out of skin. Creep was holding up red rose. Stared at him aghast as he removed ridiculous sunglasses, smirking, to reveal Barbara Cartland-like pair of false eyelashes. Creep was Wild Boy. Rushed out in horror followed by Jude and Shazzer collapsing in giggles.

Tuesday 6 May

9st 2 (1lb phantom baby?), Mark thoughts: better, progress on hole in wall by Gary: static i.e. none.

7 p.m. V. depressed. Just left message for Tom to ask if he is mad too. Realize have to learn to love self and live in moment, not obsess but think of others and be complete in self but just feel awful. Really miss Mark so much. Cannot believe he is going to go out with Rebecca. What did I do? Obviously there is something wrong with me. Just getting older and older and is clear nothing is ever going to work out so might as well just accept am always going to be alone and never have any children. Oh look, must pull self together. Gary will be here soon.

7.30 p.m. Gary is late.

7.45 p.m. Still no sign of bloody Gary.

8 p.m. Still no Gary.

8.15 p.m. Gary has not bloody well turned up. Ooh, telephone, must be him.

8.30 p.m. Was Tom saying that he was very mad and so was the cat, which had started pooing on the carpet. Then he said something rather surprising.

'Bridge?' he said. 'Do you want to have a baby with me?'

'What?'

'A baby.'

'Why?' I said, suddenly getting alarming image of having sex with Tom.

'Well . . .' He thought for a minute. 'I'd quite like to have a baby and see my line extended but, one I'm too selfish to look after it and, two: I'm a pouf. But you'd be good at looking after it if you didn't leave it in a shop.'

Love Tom. Is as if he sort of sensed the way I'm feeling. Anyway, he said to think about it. Is just an idea.

8.45 p.m. I mean why not? Could keep it at home in a little basket. Yes! Just imagine waking up in the morning with a lovely little creature next to me to snuggle up to and love. And we could do all things together like going to the swings and Woolworth's to look at the Barbie things and home would become a lovely peaceful baby-powder smelling haven. And if Gary turns up baby could sleep in spare bedroom. Maybe if Jude and Shazzer had babies too we could live in a community together and . . . Oh shit. Have set wastebin on fire with fag end.

Saturday 10 May

9st 3 (phantom baby already gigantic, given age), cigarettes 7 (not necessary to stop for phantom pregnancy, surely?), calories 3,255 (eating for one plus tiny phantom), positive thoughts 4, progress on hole in wall by Gary: none.

11 a.m. Just been out for fags. Is suddenly, freakishly, really, really hot. Is fantastic! Some men are actually wandering round the streets in swimming trunks!

11.15 a.m. Just because it is summer is no reason life should fall into disarray with flat chaotic, in-tray ranging out of control, bad smells everywhere. (Ugh. Is really bad on stairs now.) Am going to change all this by spending today clearing up flat and doing in-tray. Must get things ordered ready to welcome new life into world.

11.30 a.m. Right. Will start by moving all piles of newspapers into one central pile.

11.40 a.m. Ugh, though.

12.15 p.m. Maybe will do in-tray first.

12.20 p.m. Clearly impossible without getting properly dressed.

12.25 p.m. Not keen on look in shorts. Too sporty somehow. Need little slippy dress thing.

12.35 p.m. Now where is it?

12.40 p.m. Just needs washing through and hanging out to dry. Then can get on.

12.55 p.m. Hurrah! Am going swimming to Hampstead Ponds with Jude and Shazzer! Have not done legs but Jude says pond is ladies only and teeming with lesbians who consider it mark of gay pride to be as hairy as yetis. Hurrah!

Midnight. Was fantastic at ponds, like painting of sixteenth-century nymphs only rather more of them than would expect in Dorothy Perkins swimsuits. V. old-fashioned, with wooden decking and lifeguards. Swimming in natural environment with mud on bottom* totally new sensation.

Told them what Tom had said about the Babyfather idea.

'My God!' said Shaz. 'Well, I think it's a good idea. Except that on top of "Why aren't you married?" you'd have "Who's the father?" to contend with.'

'I could say it was an immaculate conception,' I suggested.

'I think all this would be extremely selfish,' said Jude coldly.

There was a stunned pause. We peered at her, trying to work out what was going on.

'Why?' said Shaz eventually.

'Because a child needs two parents. You would be doing it to satisfy yourself when actually you're just too selfish to have a relationship.'

Blimey. I could see Shaz taking out a sub-machine gun and gunning her down. Next thing Shaz was off on one, ranting away with a no-holds-barred sphere of eclectic cultural reference.

'Look at the Caribbean,' she ranted while the other girls looked round in alarm and I thought, mmm. Caribbean. Lovely luxury hotel and white sand.

'The womenfolk bring the children up in compounds,' Shaz declared. 'And the men just turn up sometimes and

* bottom of pond, not own bottom

shag them, and now the women are getting economic power and there are pamphlets saying "Men at Risk" because they're losing their role just like they are ALL OVER THE FUCKING WORLD.'

Sometimes wonder if Sharon really is quite such a Ph.D.-style authority on, well, everything, as she pretends to be.

'A child needs two parents,' said Jude doggedly.

'Oh for God's sake that's a completely narrow, paternalistic, unrealistic, partisan Smug-Middle-Class-Married-Parent view,' hissed Shaz. 'Everyone knows a third of all marriages end in divorce.'

'Yes!' I said. 'Being with one mother who loves you is bound to be better than being the product of a bitter divorce. Children need relationships and life and people around but it doesn't have to be a husband.' Then suddenly remembering something my – ironically enough – mother always comes out with I said, 'You can't spoil a child by loving it.'

'Well, there's no need to gang up on me about it,' said Jude huffily, 'I'm only giving my view. Anyway, I've got something to tell you.'

'Oh yeah? What?' said Shaz. 'You believe in keeping human slaves?'

'Vile Richard and I are getting married.'

Shazzer and I gawped in mute horror as Jude looked down, blushing winningly.

'I know, isn't it wonderful? I think when I chucked him the last time he realized you don't know what you've got till it's gone – and that finally jerked him into being able to commit!'

'Finally jerked him into realizing he'd have to get a

bloody job if he couldn't live off you any more, more like,' muttered Shaz.

'Er, Jude,' I said. 'Did you just say you were going to marry Vile Richard?'

'Yes,' said Jude. 'And I wondered – will you two be bridesmaids?'

Sunday 11 May

9st 2 (phantom baby departed in horror at impending wedding), alcohol units 3, cigarettes 15 (may as well smoke and drink freely now), Mark fantasies 2 only (excellent).

Shaz just called and both agreed that whole thing is doom. Doom. And that Jude must not marry Vile Richard because:

a) He is mad.
b) He is vile: Vile by name and vile by nature.
c) Is intolerable to have to dress up as pink puffballs and walk down aisle with everybody watching.

Am going to call Magda and tell her.

'What do you think?' I said.

'Hmm. It doesn't seem like a very promising idea. But you know, people's relationships are quite mysterious,' she said enigmatically. 'No one from the outside ever really understands what makes them work.'

Conversation then moved on to the Babymother idea at which Magda unaccountably seemed to brighten.

'You know what, Bridge? I think you should try it out first, I really do.'

'What do you mean?'

'Well, why don't you look after Constance and Harry for an afternoon and see how it goes. I mean I've often thought time-share was the answer for modern woman-hood.'

Blimey. Have promised to have Harry, Constance and the baby next Saturday while she has her highlights done. Also she and Jeremy are having a garden party in six weeks' time for Constance's birthday and she asked if I wanted her to invite Mark. I said yes. You see he has not seen me since February and it will be really good for him to see how I have changed and how calm and poised and full of inner strength I am now.

Monday 12 May

Got into work to find Richard Finch in a foul hyperactive mood, jumping around the room chewing and shouting at everyone. (Sexy Matt, who was looking particularly like a DKNY model this morning, told Horrid Harold he thought that Richard Finch was on cocaine.)

Anyway, it turned out the channel controller had turned down Richard's idea to replace the breakfast news slot with live 'warts and all' coverage of the Sit Up Britain team's morning meeting. Considering the Sit Up Britain's last morning 'meeting' consisted of an argument about which of our presenters was going to cover the lead story; and the lead story was about which presenters were going to be presenting the BBC and ITV news, I don't think it would have been a very interesting programme; but Rich-ard was really pissed off about it.

'Do you know what's the trouble with the news?' he was saying, taking his gum out of his mouth and flinging it in the vague direction of the bin. 'It's boring. Boring, boring, bloody boring.'

'Boring?' I said. 'But we're just seeing the launch of the first Labour government for . . . for several years!'

'My God,' he said, whipping off his Chris Evans-type glasses. 'Have we got a new Labour government? Have we really? Everyone! Everyone! Gather round. Bridget's got a scoop!'

'And what about the Bosnian Serbs?'

'Oh wake up and smell the de-caf cap,' whined Patchouli. 'So they want to carry on shooting at each other behind bushes? So? It's just so, like, five minutes ago.'

'Yeah, yeah, yeah,' said Richard with mounting excitement. 'People don't want dead Albanians in headscarves, they want people. I'm thinking *Nationwide*. I'm thinking Frank Bough, I'm thinking skateboarding ducks.'

So now we all have to think up Human Interest like snails that get drunk or old people going bunjee jumping. I mean how are we supposed to organize a geriatric bunjee jump by . . . Ah, telephone! That'll be the Mollusc and Small Amphibian Association.

'Oh, hello, darling, guess what?'

'Mum,' I said dangerously, 'I've told you . . .'

'Oh I know, darling. I just rang to tell you something very sad.'

'What?' I said sulkily.

'Wellington's going home. His speech at the Rotary was fantastic. Absolutely fantastic. Do you know, when he talked about the conditions the children in his tribe live in Merle Robertshaw was actually crying! Crying!'

'But I thought he was raising money for a jet-ski bike.'

'Oh he is, darling. But he came up with this marvellous scheme which is right up the Rotary's street. He said if they donated money he'd not only give the Kettering branch a ten per cent share in the profits, but if they'd give half of that to his village school he'd match it with another five per cent of his profits. Charity and small business – isn't that clever? Anyway they raised four hundred pounds and he's going back to Kenya! He's going to build a new school! Imagine! Just because of us! He did a lovely slide show with Nat King Cole's "Nature Boy" underneath it. And at the end he said "*Hakuna Matata!*", and we've adopted it as our motto!'

'That's great!' I said, then saw Richard Finch staring crossly in my direction.

'Anyway, darling, we thought you—'

'Mum,' I interrupted, 'do you know any old people who do interesting things?'

'Honestly, what a silly question. All old people do interesting things. Look at Archie Garside – you know Archie – who used to be deputy spokesman on the governors. He's a parachute jumper. In actual fact I think he's doing a sponsored parachute jump for the Rotary tomorrow and he's ninety-two. A ninety-two-year-old parachute jumper! Imagine!'

Half an hour later I set off towards Richard Finch's desk, a smug smile playing about my lips.

6 p.m. Hurrah! Everything is lovely! Am completely back in Richard Finch's good books and am going off to Kettering to film parachute jump. And not only that, but I am going to direct it, and it is going to be the lead item.

Tuesday 13 May

Do not want to be stupid TV career woman any more. Is heartless profession. Had forgotten the nightmare of TV crews when allowed to interact freely with trusting media-virgin members of the public. Was not allowed to direct the item as deemed too complex, so was left on the ground while bossy career-crazed Greg was sent up in the plane to do it. Turned out Archie did not want to jump as could not see a good landing spot. But Greg went on and on saying, 'Come on, mate, we're losing the light,' and eventually pressurized him to jump towards a soft-looking ploughed field. Unfortunately, however, it wasn't a ploughed field, it was a sewerage works.

Saturday 17 May

9st 3, alcohol units 1, cigarettes 0, dashed baby-fantasies 1, dashed Mark Darcy fantasies: all the ones about him seeing self again realizing how changed, poised i.e. thin, well-dressed, etc. am, and falling in love with self again 472.

Completely exhausted by working week. Almost too drained to get out of bed. Wish could get someone to go downstairs and fetch paper, also chocolate croissant and cappuccino. Think will stay in bed, read *Marie Claire*, and do nails, then maybe see if Jude and Shazzer fancy going to Jigsaw. Would really like to get something new for when see Mark again next week, as if to stress am changed . . . Gaaah! Doorbell. Who in their right mind would ring on someone's doorbell at 10 o'clock on Saturday morning? Are they completely insane?

Later. Staggered to entryphone. It was Magda, who shouted chirpily, 'Say hello to Auntie Bridget!'

Lurched in horror, dimly remembering offer to spend Saturday taking Magda's infants to the swings while she spends day having hair done and lunching with Jude and Shazzer like single girl.

Panicking, I pressed the buzzer, flung on only dressing gown could find – unsuitable, v. short, translucent – and started running round the flat to remove ashtrays, mugs of vodka, broken glass etc., etc.

'Fwoff. Here we are! I'm afraid Harry's got a bit of a snuffle, haven't we?' crooned Magda, clunking up the stairs, festooned with pushchairs and bags like a homeless person. 'Ooof. What's that smell?'

Constance, my goddaughter, who is three next week, said she had brought me a present. She seemed very pleased indeed with her gift choice and sure that I would like it. Unwrapped it excitedly. It was a fireplace catalogue.

'I think she thought it was a magazine,' whispered Magda.

Demonstrated massive delight. Constance beamed smugly and gave me a kiss, which I liked, then sat down happily in front of the *Pingu* video.

'Sorry. I'm going to have to dump and dash, I'm late for my highlights,' said Magda. 'There's everything you need in the bag under the pram. Don't let them fall out of the hole in the wall.'

It all seemed fine. The baby was asleep, Harry, who is nearly one, was sitting in the double pushchair next to him, holding a very battered rabbit and looking as if he was about to fall asleep too. But the second the door slammed downstairs, Harry and the baby began to scream blue murder, writhing and kicking when I tried to pick them up, like violent deportees.

Found self trying to do anything (though obviously not gagging with tape) to make them stop: dancing, waving and pretending to blow imaginary trumpet to no avail.

Constance looked up solemnly from the video, removing her own bottle from her mouth. 'They're probably thirsty,' she said. 'You can see through your nightie.'

Humiliated at being out-earth-mothered by someone not quite three, I found the bottles in the bag, handed them over and sure enough both babies stopped crying and sat there sucking, busily watching me from beneath lowered brows as if I were someone very nasty from the Home Office.

I tried to slip next door to put some clothes on, at which they took the bottles out and started yelling again. Finally, I ended up dressing in the sitting room while they watched intently as if I were a bizarre reverse striptease artist.

After forty-five minutes of Gulf War-style operation to get them, plus the prams and bags, downstairs, we reached the street. Was very nice when we got to the swings. Harry, as Magda says, has not mastered the human language yet but Constance developed a very sweet, all-adults-together confidential tone with me, saying, 'I think he wants to go on the swing,' when he talked gibberish, and when I bought a packet of Minstrels saying solemnly, 'I don't think we'd better tell people about this.'

Unfortunately, for some reason when we got to the front door, Harry started sneezing and a huge web of projectile green snot seemed to fly into the air then flop back over his face like something from *Dr Who*. Constance then gagged in horror and threw up on my hair and the baby started screaming, which set the other two off. Desperately trying to calm the situation, I bent down, wiped the snot off Harry, and put his dummy back into his mouth while beginning a soothing rendition of 'I Will Always Love You'.

For a miraculous second, there was silence. Thrilled with my gifts as a natural mother, I launched into a second verse, beaming into Harry's face, at which he abruptly pulled the dummy out of his mouth and shoved it into mine.

'Hello again,' said a manly voice as Harry started to scream once more. I turned round, dummy in mouth and sick all over hair to find Mark Darcy looking extremely puzzled.

'They're Magda's,' I said eventually.

'Ah, I thought it was all a bit quick. Or a very well-kept secret.'

'Who's that?' Constance put her hand in mine, looking up at him suspiciously.

'I'm Mark,' he said. 'I'm Bridget's friend.'

'Oh,' she said, still looking suspicious.

'She's got the same expression as you anyway,' he said, looking at me in a way I couldn't fathom. 'Can I give you a hand upstairs?'

Ended up with me carrying the baby and holding Constance's hand and Mark bringing the pushchair and holding Harry's hand. For some reason neither of us could speak, except to the children. But then I was aware of voices on the stairs. Rounded the corner and there were two policemen emptying the hall cupboard. They'd had a complaint from next door about the smell.

'You take the children upstairs, I'll deal with this,' said Mark quietly. Felt like Maria in *The Sound of Music* when they've been singing in the concert and she has to get the children into the car while Captain Von Trapp confronts the Gestapo.

Talking in a cheery, fraudulently confident whisper, I put the *Pingu* video back on, gave them all some sugar-free Ribena in their bottles and sat on the floor between them, which they seemed more than contented about.

Then policeman appeared clutching a holdall I recognized as mine. He pulled a polythene bag of stinking blood-smeared flesh accusingly from the zip pocket with his gloved hand and said, 'Is this yours, miss? It was in the hall cupboard. Could we ask you a few questions?'

I got up, leaving the children staring rapt at *Pingu* as Mark appeared in the doorway.

'As I said, I'm a lawyer,' he said pleasantly to the young policemen, with just the merest steely hint of 'so you'd better watch what you're doing' in his voice.

Just then the phone rang.

'Shall I get that for you, miss?' said one of the officers suspiciously, as if it might be my bits-of-dead-person supplier. I just couldn't work out how blood-stained flesh had got in my bag. The policeman put the phone to his ear, looked completely terrified for a moment, then shoved the phone at me.

'Oh, hello, darling, who's that? Have you got a man in the house?'

Suddenly the penny dropped. The last time I used that bag was when I went to Mum and Dad's for lunch.

'Mother,' I said, 'when I came down for lunch, did you put anything in my bag?'

'Yes, in actual fact I did, come to mention it. Two pieces of fillet steak. And you never said thank you. In the zip pocket. I mean as I was saying to Una, it's not cheap isn't fillet steak.'

'Why didn't you tell me?' I hissed.

Finally managed to get a totally un-penitent mother to confess to the policemen. Even then they started saying they wanted to take the fillet steak off for analysis and maybe hold me for questioning at which Constance started crying, I picked her up, and she put her arm round my neck, holding on to my jumper as if I were about to be wrested from her and thrown in a pit with bears.

Mark just laughed, put his hand on one of the policemen's shoulder and said, 'Come on, boys. It's a couple of pieces of fillet steak from her mother. I'm sure there's better things you could be doing with your time.'

The policemen looked at each other, and nodded, then they started closing their notebooks and picking their helmets up. Then the main one said, 'OK, Miss Jones, just keep an eye on what your mother puts in your bag in future. Thanks for your help, sir. Have a good evening. Have a good evening, miss.'

There was a second's pause when Mark stared at the hole in the wall, looking unsure what to do, then he suddenly said, 'Enjoy *Pingu*,' and bolted off down the stairs after the policemen.

Wednesday 21 May

9st 1, alcohol units 3 (v.g.), cigarettes 12 (excellent), calories 3,425 (off food), progress of hole in wall by Gary 0, positive thoughts about furnishing fabric as special-occasion-wear look 0.

Jude has gone completely mad. Just went round to her house to find entire place strewn with bridal magazines, lace swatches, gold-sprayed raspberries, tureen and grapefruit-knife brochures, terracotta pots with weeds in and bits of straw.

'I want a gurd,' she was saying. 'Or is it a yurd? Instead of a marquee. It's like a nomad's tent in Afghanistan with rugs on the floor, and I want long-stemmed patinated oil-burners.'

'What are you wearing?' I said, leafing through pictures of embroidered stick-thin models with flower arrangements on their heads and wondering whether to call an ambulance.

'I'm having it made. Abe Hamilton! Lace and lots of cleavage.'

'What cleavage?' muttered Shaz murderously.

'That's what they should call *Loaded* magazine.'

'I'm sorry?' said Jude coldly.

'"What Cleavage?"' I explained. 'Like *What Car?*'

'It's not *What Car?* it's *Which Car?*' said Shaz.

'Girls,' said Jude, over-pleasantly, like a gym mistress about to make us stand in the corridor in our gym knickers, 'can we get on?'

Interesting how 'we' had crept in. Suddenly was not Jude's wedding but our wedding and we were having to do all these lunatic tasks like tying straw round 150 patinated oil-burners and going away to a health farm to give Jude a shower.

'Can I just say something?' said Shaz.

'Yes,' said Jude.

'DON'T BLOODY MARRY VILE RICHARD. He's an unreliable, selfish, idle, unfaithful fuckwit from hell. If you marry him, he'll take half your money and run off with a bimbo. I know they have the pre-nuptial agreements but . . .'

Jude went all quiet. Suddenly realized – feeling her shoe hit my shin – I was supposed to back Shazzie up.

'Listen to this,' I said hopefully, reading from the *Bride's Wedding Guide*. '"Best Man: the groom should ideally choose a level-headed responsible person . . ."'

I looked round smugly as if to prove Shaz's point but the response was chilly. 'Also,' said Shaz, 'don't you think a wedding puts too much pressure on a relationship? I mean it's not exactly playing hard to get, is it?'

Jude breathed in deeply through her nose while we watched, on tenterhooks.

'Now!' she said eventually, looking up with a brave smile. 'The bridesmaids' duties!'

Shaz lit a Silk Cut. 'What are we wearing?'

'Well!' gushed Jude. 'I think we should have them made. And look at this!' It was an article entitled '50 Ways to Save Money on the Big Day'. '"For bridesmaids, furnishing fabrics can work surprisingly well"!'

Furnishing fabrics?

'You see,' Jude was going on, 'with the guest list it says, don't feel you have to invite guest's new partners – but the minute I mentioned it she said, "Oh *we'd* love to come."'

'Who?' I said.

'Rebecca.'

I looked at Jude, dumbstruck. She wouldn't. She wouldn't expect me to walk down the aisle dressed as a sofa while Mark Darcy sat with Rebecca, would she?

'And I mean they have asked me to go on holiday with them. Not that I would go, of course. But I think Rebecca was a bit hurt that I hadn't told her before.'

'What?' exploded Shazzer. 'Have you no concept of the meaning of the word "girlfriend"? Bridget's your best friend joint with me, and Rebecca has shamelessly stolen Mark, and instead of being tactful about it, she's trying to hoover everyone into her revolting social web so he's so woven in he'll never get away. And you're not taking a bloody stand. That's the trouble with the modern world – everything's forgivable. Well, it makes me sick, Jude. If that's the sort of friend you are you can walk down the aisle with Rebecca behind you wearing Ikea curtains and not us. And then see how you like it. And you can stuff your yurd, gurd, turd or whatever it is up your bum!'

So now Sharon and I are not speaking to Jude. Oh dear. Oh dear.

9

Social Hell

Sunday 22 June

9st 3, alcohol units 6 (felt I owed it to Constance), cigarettes 5 (v.g.), calories 2,455 (but mainly items covered in orange icing), escaped barn animals 1, attacks on self by children 2.

Yesterday was Constance's birthday party. Arrived about an hour late and made my way through Magda's house, following the sound of screaming into the garden where a scene of unbridled carnage was underway with adults chasing after children, children chasing rabbits and, in the corner, a little fence behind which were two rabbits, a gerbil, an ill-looking sheep and a pot-bellied pig.

I paused at the French windows, looking around nervously. Heart lurched when located him, standing on his own, in traditional Mark Darcy party mode, looking detached and distant. He glanced towards the door where I was standing and for a second we were locked in each other's gaze before he gave me a confused nod, then looked away. Then I noticed Rebecca crouched down beside him with Constance.

'Constance! Constance! Constance!' Rebecca was cooing,

waving a Japanese fan in her face at which Constance was glowering and blinking crossly.

'Look who's come!' said Magda, bending down to Constance and pointing across at me.

A surreptitious smile crept across Constance's face and she set off determinedly, if slightly wobbly, towards me, leaving Rebecca looking foolish with the fan. I bent down when she got near and she put her arm round my neck and pressed her little hot face against mine.

'Have you brought me a present?' she whispered.

Relieved that this blatant example of cupboard love was inaudible to anyone but me I whispered, 'Might have done.'

'Where is it?'

'In my bag.'

'Shall we go and get it?'

'Oh, isn't that sweet?' I heard Rebecca coo and looked up to see her and Mark watching as Constance took me by the hand and led me into the cool of the house.

Was quite pleased with Constance's present actually, a packet of Minstrels and a pink Barbie tutu with a gold and pink net sticking-out skirt, which had had to trawl two branches of Woolworth's to find. She liked it very much and naturally – as would any woman – wished to put it on immediately.

'Constance,' I said when we had admired it from every angle, 'were you pleased to see me because of me or because of the present?'

She looked at me under lowered brows. 'The present.'

'Right,' I said.

'Bridget?'

'Yes.'

'You know in your house?'

'Yes.'

'Why haven't you got any toys?'

'Well, because I don't really play with that *sort* of toy.'

'Oh. Why haven't you got a playroom?'

'Because I don't do that sort of playing.'

'Why haven't you got a man?'

Couldn't believe it. Had only just walked into the party and was being Smug Marrieded by someone who was three.

Had long quite serious conversation then, sitting on the stairs, about everyone being different and some people being Singletons, then heard a noise and looked up to see Mark Darcy looking down at us.

'Just, er. The loo is upstairs, I assume?' he said uninterestedly. 'Hello, Constance. How's Pingu?'

'He isn't real,' she said, glowering at him.

'Right, right,' he said. 'Sorry. Stupid of me to be so' – he looked straight into my eyes – 'gullible. Happy birthday, anyway.' Then he made his way past us without even giving me a kiss hello or anything. 'Gullible'. Did he still think I was unfaithful with Gary the Builder and the dry-cleaning man? Anyway, I thought, I don't care. It doesn't matter. Everything's fine and I'm completely over him.

'You look sad,' said Constance. She thought for a moment, then took a half-sucked Minstrel out of her mouth and put it in mine. We decided to go back outside to show off the tutu, and Constance was immediately swept up by a maniacal Rebecca.

'Ooh, look, it's a fairy. Are you a fairy? What kind of fairy are you? Where's your wand?' she gabbled.

'Great present, Bridge,' said Magda. 'Let me get you a drink. You know Cosmo, don't you?'

'Yes,' I said, heart sinking, taking in the quivering jowls of the enormous merchant banker.

'So! Bridget, great to see you!' bellowed Cosmo, eyeing me up and down leerily. 'How's work?'

'Oh, great actually,' I lied, relieved that he wasn't launching straight into my love life. How things had moved on! 'I'm working in TV now.'

'TV? Marvellous! Bloody marvellous! Are you in front of the camera?'

'Only occasionally,' I said in the sort of modest tone that suggested I was practically Cilla Black but didn't want anyone to know.

'Oh! A celebrity, eh? And' – he leaned forward in a concerned manner – 'are you getting the rest of your life sorted out?'

Unfortunately at that moment Sharon happened to be passing. She stared at Cosmo, looking like Clint Eastwood when he thinks somebody is trying to double-cross him.

'What kind of question is that?' she growled.

'What?' said Cosmo, looking round at her, startled.

'"Are you getting the rest of your life sorted out?" What do you mean by that exactly?'

'Well, ah, you know . . . when is she going to get . . . you know . . .'

'Married? So basically just because her life isn't exactly like yours you think it isn't sorted out, do you? And are you getting the rest of your life sorted out, Cosmo? How are things going with Woney?'

'Well I . . . well,' huffed Cosmo, going bright red in the face.

'Oh, I am sorry. We've obviously hit a sore spot. Come on, Bridget, before I put my big foot in it again!'

'Shazzer!' I said, when we were at a safe distance.

'Oh, come on,' she said. 'Enough, already. They just can't go around randomly patronizing people and insulting their lifestyles. Cosmo probably wishes Woney would lose four stone and stop doing that shrieking laugh all day but we don't just assume that the minute we've met him, and decide it's our business to rub it in, do we?' An evil gleam came into her eye. 'Or maybe we should,' she said, grabbing hold of my arm and changing direction back towards Cosmo, only to be confronted by Mark and Rebecca and Constance again. Oh Christ.

'Who do you think is older, me or Mark?' Rebecca was saying.

'Mark,' said Constance sulkily, looking from side to side as if planning to bolt.

'Who do you think is older, me or Mummy?' Rebecca went on playfully.

'Mummy,' said Constance disloyally, at which Rebecca gave a tinkly little laugh.

'Who do you think is older, me or Bridget?' said Rebecca, giving me a wink.

Constance looked up at me doubtfully while Rebecca beamed at her. I nodded quickly at Rebecca.

'You,' said Constance.

Mark Darcy let out a burst of laughter.

'Shall we play fairies?' Rebecca trilled, changing tack, trying to take Constance by the hand. 'Do you live in a fairy castle? Is Harry a fairy too? Where are your fairy-wairy friends?'

'Bridget,' said Constance, looking at me levelly, 'I think you'd better tell this lady I'm not really a fairy.'

Later on, as I was recounting this to Shaz, she said darkly, 'Oh God. Look who's here.'

Across the garden was Jude, radiant in turquoise, chatting to Magda but without Vile Richard.

'The girls are here!' said Magda gaily. 'Look! Over there!'

Shaz and I stared down studiously into our glasses as if we hadn't noticed. When we looked up, Rebecca was bearing down on Jude and Magda mwah-mwahing like a social-climbing literary wife who's just spotted Martin Amis talking to Gore Vidal.

'Oh Jude, I'm so happy for you, it's wonderful!' she gushed.

'I don't know what that woman's on but I want some of it,' muttered Sharon.

'Oh, you and Jeremy must come, no you must. You absolutely must,' Rebecca was going now. 'Well, bring them! Bring the children! I love children! Second weekend in July. It's my parents' place in Gloucestershire. They'll love the pool. All sorts of lovely, lovely people are coming! I've got Louise Barton-Foster, Woney and Cosmo . . .' Snow White's step-mother, Fred and Rosemary West and Caligula, I thought she might go on.

'. . . Jude and Richard, and Mark'll be there of course, Giles and Nigel from Mark's office . . .'

I saw Jude glance in our direction. 'And Bridget and Sharon?' she said.

'What?' said Rebecca.

'You've invited Bridget and Sharon?'

'Oh.' Rebecca looked flustered. 'Well, of course, I'm

not sure we've got enough bedrooms but I suppose we could use the cottage.' Everyone stared at her. 'Yes, I have!' She looked round wildly. 'Oh, there you two are! You're coming on the twelfth, aren't you?'

'Where?' said Sharon.

'To Gloucestershire.'

'We didn't know anything about it,' said Sharon loudly.

'Well. You do now! Second weekend in July. It's just outside Woodstock. You've been before, haven't you, Bridget?'

'Yes,' I said, colouring, remembering that hideous weekend.

'So! That's great! And you're coming, Magda, so . . .'

'Um . . .' I began.

'We'd love to come,' said Sharon firmly, treading on my foot.

'What? What?' I said when Rebecca had whinnied off.

'Of course we're bloody well going,' she said. 'You're not letting her hijack all your friends just like that. She's trying to bludgeon everyone into some ridiculous social circle of suddenly-needed nearly-friends of Mark's ready for the two of them to plop into like King and Queen Buzzy-bee.'

'Bridget?' said a posh voice. I turned to see a shortish sandy-haired guy in glasses. 'It's Giles, Giles Benwick. I work with Mark. Do you remember? You were terribly helpful on the phone that night when my wife said she was leaving.'

'Oh, yes, Giles. How are you?' I said. 'How's everything going?'

'Oh, not very good, I'm afraid,' said Giles. Sharon disappeared with a backwards look, at which Giles launched into a long, detailed, and thorough account of his marital break-up.

'I so much appreciated your advice,' he said, looking at me very earnestly. 'And I did buy *Men are from Mars, Women are from Venus*. I thought it was very, very, very good, though it didn't seem to alter Veronica's point of view.'

'Well, it's more dealing with dating than divorce,' I loyally-to-the-Mars-and-Venus-concept said.

'Very true, very true,' conceded Giles. 'Tell me: have you read *You Can Heal Your Life* by Louise Hay?'

'Yes!' I said delightedly. Giles Benwick really did seem to have an extensive knowledge of the self-help book world and I was very happy to discuss the various works with him, though he did go on a bit. Eventually Magda came over with Constance.

'Giles, you really must come and meet my friend Cosmo!' she said, rolling her eyes discreetly at me. 'Bridge, would you mind looking after Constance for a mo?'

I knelt down to talk to Constance, who seemed to be worried about the aesthetic effect of chocolate smears on a tutu. Just as we had both firmly convinced ourselves that chocolate smears on pink were attractive, unusual and a positive design asset, Magda reappeared. 'I think poor old Giles's got a bit of a crush on you,' she said wryly and took Constance off for a poo. Before I'd got up again someone started smacking my bottom.

I turned round – thinking, I confess, maybe Mark Darcy! – to see Woney's son William and his friend, giggling evilly.

'Do it again,' said William and his small friend started

smacking again. Tried to get up but William – who's about six and big for his age – launched himself on to my back and wrested his arms around my neck.

'Stoppit, William,' I said with an attempt at authority but at that moment there was a commotion at the other side of the garden. The pot-bellied pig had broken free and was rushing backwards and forwards letting out a high-pitched noise. There was mayhem as parents rushed for their offspring but William was still clinging tight to my back and the boy was still smacking my bottom and shrieking with *Exorcist*-style laughter. I tried to get William off, but he was surprisingly strong and clung on. My back was really hurting.

Then suddenly William's arms were released from round my neck. I felt him being lifted away and then the smacking stopped. For a moment I just hung my head, trying to get my breath back and recover my composure. Then I turned to see Mark Darcy walking away with a writhing six-year-old boy under each arm.

For a while the party was entirely taken over by the recapturing of the pig, and Jeremy giving the petting zookeeper a bollocking. The next I saw of Mark, he was wearing his jacket and saying goodbye to Magda at which Rebecca rushed over and started saying goodbye as well. I looked away quickly and tried not to think about it. Then suddenly Mark was coming over to me.

'I'm, er, off now, Bridget,' he said. Could swear I saw him glance down at my tits. 'Don't leave with any pieces of meat in your handbag, will you?'

'No,' I said. For a moment we just looked at each other. 'Oh, thank you, thank you for . . .' I nodded to where the incident had happened.

'Not at all,' he said softly. 'Any time you want me to get a boy off your back.' And as if on cue, bloody Giles Benwick reappeared carrying two drinks.

'Oh, are you off, old boy?' he said. 'I was just about to pump Bridget for some more of her seasoned advice.'

Mark looked quickly from one of us to the other.

'I'm sure you'll be in very good hands,' he said abruptly. 'See you in the office on Monday.'

Fuck, fuck, fuck. How come nobody ever flirts with me except when Mark is around?

'Back in the old torture chambers, eh?' Giles was saying, clapping him on the back. 'On it goes. On it goes. Off you go then.'

Head was in a whirl while Giles went on and on about sending me a copy of *Feel the Fear and Do It Anyway*. He was very keen to know if Sharon and I were going to Gloucestershire on the twelfth. But the sun seemed to have gone in, there was a lot of crying and 'Mummy will smack'ing going on and everyone seemed to be leaving.

'Bridget.' It was Jude. 'Do you want to come to 192 for a . . .'

'No we don't,' snapped Sharon. 'We're going for a post-mortem.' Which was a lie as Sharon was meeting Simon. Jude looked stricken. Oh God. Bloody Rebecca has ruined bloody everything. Though must remember not to blame others but take responsibility for everything that happens to self.

Tuesday 1 July

9st 1 (is working!), progress on hole in wall by Gary 0.

I think I had better accept it now. Mark and Rebecca are an item. Is nothing I can do about it. Have been reading *The Road Less Travelled* some more and realize you can't have everything you want in life. Some of what you want but not everything you want. Is not what happens to you in life that counts but how you play the cards you are dealt. Am not going to think about the past and procession of disasters with men. Am going to think about the future. Oooh goody, telephone! Hurrah! You see!

Was Tom just ringing up for a moan. Which seemed nice. Until he said, 'Oh, by the way, I saw Daniel Cleaver earlier on tonight.'

'Oh really, where?' I trilled, in a gay yet strangled voice. Realize am new me and dating embarrassments of past – e.g., just to pluck an example out of the air, finding a naked woman on Daniel's roof last summer when was supposed to be going out with him – would never happen to new me. Even so, however, did not want spectre of Daniel humiliation rearing up alarmingly in manner of Loch Ness monster, or erection.

'In the Groucho Club,' said Tom.

'Did you talk to him?'

'Yes.'

'What did you say?' I asked dangerously. Whole point about exes is that friends should punish and ignore them, not try to get on with both sides in manner of Tony and Cherie with Charles and Diana.

'Oof. I can't remember now, exactly. I said, um: "Why were you so horrible to Bridget when she is so nice?"'

There was something about the way he said this in manner of a parrot that suggested he may not have been quoting himself strictly word for word.

'Good,' I said, 'very good.' I paused, determined to leave it at that and change the subject. I mean what do I care what Daniel said?

'So what did he say?' I hissed.

'He said,' said Tom, then started laughing. 'He said . . .'

'What?'

'He said . . .' He was practically crying with laughter now.

'What? What? WHAAAAAAAAT?'

'"How can you go out with someone who doesn't know where Germany is?"'

I let out a high-pitched hyena laugh, almost as one does when one hears one's grandmother has died and believes it to be a joke. Then the reality hit me. I clutched the side of the kitchen table, mind reeling.

'Bridge?' said Tom. 'Are you all right? I was only laughing because it's so . . . ridiculous. I mean of course you know where Germany is . . . Bridge? Don't you?'

'Yes,' I whispered weakly.

There was a long, awkward pause while I tried to come to terms with what had happened i.e. Daniel had chucked me because he thought I was stupid.

'So, then,' said Tom, brightly. 'Where is it . . . Germany?'

'Europe.'

'Yeah, but, like, where in Europe?'

Honestly. In the modern age it is not necessary to know where countries actually are since all that is required is to purchase a plane ticket to one. They do not exactly ask you at the travel agent's which countries you will be flying over before they will give you the ticket, do they?

'Just give us a ballpark position.'

'Er,' I stalled, head down, eyes flicking round the room to see if there might be an atlas at large.

'Which countries do you think Germany might be near?' he pressed on.

I thought about it carefully. 'France.'

'France. I see. So Germany is "near France", is it?'

Something about the way Tom said this made me feel I'd made some cataclysmic gaff. Then it occurred to me that Germany is of course connected to Eastern Germany and therefore it is far more likely to be close to Hungary, Russia or Prague.

'Prague,' I said. At which Tom burst out laughing.

'Anyway, there's no such thing as general knowledge any more,' I said indignantly. 'It has been proved by articles that the media has created such a great sea of knowledge that everyone cannot possibly have the same selection of it.'

'Never mind, Bridge,' said Tom. 'Don't worry about it. Do you want to see a movie tomorrow?'

11 p.m. Yes, am just going to go to movies now and read books. What Daniel may or may not have said is a matter of supreme indifference to me.

11.15 p.m. How dare Daniel go round bad-mouthing me! How did he know I don't know where Germany is? We never even went near it. Furthest we got to was Rutland Water. Huh.

11.20 p.m. Anyway, I am really nice. So there.

11.30 p.m. Am horrible. Am stupid. Am going to start studying *The Economist* and also go to evening classes and read *Money* by Martin Amis.

11.35 p.m. Harhar. Have found atlas now.

11.40 p.m. Hah! Right. I am going to ring up that bastard.

11.45 p.m. Just dialled Daniel's number.

'Bridget?' he said, before I had time to say anything.

'How did you know it was me?'

'Some surreal sixth sense,' he drawled amusedly. 'Hang on.' I heard him lighting a fag. 'So go on then.' He inhaled deeply.

'What?' I muttered.

'Tell me where Germany is.'

'It is next to France,' I said. 'And also Holland, Belgium, Poland, Czechoslovakia, Switzerland, Austria and Denmark. And it has a sea coast.'

'Which sea?'

'North Sea.'

'And?'

I stared at the atlas furiously. It didn't say the other sea.

'OK,' he said. 'One sea out of two is fine. So do you want to come round?'

'No!' I said. Honestly. Daniel is absolutely the limit. Am not going to get involved with all that again.

Saturday 12 July

20st 12 (feel like, compared to Rebecca), no. of pains in back from vile foam mattress 9, no. of thoughts involving Rebecca and natural disasters, electrical fires, floods, and professional killers: large, but proportionate.

Rebecca's house, Gloucestershire. In horrible guest cottage. Why did I come here? Why? Why? Sharon and I left it quite late and so arrived ten minutes before dinner. This did not go down very well with Rebecca, who trilled, 'Oh, we'd almost given you up for lost!' in manner of Mum or Una Alconbury.

We were staying in a servants' cottage, which I decided was good as no danger of bumping into Mark in corridors, until we got into it: is all painted green with foam rubber single beds and Formica headboards, in sharp contrast to last time was here, staying in lovely hotel-style room with own bathroom.

'Typical Rebecca,' grumbled Sharon. 'Singletons are second-class citizens. Rub it in.'

We teetered in late for dinner, feeling like a pair of garish divorcees because we'd put our make-up on so quickly. Dining room looked as breathtakingly grand as ever, with a huge inglenook fireplace at the end and twenty people sitting round an ancient oak dining table lit by silver candelabras and festooned with flower arrangements.

Mark was at the head of the table, sitting between Rebecca and Louise Barton-Foster and deep in conversation.

Rebecca appeared not to notice we'd come in. We

stood staring awkwardly at the table till Giles Benwick bellowed, 'Bridget! Over here!'

I was put between Giles and Magda's Jeremy, who seemed to have forgotten I ever went out with Mark Darcy and launched things off by going, 'So! Looks like Darcy's gone for your friend Rebecca, then. Funny because there was this bit of totty, Heather someone, friend of Barky Thompson's, who seemed to be fancying a bit of a crack at the old bugger.'

The fact that Mark and Rebecca were in earshot had clearly escaped Jeremy, but not me. I was trying to concentrate on his conversation and not listen to theirs, which had turned to a villa holiday Rebecca was organizing in Tuscany in August with Mark – as seemed to be the assumption – to which everybody simply *must* come, except presumably me and Shaz.

'What's that, Rebecca?' bellowed some terrible hooray I vaguely remembered from the skiing. Everyone looked at the fireplace where a new-looking family crest was engraved with the motto '*Per Determinam ad Victoriam*'. It was quite strange to have a crest since Rebecca's family are not members of the aristocracy but something big in estate agents Knight, Frank and Rutley.

'*Per Determinam ad Victoriam*?' roared the hooray. 'Through ruthlessness to victory. That's our Rebecca for you.'

There was a huge roar of laughter and Shazzer and I exchanged a gleeful little look.

'Actually it's through determination to success,' said Rebecca icily. Glanced up at Mark, a trace of a smile just disappearing behind his hand.

Somehow got through the meal, listening to Giles

talking very slowly and analytically about his wife and tried to keep my mind away from Mark's end of the table by sharing my self-help book knowledge.

Was desperate to get off to bed and escape the whole painful nightmare, but we all had to go through to the big room for dancing.

I started looking through the CD collection to distract me from the sight of Rebecca slowly rotating Mark round the floor, her arms round his neck, eyes darting contentedly round the room. I felt sick, but I wasn't going to show it.

'Oh, for God's sake, Bridget. Have some common sense,' said Sharon, barging up to the CDs, removing 'Jesus to a Child' and putting some frenetic garage acid medley on instead. She strode on to the floor, swept Mark away from Rebecca and started dancing with him. Actually Mark was quite funny, laughing at Shazzer's attempts to make him trendy. Rebecca looked as though she had eaten a tiramisu and only just checked the fat units.

Suddenly Giles Benwick grabbed hold of me and started to rock and roll me wildly, so I found myself being flung around the room with a fixed grin on my face, head bouncing up and down like a rag doll being shagged.

After that I literally couldn't stand it any longer.

'I'm going to have to go,' I whispered to Giles.

'I know,' he said conspiratorially. 'Shall I walk you back to the cottage?'

Managed to put him off and ended up teetering across the gravel in my Pied à Terre slingbacks and sinking gratefully into even this ludicrously uncomfortable bed. Mark is probably at this moment getting into bed with

Rebecca. Wish I was anywhere else but here: the Kettering Rotary summer fête, the Sit Up Britain morning meeting, the gym. But is own fault. I decided to come.

Sunday 13 July

22st 10, alcohol units 0, cigarettes 12 (all secret), people rescued from water accidents 1, people who shouldn't have been rescued from said water accidents but left in water to go all wrinkly 1.

Bizarre, thought-provoking day.

After breakfast, I decided to escape and wandered round the water garden, which was quite pretty, with shallow rivulets between grassy banks and under little stone bridges, surrounded by a hedge with all the fields beyond. I sat down on a stone bridge, looking at the stream, and thinking how it all didn't matter because there would always be nature, and then I heard voices approaching behind the hedge.

'. . . Worst driver in the world . . . Mother's constantly . . . correct him but . . . no concept . . . of steering accuracy. He lost his no-claims bonus forty-five years ago and never got it back since.' It was Mark. 'If I was my mother I'd refuse to go in the car with him, but they won't be parted. It's rather endearing.'

'Oh, I love that!' Rebecca. 'If I were married to someone I really loved I would want to be with them constantly.'

'Would you?' he said eagerly. Then he went on. 'I think, as you get older, then . . . the danger is if you've been single for a time, you get so locked into a network of friends – this is particularly true of women – that it hardly leaves room for a man in their lives, emotionally as much as anything because their friends and their views are their first point of reference.'

'Oh, I quite agree. For me, of course I love my friends, but they're not top of my list of priorities.'

You're telling me, I thought. There was silence, then Mark burst out again.

'This self-help book nonsense – all these mythical rules of conduct you're presumed to be following. And you just know every move you make is being dissected by a committee of girlfriends according to some breathtakingly arbitrary code made up of *Buddhism Today*, *Venus and Buddha Have a Shag* and the *Koran*. You end up feeling like some laboratory mouse with an ear on its back!'

I clutched my book, heart pounding. Surely this couldn't be how he saw what had happened with me?

But Rebecca was off on one again. 'Oh, I quite agree,' she gushed. 'I have no time for all that stuff. If I decide I love someone then nothing will stand in my way. Nothing. Not friends, not theories. I just follow my instincts, follow my heart,' she said in new simpery voice, like a flower girl-child of nature.

'I respect you for that,' said Mark quietly. 'A woman must know what she believes in, otherwise how can you believe in her yourself?'

'And trust her man above all else,' said Rebecca in yet another voice, resonant and breath-controlled, like an affected actress doing Shakespeare.

Then there was an excruciating silence. I was dying, dying frozen to the spot, assuming they were kissing.

'Of course I said all this to Jude,' Rebecca started up again. 'She was so concerned about everything Bridget and Sharon had told her about not marrying Richard – he's such a great guy – and I just said, "Jude, follow your heart."'

I gawped, looking to a passing bee for reassurance. Surely Mark couldn't be slaveringly respectful of this?

'Ye-es,' he said doubtfully. 'Well I'm not sure . . .'

'Giles seems to be very keen on Bridget!' Rebecca burst in, obviously sensing she had veered off course.

There was a pause. Then Mark said, in an unusually high-pitched voice, 'Oh really. And is . . . is this reciprocated?'

'Oh, you know Bridget,' said Rebecca airily. 'I mean Jude says she's got all these guys after her' – Good old Jude, I started to think – 'but she's so screwed up she won't – well, as you say, she can't get it together with any of them.'

'Really?' Mark jumped in. 'So have there been . . .'

'Oh, I think – you know – but she's so bogged down in her rules of dating or whatever it is that no one's good enough.'

Could not work out what was going on. Maybe Rebecca was trying to make him stop feeling guilty about me.

'Really?' said Mark again. 'So she isn't . . .'

'Oh, look, there's a duckling! Oh, look, a whole brood of ducklings! And there's the mother and father. Oh, what a perfect, perfect moment! Oh, let's go look!'

And off they went, and I was left, breathless, mind racing.

After lunch, it was boiling hot and everyone decamped

under a tree at the edge of the lake. It was an idyllic, pastoral scene: an ancient stone bridge over the water, willows overhanging the grassy banks. Rebecca was triumphant. 'Oh, this is such fun!! Isn't it, everyone? Isn't it fun?'

Fat Nigel from Mark's office was fooling about heading a football to one of the hoorays, huge stomach quivering in the bright sunlight. He made a lunge, missed and plunged head-first into the water, displacing a giant wave.

'Yesss!' said Mark, laughing. 'Breathtaking incompetence.'

'It's lovely, isn't it?' I said vaguely to Shaz. 'You expect to see lions lying down with lambs.'

'Lions, Bridget?' said Mark. I started. He was sitting right at the other side of the group, looking at me through a gap in the other people, raising one eyebrow.

'I mean like in psalm whatsit,' I explained.

'Right,' he said. There was a familiar teasing look in his eye. 'Do you think you might be thinking of the Lions of Longleat?'

Rebecca suddenly leaped to her feet. 'I'm going to jump off the bridge!'

She looked round beaming expectantly. Everyone else was in shorts or little dresses, but she was naked except for a tiny sliver of Calvin Klein brown nylon.

'Why?' said Mark.

'Because attention was diverted from her for five minutes,' breathed Sharon.

'We used to do it when we were little! It's heaven!'

'But the water's very low,' said Mark.

It was true, there was a foot and a half of baked earth all the way round the water line.

'No, no. I'm good at this, I'm very brave.'

'I really don't think you should, Rebecca,' said Jude.

'I have made up my mind. I am resolute!' she twinkled archly, slipped on a pair of Prada mules, and sashayed off towards the bridge. Happily, there was a bit of mud and grass attached to her upper right-hand buttock, which greatly added to the effect. As we watched, she took off the mules, held them in her hand and climbed on to the edge of the parapet.

Mark had got to his feet, looking worriedly at the water and up at the bridge.

'Rebecca!' he said. 'I really don't think . . .'

'It's all right, I trust my own judgement,' she said playfully, tossing her hair. Then she looked upwards, raised her arms, paused dramatically and jumped.

Everyone stared as she hit the water. The moment came when she should have reappeared. She didn't. Mark started towards the lake just as she broke the surface screaming.

He ploughed off towards her as did the other two boys. I reached in my bag for my mobile.

They pulled her to the shallows and eventually, after much writhing and crying, Rebecca came limping to shore, supported between Mark and Nigel. It was clear that nothing too terrible could have happened.

I got up and handed her my towel. 'Shall I dial 999?' I said as a sort of joke.

'Yes . . . yes.'

Everyone gathered round staring at the injured hostess's foot. She could move her toes, daintily and professionally painted in Rouge Noir, so that was a blessing.

In the end I got the number of her doctor, took the

out-of-surgery hours number from the answerphone, dialled it and handed the phone to Rebecca.

She spoke at length to the doctor, moving her foot according to his instructions and making a great range of noises, but in the end it was agreed there was no breakage, not really a sprain, just a slight jar.

'Where's Benwick?' said Nigel, as he dried himself and helped himself to a big slug of chilled white wine.

'Yes, where is Giles?' said Louise Barton-Foster. 'I haven't seen him all morning.'

'I'll go and see,' I said, grateful to get away from the hellish sight of Mark rubbing Rebecca's delicate ankle.

It was nice to get into the cool of the entrance hall with its sweeping staircase. There was a line of statues on marble plinths, oriental rugs on the flagstone floor, and another of the giant garish crests above the door. I stood for a moment, relishing the peace. 'Giles?' I said and my voice echoed round and round. 'Giles?'

There was no reply. I had no idea where his room was, so set off up the magnificent staircase.

'Giles!'

I peeked into one of the rooms and saw a gigantic carved-oak four-poster bed. The whole room was red and it looked out over the scene with the lake. The red dress Rebecca had been wearing at dinner was hanging over the mirror. I looked at the bed and felt as though I had been punched in the stomach. The Newcastle United boxer shorts I bought Mark for Valentine's Day were neatly folded on the bedspread.

I shot out of the room and stood with my back to the door, breathing unsteadily. Then I heard a moan.

'Giles?' I said. Nothing. 'Giles? It's Bridget.'

The moaning noise came again.

I walked along the corridor. 'Where are you?'

'Here.'

I pushed open the door. This room was lurid green and hideous with huge lumps of dark wood furniture everywhere. Giles was lying on his back with his head turned to one side, moaning slightly, the telephone off the hook beside him.

I sat on the bed and he opened his eyes slightly and closed them again. His glasses were skew-whiff on his face. I took them off.

'Bridget.' He was holding a bottle of pills.

I took them from him. Temazepam.

'How many have you taken?' I said, taking his hand.

'Six . . . or four?'

'When?'

'Not long . . . about . . . not long.'

'Make yourself sick,' I said, thinking that they always pumped overdosed people's stomachs.

We went together into the bathroom. It wasn't attractive, frankly, but then I gave him lots of water and he flopped back on the bed and started to sob quietly, holding my hand. He had called Veronica, his wife, it emerged groaningly, as I stroked his head. And he had lost all sense of himself and self-respect by begging her to come back, thereby undoing all his good dignified work of the last two months. At this, she'd announced she definitely wanted a divorce and he felt desperate, which I could totally relate to. As I told him, it was enough to drive anyone to the Temazepam.

There were footsteps in the corridor, a knock, and then Mark appeared in the doorway.

'Will you ring the doctor again?' I said.

'What's he taken?'

'Temazepam. About half a dozen. He's been sick.'

He stepped out in the corridor. There were more voices. I heard Rebecca go 'Oh, for God's sake!' and Mark trying to quieten her down, then more low mumbling.

'I just want everything to stop. I don't want to feel like this. I want it all just to stop,' moaned Giles.

'No, no,' I said. 'You have to have hope and confidence that everything will turn out all right, and it will.'

There were more footsteps and voices in the house. Then Mark reappeared.

He gave a half smile. 'Sorry about that.' Then he looked serious again. 'You're going to be all right, Giles. You're in good hands here. The doctor'll be round in fifteen minutes but he said nothing to worry about.'

'Are you OK?' he said to me.

I nodded.

'You're being great,' he said. 'A rather more attractive version of George Clooney. Will you stay with him till the doctor comes?'

When the doctor had finally sorted Giles out half the people seemed to have left. Rebecca was sitting tearfully in the baronial hall with her foot up, talking to Mark, and Shaz was standing at the front door, smoking a cigarette, with both our bags packed.

'It's just so inconsiderate,' Rebecca was saying. 'It's ruined the whole weekend! People should be strong and resolute, it's so . . . self-indulgent and self-obsessed. Don't just say nothing, don't you think I'm right?'

'I think we should . . . talk about it later,' said Mark.

After Shaz and I had said our goodbyes and were putting our bags in the car, Mark came out to us.

'Well done,' he barked. 'Sorry. God, I sound like a sergeant major. The surroundings are getting to me. You were great, back there, with . . . with . . . well, with both of them.'

'Mark!' Rebecca yelled. 'I've dropped my walking stick.'

'Fetch!' said Sharon.

For a split second a look of pure embarrassment flashed across Mark's face, then he recovered himself and said, 'Well, nice to see you, girls, drive safely.'

As we drove away, Shaz was giggling gleefully at the idea of Mark spending the rest of his life forced to run around after Rebecca, following her orders and fetching sticks like a puppy, but my mind was turning round and round the conversation I'd overheard behind the hedge.

10

Mars and Venus in the Dustbin

Monday 14 July

9st 4, alcohol units 4, cigarettes 12 (no longer priority), calories 3,752 (pre-diet), self-help books scheduled for dustbin 47.

8 a.m. In turmoil. Surely it cannot be that reading self-help books to improve my relationship has destroyed the whole relationship? Feel like entire life's work has been a failure. But if is one thing have learned from self-help books is how to let go of the past and move on.

About to be thrown out:
What Men Want
How Men Think and What They Feel
Why Men Feel They Want What They Think They Want
The Rules
Ignoring the Rules
Not Now, Honey, I'm Watching the Game
How to Seek and Find the Love You Want
How to Find the Love You Want Without Seeking It
How to Find You Want the Love You Didn't Seek
Happy to be Single
How not to be Single

If Buddha Dated
If Mohammed Dated
If Jesus Dated Aphrodite
The Famished Road by Ben Okri (not strictly self-help book, as far as know, but will never read the bloody thing anyway)

Right. All going in the bin plus the other thirty-two. Oh God, though. Cannot bear to throw out *The Road Less Travelled* and *You Can Heal Your Life*. Where else is one to turn for spiritual guidance to deal with problems of modern age if not self-help books? Also maybe should give to Oxfam? But no. Must not ruin relationships of others, especially in Third World. Would be worse than behaviour of tobacco giants.

Problems
Hole in wall of flat.
Finances in negative position owing to second mortgage for hole in wall of flat.
Boyfriend going out with Other Woman.
Not speaking to joint best friend as is going on holiday with boyfriend and Other Woman.
Work crap but necessary owing to second mortgage for hole in wall of flat.
Badly need holiday owing to boyfriend/friends/hole in wall of flat/professional and financial crises but no one to go on holiday with. Tom is going back to San Francisco. Magda and Jeremy are going to Tuscany with Mark and fucking Rebecca and probably Jude and Vile Richard too for all I know. Shazzer being evasive presumably waiting to see if Simon will agree to go somewhere with her if sleep in twin beds (not under five foot), hoping he will get into hers.

Also no money to go on holiday owing to financial crisis owing to hole in wall of flat.

No. Am not going to weaken. Have been too swayed this way and that by everyone else's ideas. They are going. In. The. Bin. I am Going. To stand on. Own. Two. Feet.

8.30 a.m. Flat is purged of all self-help books. Feel empty and spiritually at sea. But surely some of information will have stayed in head?

Spiritual principles have garnered from self-help book study (non-dating based):

1. Importance of positive thought cf.: *Emotional Intelligence, Emotional Confidence, The Road Less Travelled, How to Rid Your Thighs of Cellulite in 30 Days,* Gospel according to St Luke, Ch. 13.
2. Importance of forgiveness.
3. Importance of going with flow and instincts rather than trying to squeeze everything into shape and organize everything.
4. Importance of confidence in self.
5. Importance of honesty.
6. Importance of enjoying present moment and not fantasizing or regretting things.
7. Importance of not being obsessed with self-help books.

So solution is to:

1. Think what a nice time am having writing lists of problems and spiritual solutions instead of planning ahead and . . .

Gaaah! Gaaah! Is 8.45! Am going to miss morning meeting and not have time for cappuccino.

10 a.m. In work. Thank God have got cappuccino to help self through aftermath of hell of buying cappuccino when late. Is bizarre how cappuccino queue thing gives whole areas of London appearance of war- or communism-torn culture with people standing patiently in huge queues for hours as if waiting for bread in Sarajevo while others sweat, roasting and grinding, banging metal things full of gunge around, with steam hissing. Is odd when people generally show less and less willingness to wait for anything that should be prepared to do so for this one thing: as if in cruel modern world is only thing one can really trust and hold on to . . . Gaaah!

10.30 a.m. Loos, work. Was Richard Finch bellowing at self. 'Come on, Bridget. Don't be coy,' the great lump roared in front of everyone, twitching and chewing in now-obvious post-cocaine-binge frenzy. 'When are you going?'

'Er . . .' I said, hoping I could ask Patchouli, 'Where?' later.

'You have no idea what I'm talking about, do you? It is literally unbelievable. When are you going on holiday? If you don't fill it in on the chart now you won't be going.'

'Oh, um, yar,' I said airily.

'No charto no departo.'

'Sure, sure, yar, just need to check out the dates,' I said clenching my teeth. As soon as the meeting was over, shot in here to loos for cheering cigarette. Does not matter if am only person in whole office not going on holiday. It does not. Does not mean am social outcast. Definitely. All is well in my world. Even if do have to do item on surrogacy, again.

6 p.m. Nightmare day trying to get women in to talk about quease-inducing egg-hatching permutations. Cannot face thought of going straight home to building site. Is gorgeous, soft sunny evening. Maybe will go for a walk on Hampstead Heath.

9 p.m. Unbelievable. Unbelievable. Just shows if you stop struggling to work everything out, and go with Flow in Zen-like positive way, solutions appear.

Was just walking along path towards the top of Hampstead Heath thinking how fantastic London is in the summer with people loosening their ties after work and spreading out shaggily in the sunshine when eye was caught by a happy-looking couple: she on her back with her head on his stomach, him smiling, and stroking her hair while he talked. Something about them looked familiar. As I got closer, I saw that it was Jude and Vile Richard.

Realized had never seen them alone together before – well, obviously because if I'd been there they wouldn't have been. Suddenly Jude burst out laughing at something Vile Richard had said. She looked really happy. I hesitated, wondering whether to walk past or go back, then Vile Richard said, 'Bridget?'

I paused, frozen, and Jude looked up and gawped unattractively.

Vile Richard got to his feet brushing the grass off him.

'Hey, good to see you, Bridget,' he said with a grin. Realized had always seen him before in Jude-based social situations, when I'd been flanked by Shazzer and Tom and he'd been chippily resentful.

'I'm just going off for some wine, you sit down with Jude. Oh, come on, she won't eat you. She won't touch anything with dairy.'

When he'd gone, Jude smiled sheepishly. 'I'm not pleased to see you or anything.'

'Not pleased to see you either,' I said gruffly.

'So do you want to sit down?'

'All right,' I said, kneeling down on the rug at which she biffed me awkwardly on the shoulder nearly knocking me over.

'I missed you,' she said.

'Shut-urrrrp,' I said out of the corner of my mouth. For a moment, thought I was going to cry.

Jude apologized for being insensitive about Rebecca. She said she'd just got carried away by the thought of anyone who was pleased she was marrying Vile Richard. Turns out she and Vile Richard are not going to Tuscany with Mark and Rebecca, even though they were invited, because Vile Richard said he didn't want to be bossed around by a deranged social engineer and he'd rather they just went on their own. Found self unaccountably warming to Vile Richard. I said I was sorry for falling out over something so stupid as whole Rebecca thing.

'It wasn't stupid. You were really hurt,' said Jude. Then she said they were delaying the wedding because it had all got so complicated but she still wanted me and Shaz to be bridesmaids. 'If you want to,' she said shyly. 'But I know you don't like him.'

'You really love him, don't you?'

'Yes,' she said happily. Then she looked anxious. 'But I don't know if I'm doing the right thing. It says in *The Road Less Travelled* that love isn't something you feel but something you decide to do. And also in *How to Get the Love You Want* that if you go out with someone who doesn't properly earn their own living and accepts help from his parents then they haven't de-parented and it'll never work.'

What was going through my head was the Nat King Cole song my dad was playing in the shed. *'The greatest thing . . . you'll ever learn . . .'*

'Also I think he's an addict because he smokes dope and addicts can't form relationships. My shrink says . . .'

'. . . *is how to love and be loved in return.*'

'. . . I shouldn't have a relationship for at least a year because I'm a relationship addict,' Jude went on. 'And you and Shaz just think he's a fuckwit. Bridge? Are you listening to me?'

'Yes, yes, sorry. If it feels right I think you should go with it.'

'Exactly,' said Vile Richard, towering above us like Bacchus with a bottle of Chardonnay and two packets of Silk Cut.

Had fantastic time with Jude and Vile Richard and all piled into taxi and went back together. Once home, immediately called Shazzer to tell her the news.

'Oh,' she said when I'd fully explained the Zen-like miracle workings of Flow. 'Er, Bridge?'

'What?'

'Do you want to go on holiday?'

'I thought you didn't want to go with me.'

'Well, I just thought I'd wait till . . .'

'Till what?'

'Oh, nothing. But anyway . . .'

'Shaz?' I prodded.

'Simon's going to Madrid to see some girl he met on the Internet.'

Was torn between sorriness for Sharon, huge excitement about having someone to go on holiday with, and feelings of inadequacy for not being 6ft architect with penis when could not be further from same.

'Baaah. It's just pashmina-ism. She'll probably turn out to be a man,' I said to make Shazzie feel better.

'But anyway,' she said lightly, after a pause which sent huge pain vibes down the phone, 'I've found these fantastic flights to Thailand for only £249 and we could go to Koh Samui and be hippies and it would hardly cost us anything!'

'Hurrah!' I said. 'Thailand! We can study Buddhism and have a spiritual epiphany.'

'Yes!' said Shaz. 'Yes! And we're not having anything to do with any BLOODY MEN.'

So, you see . . . Oh, telephone. Maybe Mark Darcy!

Midnight. Phone call was from Daniel, sounding different from usual, though still, obviously, drunk. He said he was really down because things were going badly at work, and he was sorry about the Germany thing. He accepted that I was actually very good on geography and could we have dinner on Friday? Just to talk. So said yes. Feel v.g. about same. Why should I not be friend to Daniel in his hour of need? One must not harbour resentment as that only holds one back but must forgive.

Also as Jude and Vile Richard shows – people can change and I *was* really crazy about him.

And am v. lonely.

And is just dinner.

Am definitely not going to sleep with him though.

Friday 18 July

9st 1 (excellent omen), condoms attempted to purchase 84, condoms purchased 36, usable condoms purchased 12 (should be plenty, think. Especially as not intended for actual use).

2 p.m. Am going out in lunch hour to buy some condoms. Not going to sleep with Daniel or anything. Is just to be on safe side.

3 p.m. Condom expedition proved total failure. Initially was totally enjoying sudden feeling of being condom consumer. When do not have sex life always feel sad when passing condom section as whole side of life that is denied to me. However, when got to counter found bewildering range of varied condoms: Ultra Safe 'for extra sensitivity', Variety Pack 'for extra choice' (alluring Kellogg's-style suggestion), Ultra Fine 'spermicidally lubricated', Gossamer, 'lubricated with a gentle lubricant without' (horrible repulsive word coming up) 'spermicide', Natural styled for Extra Comfort (does that mean bigger – then what if too big?). Stared downwards furiously looking under eyelashes at condom array. Surely what one would want is Extra Sensitivity and Extra Comfort and Ultra Fine so why does one have to choose between?

'Can I help you?' said nosy chemist with knowing smirk. Obviously could not say I wanted condoms, as tantamount to announcing 'Am about to have sex': almost as when people are walking round obviously pregnant and is like saying 'Look, everyone, I have had sex.' Cannot believe condom industry whose very existence is virtual admission that everyone has sex all the time (apart from me), instead of continuing pretence that no one does, which is surely more normal in our land.

Anyway. Just bought some Bradasols.

6.10 p.m. Irritatingly detained at work till 6 p.m. and now chemist's is shut and have not got condoms. I know: will go to Tesco Metro. Will surely have as is store designed for impulsive Singletons.

6.40 p.m. Wandered surreptitiously up and down toothpaste aisle. Zilch. Eventually, in desperation, sidled up to supervisor-style lady and whispered, with an attempt at all-lads-together, one-eyebrow-raised smirk, 'Where are your condoms?'

'We are going to do them,' she said thoughtfully. 'Maybe in a couple of weeks.'

'Fat lot of good that is to me!' I felt like yelling. 'What about tonight?' Though am not going to sleep with him, obviously!

Huh. *Soi-disant* modern, urban, Singleton-directed store. Humph.

7 p.m. Just went to local stinky double-price corner shop. Could see condoms behind counter with cigarettes and vile tights but decided against as whole setting too sordid.

Wish to purchase condom product in pleasant clean Boots-style environment. Also parlous choice. Just Premium Quality Teat-Ended.

7.15 p.m. Have had brainwave. Will go to petrol station, wait in queue whilst secretly looking at condoms then . . . Actually must not conform to outdated male stereotypes feeling forward or sluttish for carrying condoms. All clean girls have condoms. Is hygiene.

7.30 p.m. Lalala. Have dunnit. Was easy. Actually managed to grab two packets: one Variety Pack (spice of life) and Improved Ultra Lightweight Latex Teat Ended for Even Greater Sensitivity. Assistant looked startled at range and quantity of condom choice yet strangely respectful: probably thought was biology teacher or similar purchasing condoms to teach early developing school pupils.

7.40 p.m. Startled by frank drawings in instruction leaflet, which disturbingly made me think about not Daniel but Mark Darcy. Hmmm. Hmmm.

7.50 p.m. Bet they had a difficult time deciding on sizing of pictures not to make anyone feel crestfallen or overarrogant. Variety Pack is insane. 'Mates coloured condoms are vibrantly coloured for extra fun.' Extra fun? Suddenly get garish image of couples with vibrantly coloured rude bits wearing paper hats, hooting with gay sexy laughter and hitting each other with balloons. Think will throw mad Variety Pack away. Right, better get ready. Oh God, telephone.

8.15 p.m. Oh bloody hell. Was Tom moaning that he'd lost his mobile and thought he left it round here. Forced me to look all over for it, even though was really late, but could not find it and eventually suspected might have thrown it away with the self-help books and newspapers.

'Well, can you go and get it?' he said eagerly.

'I'm really late. Can't I do it tomorrow?'

'But what if they empty the bins? What day do they come?'

'Tomorrow morning,' I said with a sinking, bitter heart. 'But the thing is, they're those big communal dustbins and I don't know which one it's in.'

Ended up flinging long leather jacket on top of bra and knickers and going out into street to wait till Tom rang the phone so could find out which it was in. Was just standing on wall peering into the dustbins when a familiar voice said, 'Hello.'

Turned round and there was Mark Darcy.

He glanced down and I realized was standing with – fortunately co-ordinated – underwear on full display.

'What are you doing?' he said.

'I'm waiting for the dustbin to ring,' I replied with dignity, pulling jacket around self.

'I see.' There was a pause. 'Have you been waiting . . . long?'

'No,' I said carefully. 'A normal amount of time.'

Just then one of the dustbins started to ring. 'Ah, that'll be for me,' I said and started to try to reach into it.

'Please, allow me,' said Mark, put down his briefcase, leapt, rather agilely on to the wall, reached into the dustbin and picked out the phone.

'Bridget Jones's phone,' he said. 'Yes of course, I'll put her on.'

He handed it to me. 'It's for you.'

'Who's that?' hissed Tom, hysterical with excitement. 'Sexy voice – who is it?'

I put my hand over the earpiece. 'Thank you so much,' I said to Mark Darcy who had picked a handful of self-help books out of the bin and was looking at them with a puzzled expression.

'Not at all,' he said, putting the self-help books back. 'Er . . .' He paused, looking at my leather jacket.

'What?' I said, heart racing.

'Oh, nothing, er, just, um, well, nice to see you.' He hesitated. 'Well . . . nice to see you again.' Then he gave an attempt at a smile, turned and started to walk off.

'Tom, I'll call you back,' I said into the protesting mobile. My heart was beating wildly. By all the laws of dating etiquette I should just let him go but I was thinking about the overheard conversation behind the hedge. 'Mark?'

He turned round looking full of emotion. For a moment we just stared at each other.

'Hey! Bridge! Are you coming out for dinner without a skirt?'

It was Daniel, walking up, early, behind me.

I saw Mark take him in. He gave me a long, painful look then turned on his heel and strode away.

11 p.m. Daniel had not spotted Mark Darcy – both fortunately and unfortunately because on the one hand did not need to explain what he was doing there but on other hand could not explain why was feeling so churned up. The minute we got in the flat Daniel started trying to kiss me. It felt very strange not to want him to after all the time I spent last year desperately wanting him to and wondering why he wasn't.

'OK, OK,' he said, holding out his hands, palms towards me. 'No problem.' He poured us both a glass of wine and sat down on the sofa, long lean legs all sexy in his jeans. 'Look. I know I hurt you, and I'm sorry. I know you're feeling defensive but I'm different now, I really am. Come and sit down here.'

'I'll just go put my clothes on.'

'No. No. Come here,' he said, patting the sofa beside him. 'Come on, Bridge. I won't lay a finger on you, I promise.'

I sat down gingerly, pulling my jacket around me, hands folded primly on my knee.

'There, there,' he said. 'Now come on, have a drink of this and just relax.'

He put his arm gently round my shoulders.

'I'm haunted by the way I treated you. It was unforgivable.' It was so lovely to be held again. 'Jones,' he whispered tenderly. 'My little Jones.'

He pulled me to him, laying my head against his chest. 'You didn't deserve it.' The old familiar scent of him wafted over me. 'There. Just have a bit of a cuddle. You're all right now.'

He was stroking my hair, stroking my neck, stroking my back, he started slipping my jacket off my shoulders, his hand reached down and with one flick, he'd undone my bra.

'Stoppit!' I said trying to pull the coat back round me.

'Honestly, Daniel.' I was half laughing. I suddenly saw his face. He wasn't laughing.

'Why?' he said, pulling the jacket roughly off my shoulders again. 'Why not? Come on.'

'No!' I said. 'Daniel, we're just going out for dinner. I don't want to kiss you.'

He dropped his head forward, breathing unsteadily, then sat up, head back, eyes closed.

I got to my feet, pulling my coat around me, and walked to the table. When I looked back, Daniel had his head in his hands. I realized he was sobbing.

'I'm sorry, Bridge. I've been promoted downstairs. Perpetua's got my job. I feel redundant, and now you don't want me. No girls will want me. Nobody wants a man at my age without a career.'

I stared at him in astonishment. 'And how do you think I felt last year? When I was bottom of the pile in that office and you were messing me around and making me feel like a re-tread?'

'Re-tread, Bridge?'

Was going to explain about the re-tread theory, but something made me decide I just wouldn't bother.

'I think it'd be best if you go now,' I said.

'Oh, come on, Bridge.'

'Just go,' I said.

Hmm. Anyway. Will just detach from whole thing. Glad am going away. Will be able to free self's head of all men issues in Thailand and concentrate on self.

Saturday 19 July

9st 3 (why? On bikini-purchase day, why?), confusing thoughts about Daniel: too many, bikini bottoms fitted into 1, bikini tops fitted into: half, rude thoughts about Prince William 22, no. of times wrote 'Prince William and his lovely date Miss Bridget Jones at Ascot' on Hello! *magazine 7.*

6.30 p.m. Bloody, bloody, bloody. Have spent all day in changing rooms of Oxford Street trying to squeeze my breasts into bikini tops designed for people with breasts either arranged one on top of the other in the centre of their chests or one under each arm, with the harsh downlighting making me look like River Cafe frittata. Obvious solution is one-piece but then will return with already squashily textured stomach highlighted against rest of body by whiteness.

Urgent bikini diet weight-loss target programme: week 1

Sun 20 July	9st 3
Mon 21 July	9st 2
Tues 22 July	9st 1
Wed 23 July	9st 0
Thurs 24 July	8st 13
Fri 25 July	8st 12
Sat 26 July	8st 11

Hurray! So by a week today will be almost down to target weight so then, with body-bulk thus adjusted, all will need to do is alter texture and arrangement of fat through exercise.

Oh fuck. Will never work. Am only sharing a room

and probably bed with Shaz. Will concentrate instead on my spirit. Anyway Jude and Shaz are coming round soon. Hurrah!

Midnight. Lovely evening. V. nice to be back with girls again, though Shaz whipped herself up into such a frenzy of indignation about Daniel was all I could do to stop her ringing the police and having him arrested for date rape.

'Redundant? You see?' she was ranting. 'Daniel's an absolute archetype of fin-de-millennium male. It's becoming clear to him that women are the superior race. He's realizing he has no role or function so what does he do? He turns to violence.'

'Well, he only tried to kiss her,' said Jude mildly, flicking idly through the pages of *What Marquee*.

'Pah! That's exactly the point. She's bloody lucky he didn't burst into her bank dressed as an Urban Warrior and kill seventeen people with a sub-machine gun.'

Just then the phone rang. It was Tom, not, unaccountably, ringing to thank me for sending his mobile back after all the bloody trouble the pesky item has caused but wanting my mum's phone number. Tom seems to be quite pally with Mum, seeing her in what I suspect is a Judy Garland/Ivana Trump kitsch sort of way (which is odd since only last year I remember Mum lecturing me on how gayness was 'just laziness, darling, they simply can't be bothered to relate to the opposite sex' – but then that was last year). Suddenly feared that Tom was going to ask my mother to perform 'Non, Je Ne Regrette Rien' in a sequinned dress in a club called Pump, which she would – naively yet egomaniacally – agree to, thinking it was something to do with ancient machinery in Cotswold Mill Houses.

'What do you want it for?' I said suspiciously.

'Isn't she in a book club?'

'Dunno. Anything's possible. Why?'

'Jerome's sensing his poems are ready, so I'm finding him book club venues. He did one last week in Stoke Newington and it was awesome.'

'Awesome?' I said, doing a bulging-cheeked vomit face at Jude and Shaz. Ended up giving Tom the number in spite of reservations, as suspect Mum might be needing another diversion now Wellington has gone.

'What is it about book clubs?' I said when I'd put the phone down. 'Is it just me, or have they suddenly sprung up from nowhere? Should we be in one or do you have to be Smug Married?'

'You have to be Smug Married,' said Shaz definitively. 'That's because they fear their minds are being sucked dry by the paternalistic demands of . . . Oh my God, look at Prince William.'

'Let me look,' interrupted Jude, snatching the copy of *Hello!* with its photo of the lithe young royal whipper-snapper. Tried not to snatch it myself. Although, clearly, wish to admire as many pictures of Prince William as possible, preferably in a range of outfits, realize urge is both intrusive and wrong. Cannot, though, ignore impression of great things fermenting around in young royal brain, and sense that, at maturity, will rise up like ancient knight of Round Table thrusting sword in air and creating dazzling new order, which will make President Clinton and Tony Blair look like passé elderly gentlemen.

'How young is too young, would you say?' said Jude dreamily.

'Too young to be your legal son,' said Shaz definitively as if was already part of government statute: which suppose it is, come to think of it, depending how old you are. Just then the phone rang again.

'Oh, hello, darling. Guess what?' My mother. 'Your friend Tom – you know the "homo" – well, he's bringing a poet to read at the Lifeboat Book Club! He's going to read us romantic poems. Like Lord Byron! Isn't that fun?'

'Er . . . yes?' I floundered.

'Actually, it's nothing special,' she sniffed airily. 'We often have visiting authors.'

'Really? Like who?'

'Oh, lots of them, darling. Penny's *very* good friends with Salman Rushdie. Anyway, you will be coming, darling, won't you?'

'When is it?'

'A week on Friday. Una and I are doing vol-au-vents hot with Chunky Chicken.'

A sudden fear convulsed me. 'Are Admiral and Elaine Darcy coming?'

'Durr! No boys allowed, silly. Elaine's coming but the chaps are turning up later.'

'But Tom and Jerome are coming.'

'Oh, they're not boys, darling.'

'Are you sure Jerome's poems will be the sort of thing that . . .'

'Bridget. I don't know what you're trying to say. We weren't born yesterday, you know. And the whole point about literature is free expression. Ooh, and I think

Mark's coming along later. He's up doing Malcolm's will with him – you never know!'

Friday 1 August

9st 3 (total failure of bikini diet), cigarettes 19 (diet aid), calories 625 (not too late, surely).

6.30 p.m. Grr. Grrr. Leaving for Thailand tomorrow, nothing is packed and had failed to realize that 'a week on Friday' for book club is to-bloody-night. Really, really do not want to drive all way to Grafton Underwood. Is hot steamy evening and Jude and Shaz are going to lovely party at River Cafe. Obviously, though, is important to support Mum, Tom's love life, Art etc. Is respecting self by respecting others. Also does not matter if tired tomorrow when get on plane as going on holiday. Sure trip-preparation will not take long as only need capsule wardrobe (just a couple of bodies and a sarong!) and packing always expands to fill the time available so best use of time, surely, is to make time available v. short. Yes! You see! So will do everything!

Midnight. Just back. Arrived v. late owing to typical motorway signpost debacle (if war today, better, surely, to confuse Germans by leaving signposts up?). Was greeted by Mum, wearing a very strange maroon velvet kaftan which presume she intended to be literary.

'How's Salman?' I said as she tut-tutted about my lateness.

'Oh, we decided to do chicken instead,' she said sniffily, leading me through the ripply-glassed French doors, into the lounge where the first thing I noticed was a garish new 'family crest' above the fake stone fireplace saying *'Hakuna Matata'*.

'Shh,' said Una, holding a finger up, enraptured.

Pretentious Jerome, pierced nipple clearly visible through black wet-look vest, was standing in front of the cut-glass dish collection, bellowing belligerently: 'I watch his hard, bony, horny, hams. I watch, I want, I grab,' at a semi-circle of appalled Jaeger-be-two-pieced Lifeboat Luncheon Book Club ladies on reproduction Regency dining chairs. Across the room I saw Mark Darcy's mum, Elaine, sporting an expression of suppressed amusement.

'I want,' Jerome bellowed on. 'I seize his horny, hairy, hams. I have to have. I heave, I hump, I . . .'

'Well! I think that's been absolutely smashing!' said Mum, jumping to her feet. 'Does anyone fancy a vol-au-vent?'

Is amazing the way the world of middle-class ladies manages to smooth everything into its own, turning all the chaos and complication of the world into a lovely secure mummy stream, rather as lavatory cleaner turns everything in the toilet pink.

'Oh, I love the spoken and written word! It makes me feel so free!' Una was gushing to Elaine as Penny Husbands-Bosworth and Mavis Enderbury fussed over Pretentious Jerome as if he were T. S. Eliot.

'But I hadn't finished,' whined Jerome. 'I wanted to do "Fister Contemplations" and "The Hollow Men-Holes".'

Just then there was a roar.

'*If you can keep your head when all about you are losing theirs and blaming it on you.*' It was Dad, and Admiral

Darcy. Both paralytic. Oh God. Every time I see Dad these days, he seems to be completely pissed, in bizarre father-daughter role-reversal scenario.

'*If you can trust yourself when all men doubt you,*' Admiral Darcy bellowed, leaping on to a chair to a flutter from the assembled ladies.

'*And make allowance for their doubting too,*' added Dad, almost tearfully, leaning against the Admiral for support.

The pissed duo proceeded to recite the whole of Rudyard Kipling's 'If' in manner of Sir Laurence Olivier and John Gielgud to the fury of Mum and Pretentious Jerome who started throwing simultaneous hissy fits.

'It's typical, typical, typical,' hissed Mum as Admiral Darcy, on his knees, beating his breast, intoned, 'Or being lied about, don't deal in lies.'

'It's regressive, colonialist doggerel,' hissed Jerome.

'*If you can force your heart, and nerve and sinew.*'

'I mean it fucking rhymes,' re-hissed Jerome.

'Jerome, I will not have that word in my house,' also re-hissed Mum.

'*To serve their turn long after they are gone,*' said Dad, then flung himself on the swirly carpet in mock death.

'Well, why did you invite me then?' hissed Jerome really hissily.

'*And so keep on, when there is nothing in you,*' roared the Admiral.

'*Except your nerve,*' growled Dad from the carpet. '*Which says to you*' – he leapt to his knees and raised his arms – '*hold on*!'

There was a huge cheer and round of applause from

the ladies as Jerome flounced out slamming the door and Tom rushed after him. I looked despairingly back at the room straight into the eyes of Mark Darcy.

'Well! That was interesting!' said Elaine Darcy, coming to stand by me as I bent my head, trying to recover my composure. 'Poetry uniting the old and young.'

'The pissed and sober,' I added.

At this Admiral Darcy lurched over, clutching his poem.

'My dear, my dear, my darling!' he said, lunging at Elaine. 'Oh here's what's-her-name,' he said, peering at me. 'Lovely! Mark's arrived, that's my boy! Come to pick us up, sober as a judge. All on his own. I don't know!' he said.

They both turned to look at Mark who was sitting at Una's threepenny-bit occasional table, scribbling something, watched over by a blue-glass dolphin.

'Writing my will for me at a party! I don't know. Work, work, work!' roared the Admiral. 'Brought this bit of totty along, what was 'er name, m'dear, Rachel, was it? Betty?'

'Rebecca,' Elaine said tartly.

'And the next thing she's nowhere to be seen. Ask him what's happened to her, and he mumbles! Can't stand a mumbler! Never could.'

'Well, I don't think she was really . . .' murmured Elaine.

'Why not! Why not! Perfectly good! I don't know! Fussing about this, that and the other! I hope you young ladies are not always flitting hither and thither like these young fellers seem to be!'

'No,' I said ruefully. 'In fact if we love someone it's

pretty hard to get them out of our system when they bugger off.'

There was a crash behind. I turned to see that Mark Darcy had knocked over the blue-glass dolphin, which in turn had dislodged a vase of chrysanthemums and a photo frame, creating a melee of shattered glass, flowers and bits of paper, the hideous dolphin itself remaining miraculously intact.

There was a commotion as Mum and Elaine and Admiral Darcy all rushed at the scene, the Admiral striding around and bellowing, Dad trying to bounce the dolphin on to the floor saying, 'Get rid of the bloody thing,' and Mark grabbing at his papers and offering to pay for everything.

'Are you ready to go, Dad?' muttered Mark, looking deeply embarrassed.

'No, no, in your own time, I've been in very good company, with Brenda here. Get me another port, will you, son?'

There was an awkward pause as Mark and I looked at each other.

'Hello, Bridget,' Mark said abruptly. 'Come on, Dad, I really think we should go.'

'Yes, come along, Malcolm,' said Elaine, taking his arm affectionately. 'Or you'll be widdling on the carpet.'

'Oh, widdling, widdling, I don't know.'

The three of them made their goodbyes, Mark and Elaine easing the Admiral out of the door. I watched, feeling empty and flat, then suddenly Mark reappeared and headed towards me.

'Ah, forgot my pen,' he said, picking up his Mont Blanc

from the occasional table. 'When are you going to Thailand?'

'Tomorrow morning.' For a split second I could swear he looked disappointed.

'How did you know I was going to Thailand?'

'Grafton Underwood speaks of nothing else. Have you packed?'

'What do you think?'

'Not a single pant,' he said wryly.

'Mark,' bellowed his father. 'Come on, boy, thought it was you who was keen to be off.'

'Coming,' said Mark, glancing over his shoulder. 'This is for you.' He handed me a scrumpled piece of paper, flashed me a . . . er . . . penetrating look, then left.

I waited till no one was watching then unfolded the sheet with shaking hands. It was just a copy of Dad and Admiral Darcy's poem. What did he give me that for?

Saturday 2 August

9st 2 (huh, total pre-holiday diet failure), alcohol units 5, cigarettes 42, calories 4,457 (total despair), items packed 0, ideas as to whereabouts of passport 6, passport whereabout ideas proved to have any substance whatsoever 0.

5 a.m. Why oh why am I going on holiday? I will spend the entire holiday wishing Sharon were Mark Darcy, and she that I were Simon. It's 5 o'clock in the morning. My entire bedroom is covered in wet washing, biros, and polythene bags. I do not know how many bras to take, I cannot find my little black Jigsaw dress without which I cannot go or my other pink jelly mule, I haven't got any traveller's cheques yet and do not think my credit card is working. There are now only 1.5 hours left till I have to leave the house and everything will not fit into the suitcase. Maybe will have cigarette and look at brochure for calming few minutes.

Mmm. Will be lovely just to lie and sunbathe to get all brown on beach. Sunshine and swimming and . . . Oooh. Answerphone light is flashing. How come did not notice?

5.10 a.m. Pressed ANSWER PLAY.

'Oh Bridget, it's Mark. Just wondered. You do realize it's the rainy season in Thailand? Maybe you should pack an umbrella.'

11

Thai Takeaway

Sunday 3 August

Weightless (in air), alcohol units 8 (but in-flight so cancelled out by altitude), cigarettes 0 (desperate: no-smoking seat), calories 1 million (entirely made up of things would never have dreamt of putting in self's mouth were they not on in-flight tray), farts from travelling companion 38 (so far), variations in fart aroma 0.

4 p.m. English time. In aeroplane in sky. Having to pretend to be very busy wearing walkman and writing as ghastly man next to self in pale brown synthetic-type suit keeps trying to talk to me in between silent but deadly farting. Tried pretending to have fallen asleep whilst holding nose but after a few minutes ghastly man tapped me on the shoulder and said, 'Do you have any hobbies?'

'Yes, napping,' I replied but even that didn't put him off and within seconds I was plunged into the murky world of early Etruscan coinage.

Sharon and I are separated as we were so late for plane that there were only separate seats left and Shazzer was in complete grump with me. She seems, however, to have unaccountably got over it, which has clearly nothing to do with fact that she is sitting next to Harrison Ford-style stranger with jeans and crumpled khaki shirt, laughing like drain (weird expression, surely?) at everything he says. This, in spite of the fact that Shaz hates all men for losing their roles and turning to pashmina-ism and mindless violence. I, meanwhile, am stuck to Mr Synthetic Fabric Fart Machine, and cannot have cigarette for twelve hours. Thank God have got Nicorette.

Non-v.g. start but still v. excited re: Thailand trip. Sharon and I are going to be *travellers* rather than tourists i.e. not stay in hermetically sealed tourist enclaves but really experience the religion and culture.

Holiday Aims:

1. Be hippy-style traveller.
2. Lose weight through mild, ideally not life-threatening dysentery.
3. Get subtle biscuit-style suntan – not bright orange in manner of Sheryl Gascoigne, or melanoma- or wrinkle-inducing.
4. Have nice time.
5. Find self, also sunglasses. (Hopefully are in suitcase.)
6. Swim and sunbathe (sure only rains in short tropical bursts).
7. See temples (not too many, though, hope).
8. Have spiritual epiphany.

Monday 4 August

8st 7 (weighing no longer possible, so can select weight according to mood: excellent advantage of travel), calories 0, minutes not spent on toilet 12 (feels like).

2 a.m. local time. Bangkok. Shazzer and I are trying to get to sleep in worst place I have ever been in. Think am going to suffocate and stop breathing. When we flew in over Bangkok there was thick grey cloud and it was pissing rain. The Sin Sane (Sin Sae) Guest House has no toilets, just hideous stinking holes in ground in cubicles. Open window and fan make no difference whatsoever since air is nearest possible thing to warm water without actually being it. There is disco underneath (hotel, not toilet) and in pauses can hear everyone in entire street moaning and not able to get to sleep either. Feel like great white flobbering bloated thing. Hair has first turned into feathers then become plastered down on face. Worst of it is, Sharon is wittering on about Harrison Ford-style airline stranger.

'. . . So well travelled . . . was on Sudan Airways when the pilot and co-pilot decided to shake hands with all the passengers and the cockpit door shut behind them! They had to hack it down with an axe. So witty. He's staying at the Oriental – he said to come over.'

'I thought we didn't want anything to do with men,' I said grumpily.

'No, no, I just think if we're in a strange place it's useful to talk to someone really well travelled.'

6 a.m. Finally got to sleep at 4.30 only to be woken at 5.45 by Sharon bouncing on the bed saying we should go to a temple and watch the sunrise (through 300ft of cloud?). Cannot go on. Gaah! Something v. horrible seems to be going on in stomach. Keep having little eggy burps.

11 a.m. Sharon and I have been up for five hours, four and a half of which have been spent taking it in turns to go to the 'toilet'. Sharon says suffering and simple life is part of spiritual epiphany. Physical comfort is not only unnecessary but an impediment to spirituality. We are going to meditate.

Noon. Hurrah! We have checked into the Oriental Hotel! Realize will cost more for one night than week in Corfu but is emergency and what are credit cards for? (Shazzer's is still working and she says I can pay her back. Wonder if is all right to have spiritual epiphany on someone else's credit card?)

Both agreed hotel marvellous and changed immediately into powder-blue bathrobes and played with bubble bath etc. Also Shazzer says it is not necessary to completely rough it all the time in order to be a traveller since it is the contrast between worlds and lifestyles that makes one have a spiritual epiphany. Could not agree more. Greatly appreciate, for example, simultaneous presence of toilet and bidet in view of current stomach scenario.

8 p.m. Shazzer was asleep (or dead from dysentery), so decided to go out for walk on terrace of hotel. Was just beautiful. Stood in inky darkness with soft warm breezes lifting plastered-down feathers off face, looking over bend in Chao Phraya river – and all twinkly lights and lurking oriental-style boats. Flying is marvellous thing – only 24 hours ago was sitting on bed at home surrounded by wet washing – now all is unbelievably exotic and romantic. Was just about to light cigarette when suddenly posh gold lighter appeared under nose. Glanced at the face in the matchlight and made odd noise. Was the airline Harrison Ford! Waiter brought gin and tonics that seemed quite strong. Harrison Ford, or 'Jed', explained was v. important to take quinine in tropics. Could quite see why Shaz was going on about him. He asked what our plans were. Told him we had decided to go to hippy island of Koh Samui to stay in hut and have spiritual epiphany. He said he might come too. I said Sharon would like that (as obviously he was hers though did not say that to Harrison Ford), and maybe I should go wake her up. By this time was feeling rather woozy what with all the quinine then panicked as he brushed one finger gently down the side of my cheek and leaned towards me.

'Bridget,' hissed a voice, 'call yourself a bloody friend.'

Oh no, oh no. Was Shazzer.

Thursday 7 August

8st 6 or maybe 2?, cigarettes 10, appearances by the sun 0.

Koh Samui Island, Thailand. (Hmm: rhymes in manner of rap song or similar.)

Have arrived at v. idyllic – apart from teeming rain – hippy beach: lovely crescent of sand and little huts on stilts and restaurants all along it. The huts are made of bamboo with balconies overlooking the sea. Things are still rather frosty between me and Shaz and she has developed an irrational aversion to 'Boys Who Have Huts Near One' with the result that even though we have not yet been here eighteen hours we have had to move huts three times in rain. The first time it was fair enough as after three minutes the boys came over and tried to sell us something that was either heroin, opium, or fudge.

Then we moved to a new hut-hotel where the boys in the next hut looked v. clean-cut in manner of biochemists or similar. Unfortunately, however, the biochemists came over and told us someone had hanged himself in our hut three days ago at which Shazzer insisted we leave. By this time it was pitch black. The biochemists had offered to help with our bags but Shaz would have none of it and we had to tramp along the beach with rucksacks for ages. The upshot of it was, having travelled about 20,000 miles to wake up by the sea, we ended up in a hut overlooking the back of a restaurant and a ditch. So now we have to go up and down the beach looking for another hut that is on the sea but does not have the wrong sort of boys near it, or post-hanging karma. Bloody Shazzer.

11.30 p.m. Argor, es wor blurry brill in ganja restaurant, Shazz blurry fantastic. Bessfrien.

Friday 8 August

8st 0 (marvellous by-product of stomach explosion), alcohol units 0, cigarettes 0 (v.g.), magic mushrooms 12 (mmmmm wooooo weeeeee).

11.30 a.m. When woke up, admittedly quite late, found myself alone. Could not find Shaz anywhere in the hut, so came out on the balcony and looked around. Worryingly, the frightening Swedish girls next door seemed to have been replaced by a Boy Who Has Hut Near One but clearly this could not be my fault as travellers constantly coming and going. Put on prescription sunglasses as lenses not in yet and on closer inspection, Boy Who Newly Had Hut Near One turned out to be airline Harrison Ford-lookalike-Oriental-Hotel-snogger. As I watched he turned round and smiled at someone coming out of his hut. It was Shazzer, revealing whole 'be careful while travelling, avoid Boys Who Have Huts Near One' philosophy to contain gigantic 'unless they're really attractive' caveat.

1 p.m. Jed is taking us both to the café for a magic mushroom omelette! Initially we were doubtful as strictly against classified substances but Jed explained magic mushrooms are not drugs but natural and will provide a gateway to our spiritual epiphany. V. excited.

2 p.m. I am beautiful in a striking, exotic way, beautiful and part of all colours and life with its laws. When lie on the sand and look at the sky through my army hat pinpricks of light shine through and it is the most beautiful, beautiful, precious thing in imagery. Shazzer is beautiful. I will take my hat into the sea so the beauty of the sea will combine with the precious pinpricks of light like jewels.

5 p.m. In ganja restaurant on own. Shazzer is not speaking to me. After the magic mushroom omelette, nothing happened initially but on the way back to our hut everything suddenly began to seem most amusing and I unfortunately began to giggle uncontrollably. Shaz, however, did not seem to be joining in the joke. On arrival at our latest hut I decided to put my hammock up outside, using thin string, which broke, so that I landed on the sand.

This seemed at the time so very amusing I immediately wanted to do it again and, Shazzer is claiming, re-performed amusing hammock-crash repeatedly for forty-five minutes finding the amusingness undiminished by repetition. Jed had been in the hut with Shaz but gone off for a swim so I decided to go in to find her. She was lying on the bed moaning, 'I'm ugly, ugly, ugly, ugly.' Alarmed by Shazzer's contrasting-with-own-mood self-loathing, hurried towards her to cheer her up. On the way, however, caught sight of self in the mirror and had never seen a more beautiful or entrancing creature in entire life.

Shaz alleges that for the next forty minutes kept attempting to rouse her spirits but I became repeatedly distracted by sight of self in the mirror, striking poses and beseeching Shaz to admire me. Shaz, meanwhile, was suffering total trauma believing her entire face and body to be grievously deformed. I went off to get her some food and returned giggling with a banana and Bloody Mary, telling her the waitress in the restaurant had a lampshade on her head, then returned besottedly to my station at the mirror. Following this, Shaz claims, I lay on the beach for two and a half hours staring up at army hat and waving fingers softly in the air while she contemplated suicide.

All can remember was being in midst of happiest time of life, sure that had understood deep, permanent laws of life and that all that was necessary was to get into deep Flow state – as fully described in *Emotional Intelligence* – thereby to go along with Laws in Zen-like fashion, then suddenly it was as if a switch had been turned off. Returned to hut and instead of radiant Buddha/Yasmin Le

Bon-type female incarnation in mirror it was just me, bright red and sweating in the face, one side of hair plastered down my head and the other side sticking out in peaks and horns, and Shaz on the bed looking at me with the expression of an axe-murderer. V. sad and ashamed of behaviour but it was not me, it was the mushrooms.

Maybe if I go back to the hut and talk about spiritual epiphanies she will not be so grumpy.

Friday 15 August

8st 1 (in slightly rounder mood today), alcohol units 5, cigarettes 25, spiritual epiphanies 0, disasters 1.

9 a.m. We have had a fantastic holiday though not a spiritual epiphany. Felt a bit left out because Shaz was often with Jed, but the sun made really quite a few appearances so swam and sunbathed when they were shagging, and at night the three of us had dinner. Shaz is a bit heartbroken because Jed left last night to go on to some other islands. We are going to have cheer-up breakfast (though not magic mushrooms) and then can be just the two of us again and have fun. Hurrah!

11.30 a.m. Oh my bloody God and fuck. Sharon and I have just got back to our hut to find our padlock was open and our rucksacks have gone missing. Definitely left it locked but they must have broken in. Fortunately we had our passports and not all the stuff was actually in the bags but our air tickets and traveller's cheques appear to be no longer there. Shazzer's card is not working after

Bangkok with all shopping etc. We only have $38 between us and the flight to London from Bangkok is on Tuesday and we are hundreds of miles away on an island. Sharon is crying and I keep trying to cheer her up to little effect.

Whole scenario reminiscent of *Thelma and Louise* when Thelma sleeps with Brad Pitt who steals all their money and Geena Davis is saying it's all right and Susan Sarandon is crying and saying, 'It is not all right. Thelma, it is definitely not all right.'

Even to fly to Bangkok in time for the plane will cost us $100 each, and then who knows if they would believe us at Bangkok airport about lost tickets or whether we could . . . Oh God. Must keep head and spirits up. Just suggested to Shazzer that we go back to the ganja restaurant and have a couple of Bloody Marys and sleep on it and she went mental.

The trouble is part of me is frantic and part of me thinks it is brilliant to have a crisis and adventure and it is such a change from worrying about the circumference of my thighs. Think I will just sneak out and get the Bloody Marys. Might as well cheer ourselves up. Can't do anything about it till Monday anyway as everything closed: short of going to a bar and raising money by doing exotic dances with ping-pong balls coming out of us but somehow do not think we would stand up to the competition.

1 p.m. Hurrah! Shazzza I going tor live in KohSamui like hippies off bananas sell shells onsbeach. IIs y spiritual epiphany. Blurry brilli. Nothing but selves to re on. Spirtal.

5 p.m. Hmm. Shaz is still asleep, which I am glad about as she seems to be taking things rather hard. This, I feel, is an opportunity to test our self-reliance. I know. Am going to go to the big hotel and enquire at reception as to what facilities are available to deal with a crisis. For example I could ring the traveller's cheque company. But then we'll never get the refund in time. No, no. Keep positive.

7 p.m. You see. As long as you keep your spirits up something always comes along to get you out of a hole. Who should I bump into in the hotel foyer but Jed! He said his trip to the other islands had been rained off, he was going back to Bangkok later tonight and was just about to come to see us to say hi before he goes. (Think Shaz might be a bit upset he didn't come to find her straight away, but still. Maybe he thought we'd already gone or . . . Look, I am *not* going to start obsessing on behalf of Sharon.)

Anyway, Jed was really sympathetic, though did say we should never have left anything valuable in the hut, even if it was padlocked. He gave me a bit of a lecture (bloody sexy, sort of father/priest figure) then said we'd be pushing it to get to Bangkok in time for Tuesday's flight, as all the flights from here today and tomorrow were full, but he would try to get us tickets for the overnight train tomorrow, which should make the connection. Also offered to give us some money for taxis and to pay the hotel here. He thought if we rang the travel agent in London first thing Monday they would definitely re-issue the tickets to pick up at the airport.

'We'll pay you back,' I said gratefully.

'Hey, don't worry,' he said. 'It's not very much.'

'No, we will,' I insisted.

'Well, when you can afford it,' he laughed.

He is a generous, wealthy dreamgod, though obviously money not important. Except when missing in crisis.

Monday 18 August

On train from Surat Thani Koh Samui to Bangkok. Is quite nice on the train, watching all the paddy fields and people with triangular hats go by. Every time it stops, people come up to the windows offering us chicken saté, which is delicious. Cannot stop thinking about Jed. He was so kind and there for us in way that reminded self of Mark Darcy when not gone off with Rebecca. He even gave us one of his bags to put our stuff in that wasn't nicked and all his little shampoos and soaps from his various hotels. Shaz is happy because they've swapped numbers and addresses and are going to see each other as soon as she gets back. In fact, to be perfectly honest about it, Shazzer is smug to the point of insufferability. Is good though, as she had horrible time with Simon. Always suspected she did not hate all men, just crap ones. Oh God. Hope we get the plane in time.

Tuesday 19 August

11 a.m. Bangkok airport. A terrible nightmare seems to be happening. Blood all seems to be racing through my head and I can hardly see. Shaz went on ahead of me to hold up the plane while I brought the luggage. Had to walk past an official with a dog on a leash, which was straining at my bag and barking. The airline officials all started jabbering, and then an army woman took me and the bag away to a separate room. They emptied the holdall, then took a knife and slashed open the lining, and inside was a polythene bag full of white powder. And then . . . Oh God. Oh God. Someone help me.

Wednesday 20 August

6st, alcohol units 0, cigarettes 0, calories 0, likelihood of ever eating Thai takeaway again 0.

11 a.m. Police custody, Bangkok. Calm. Calm. Calm. Calm.

11.01 a.m. Calm.

11.02 a.m. Am wearing leg irons. Am wearing LEG IRONS. Am in stinking Third-World cell with eight Thai prostitutes and a potty in the corner. Feel like am going to faint in heat. This cannot be happening.

11.05 a.m. Oh God. It's all falling into place what has

happened. Cannot believe anyone could be so callous, to sleep with someone then nick all their things and dupe their friend into being a pigeon. Is unbelievable. Anyway, I expect the British Ambassador will be here soon to explain everything and get me out.

Noon. Becoming slightly anxious about whereabouts of British Ambassador.

1 p.m. Sure the British Ambassador will be along after his lunch break.

2 p.m. Maybe the British Ambassador has been held up, perhaps by a more pressing case of real drug trafficking as opposed to an innocent dupe.

3 p.m. Oh my bloody God and fuck. I hope they have bloody well *told* the British Ambassador. Surely Shazzer will have raised the alert. Maybe they have got Shazzer as well. But where is she?

3.30 p.m. Look, have got to, got to keep myself together. All I have got now is myself. Fucking Jed. Must not hold on to resentment . . . Oh God, I'm so hungry.

4 p.m. Guard just came by with some disgusting rice and some personal effects was allowed to keep – one pair of knickers, a photo of Mark Darcy and another of Jude showing Shazzer how to have an orgasm and a screwed up bit of paper from jeans pocket. Tried to ask guard about British Ambassador but he just nodded and said something I couldn't understand.

4.30 p.m. You see. Even when things seem bad, still enlightening things happen. Screwed up paper was Dad's poem from book club that Mark gave me. Is literature. Am going to read it and think of finer things.

'If' by Rudyard Kipling

If you can keep your head when all about you
    Are losing theirs and . . .

Oh my God. Oh my GOD. Do they still have beheading in Thailand?

Thursday 21 August

5st (v.g. but imaginary), alcohol units 14 (but also imaginary), cigarettes 0, calories 12 (rice), no. of times wish had gone to Cleethorpes instead 55.

5 a.m. Hideous night huddled on flea-infested old sack stuffed with socks masquerading as mattress. Funny how quickly you get used to being dirty and uncomfortable. Is the smell that is the worst. Managed to sleep for a couple of hours, which was great except for moment when woke up and remembered what happened. Still no sign of British Ambassador. Sure it is just a mistake and will all be OK. Must keep spirits up.

10 a.m. A guard just appeared at the door with a Sloaney-looking chap in a pink shirt.

'Are you the British Ambassador?' I yelled, practically flinging myself on him.

'Ah. No. Assistant to the Consul. Charlie Palmer-Thompson. Jolly good to meet you.' He shook my hand in a manner that would have been reassuringly British had he not involuntarily wiped it on his trousers afterwards.

He asked me what happened and took down the details in a Mulberry leather-bound notebook, saying things like 'Yar, yar. Oh Christ, how frightful,' as if I were telling him a polo anecdote. Started to panic as (a) did not seem quite to grasp the gravity of the situation, (b) did not seem – not to be snobbish or anything – exactly brain of Britain and (c) did not seem nearly as certain as I would have liked that this was all a mistake and I was about to be released any second.

'But why?' I said, having told him the whole story again. Explained how Jed must have broken into the hut himself and planned the whole thing.

'Well, you see the bore is' – Charlie leaned forward confidentially – 'everyone who comes in here has some sort of story, usually pretty much along the lines of yours. So unless this bloody Jed character makes a full confession it's a bit of a sticky wicket.'

'Am I going to get the death penalty?'

'Good God, no. Bloody hell. Shouldn't think so. Worst you'd be looking at is about ten years.'

'TEN YEARS? But I haven't done anything.'

'Yar, yar, it's a bastard, I know,' he said, nodding earnestly.

'But I didn't know it was there!'

'Sure, sure,' he said, looking as if he'd got himself into a slightly awkward situation at a drinks party.

'Will you do everything you can?'

'Absolutely,' he said, getting up. 'Yar.'

He said he would bring me a list of lawyers to choose from and he could make two calls on my behalf, just to give the details of what had happened. Was in quite a quandary. Best person, practically speaking, would be Mark Darcy but really did not like idea of admitting have got into mess again, especially after he sorted out all the Mum and Julio stuff last year. In the end I plumped for Shazzer and Jude.

Feel like my fate is now in the hands of some fresh-out-of-Oxbridge Sloane. God, it is so awful in here. So hot and stinking and weird. I feel like nothing's real.

4 p.m. Very black. All my life I have had the feeling something terrible was about to happen and now it has.

5 p.m. Mustn't get down. Must keep my mind off it all. Maybe will read poem, and try to ignore first two lines:

'If' by Rudyard Kipling

If you can keep your head when all about you
  Are losing theirs and blaming it on you;
If you can trust yourself when all men doubt you,
  But make allowance for their doubting too;
If you can wait, and not be tired by waiting,
  Or, being lied about, don't deal in lies,
Or, being hated, don't give way to hating,
  And yet don't look too good, nor talk too wise;

If you can dream – and not make dreams your master;
  If you can think – and not make thoughts your aim;
If you can meet with Triumph and Disaster
  And treat those two impostors just the same;

If you can bear to hear the truth you've spoken
  Twisted by knaves to make a trap for fools,
Or watch the things you gave your life to broken,
  And stoop and build 'em up with worn-out tools;

If you can make one heap of all your winnings
  And risk it on one turn of pitch-and-toss,
And lose, and start again at your beginnings
  And never breathe a word about your loss;
If you can force your heart and nerve and sinew
  To serve your turn long after they are gone,
And so hold on when there is nothing in you
  Except the Will which says to them: 'Hold on!'

If you can talk with crowds and keep your virtue,
  Or walk with Kings – not lose the common touch;
If neither foes nor loving friends can hurt you;
  If all men count with you, but none too much;
If you can fill the unforgiving minute
  With sixty seconds' worth of distance run –
Yours is the Earth and everything that's in it,
  And – which is more – you'll be a Man, my son!

Poem is good. Very good, almost like self-help book. Maybe that is why Mark Darcy gave it to me! Maybe he sensed I might get into danger! Or maybe he was just trying to tell me something about my attitude. Bloody cheek. Not sure about sixty seconds' worth of distance run anyway, or if actually want to be man. Also is a bit hard to treat this disaster the same as triumphs as have not had any triumphs that can think of, but still. Will force heart and nerve and sinew to serve turn etc. in manner of First World War or jungle soldier or whatever Rudyard Kipling was and just hold on. At least am not being shot at or having to go over top. And also am not spending any money in jail so actually helping financial crisis. Yes, must look on positive side.

Good things about being in jail:

1. Not spending any money.
2. Thighs have really gone down and have probably lost at least half a stone without even trying.
3. Will be good for hair to leave it without washing such as have never been able to do before as too mad to go out of door.

So when go home will be thin, with shiny hair and less broke. But when will I go home? When? I'll be old. I'll be dead. If I am here for ten years I will never be able to have any children. Unless I take a fertility drug when I get out and have eight. I'll be a lonely, broken old woman shaking my fist at street urchins who put turds through the letter box. But maybe I could have a child while in prison? I could get the Assistant to the British Consul somehow to impregnate me. But where would I get hold of folic acid in jail? The baby would grow up stunted. Must stop this. Stoppit. Stoppit. Am catastrophizing.

But it is a catastrophe.

Will read poem again.

Friday 22 August

Calories 22, unforgiving minutes filled with distance run 0.

8 p.m. Women's Correctional Institute, Bangkok. This morning they came and moved me from police custody to proper prison. In despair. Feel as if this means they have given up on me and accepted I'm done for. Cell is big filthy room with at least sixty women squeezed in. Seems that any power or individuality is being relentlessly peeled away as get filthier and filthier and more exhausted. Cried today for first time in four days. I feel like I'm slipping through the net. I feel like I'm going to get forgotten now and just languish here, a wasted life. Will try to sleep. Would be so great to sleep.

11 p.m. Aargh. Had just got off to sleep when was woken by something sucking my neck. It was the Lesbian Ring who had got me. They all started kissing and groping bits of me. I could not bribe them to stop because I had already given away my Wonderbra and no way was I going round with no knickers. I could not scream for the guard as that is the worst thing you can do here. So I had to swap my jeans for a filthy old sarong. Although obviously I felt violated, part of me could not help but feel it was so nice just to be touched. Gaaah! Maybe I am a lesbian? No. Don't think so.

Sunday 24 August

Minutes spent crying 0 (hurrah!).

Much more cheerful since sleep. Think will find Phrao. Phrao is my friend as she was transferred at same time as me and I lent her my Wonderbra. Even though she has no breasts to put in it she seems to like it – she is always walking around in it saying 'Madonna'. Cannot help thinking it is cupboard love or underwear drawer love but beggars can't be choosers and it is nice to have a friend. Also do not want it to be like when Beirut hostages got out and it was obvious no one really liked Terry Waite.

You see, you can get used to anything if you try. Am not going to give in to being all mopey. Sure they must be doing something at home. Shazzer and Jude will be organizing newspaper campaigns like for John McCarthy and standing outside the House of Commons with banners with my head on, holding up torches.

There must be something I can do. It seems to me if getting out depends on catching Jed and extracting a confession then there ought to be a bit more bloody effort put into catching and extracting.

2 p.m. Hurrah! Am suddenly most popular girl in cell. Was quietly teaching Phrao words to Madonna songs as she is obsessed with Madonna, when a little group started forming round us. Seemed to be considered some kind of goddess as knew words to *Immaculate Collection* all the way through. Ended up being forced by popular demand to perform 'Like a Virgin' standing on a pile of mattresses wearing the Wonderbra and sarong and using a Tampax as a microphone at which point the guard started shouting in a high-pitched voice. Looked up to see the representative to the British Consul had just been let in.

'Ah, Charlie,' I said graciously, getting down off the mattress and hurrying towards him, whilst trying to pull the sarong up over the bra and retain my dignity. 'So glad you've come! We've got lots to talk about!'

Charlie did not appear to know which way to look but seemed to keep plumping for the Wonderbra direction.

He brought me a kit from the British Embassy with water, biscuits, sandwiches, insect repellent, some more pens and paper and, best of all, soap.

Was completely overcome. Was the best present I had ever had in life.

'Thank you, thank you, I can't thank you enough,' I said emotionally, on the verge of flinging my arms round him, and taking him roughly against the bars.

'No problem, standard issue, actually. Would have brought you one before but all the bloody totty in the office kept woofing the sandwiches.'

'I see,' I said. 'Now, Charlie. Jed.'

Blank stare.

'You remember Jed?' I said in a Listen-With-Mother voice. 'The guy who gave me the bag? It's very important that we catch him. I'd like you to take down lots more details about him and then send me someone from the Drug Squad who can spearhead the search.'

'Right,' said Charlie seriously yet at the same time deeply unconvincingly. 'Right.'

'Now come along,' I said, turning into a Peggy Ashcroft-style figure from the last days of the Raj who was about to rap him over the head with an umbrella. 'If the Thai authorities are so keen to set an example over drugs that they're locking up innocent Westerners without trial, they've got to at least show an interest in catching the drug traffickers.'

Charlie stared up at me thickly. 'Yar, right, right,' he said, furrowing his brows and nodding heartily, not the faintest glimmer of understanding illuminating his gaze.

After had explained it a few more times Charlie suddenly saw the light.

'Yar, yar. See what you mean. Yar. They've got to go after the guy that put you in here because otherwise it looks as though they're not making an effort.'

'Exactly!' I said, beaming, delighted at my handiwork.

'Right, right,' said Charlie, getting to his feet, still wearing his very earnest expression. 'I'm going to get them to get moving on this right now.'

Was watching him leave, marvelling at how such a creature could have risen through the ranks of the British diplomatic service. I suddenly had a brainwave.

'Charlie?' I said.

'Yar,' he said, looking down to check that his flies weren't undone.

'What does your father do?'

'Dad?' Charlie's face brightened. 'Oh, he works in the Foreign Office. Bloody old fart.'

'Is he a politician?'

'No, civil servant actually. Used to be Douglas Hurd's right-hand man.'

Checking swiftly that the guards weren't looking, I leaned forward.

'How's your career going here?'

'Bit bloody static, to be perfectly honest,' he said cheerily. 'Black bloody hole of Calcutta, unless you get down to the islands of course. Oh sorry.'

'Wouldn't it be really good for you if you pulled off a diplomatic coup?' I began temptingly. 'Why don't you just give your dad a little call . . .'

Monday 25 August

7st 2 (attention-seeking thinness), no. of – oh fuck it, brain has dissolved. Good for slimming, surely.

Noon. Bad, low day. Must have been mad to think I could influence anything. Am bitten to death by mosquitoes and fleas. Am nauseous and feeble with constant diarrhoea, which is difficult in view of potty situation. In a way is quite good, though, as light-headedness makes everything unreal: much better than reality. Wish could sleep. So hot. Maybe have got malaria.

2 p.m. Bloody Jed. I mean how could anyone be so . . . ? But mustn't hold on to resentments or will harm self. Detach. I do not wish him ill, I do not wish him well. I detach.

2.01 p.m. Bloody fucking dog pig black-livered bastard from hell. I hope his face gets put on a porcupine.

6 p.m. Result! Result! An hour ago the guard came in and hustled me out of the cell. Fantastic to get out and away from the stink. Was taken to a small interview room with a wood-effect Formica table, a grey metal filing cabinet and a copy of a Japanese gay porn magazine, which the guard hurriedly removed as a short, distinguished middle-aged Thai man entered and introduced himself as Dudwani.

He turned out to be Drug Squad and a pretty hard nut. Good old Charlie.

I started on the details of the story, the flights Jed had

arrived on and probably left on, the bag, the description of Jed.

'So surely you can trace him from this?' I concluded. 'There must be his fingerprints on the bag.'

'Oh, we know where he is,' he said dismissively. 'And he has no fingerprints.' Ieuw. No fingerprints. Like having no nipples or something.

'So why haven't you captured him?'

'He is in Dubai,' he said dispassionately.

Suddenly I felt really quite annoyed.

'Oh, he's in Dubai, is he?' I said. 'And you know all about him. And you know he did it. And you know I didn't do it and he made it look as though I did and I didn't. But you go home to your lovely saté sticks and wife and family in the evening and I'm stuck here for the rest of my childbearing years for something I didn't do just because you can't be bothered to get someone to confess to something I didn't do.'

He looked at me in consternation.

'Why don't you get him to confess?' I said.

'He is in Dubai.'

'Well, get somebody else to confess, then.'

'Miss Jones, in Thailand, we . . .'

'Someone must have seen him break into the hut or broke in for him. Someone must have sewn the drugs into the lining. It was done with a sewing machine. Go investigate it like you're supposed to do.'

'We are doing everything we can,' he said coldly. 'Our government takes any breach of the drug codes very seriously.'

'And my government takes the protection of its citizens very seriously,' I said, thinking for a moment of Tony

Blair and imagining him striding in and coshing the Thai official on the head.

The Thai man cleared his throat to speak. 'We . . .'

'And I am a journalist,' I interrupted him. 'On one of Great Britain's top television current affairs programmes,' I said, trying to fight back a vision of Richard Finch going 'I'm thinking Harriet Harman, I'm thinking black underwear, I'm thinking . . .'

'They are planning a vigorous campaign on my behalf.'

Mental cut to Richard Finch: 'Oh, Bridget droopy bikini hasn't come back from her holiday, has she? Snogging on the beach, forgot to get the plane.'

'I have connections in the highest ranks of government and I *think*, given the current climate' – I paused to give him a meaningful stare, I mean the current climate's always *something*, isn't it? – 'it would look very bad indeed in our media if I were imprisoned in these frankly appalling conditions for a crime I plainly and by your own admission did not commit, while the police force here are failing to enforce their own laws with their own people and properly investigate the crime.'

Gathering my sarong around me with tremendous dignity, I sat back and gave him a cool stare.

The official shuffled in his seat, looked at his papers. Then he looked up, pen poised.

'Miss Jones, can we go back to the moment at which you realized your hut had been broken into?'

Hah!

Wednesday 27 August

8st, cigarettes 2 (but at hideous price), fantasies involving Mark Darcy/Colin Firth/Prince William bursting in saying: 'In the name of God and England, release my future wife!': constant.

Worrying two days with nothing. No word, no visits, just constant requests to perform Madonna songs. Repeated reading of 'If' only means of keeping nerve. Then this morning Charlie appeared – in a new mood! Extremely earnest, top level and overconfident, with another kit containing cream cheese sandwiches that – given earlier flight of fantasy about in-jail impregnation – found self not really wanting to eat.

'Yar. Things are starting to move,' said Charlie with the heavy air of a government agent burdened with explosive MI5 secrets. 'Bloody good actually. We've had movements from the Foreign Office.'

Trying not to think about tiny top-level turds in boxes, I said, 'Did you speak to your dad?'

'Yar, yar,' he said. 'They know all about it.'

'Has it been in the papers?' I said excitedly.

'No, no. Hush-hush. Don't want to rock the boat. Anyway. There's some mail for you. Your friends got it to Dad. Bloody attractive actually, Dad says.'

I opened the big brown Foreign Office envelope, hands shaking. First was a letter from Jude and Shaz, rather carefully written almost in code, as if they thought spies might read it.

Bridge,

Don't worry, we love you. We're gonna get you out of there. Jed tracked down. Mark Darcy helping (!).

Heart leaped. Was best news possible (apart, obviously, from ten-year jail sentence being lifted).

Remember Inner Poise and diet potential of jail. 192 soon. Repeat do not worry. Girls on top.
All our love,
Jude and Shaz

Looked at letter, blinking with emotion, then tore eagerly at the other envelope. Maybe from Mark?

Was written on reverse of long concertina of views of Lake Windermere and said:

Visiting Granny in St Anne's and touring the Lakes. Weather a bit mixed but super factory shops. Daddy has bought a sheepskin gilet! Could you call Una and check that she's put the timer on?
Love,
Mum

Saturday 30 August

8st (hope), alcohol units 6 (hurrah!), cigarettes 0, calories 8,755 (hurrah!), no. of times checked bag to make sure no drugs in same 24.

6 a.m. On plane. Going home! Free! Thin! Clean! Shiny-haired! In own clean clothes! Hurrah! Have got tabloids and *Marie Claire* and *Hello!* All is marvellous.

6.30 a.m. Unaccountable plummet. Is disorientating being squashed on plane again in darkness with everyone asleep. Feel huge pressure to be euphoric but feel really freaked out. Guards came last night and called me out. Was taken to room and given clothes back, met by a different embassy official called Brian with strange short-sleeved nylon shirt and wire specs. He said there'd been a 'development' in Dubai and pressure from the highest level in the Foreign Office and they had to get me out of the country immediately before the climate changed.

Was all strange in the embassy. No one there except Brian who showed me straight to a very bare old-fashioned bathroom where there was a little pile of all my things and said to have a shower and change, but be really quick.

Couldn't believe how thin I had got, but there was no hairdryer so hair was still pretty mad. Obviously not important but would have been good to look nice on return. Was starting with make-up when Brian knocked on the door saying that we really had to leave.

Was all a blur, rushed out in steamy night to car, rushing through streets full of goats and tuk-tuks and honking and people with entire families on one bicycle.

Couldn't believe cleanliness of airport. Did not have to go through normal channel but some special embassy route, everything all stamped and cleared. When got to the gate, whole area was empty, plane ready to leave with just one guy in a luminous yellow jacket waiting for us.

'Thank you,' I said to Brian. 'Thank Charlie for me.'

'I will,' he said wryly. 'Or his dad anyway.' Then he handed me my passport and shook my hand in really quite a respectful way such as was not at all used to even before incarceration.

'You did very well,' he said. 'Well done, Miss Jones.'

10 a.m. Just been to sleep. Really excited about return. Have actually had spiritual epiphany. Everything is going to be different now.

New post-spiritual epiphany life resolutions:

1. Not start smoking or drinking again as have not had drink for eleven days and only two cigarettes (do not want to go into what had to do to get them). Though may just have small bottle of wine now. As obviously need to celebrate. Yes.
2. Not rely on men but on self. (Unless Mark Darcy wants to go back out with me. Oh God, hope so. Hope he realizes still love him. Hope it was him who got me out. Hope he is there at airport.)
3. Not bother about stupid things e.g. weight, mad hair, who Jude invited to wedding.
4. Not discard advice of self-help books, poems etc. but limit it to key things e.g. optimism, not freaking out, forgiving (though maybe not Fucking Jed as shall now be known).
5. Be more careful about men as are plainly – if evidence of Fucking Jed not to mention Daniel anything to go by – dangerous.
6. Not take shit from people i.e. Richard Finch, but have confidence in self-reliance.
7. Be more spiritual and stick to spiritual principles.

Goody, now can look at *Hello!* and tabloids.

11 a.m. Mmm. Fantastic spreads of newly rounded Diana and hairy Dodi. Humph, though. Just when I am thin she starts trend for newly roundedness. Great. Glad she is happy but not sure he is right for her somehow. Hope she is not just going out with him because he is not being a fuckwit. Understand, though, if she is.

11.15 a.m. Does not seem to be anything in papers about me – though as Charlie said, it was all hush-hush and kept under wraps by government so as not to interfere with Thai relations, imports of peanut sauce etc.

11.30 a.m. Brown is this season's black! Just glanced through *Marie Claire*.

11.35 a.m. Though really should be brown is this season's grey as grey was last season's black. Yes.

11.40 a.m. V. bad disaster though, as no. of brown items in wardrobe 0, though maybe some money will come in manner of unexpected release.

11.45 a.m. Mmm. Wine delicious after so long. Really goes to head.

12.30 p.m. Yuk. Feel slightly sick after tabloid gorging. Had forgotten depressed, ashamed feeling you get afterwards like hangover – and sense of world being turned into same horrible tale over and over again where people get set up as good then turn out to be evil and bad.

Particularly enjoyed, at time, priest-turned-shagging-fuckwit story. Is always so enjoyable when other people behave badly. Feel, however, that founders of support group for victims of shagging priest (because 'women who have relationships with priests often have no one to turn to') are being rather partisan. What about others who have no one to turn to? Should surely also be support groups for women who have been victims of shagging Tory ministers, members of British national sporting teams who have slept with members of the Royal family, Roman Catholic clergy who have slept with celebrities or members of the Royal family, and celebrities who have slept with members of the public who have confessed their story to members of the Roman Catholic clergy who have then sold the story to the Sunday papers. Maybe I will sell story to Sunday papers and that is where money will come from. No, that is wrong, you see spirituality has already been infested by tabloid mentality.

Maybe will write book though. Maybe will get hero's return in England like John McCarthy and write a book called *Some Other Cloud Formation* or other meteorological phenomenon. Maybe will get hero's welcome with Mark, Jude, Shazzer, Tom, and parents and crowds of waiting photographers and Richard Finch grovellingly begging for exclusive interview. Had better not get too pissed. Hope am not going to go all mad. Feel like I should be met by police or counsellors or something and taken to a secret base for de-briefing. Think will have little sleep.

9 p.m. (UK time now.) Arrived at Heathrow with clouting post-flight hangover trying to purge clothes of remnants of bread and pink toothpaste fraudulently offered as airline dessert, rehearsing lines, in preparation for waiting press phalanx – 'It was a nightmare. A living nightmare. A thunderbolt out of the blue. I feel no hatred (bitterness?) for if others are warned of the dangers of one's friends sleeping with strange men, my incarceration will not have been wasted (in vain?).' Whole time, however, did not think waiting phalanx would actually be there. Passed through customs without incident and looked around excitedly for familiar faces, only to be engulfed by – well, press phalanx. Crowd of photographers and journalists with flashguns. Mind went completely blank and could not think what to say or do except parrot 'no comment', in manner of government minister who has been caught shagging prostitute, and keep walking, pushing the trolley, thinking my legs were going to collapse under me. Then suddenly the trolley was taken away, and someone put their arm round me saying, 'It's all right, Bridge, we're here, we've got you, it's all right.'

It was Jude and Shazzer.

Sunday 31 August

8st 2 (Yess! Yess! Triumphant culmination of 18-year diet, though perhaps at unwarranted cost), alcohol units 4, calories 8,995 (deserved, surely), progress on hole in wall made by Gary the Builder 0.

2 a.m. My flat. So nice to be home. So nice to see Jude and Shazzer again. At airport, policeman took us through the crowd to an interview room where there were Drug Squad people and a man from the Foreign Office who started asking lots of questions.

'Look, can't this bloody well wait?' burst out Shaz indignantly after about a minute. 'Can't you see the state she's in?'

Men seemed to think it was necessary to carry on but eventually became so terrified of Shazzer's growls of 'Are you men or monsters?' and threats to report them to Amnesty International that they gave us a policeman to take us back to London.

'Just be careful who you get mixed up with next time, ladies,' said the Foreign Office man.

'Oh please,' said Shaz, just as Jude was saying, 'Oh quite right officer,' and launching into a professional woman vote-of-thanks-style speech.

Back in my flat, the fridge was full of food, there were pizzas waiting to go in the oven, Milk Tray and Dairy Box, smoked salmon pinwheels, packets of Minstrels, and bottles of Chardonnay. There was a big sign on the polythene hole in the wall saying 'Welcome back, Bridget.' And a fax from Tom – who has *moved in* with the customs guy in San Francisco – saying:

> *DARLING, DRUGS ARE POWDER OF SATAN. JUST SAY NO! ASSUME YOU WILL NOW BE THINNEST EVER. GIVE UP ALL MEN IMMEDIATELY AND BECOME GAY. COME HERE AND LIVE WITH US IN CALIFORNIAN GAY SEX-SANDWICH THREESOME. HAVE BROKEN JEROME'S HEART! HAHAHAHA.*
>
> *CALL ME. LOVE YOU. WELCOME BACK.*

Also Jude and Shaz had cleaned all the packing mess up from the bedroom floor and put clean sheets on the bed and fresh flowers and Silk Cut on the bedside table. Love the lovely girls. And the lovely self-obsessed Tom.

They ran me a bath and brought me in a glass of champagne and I showed them my flea bites. Then I got into my pyjamas and we all sat on the bed with cigarettes, champagne and Cadbury's Milk Tray and started going through everything that had happened but think I must have just fallen asleep because now it is all dark, Jude and Shaz are not here but have left a note on my pillow saying to call them when I wake up. They are both staying at Shazzer's because Jude's flat is being done up so she and Vile Richard can live together after the wedding. Hope she has got a better builder than me. Hole in wall entirely unchanged.

10 a.m. Gaaah! Where am I? Where am I?

10.01 a.m. Strange being in bed with sheets. Nice but unreal. Oooh, have just remembered am going to be in papers. Will go fetch from shop. Will cut everything out and keep in scrapbook and show to grandchildren (if ever obtain). Hurrah!

10.30 a.m. Is unbelievable. Like dream or sick newspaper April Fool. Is unbelievable. Diana dies is just not kind of thing she would do.

11.10 a.m. Am going to put on telly and they will say it has been a mistake and she is back then we will see her coming out of the Harbour Club with all the photographers asking her what it was like.

11.30 a.m. Cannot believe it. Is so scary when is obvious no one in authority knows what to do.

Noon. At least Tony Blair is in control. Seemed to say what everyone was thinking instead of repeating 'grief and shock' over and over again in manner of parrot.

1.15 p.m. Seems like world has gone mad. Is no normality to come back to.

1.21 p.m. Why haven't Jude and Shaz rung?

1.22 p.m. Oh, maybe they think I am asleep. Will ring them.

1.45 p.m. Jude, me and Shazzer all agree that she was our national treasure and all feel very bad that everyone was so niggardly about her and she did not like being in England. Is like great big hand coming down from heaven saying, 'If you are going to squabble about her no one is going to have her.'

2 p.m. Would have to bloody happen on one day was going to be in newspapers, though. Is nothing about me, nothing.

6 p.m. Cannot believe she is dead. Keep having to look at newspaper headline again to make self believe it. Really, Princess Diana was patron saint of Singleton women because she started off like the archetypal fairy tale doing what we all thought we were supposed to do i.e. marry a handsome prince, and she was honest enough to say that life is not like that. Also it made you feel that if someone so beautiful and gorgeous could be treated like shit by stupid men and feel unloved and lonely then it wasn't because you were rubbish if it happened to you. Also she kept re-inventing herself and sorting out her problems. She was always just trying so hard like modern women.

6.10 p.m. Hmm. Wonder what people would say about me if I died?

6.11 p.m. Nothing.

6.12 p.m. Especially if what they say about me when locked in Thai jail is anything to go by.

6.20 p.m. Have just had horrible realization. Was watching television with the sound down and tabloid front page came up that looked as though it might have had actual pictures of aftermath of the crash in. Realized was horrible part of me that actually wanted to see the pictures. Clearly would not buy said newspaper even if could but ugh! Ugh! What does this mean about me? Oh God. Am terrible.

6.30 p.m. Just keep staring into space. Simply hadn't realized how much Princess Diana was part of consciousness. Is like Jude or Shazzer being there and full of life and giggly jokes and lip gloss then suddenly being something so grown-up and horror-filled and alien as dead.

6.45 p.m. Just saw on telly woman has been to garden centre and bought a tree and planted it for Princess Diana. Maybe could plant something in window box e.g. um, basil? Could get from Cullens.

7 p.m. Hmm. Basil does not seem right somehow.

7.05 p.m. Everyone is going to Buckingham Palace with floral tributes as if is long-standing tradition. Have people always done this? Is it something naff people do to try to get on the television like camping all night outside sales or good, real thing? Hmm. Feel want to go though.

7.10 p.m. Think going with flowers might be a bit creepy . . . but thing is really did like her. Was like having someone in heart of authority who was same as you. Also all huffer-puffers criticized her re: landmines etc. but if you ask me was bloody intelligent use of mad publicity. Better than doing nothing except huffing at home.

7.15 p.m. What is point of living in capital city if cannot join in great expressions of feeling? Does not seem very English thing to do but maybe everything has changed with the changing weather and Europe and Tony Blair and it is all right to express yourself. Maybe she has changed English stuffiness.

7.25 p.m. OK, am definitely going to go to Kensington Palace. Have not got any flowers, though. Will get some from petrol station.

7.40 p.m. Petrol station has sold out. Only things like Chocolate Orange and custard left. Nice but inappropriate.

7.45 p.m. Bet she would like them, though.

7.50 p.m. Have chosen copy of *Vogue*, Milk Tray, one Instants and packet of Silk Cut. Not perfect but everyone will have bought flowers and know she liked *Vogue*.

9.30 p.m. V. glad went. Felt a bit shy walking through Kensington in case people knew where was going and that was on own, but then when think about it Princess Diana was often on own.

Inside park was v. dark and gentle with everyone just walking quietly in one direction. Was no histrionics like on news. The bottom of the wall was covered with flowers and candles in the darkness and people relighting the candles that had gone out and reading messages.

Hope that she knows now after all the times she worried about not being good enough, look what everybody felt about her. Really all this should give a message to women who are worried about how they look and being rubbish and expecting so much of themselves just not to worry so much. Felt a bit embarrassed about the *Vogue* and chocolate and Instants so hid under flowers and looked at the messages, which made you think that you do not have to be a spokesman for anything to be able to express things. The best one was copied from the Bible, I think, and it said in wobbly old lady's writing: 'When I was in trouble you cared about me, when I was in danger you tried to stop it, when I was sick you visited me, when people ran away you took my hand. Whatever you did for the poorest and the smallest people I felt as if you did it for me.'

12

Strange Times

Monday 1 September

8st 2 (must make sure do not put weight back on immediately), calories 6,452.

'I knew something was wrong when I got to the gate,' Shaz was saying when she and Jude came round last night. 'But the airline people wouldn't tell me what had happened and insisted I got on the plane, then they wouldn't let me get off again, and the next thing we were taxiing along the runway.'

'So when did you find out?' I said, polishing off my Chardonnay, at which Jude immediately held out the bottle to pour me another. Was marvellous, marvellous.

'Not till we landed,' said Shaz. 'It was just the most terrible flight. I was hoping you'd just missed it, but they were being really odd and sniffy with me. Then the second I got off the plane . . .'

'She got arrested!' said Jude gleefully. 'Pissed as a fart.'

'Oh, no,' I said. 'And you were hoping Jed would be there.'

'That bastard,' said Shaz, colouring.

Somehow thought I'd better not mention Jed again.

'He had someone behind you in the queue at Bangkok,' Jude explained. 'Apparently he was waiting at Heathrow for a call and immediately got on a plane to Dubai.'

Turned out Shaz called Jude from the police station and they quickly got on to the Foreign Office.

'Then nothing happened,' said Jude. 'They started talking about you being in for ten years.'

'I remember.' I shuddered.

'We called Mark on the Wednesday night and he immediately got on to all his contacts in Amnesty and Interpol. We tried to get hold of your mum but the answerphone said she was touring the Lakes. We thought about ringing Geoffrey and Una but we decided everyone would just get hysterical and it wouldn't help.'

'Very wise,' I said.

'On the first Friday we heard you'd been transferred to proper jail . . .' said Shaz.

'And Mark got on a plane to Dubai.'

'He went to Dubai? For me?'

'He was fantastic,' said Shaz.

'And where is he? I left him a message but he hasn't rung back.'

'He's still there,' said Jude. 'Then on Monday we got a call from the Foreign Office and everything seemed to have changed.'

'That must have been when Charlie talked to his dad!' I said excitedly.

'They let us send out your mail . . .'

'And then on Tuesday we heard they'd got Jed . . .'

'And Mark called on Friday and said they'd got a confession . . .'

'Then the call came out of the blue on Saturday that you were on the plane!'

'Hurrah!' we all said, clinking glasses. Was desperate to get on to subject of Mark but did not want to appear shallow and ungrateful for all the girls had done.

'So is he still going out with Rebecca?' I burst out.

'No!' said Jude. 'He's not! He's not!'

'But what happened?'

'We don't really know,' said Jude. 'One minute it was all on, next thing Mark wasn't going to Tuscany and—'

'You'll never guess who Rebecca's going out with now,' interrupted Shaz.

'Who?'

'It's someone you know.'

'Not Daniel?' I said, feeling an odd mixture of emotions.

'No.'

'Colin Firth?'

'No.'

'Phew. Tom?'

'No. Think of someone else you know quite well. Married.'

'My dad? Magda's Jeremy?'

'Now you're getting warm.'

'What? It's not Geoffrey Alconbury, is it?'

'No.' Shaz giggled. 'He's married to Una and he's gay.'

'Giles Benwick,' said Jude suddenly.

'Who?' I gibbered.

'Giles Benwick,' confirmed Shaz. 'You know Giles, for God's sake, the one who works with Mark, who you rescued from suicide at Rebecca's.'

'He had that thing about you.'

'He and Rebecca both stayed holed up in Gloucestershire after their accidents reading self-help books and now – they are together.'

'They are as one,' added Jude.

'They are joined in the act of love,' expanded Shaz.

There was a pause while we all looked at each other, stunned at this strange act of the heavens.

'The world has gone mad,' I burst out with a mixture of wonderment and fear. 'Giles Benwick isn't handsome, he isn't rich.'

'Well, actually he is,' murmured Jude.

'But he isn't someone else's boyfriend. He isn't a status symbol in any normal Rebecca way.'

'Apart from being very rich,' said Jude.

'Yet Rebecca has chosen him.'

'That's right, that's exactly right,' said Shaz, excitedly. 'Strange times! Strange times indeed!'

'Soon Prince Philip will ask me to be his girlfriend, and Tom will be going out with the Queen,' I cried.

'Not Pretentious Jerome, but our own, dear Queen,' clarified Shaz.

'Bats will start eating the sun,' I expanded. 'Horses will be born with tails on their heads, and cubes of frozen urine will land on our roof terraces offering us cigarettes.'

'And now Princess Diana is dead,' said Shazzer, solemnly.

The mood abruptly changed. We all fell silent, trying to absorb this violent, shocking and unthinkable thought.

'Strange times,' pronounced Shaz shaking her head with heavy portentousness. 'Strange times indeed.'

Tuesday 2 September

8st 3 (will definitely stop gorging tomorrow), alcohol units 6 (must not start drinking too much), cigarettes 27 (must not start smoking too much), calories 6,285 (must not start eating too much).

8 a.m. My flat. Owing to Dianadeath Richard Finch has cancelled all the stuff they were doing on Thai Drug Girl (me) and given me two days off to sort myself out. Cannot come to terms with death or anything else come to think of it. Maybe there will be national depression now. Is end of era, no two ways about it, but also start of new era in manner of autumn term. It is a time for new beginnings.

Determined not to sink back into old ways, spending entire life checking answerphone and waiting for Mark to ring, but to be calm and centred.

8.05 a.m. But why did Mark split up with Rebecca? Why is she going out with speccy Giles Benwick? WHY? WHY? Did he go to Dubai because he still loves me? But why hasn't he rung me back? Why? Why?

Anyway. All that is irrelevant to me now. I am working on myself. I am going to get my legs waxed.

10.30 a.m. Back in flat. Turned up late (8.30 a.m.) for leg wax only to find that beautician was not coming in 'Because of Princess Diana'. Receptionist was almost sarcastic about this but, as I pointed out, who are we to judge what each individual is going through? If all this has taught us one thing it is not to judge others.

Mood was hard to sustain on way home, however, when was caught in massive traffic jam in Kensington High Street rendering normal ten-minute journey home four times normal length. When reached jam-source turned out to be road works only quite inactive and workman-free with merely sign saying: 'The men working on this road have decided to stop work for the next four days as a mark of respect to Princess Diana.'

Ooh, answerphone is flashing.

Was Mark! He sounded very faint and crackly. 'Bridget . . . only just got the news. I'm delighted you're free. Delighted. I'll be back later in the . . .' There was a loud hiss on the line, then it clicked off.

Ten minutes later, the phone rang.

'Oh, hello, darling, guess what?'

My mother. My own mother! Felt great overwhelming rush of love.

'What?' I said, feeling tears welling up.

'"Go quietly amidst the noise and haste and remember what peace there may be in silence."'

There was a long pause.

'Mum?' I said eventually.

'Shhh, darling, silence.' (More pause.) '"Remember what peace there may be in silence."'

I took a big breath, tucked the phone under my chin, and carried on making the coffee. You see what I have learned is the importance of detaching from other people's lunacy as one has enough to worry about keeping oneself on course. Just then the mobile started ringing.

Trying to ignore the first phone, which had started vibrating and yelling: 'Bridget, you'll never find equilibrium if you don't learn to work with silence,' I pressed OK on the mobile. It was my dad.

'Ah, Bridget,' he said in a stiff, military-style voice. 'Will you speak to your mother on the land-line? Seems to have got herself worked up into a bit of a state.'

She was in a state? Didn't they care about me at all? Their own flesh and blood?

There was a series of sobs, shrieks and unexplained crashes on the 'land-line'. 'OK, Dad, bye,' I said, and picked up the real phone again.

'Darling,' croaked Mum, in a hoarse, self-pitying whisper. 'There's something I have to tell you. I cannot keep it from my family and loved ones any longer.'

Trying not to dwell on the distinction between 'family' and 'loved ones', I said brightly, 'Well! Don't feel you have to tell me if you don't want to.'

'What would you have me do?' she yelled histrionically. 'Live a lie? I'm an addict, darling, an addict!'

I racked my brains as to what she could have decided she's addicted to. My mum has never drunk more than a single glass of cream sherry since Mavis Enderbury got drunk at her twenty-first birthday party in 1952 and had to be taken home on the crossbar of a bicycle belonging to someone called 'Peewee'. Her drug intake is limited to the occasional Fisherman's Friend in response to a tickly cough triggered during the bi-annual performances of Kettering Amateur Dramatic Society.

'I'm an addict,' she said again, then paused dramatically.

'Right,' I said. 'An addict. And what exactly are you addicted to?'

'Relationships,' she said. 'I'm a relationship addict, darling. I'm co-dependent.'

I crashed my head straight down on to the table in front of me.

'Thirty-six years with Daddy!' she said. 'And I never understood.'

'But, Mum, being married to someone doesn't mean . . .'

'Oh no, I'm not co-dependent on Daddy,' she said. 'I'm co-dependent on fun. I've told Daddy I . . . Ooh, must whizz. It's time for my affirmations.'

I sat staring at the cafetière, mind reeling. Didn't they know what had happened to me? Had she finally gone over the edge?

The phone rang again. It was my dad.

'Sorry about that.'

'What's going on? Are you with Mum now?'

'Well, yes, in a manner of . . . She's gone off to some class or other.'

'Where are you?'

'We're in a . . . well, it's a sort of . . . well . . . It's called "Rainbows".'

Moonies? I thought. Scientologists? Est?

'It's, um, it's a re-hab.'

Oh my God. It turns out it wasn't just me who was starting to worry about Dad's drinking. Mum said he went off into Blackpool one night when they were visiting Granny in St Anne's and turned up at the old people's home completely plastered holding a bottle of Famous Grouse, and a plastic model of Scary Spice with a pair of wind-up false teeth attached to her breast. Doctors were called and they went straight from Granny in St Anne's last week to this re-hab place, where Mum, as ever it seems, was determined not to be upstaged.

'They don't seem to think it's a major problem with the old Scotch. They said I've been masking my pain or some such about all these Julios and Wellingtons. Plan is we're supposed to indulge her addiction to "fun" together.'

Oh God.

Think it is best not to tell Mum and Dad about Thailand, just for the time being.

10 p.m. Still my flat. There, you see. Hurrah! Have spent all day tidying up and sorting out and everything is under control. All the mail is done (well, put in pile anyway). Also Jude is right. Is ridiculous to have bloody great hole in the wall after four months and a miracle no one has climbed up the back wall and broken in. Am not going to engage with Gary the Builder's nonsensical excuses any more. Have got lawyer friend of Jude's to write him a letter. You see what one can do when one is empowered new person. Is marvellous . . .

Dear Sir,

We act for Ms Bridget Jones.

We are instructed that our client entered into a verbal contract with you on or about 5 March 1997 further to which you agreed to construct an extension to our client's flat (consisting of a second study/bedroom and a roof terrace) for a (quoted) price of £7,000. Our client paid £3,500 to you on 21 April 1997 in advance of work being commenced. It was an express term of the contract that work would be completed within six weeks of this first payment being made.

You commenced work on 25 April 1997 by knocking a large 5ft x 8ft hole in the exterior wall of our client's flat. You then failed to progress the work for a period of some weeks. Our client attempted to contact you by telephone on a number of occasions leaving messages, which you did not return. You eventually returned to our client's flat on 30 April 1997 while she was out at work. However, rather than continuing with the work you had agreed to do, you simply covered the hole you had made in her exterior wall with thick polythene. Since then, you have failed to return to finish the work and have failed to respond to any of our client's numerous telephone messages requesting you to do so.

The hole you have left in the exterior wall of our client's flat renders it cold, insecure and uninsured against burglary. Your failure to carry out and complete the work you agreed to undertake constitutes the clearest possible breach of your contract with our client. You have therefore repudiated the contract, which repudiation is accepted by our client . . .

Blah, blah, rudiate woodiate gibberish gibberish . . . entitled to recover costs . . . directly responsible for any losses . . . unless we hear from you within seven days of this letter with confirmation that you will compensate our client for the losses suffered . . . as a result we are instructed to issue proceedings for breach of contract against you without further notice.

Ha. Ahahahaha! That will teach him a lesson he won't forget. Has gone in post so he will get it tomorrow. That will show him I mean business and am not going to be pushed around and disrespected any more.

Right. Now, am going to take half an hour to think up some ideas for morning meeting.

10.15 p.m. Hmmm. Maybe need to get newspapers in order to get ideas. Bit late, though.

10.30 p.m. Actually, am not going to bother about Mark Darcy. One does not need a man. Whole thing used to be that men and women got together because women could not survive without them but now – hah! Have own flat (even if hole-filled), friends, income and job (at least till tomorrow) so hah! Hahahahaha!

10.40 p.m. Right. Ideas.

10.41 p.m. Oh God. Really feel like having sex, though. Have not had sex for ages.

10.45 p.m. Maybe something on New Labour New Britain? Like after the honeymoon, when you've been going out with someone for six months and start getting annoyed with them for not doing the washing up? Scrapping student grants already? Hmm. Was so easy to have sex and go out with people when one was a student. Maybe they do not deserve bloody grants when they are just having sex all the time.

> Number of months have not had sex: 6
> Number of seconds have not had sex:
> (*How many seconds are there in a day?*)
> 60 × 60 = 3,600 × 24 =
> (*Maybe will get calculator.*)
> 86,400 × 28 = 2,419,200
> × 6 months = 14,515,200
> *Fourteen million five hundred and fifteen thousand two hundred seconds have not had sex in.*

11 p.m. Maybe I will just, like, NEVER HAVE SEX AGAIN.

11.05 p.m. Wonder what happens if you do not have sex? Is it good for you or bad?

11.06 p.m. Maybe you just, like, *seal up*.

11.07 p.m. Look, am not supposed to be thinking about sex. Am spiritual.

11.08 p.m. And then surely it is good for one to procreate.

11.10 p.m. Germaine Greer did not have children. But then what does that prove?

11.15 p.m. Right. New Labour, New . . .

Oh God. Have become a celibate.

Celibacy! The New Celibates! I mean if it's happening to me, chances are it's happening to lots of other people as well. Isn't that the whole point about zeitgeist?

'Suddenly there is less sex everywhere.' Hate, though, this about popular news coverage. Reminds me of when there was an article in *The Times* that started: 'Suddenly there are more Dining Rooms everywhere,' the same day as there was one in the *Telegraph* on 'Whatever Happened to the Dining Room?'

Right, must go to bed. Determined to be very early on first day of new me at work.

Wednesday 3 September

8st 5 (gaah, gaah), calories 4,955, no. of seconds since had sex 14,601,600 (yesterdays figure + 86,400 – a day's worth).

7 p.m. Got into office early, first day back since Thailand, expecting new concern and respect to find Richard Finch in traditional foul mood: petulant, obsessively chain-smoking and chewing with crazed look in his eye.

'Ho!' he said as I walked in. 'Ho! Ahahahahaha! What've we got in that bag, then? Opium, is it? Skunk? Have we got crack in the lining? Have we brought in some Purple Hearts? Some E for the class? Is it poppers? Is it some nice speedy speed? Hasheeeesh? Some Rokey-cokey cokey? *OHHHHH okeecokeycokeeee,*' he started to sing maniacally. '*Oooh okeecokeycokeeee. Ooooh! okeecokeycokeeee!*' An idiotic gleam in his eye, he grabbed the two researchers next to him and started rushing forwards, yelling, 'Knees bent, arms stretched, it's all in Brid-get's bag, Ra-Ra!'

Realizing our executive producer was coming down from some drug-induced frenzy, I smiled beatifically and ignored him.

'Oh, little Miss Hoity-toity today, are we? Oooh! Come on, everybody. Bridget Hoity-bottom-just-out-of-prison's here. Let's start. Let's startitdeedoodaa.'

Really, this was not at all what I had in mind. Everyone began to converge on the table, looking from the clock to me resentfully. I mean it was only twenty bloody past nine: the meeting wasn't supposed to start till half past.

Just because I start coming in early doesn't mean the meeting has to start early instead of late.

'Right then, Brrrrrridget! Ideas. What ideas have we got today to delight the breathless nation? Ten Top Smuggling Tips from the Laydee in the Know? Britain's Best Bras for stashing Charlie in the booster pads?'

If you can trust yourself when all men doubt you, I thought. Oh fuck it, I'm just going to sock him in the mouth.

He looked at me, chewing, grinning expectantly. Funnily enough the usual sniggers round the table weren't happening. In fact the whole Thailand interlude seemed to have brought a new respect from my colleagues that I was naturally delighted by.

'What about New Labour – after the honeymoon?'

Richard Finch crashed his head down on to the table and started snoring.

'Actually, I have got another idea,' I said, after a casual pause. 'About sex,' I added, at which Richard sprang to attention. (I mean just his head. At least I hope.)

'Well? Are you going to share it with us – or save it, for your chummies in the Drug Squad?'

'Celibacy,' I said.

There was an impressed silence.

Richard Finch was staring at me bulgy-eyed as if he couldn't believe it.

'Celibacy?'

'Celibacy.' I nodded smugly. 'The new celibacy.'

'What – you mean monks and nuns?' said Richard Finch.

'No. Celibacy.'

'Ordinary people not having sex,' Patchouli cut in, looking at him insolently.

Really there was a very changed atmosphere around the table. Maybe Richard had begun to go so far over the edge that no one was sucking up to him any more.

'What, because of some tantric, Buddhist thing?' said Richard sniggering, one leg twitching convulsively as he chewed.

'No,' said sexy Matt, carefully looking down at his notebook. 'Ordinary people, like us, who don't have sex for long periods of time.'

I shot a look at Matt, just as he was doing the same to me.

'What? You lot?' said Richard, looking at us incredulously. 'You're all in the first flush of youth – well, except Bridget.'

'Thanks,' I muttered.

'You're all at it like rabbits every night! Aren't you? *In, out, in, out and shake it all about,*' he sang. '*You do the Okeekokee and you turn her round, and do it to her from – be-hind!* Aren't you?'

There was a certain degree of shuffling round the table.

'Aren't you?'

More pause.

'Who here hasn't had sex in the last week?'

Everyone stared hard at their notepads.

'OK. Who *has* had sex in the last week?'

No one raised their hand.

'I don't believe this. All right. Which one of you has had sex in the last month.'

Patchouli raised her hand. As did Harold, who beamed at us all smugly from behind his spectacles. Probably lying. Or maybe just puppy-love-type shagging.

'So the rest of you . . . Jesus. You're a bunch of freaks. It can't be because you're working too hard. Celibacy. Pah! Talk about bums off seats. We're off the air because of Diana so you lot had better come up with something better than this for the rest of the season. None of this limp no-sex bollocks. We're coming back next week with a bang.'

Thursday 4 September

8st 6 (this must stop or jail sentence will have been wasted), no. of ways imagined killing Richard Finch 32 (this too must stop otherwise deterrent value of jail sentences annihilated), no. of black jackets considered buying 23, no. of seconds not had sex 14,688,000.

6 p.m. V. happy about return-to-school-autumnal-style feel of world. Going to go late-night shopping on way home: not to buy anything as financial crisis, just to try on new 'brown is black' autumn wardrobe. V. excited and determined this year to be better at shopping i.e. (a) not panic and find only thing able to buy is black jacket as only so many black jackets one girl needs and (b) get money from somewhere. Maybe Buddha?

8 p.m. Angus Steak House, Oxford Street. Uncontrollable panic attack. Shops all seem to have just slightly different versions of each thing. Throws self into thought-fug with mind unable to settle until has encompassed and catalogued all, for example, available black nylon jackets: French Connection one at £129 or high-class Michael Kors (tiny, square quilted one) at £400. Black nylon jackets in Hennes are only £39.99. Could for example buy ten Hennes black nylon jackets for price of one Michael Kors one but then wardrobe would be more riddled with more black jackets than ever and cannot buy any of them anyway.

Maybe whole image is at fault. Maybe should start wearing brightly coloured pantomime outfits in manner of Zandra Rhodes or Su Pollard. Or have a capsule wardrobe and just buy three very classy pieces and wear them all the time. (But what if spill or throw up on them?)

Right. Calm, calm. This is what need to buy:

Black nylon jacket (1 only)
Torque. Or maybe Tong or Tonk? Anyway, choker thing to go round neck.
'Boot leg' brown trousers (depending what 'boot leg' should turn out to mean).
Brown suit for work (or similar).
Shoes.

Was nightmare in shoe shop. Just trying on brown square-toed high-heeled 70s style shoes in Office feeling v. déjà-vu-esque for all those back-to-school times buying new shoes and fighting with bloody Mum about what they were allowed to be like. Then suddenly had horrifying realization: was not freaky sense of déjà vu – they were exactly the same shoes I had in Six Lower from Freeman Hardy Willis.

Suddenly felt like innocent dupe or stooge of fashion designers who cannot be arsed to think of new things. Worse, am now so old that young fashion buying generation no longer remember wearing things I wore as teenager. At last realize point at which ladies start going to Jaeger for two-pieces – when do not want to be reminded of lost youth by high-street fashion any more. Have now reached said point. Am going to abandon Kookaï, Agnès B, Whistles etc. in favour of Country Casuals and spirituality. Also cheaper. Am going home.

9 p.m. My flat. Feel very strange and empty. Is all very well thinking everything is going to be different when you come back but then it is all the same. Suppose I have to make it different. But what am I going to do with my life?

I know. Will eat some cheese.

The thing is, as it says in *Buddhism: The Drama of the Moneyed Monk*, the atmosphere and events around you are created by the atmosphere within you. So it is no wonder all that bad stuff – Thailand, Daniel, Rebecca etc. – happened. Must start being more inner-poised and spiritual epiphanied, then will start attracting peaceful things and kind, loving, well-balanced people. Like Mark Darcy.

Mark Darcy – when he returns – is going to see the new me, calm and centred, attracting peace and order all around me.

Friday 5 September

8st 7, cigarettes 0 (triumph), no. of seconds since had sex 14,774,400 (disaster), (must treat both impostors just the same).

8.15 a.m. Right. Up bright and early. You see, this is important: steal a march on the day!

8.20 a.m. Ooh, a package has come for me. Maybe a gift!

8.30 a.m. Mmm. Is in gift box with roses on. Maybe from Mark Darcy! Maybe he's back.

8.40 a.m. Is a lovely little gold truncated biro with my name on it. Maybe from Tiffany's! With red tip. Maybe is lipstick.

8.45 a.m. That is weird. Is no note in there. Maybe promotional lipstick from PR company.

8.50 a.m. But is not lipstick as is solid. Maybe is biro. With my name on it! Maybe invitation to party in manner of forward-thinking PR firm – perhaps launch of new magazine called *Lipstick!*, maybe product of Tina Brown! – and the invitation to glittering party will follow.

Yes, you see. Think will go to Coins and have cappuccino. Though not, of course, chocolate croissant.

9 a.m. In café now. Hmm. Delighted with the little gift but not sure is biro either. Or at least if is, is very obscurely functioning one.

Later. Oh my God. Had just sat down with cappuccino and chocolate croissant when Mark Darcy came in, just like that, as if not away at all: in his work suit, newly shaved, a little cut on his chin with toilet paper on, as traditional in the mornings. He walked to the takeaway counter and put his briefcase down as if looking around for something or someone. He saw me. There was a long moment when his eyes softened (though not, obviously, melting like goo). He turned to deal with the cappuccino. Quickly made myself even more calm and centred seeming. Then he came towards my table, looking much more businesslike. Felt like throwing my arms round him.

'Hello,' he said brusquely. 'What have you got there?' – nodding at the gift.

Hardly able to speak with love and happiness, I handed him the box.

'I don't know what it is. I think it might be a biro.'

He took the little biro out of the box, turned it round, put it back like, well, a shot, and said, 'Bridget, this isn't a promotional biro, it's a fucking bullet.'

Later still. OhmyChristalive. Was no time to discuss Thailand, Rebecca, love, anything.

Mark grabbed a napkin, took hold of the lid of the box and replaced it.

'*If you can keep your head when all about you . . .*' I whispered to myself.

'What?'

'Nothing.'

'Stay here. Don't touch it. It's a live bullet,' said Mark. He slipped out into the street, and glanced up and down in manner of TV detective. Interesting how everything in real-life police drama reminds one of TV, rather in same way picturesque holiday scenes remind one of postcards or . . .

He was back. 'Bridget? Have you paid up? What are you doing? Come on.'

'Where?'

'The police station.'

In the car started to gabble, thanking him for everything he'd done and saying how much the poem had helped me in jail.

'Poem? What poem?' he said, swinging into Kensington Park Road.

'The "If" poem – you know – *force your heart and nerve and* . . . oh God I'm really sorry you had to go all the way to Dubai, I'm so grateful, I. . .'

He stopped at the lights and turned to me.

'That's absolutely fine,' he said gently. 'Now stop auto-wittering gibberish. You've had a big shock. You need to calm down.'

Humph. Whole idea was he was supposed to notice how calm and centred I am, not be telling me to calm down. Tried to calm down, but was very difficult when all could think was: someone wants to kill me.

When we got to the police station it was slightly less like a TV drama because everything was tatty and dirty and nobody seemed the slightest bit interested in us. The police officer on the desk tried to make us wait in the waiting room but Mark insisted we were taken upstairs. We ended up sitting in a great big dingy office with nobody in it.

Mark made me tell him everything that had happened in Thailand, asking me if Jed had mentioned anyone he knew in the UK, if the packet had come with the normal post, if I'd noticed anyone strange hanging around since I got back.

Felt a bit stupid telling him about how trusting we'd been with Jed, thinking he was going to tell me off, but he was really sweet.

'The worst you and Shaz could be accused of was breathtaking stupidity,' he said. 'You did very well in jail, I heard.'

Although he was being sweet, he wasn't being . . . well it all seemed on a very businesslike footing, not like he wanted to get back together or talk about anything emotional.

'Do you think you'd better call work?' he said, looking at his watch.

My hand shot to my mouth. Tried to tell self it would not matter whether I still had a job or not if I was dead but it was twenty past ten!

'Don't look like you've just accidentally eaten a child,' said Mark laughing. 'For once you've got a decent excuse for your pathological lateness.'

I picked up the phone and dialled Richard Finch's direct line. He answered straight away.

'Oooh, it's Bridget, is it? Little Miss Celibacy? Two days back and she's playing truant. Where are you, then? Shopping, are we?'

If you can trust yourself when all men doubt you, I thought. If you can . . .

'Playing with a candle, are we? Candles out, girls!' He made a loud popping noise.

Stared at phone in horror. Could not work out whether Richard Finch has always been like this and I was different, or whether he was getting into some terrible drug-induced downward spiral.

'Give it to me,' said Mark.

'No!' I said, grabbing the phone back and hissing, 'I'm a person in my own right.'

'Of course you are, darling, just not in your own right mind,' murmured Mark.

Darling! He called me darling!

'Bridget? Fallen asleep again, have we? Where are you?' chortled Richard Finch.

'I'm in the police station.'

'Ooh, back on the rokeekoke cokee? Jolly good. Got some for me?' he chuckled.

'I've had a death threat.'

'Oooh! That's a good one. You'll get a death threat from me in a minute. Hahahaha. Police station, eh? That's what I like to see. Nice stable drug-free respectable employees on my team.'

That was it. That was just about enough. I took a big breath.

'Richard,' I said grandly. 'That, I'm afraid, is like the kettle calling the frying pan dirty bottom. Except that I haven't got a dirty bottom because I don't take drugs. Not like you. Anyway, I'm not coming back. Bye.' And I put the phone down. Hah! Hahahaha! I thought briefly before remembering the overdraft. And the magic mushrooms. Except not strictly drugs, as natural mushrooms.

Just then, a policeman appeared, rushing by and completely ignoring us. 'Look!' said Mark banging his fist down on the desk. 'We've got a girl with a live bullet with her name on here. Can we see some action?'

The policeman stopped and looked. 'It's the *funeral*

tomorrow,' he said huffily. 'And we've got a knifing in Kensal Rise. I mean there are other people who have already *been* murdered.' He tossed his head and flounced out.

Ten minutes later the detective who was supposed to be dealing with us came in with a computer printout.

'Hello. I'm DI Kirby,' he said, without looking at us. He stared at the printout for a while, then up at me, raising his eyebrows.

'This is the Thailand file, I take it?' said Mark, looking over his shoulder. 'Oh I see . . . that incident in . . .'

'Well, yes,' said the detective.

'No, no, that was just a piece of fillet steak,' said Mark.

The policeman was looking at Mark oddly.

'It was left in a shopping bag by my mother,' I explained, 'and was starting to decay.'

'You see? There? And this is the Thai report,' Mark said, leaning over the form.

The detective put his arm around the form protectively, as if Mark were trying to copy his homework. Just then the phone rang. DI Kirby picked it up.

'Yes. I want to be in a squad car on Kensington High Street. Well, somewhere near the Albert Hall! When the cortège sets off. I want to pay my last respects,' he said in an exasperated voice. 'What's DI fucking Rogers doing there? OK, well, Buckingham Palace, then. What?'

'What did the report say about Jed?' I whispered.

'"Jed" he said his name was, did he?' scoffed Mark. 'Roger Dwight, actually.'

'OK then, Hyde Park Corner. But I want it at the front of the crowd. Sorry about that,' said DI Kirby, putting the phone down, and assuming the sort of overcompensatory efficient air I identified totally with from when I am late for work. 'Roger Dwight,' the detective said. 'It's kind of pointing that way, isn't it?'

'I'd be very surprised if he's managed to organize anything himself,' said Mark. 'Not from Arabian custody.'

'Well, there are ways and means.'

Was absolutely infuriating the way Mark was talking to the policeman over my head. Almost as if I were some kind of bimbo or half-wit.

'Excuse me,' I said bristling. 'Could I possibly participate in this conversation?'

'Of course,' said Mark, 'as long as you don't bring up any bottoms or frying pans.'

Saw the detective looking from one to the other of us with a puzzled air. 'He could, I guess, have organized someone else to send it,' said Mark, turning to the detective, 'but it seems somewhat unlikely, foolhardy even, given . . .'

'Well, yes, in cases of this kind. Excuse me.' DI Kirby picked up the phone. 'Right. Well, tell Harrow Road they've already *got* two cars on the route!' he said petulantly. 'No. I want to see the coffin *before* the service. Yes. Well, tell DI Rimmington to eff off. Sorry, sir.' He put the phone down again and smiled masterfully.

'In cases of this kind . . . ?' I said.

'Yes, it's unlikely that a person with serious intentions would advertise his . . .'

'You mean they'd just shoot her, right?' said Mark.

Oh *God*.

An hour later the package had gone off to be fingerprinted and DNA'd and I was still being questioned.

'Is there anyone outside from the Thai connection who

has a grudge against you, young lady?' said DI Kirby. 'An ex-lover perhaps, a rejected suitor?'

Was delighted by being called 'young lady'. You see may not be in first flush of youth but . . .

'Bridget!' said Mark. 'Pay attention! Is there anyone who might want to hurt you?'

'There are lots of people who have hurt me,' I said, looking at Mark and racking my brains. 'Richard Finch. Daniel – but I don't think either of them would do this,' I said uncertainly.

Did Daniel think I'd been talking about that night we were supposed to have dinner? Was he so annoyed about being rejected? Surely that would be a bit of an over-reaction? But then maybe Sharon was right about fin-de-millennium males losing their roles.

'Bridget?' said Mark, gently. 'Whatever you're thinking, I think you should tell DI Kirby.'

Was so embarrassing. Ended up going into whole Daniel lingerie and jacket evening while DI Kirby took down details with a poker face. Mark didn't say anything when I was talking but he looked really angry. Noticed the detective kept looking hard at him.

'Have you been involved with any low-life characters at all?' said DI Kirby.

The only person I could think of was Uncle Geoffrey's possible rent boy, but that was ridiculous because the rent boy didn't know me from Adam.

'You're going to have to move out of your flat. Is there anywhere you can go?'

'You can stay with me,' Mark said suddenly. My heart leapt. 'In one of the spare rooms,' he added quickly.

'Could you give me a moment, sir,' said the Detective

Inspector. Mark looked dropped on, then said, 'Of course,' and abruptly left the room.

'I'm not sure staying with Mr Darcy would be wise, miss,' said the detective, glancing at the door.

'Yeah, you might be right,' I said, thinking he was taking a fatherly interest and suggesting, as a man, that I should keep the air of mystery and unavailability and let Mark be the pursuer, but then I remembered was not supposed to be thinking like that any more.

'What exactly is your past relationship with Mr Darcy?'

'Well!' I said and started the story.

DI Kirby seemed oddly suspicious about the whole thing. The door opened again at the moment he was saying, 'So Mr Darcy *just happened* to be in the coffee bar, did he? On the morning you got the bullet?'

Mark came and stood in front of us.

'OK,' he said wearily, looking at me as if to say, 'You are the source of all that is opposite to serene.' 'Print me, DNA me, let's get this out of the way.'

'Oh, I'm not saying it was you, sir,' said the detective hurriedly. 'It's just we have to eliminate the . . .'

'All right, all right,' said Mark. 'Let's go get on with it.'

13

Gaaah!

Friday 5 September, still

8st 8, no. seconds since had sex: no longer care, no. of minutes stayed alive since death threat 34,800 (v.g.).

6 p.m. Shazzer's flat. Looking out of window. It can't be Mark Darcy. That's ridiculous. It can't be. It must be something to do with Jed. I mean, he's probably got a whole ring of contacts here, desperate for drugs whom I have deprived of their livelihood. Or Daniel? But surely he wouldn't do something like that. Maybe it's just some nut. But a nut who knows my name and address? Someone wants to kill me. Someone has bothered to get a live bullet and engrave my name on it.

Must keep calm. Calm, calm. Yes. Must keep head when all around you . . . Wonder if they have bulletproof vests in Kookai?

Wish Shaz would come back. Am all disorientated. Shazzer's flat is tiny, and messy at the best of times, especially as all open-plan, but with two of them here the floor and every surface seems completely covered with Agent Provocateur bras, leopardskin ankle boots, Gucci carrier bags, faux Prada handbags, tiny Voyage cardigans and odd strappy shoes. V. confused. Maybe will find space somewhere and lie down.

After they took Mark away DI Kirby repeated that I mustn't stay in my flat and took me back there to collect some things, but trouble was did not have anywhere to stay. Mum and Dad were still in rehab. Tom's flat would have been ideal but couldn't find his San Francisco number anywhere. Tried both Jude and Shaz at work but they were both out at lunch.

Was awful really. Was leaving messages everywhere while the police stamped around getting things to fingerprint and looking for clues.

'What's this hole doing in the wall, miss?' said one of the policemen, as they wandered around, dusting things.

'Oh, it, um, got left,' I said vaguely. Just then the phone rang. Was Shaz who said I could stay and told me where spare key was hidden.

Think will have little sleep.

11.45 p.m. Wish did not keep waking up in night, though is v. comforting having Jude and Shaz asleep in the room too like babies. Was v. nice when they came home from work. Had pizzas and I went to sleep really early. No word from or about Mark Darcy. At least have got panic button. Is nice. Is remote-control operated by a little suitcase. Just think if I press it lithe young policemen will come round in uniform to save me!!!! Mmm. Delicious thought . . . v. sleepy . . .

Saturday 6 September

8st 9, cigarettes 10, alcohol units 3, calories 4,255 (might as well enjoy life while still lucky enough to have it), minutes since had sex 16,005,124,00 (must, therefore do something about this).

6 p.m. Me, Jude and Shaz spent all day watching Princess Diana's funeral. All agreed it was like funeral of someone you know, only on somewhat grander scale, so that afterwards you feel as though you have been put through a wringer, but also as though something has been let out of you. Just so pleased that they managed to get everything right. It was all good. Beautiful and really good as if the establishment has really got the message at last, and our country can do things properly again.

Whole thing seems like Shakespearean tragedy or ancient legend, especially with sparring between two great noble houses of Spencer and Windsor. Definitely feel ashamed for working on stupid daytime TV programme where we have often devoted entire afternoons to Diana's hair. Will change life. If establishment can change so can I.

Bit lonely now, though. Jude and Shaz went out into the streets as said they had cabin fever. We tried ringing the police station, as am not allowed out without a policeman, but eventually, after forty-five minutes, we got through to a woman on central switchboard who said everyone was busy. Told Jude and Shaz definitely did not mind if they went out without me as long as they brought back a pizza. Ah. Telephone.

'Oh, hello, darling, it's Mummy here.'

Mummy! Anyone would think I was about to do a poo-poo in her hand.

'Where are you, Mother?' I said.

'Oh, I've come out, darling.'

For a second I thought she was telling me she was a lesbian and was going to set up home with Uncle Geoffrey in a gay, sexless marriage of convenience.

'We're back home. Everything's sorted out and Daddy's going to be fine. I don't know! Drinking all that time in his shed when I thought it was the tomatoes. Mind you, Gordon Gomersall had exactly the same thing, you know, and Joy had no idea. It's a disease, they say now. What did you think of the funeral?'

'Very nice,' I said. 'Now what's going on?'

'Well, darling . . .' she began, then there was a kerfuffle and Dad came on the phone.

'It's all right, love. I've just got to stay off the booze,' he said. 'And they were trying to get Pam out of there from day one.'

'Why?' I said, a lurid vision of my mother seducing a procession of eighteen-year-old drug addicts loomed up before my eyes.

He chuckled. 'They said she was too normal. Let me give you back.'

'Honestly, darling. It was all complete silly-daft nonsense charging these celebrity type of people loads of money to tell them things everybody knows already!'

'What kind of things?'

'Oooh, hang on. I'll just turn the chicken over.'

I held the phone away from my ear, trying not to think

about what kind of bizarre dish would involve an upside-down chicken.

'Oof. There we go.'

'What things did they tell you?'

'Well, in the mornings we all had to sit in a circle and say all kinds of silly things.'

'Like . . . ?'

'Oh, durrr! You know. My name's Pam and I'm a whatever!'

What? I wondered . . . ever? Madly over-confident nightmare? Lump-free gravy obsessive? Girl-child torturess?

'The things they were coming out with! "Today I will be confident in myself, I will not worry about other people's opinions of me." On and on and on. I mean, honestly, darling. If someone isn't confident in themselves they're not going to get anywhere, are they?' she said, roaring with laughter. 'Durrr! Not confident in yourself! I don't know! Why would anyone go around worrying about what anyone else is thinking about them?'

I looked worriedly from side to side. 'So what did you say for your affirmations?'

'Oh, I wasn't allowed to say anything. Well, at least I was, darling.'

'What? What did you have to say?'

Heard my dad laughing in the background. He sounded on good form, anyway. 'Tell her, Pam.'

'Ufff. Well, I was supposed to say, "I will not allow over-confidence to blind me to reality" and, "Today I will recognize my faults as well as my assets." I mean, it was completely ridiculous, darling. Anyway, must whizz, there's the buzzer. So I'll see you on Monday.'

'What?' I said.

'Don't say what, say pardon, darling. I've made an appointment for you to have your colours done in Debenhams. I told you! Four o'clock.'

'But . . .' I mean, she didn't. When did she tell me? January?

'Got to go, darling. The Enderburys are at the door.'

Sunday 7 September

8st 10, sq feet of floorspace not covered by bras, shoes, food, bottles or lipstick 0.

10 a.m. Hurrah! Another day, and still not dead. Hideous night, though. Felt really tired after I'd been talking to Mum, so checked all the doors were locked, climbed under confusion of Shazzer's pants, camisoles and leopardskin throws and went to sleep. Didn't hear them come in, then woke up at midnight to find them asleep. Is really starting to stink in here. Also, trouble is if wake up in night all can do is lie staring quietly at ceiling so as not to wake them up by knocking things over.

Ooh. Telephone. Best pick it up so as not to wake them.

'Well, they've realized I'm not a homicidal ex-lover.'

Hurrah! Was Mark Darcy.

'How are you?' he said considerately, given that, thanks to me, it turned out, he'd been at the police station for seven hours. 'I'd have called but they wouldn't tell me where you were till they'd cleared me.'

Tried to be cheerful but ended up telling him in a whisper that it was a bit of a squash at Shazzer's.

'Well, the offer's still open to come and stay with me,' he said off-handedly. 'Plenty of bedrooms.'

Wished he wouldn't keep rubbing it in so much that he didn't want to sleep with me. Seems to be turning into pashmina scenario and know from Shazzer and Simon how impossible that is to get out of once you start because at the merest hint of sex everyone starts panicking about 'spoiling the friendship'.

Just then, Jude yawned and turned over, dislodging a pile of shoeboxes with her foot, which crashed to the ground spilling beads, earrings, make-up and a cup of coffee into my handbag. I took a big breath.

'Thanks,' I whispered into the phone. 'I'd love to come.'

11.45 p.m. Mark Darcy's house. Oh dear. Is not going very well. Am just lying alone in strange white room with nothing in it except white bed, white blind and worrying white chair which is twice as high as it should be. Is scary here: great big empty palace with not even any food in house. Cannot seem to find or do anything without colossal mental effort as every light switch, toilet flush, etc. disguised as something else. Also is freezing cold in manner of fridge.

Strange, twilight day, drifting in and out of sleep. Keep finding self going along as normal then hitting Sleepy Pocket, almost like when aeroplanes plunge down fifty feet as if from nowhere. Cannot decide if it is still jet-lag or just trying to escape from everything. Mark had to go into work today, even though Sunday, because of missing whole day on Friday. Shaz and Jude came round about 4 with the *Pride and Prejudice* video but could not face watching lake scene after Colin Firth debacle so we just talked and read magazines. Then Jude and Shaz started looking round the house, giggling. I fell asleep and when I woke up they'd gone.

Mark came home about 9 with a takeaway for us both. Had high hopes for romantic reconciliation but was concentrating so hard on not giving the impression that I wanted to sleep with him, or in any way think staying at his house is anything other than police-type legal arrangement, that we ended up being all stiff and formal with each other in manner of doctor and patient, *Blue Peter* house inhabitants or similar.

Wish he would come in now. Is very frustrating being so close to him, and wanting to touch him. Maybe I should say something. But it seems too scary a can of worms to open, because if I tell him how I feel, and he doesn't want to get back together, it will just be hideously humiliating, given that we're living together. Also is middle of night.

Oh my God, though, maybe Mark did do it. Maybe he's going to come into the room and just, like, shoot me, and then there'll be blood all over the virgin white room in manner of virgin's blood except am not virgin. Just bloody celibate.

Must not think like that. Of course he didn't. At least have got panic button. Is so awful not being able to sleep and Mark downstairs, naked probably. Mmmm. Mmm. Wish could go downstairs and, like, ravish him. Have not had sex for . . . v. difficult sum.

Maybe he will come up! Will hear footsteps on stairs,

door will open softly and he will come and sit on the bed – naked! – and . . . oh God, am so frustrated.

If only could be like Mum and just have confidence in self and not worry what anyone else is thinking, but that is very hard when you know that someone else *is* thinking about you. They're thinking how to kill you.

Monday 8 September

8st 11 (serious crisis now), no. of death-threateners captured by police 0 (non-v.g.), no. of seconds since had sex 15,033,600 (cataclysmic crisis).

1.30 p.m. Mark Darcy's kitchen. Have just eaten huge lump of cheese for no reason. Will check calories.

Oh fuck. 100 calories an ounce. So pack is 8 oz and had already eaten a bit – maybe 2 oz – and little bit left, so have eaten 500 calories in thirty seconds. Is unbelievable. Maybe should make self sick as mark of respect to Princess Diana. Gaah! Why did mind think such tasteless thought? Oh well, might as well eat the rest of it as if to draw a line under whole sorry episode.

Think may be forced to accept truth of doctors saying diets don't work because your body just thinks it's being starved, and the minute it so much as sees any food again it gorges like a Fergie. Awake every morning now to find fat in bizarre and horrifying new places. Would not be in least surprised to find pizza dough-like strand of fat suspended between ear and shoulder or curving out at the side of one knee, rippling slightly in the wind like an elephant's ear.

Is still awkward and unresolved with Mark. When I went down this morning he'd already gone to work (not surprising as was lunchtime) but he had left a note saying to 'make myself at home' and ask anyone I want to round. Like who? Everyone is at work. It's so quiet here. Am scared.

1.45 p.m. Look, it's all fine. Definitely. Realize have no job, no money, no boyfriend, flat with hole in which cannot go to, and am living with man I love in bizarre, platonic housekeeper-style capacity in giant fridge and someone wants to kill me, but this, surely, is temporary state.

2 p.m. Really want my mum.

2.15 p.m. Have rung police and asked them to take me to Debenhams.

Later. Mum was fantastic. Well, sort of. Eventually.

She turned up ten minutes late in top-to-toe cerise, hair all bouncy and coiffed with about fifteen John Lewis carrier bags.

'You'll never guess what, darling,' she was saying as she sat down, dismaying the other shoppers with the carrier-bag spread.

'What?' I said shakily, gripping my coffee cup with both hands.

'Geoffrey's told Una he's one of these "homos", though actually he's not, darling, he's a "bi", otherwise they'd never have had Guy and Alison. Anyway, Una says she isn't the least bit bothered now he's come out with it.

Gillian Robertson up at Saffron Waldhurst was married to one for years and it was a very good marriage. Mind you, in the end they had to stop because he was hanging round these hamburger vans in lay-bys and Norman Middleton's wife died – you know, who was head of the governors at the boys' school? So in the end, Gillian . . . Oh, Bridget, Bridget. What's the matter?'

Once she realized how upset I was she turned freakishly kind, led me out of the coffee shop, leaving the bags with the waiter, got a great mass of tissues out of her handbag, took us out to the back staircase, sat us down, and told me to tell her all about it.

For once in her life she actually listened. When I'd finished she put her arms round me like a mum and gave me a big hug, engulfing me in a cloud of strangely comforting Givenchy III. 'You've been very brave, darling,' she whispered. 'I'm proud of you.'

It felt so good. Eventually, she straightened up and dusted her hands.

'Now come along. We've got to think what we're going to do next. I'm going to talk to this detective chappie and sort him out. It's ridiculous that this person's been at large since Friday. They've had plenty of time to catch him. What have they been doing? Messing around? Oh, don't worry. I've got a way with the police. You can stay with us if you want. But I think you should stay with Mark.'

'But I'm hopeless with men.'

'Nonsense, darling. Honestly, no wonder you girls haven't got boyfriends if you're going out pretending to be superdooper whizz-kids who don't need anybody unless he's James Bond, then sitting at home gibbering that you're no good with men. Oh, look at the time. Come on, we're late for your colours!'

Ten minutes later I was sitting in a Mark Darcy-esque white room in a white robe with a white towel on my head surrounded by Mum, a swathe of coloured swatches and somebody called Mary.

'I don't know,' tutted Mum. 'Wandering round on your own worrying about all these theories. Try it with the Crushed Cerise, Mary.'

'It's not me it's a social trend,' I said indignantly. 'Women are staying single because they can support themselves and want to do their careers, then when they get older all the men think they're desperate re-treads with sell-by dates and just want someone younger.'

'Honestly, darling. Sell-by dates! Anyone would think you were a tub of cottage cheese in ASDA! All that silly-daft nonsense is just in films, darling.'

'No, it's not.'

'Durrr! Sell-by date. They might pretend they want one of these bimbas but they don't really. They want a nice friend. What about Roger what's-his-name that left Audrey for his secretary? Of course she was thick. Six months later he was begging Audrey to come back and she wouldn't have him!'

'But . . .'

'Samantha she was called. Thick as two short planks. And Jean Dawson, who used to be married to Bill – you know Dawson's the butchers? – after Bill died she married a boy half her age and he's devoted to her, absolutely devoted and Bill didn't leave much of a fortune you know, because there isn't a lot of money in meat.'

'But if you're a feminist, you shouldn't need a . . .'

'That's what's so silly about feminism, darling. Anyone with an ounce of sense knows we're the superior race and the only nigger in the woodpile is—'

'Mother!'

'—when they think they can sit around when they retire and not do any housework. Now look at that, Mary.'

'I preferred the coral,' said Mary huffily.

'Well, exactly,' I said, through a large square of aquamarine. 'You don't want to go to work and then do all the shopping if they don't.'

'I don't know! You all seem to have some silly idea about getting Indiana Jones in your house loading the dishwasher. You have to train them. When I was first married Daddy went to the Bridge Club every night! Every night! *And* he used to smoke.'

Blimey. Poor Dad, I thought, as Mary held a pale pink swatch up against my face in the mirror and Mum shoved a purple one in front of it.

'Men don't want to be bossed around,' I said. 'They want you to be unavailable so they can pursue you and . . .'

Mum gave a big sigh. 'What was the point of Daddy and me taking you to Sunday School week after week if you don't know what you think about things. You just stick to what you think's right and go back to Mark and . . .'

'It's not going to work, Pam. She's a Winter.'

'She's a Spring or I'm a tin of pears. I'm telling you. Now you go back to Mark's house . . .'

'But it's awful. We're all polite and formal and I look like a dishrag . . .'

'Well, we're sorting that out, darling, aren't we, with your colours. But actually it doesn't make any difference what you look like, does it, Mary? You just have to be real.'

'That's right,' beamed Mary, who was the size of a holly bush.

'Real?' I said.

'Oh, you know, darling, like the Velveteen Rabbit. You remember! It was your favourite book Una used to read you when Daddy and I were having that trouble with the septic tank. There now, look at that.'

'D'you know, I think you're right, Pam,' said Mary, standing back in marvellment. 'She is a Spring.'

'Didn't I tell you?'

'Well, you did, Pam, and there was me with her down for a Winter! It just shows you, doesn't it?'

Tuesday 9 September

2 a.m. In bed, alone, Mark Darcy's house still. Seem to be spending entire life in entirely white rooms now. Got lost with policeman on way back from Debenhams. Was ridiculous. As said to policeman, was always taught as a child, when lost, to ask a policeman, but somehow he failed to see the humour of the situation. When eventually got back, hit another Sleepy Pocket and woke up at midnight to find house in darkness and Mark's bedroom door closed.

Maybe will go downstairs, make myself a cup of tea and watch TV in the kitchen. But what if Mark isn't back and is going out with someone and brings her home and I am like the mad aunt or Mrs Rochester drinking tea?

Keep thinking back about what Mum said about being real and the Velveteen Rabbit book (though frankly have had enough trouble with rabbits in this particular house). My favourite book, she claims – of which I have no memory – was about how little kids get one toy that they love more than all the others, and even when its fur has been rubbed off, and it's gone saggy with bits missing, the little child still thinks it's the most beautiful toy in the world, and can't bear to be parted from it.

'That's how it works, when people really love each other,' Mum whispered on the way out in the Debenhams' lift, as if she was confessing some hideous and embarrassing secret. 'But, the thing is, darling, it doesn't happen to ones who have sharp edges, or break if they get dropped, or ones made of silly synthetic stuff that doesn't last. You have to be brave and let the other person know who you are and what you feel.' The lift was now stopping at Bathroom Fittings and Fixtures. 'Oof! Well, that was fun, wasn't it!' she trilled with an abrupt change of tone, as three ladies in brightly coloured blazers squeezed themselves and their ninety-two carrier bags each in alongside us. 'You see, I knew you were a Spring.'

It's all very well for her to say. If I told a man what I really feel they would run a mile. This – just to pluck an example out of the air – is what I feel at this precise moment.

1) Lonely, tired, frightened, sad, confused and extremely sexually frustrated.

2) Ugly, as hair sticking up in imaginative peaks and shapes and face all puffy from tiredness.
3) Confused and sad as no idea if Mark still likes me or not and scared to ask.
4) V. lovingful of Mark.
6) Tired of going to bed on my own and trying to deal with everything on own.
7) Alarmed by horrifying – thought that have not had sex for fifteen million, one hundred and twenty thousand seconds.

So. To sum up what I really am is a lonely, ugly, sad act gagging for sex. Mmmm: attractive, inviting. Oh, I don't bloody well know what to do. Really fancy a glass of wine. Think will go downstairs. Will not have wine but probably tea. Unless there's some open. I mean it might actually help me sleep.

8 a.m. Crept down towards kitchen. Could not turn on lights as impossible to find designer light switches. Half hoped Mark would wake up when went past his door, but he didn't. Carried on creeping down the stairs, then froze. Was big shadow ahead like man. Shadow moved towards me. Realized it was man – great big man – and started screaming. By time had realized man was Mark – naked! – realized he was also screaming. But screaming much more than me. Screaming in complete, abandoned terror. Screaming – in a half-asleep way – as if he had just come across the most horrifying terrible scenario of his life.

Great, I thought: 'Real.' Then this is what happens when he sees me with mad hair and no make-up.

'It's me,' I said. 'It's Bridget.'

For a second I thought he was going to start screaming even more, but then he sank down on the stairs, shaking uncontrollably. 'Oh,' he said, trying to breathe deeply. 'Oh, oh.'

He looked so vulnerable and cuddly sitting there that could not resist sitting down next to him, putting arms round him and pulling him close to me.

'Oh God,' he said, nestling against my pyjamas. 'I feel such an arse.'

It suddenly struck me as really funny – I mean it was really funny being terrified out of your wits by your own ex-girlfriend. He started laughing too.

'Oh Christ,' he said. 'It's not very manly, is it, getting scared at night. I thought you were the bullet man.'

I stroked his hair, I kissed his bald patch where his fur had been loved off. And then I told him what I felt, what I really, really felt. And the miracle was, when I had finished, he told me he felt pretty much the same.

Hand in hand like the Bisto Kids, we made our way down to the kitchen and, with extreme difficulty, located Horlicks and milk from behind the baffling walls of stainless steel.

'You see, the thing is,' said Mark, as we huddled round the oven, clutching our mugs trying to keep warm, 'when you didn't reply to my note, I thought that was it, so I didn't want you to feel I was putting any pressure on. I—'

'Wait, wait,' I said. 'What note?'

'The note I gave you at the poetry reading, just before I left.'

'But it was just your dad's "If" poem.'

Was unbelievable. Turns out when Mark knocked the

blue dolphin over he wasn't writing a will he was writing me a note.

'It was my mother who said the only thing to do was to be honest about my feelings,' he said.

Tribal elders – hurrah! The note was telling me that he still loved me, and he wasn't with Rebecca, and that I should ring him that night if I felt the same and otherwise he'd never bother me with it again but just be my friend.

'So why did you leave me and go off with her?' I said.

'I didn't! It was you who left me! And I didn't even bloody realize I was supposed to be going out with Rebecca till I got to her summer house party and found myself in the same room as her.'

'But . . . so you didn't ever sleep with her?'

Was really, really relieved he had not been so callous as to wear my Newcastle United underpants gift for prearranged shag with Rebecca.

'Well.' He looked down and smirked. 'That night.'

'What?' I exploded.

'I mean one's only human. I was a guest. It seemed only polite.'

I started trying to hit him around the head.

'As Shazzer says, men have these desires eating away at them *all* the time,' he went on dodging the blows. 'She just kept inviting me to things: dinner parties, children's parties with barnyard animals, holidays—'

'Yur, right. And you didn't fancy her at all!'

'Well, she's a very attractive girl, it would have been odd if . . .' He stopped laughing, took hold of my hands and pulled me to him.

'Every time,' he whispered urgently, 'every time I

hoped you'd be there. And that night in Gloucestershire, knowing you were fifty feet away.'

'Two hundred yards in the servants' quarters.'

'Exactly where you belong and where I intend to keep you till the end of your days.'

Fortunately he was still holding me tight, so could not hit him any more. Then he said the house was big, cold and lonely without me. And he really liked it best in my flat where it was cosy. And he said that he loved me, he wasn't exactly sure why, but nothing was any fun without me. And then . . . God, that stone floor was cold.

When we got up to his bedroom noticed a little pile of books beside his bed. 'What are these?' I said, not believing my eyes. '*How to Love and Lose but Keep Your Self-Esteem? How to Win Back the Woman You Love? What Women Want? Mars and Venus on a Date?*'

'Oh,' he said sheepishly.

'You bastard!' I said. 'I threw all mine away.' Fist fight broke out again, then one thing led to another and we just shagged, like, *all night!!!*

8.30 a.m. Mmm. Love looking at him when he's asleep.

8.45 a.m. Wish he would wake up now, though.

9 a.m. Will not actually *wake* him up, but maybe he will wake up himself just through thought vibes.

10 a.m. Suddenly Mark sat bolt upright and looked at me. Thought he was going to tell me off or start screaming again. But he smiled sleepily, sank back down and pulled me roughly to him.

'Sorry,' I said afterwards.

'Yes, you should be, you dirty little bitch,' he murmured hornily. 'What for?'

'Waking you up by staring.'

'You know what?' he said. 'I kind of missed it.'

Ended up staying in bed quite a long time after that, which was fine because Mark didn't have any appointments that couldn't wait and I didn't have any appointments ever again for the rest of life. Just at a crucial moment, though, the phone rang.

'Leave it,' gasped Mark, carrying on. The answerphone boomed out.

'Bridget, Richard Finch here. We're doing an item on the New Celibacy. We were trying to find a personable young woman who hadn't had sex for six months. Didn't have any joy. So I thought we'd settle just for any old woman who can't get laid and try you. Bridget? Pick up the phone. I know you're there, your loopy mate Shazzer told me. Bridget. Bridguuuuuuuurt. BRIDGURRRRRRRRRRRT!'

Mark paused in his activities, raised one eyebrow in manner of Roger Moore, picked up the phone, murmured, 'She's just coming, sir,' and dropped it into a glass of water.

Friday 12 September

Minutes since had sex 0 (hurrah!).

Dreamy day, highlight of which was going to Tesco Metro with Mark Darcy. There was no stopping him putting things into the trolley: raspberries, tubs of Pralines and Cream Häagen-Daaz, and a chicken with a label on saying 'extra fat thighs'.

When we got to the checkout it was £98.70.

'That's incredible,' he said, taking out his credit card, shaking his head in disbelief.

'I know,' I said ruefully, 'do you want me to chip in?'

'God, no. This is amazing. How long will this food last for?'

I looked at it doubtfully. 'About a week?'

'But that's incredible. That's extraordinary.'

'What?'

'Well, it cost less than a hundred quid. That's less than dinner at Le Pont de la Tour!'

Cooked the chicken with Mark and he was really quite carried away, pacing around the room expansively, in between chopping.

'I mean it's been such a great week. This must be what people do all the time! They go to work, and then they come home and the other person's there, and then they just chat and watch the television and they *cook food*. It's amazing.'

'Yes,' I said, looking from side to side wondering if actually he might be mad.

'I mean, I haven't rushed to the answerphone once to see if anyone's aware of my existence in the world!' he said. 'I don't have to go sit in some restaurant with a book, and think I could end up dying alone and . . .'

'. . . Being found three weeks later half eaten by an Alsatian?' I finished for him.

'Exactly, exactly!' he said, looking at me as if we had just discovered electricity simultaneously.

'Will you excuse me a minute?' I said.

'Of course. Er, why?'

'I'll just be a moment.'

Was just rushing upstairs to call Shazzer with the ground-breaking news that maybe they are not the unattainable strategic adversary aliens after all, but just like us, when the phone rang downstairs.

Could hear Mark talking. He seemed to be on for ages, so could not ring Shazzer and eventually, thinking, 'bloody inconsiderate', went down to the kitchen.

'It's for you,' he said, holding out the phone. 'They've got him.'

Felt as if I'd been hit in the stomach. Mark held my hand as I took the phone, shaking.

'Hello, Bridget, DI Kirby here. We're holding a suspect over the bullet. We've obtained a DNA match with the stamp and the cups.'

'Who is it?' I whispered.

'Does the name Gary Wilshaw mean anything to you?'

Gary! Oh my God. 'He's my builder.'

Turned out Gary was wanted for a number of petty thefts from houses he'd been doing up, and was arrested and fingerprinted early this afternoon.

'We have him in custody,' said DI Kirby. 'We haven't obtained a confession as yet but, now we can go ahead on the connection, I'm pretty confident. We'll let you know and then you'll be safe to go back to your flat.'

Midnight. My flat. Oh blimey. DI Kirby called back half an hour later and said Gary had made a tearful confession, and we could go back to the flat, not to worry about anything, and remember there was a panic button in the bedroom.

We finished the chicken then went over to my place, lit the fire, and watched *Friends*, then Mark decided to have a bath. The doorbell rang when he was in there.

'Hello?'

'Bridget, it's Daniel.'

'Um.'

'Can you let me in? It's important.'

'Hang on, I'll come down,' I said, glancing towards the bathroom. Thought I'd better sort things out with Daniel but did not want to risk incensing Mark. The minute I opened the front door I knew I'd done the wrong thing. Daniel was drunk.

'So you put the police on me, did you?' he slurred.

I started inching backwards away from him while maintaining eye contact, as if he were a rattlesnake.

'You were naked under that coat. You . . .'

Suddenly there was a great bounding of footsteps on the stairs, Daniel looked up and – *wham* – Mark Darcy had socked him in the mouth, and he was slumped against the front door, blood coming out of his nose.

Mark looked rather startled. 'Sorry,' he said. 'Um . . .' Daniel started trying to get up and Mark rushed over and helped him up. 'Sorry about that,' he said again politely. 'Are you all right, can I get you, um . . .?'

Daniel just rubbed his nose and looked dazed.

'I'll be off then,' he mumbled resentfully.

'Yes,' said Mark. 'I think that's best. Just make sure you leave her alone. Or, um, I'll have to, you know, do it again.'

'Yup. Right,' said Daniel obediently.

Once back in the flat, doors barred, it got pretty wild on the bedroom front. Could not bloody believe it when the doorbell rang again.

'I'll go,' said Mark with a heavy air of manly responsibility, wrapping a towel round him. 'It'll be Cleaver again. You stay here.'

Three minutes later there was bounding of feet outside and the bedroom door burst open. Nearly screamed when DI Kirby put his head round. Pulled the blankets up to my chin, and followed his eye, scarlet with embarrassment, along the trail of clothes and underwear leading to the bed. He closed the door behind him.

'You're all right now,' DI Kirby said in a calm, reassuring voice as if I were about to jump off a tall building. 'You can tell me, you're safe, I've got people holding him outside.'

'Who – Daniel?'

'No, Mark Darcy.'

'Why?' I said, completely confused.

He glanced back at the door. 'Miss Jones, you pressed the panic button.'

'When?'

'About five minutes ago. We got a repeated, increasingly frantic signal.'

I looked up to where I'd hung the panic button on the bedpost. Not there. I fumbled sheepishly in the bedclothes beneath it, and produced the orange device.

DI Kirby looked from the button, to me, to the clothes on the floor, then grinned.

'Right, right. I see.' He opened the door. 'You can come back in, Mr Darcy, if you still have the, er, energy.'

There was much smirking amongst the policemen as the situation was euphemistically explained.

'OK. We're off. Enjoy yourselves,' said DI Kirby as the policemen trundled back down the stairs. 'Oh, just one thing. The original suspect, Mr Cleaver.'

'I didn't know Daniel was the original suspect!' I said.

'Well. We've attempted to question him on a couple of occasions and he did seem quite angrily resistant. It might be worth a call to smooth things over.'

'Oh, thanks,' said Mark sarcastically, trying to be dignified in spite of the fact that his towel was slipping. 'Thanks for telling us now.'

He saw DI Kirby out and could hear him explaining about the punch-up and DI Kirby saying to keep him informed of any problems and all stuff about deciding whether to press charges against Gary.

When Mark came back in I was sobbing. I'd just suddenly started and once I'd started for some reason I couldn't stop.

'It's all right,' said Mark, holding me tight, stroking my hair. 'It's all over. It's all right. Everything's going to be all right.'

14

For Better or Worse?

Saturday 6 December

11.15 a.m. Claridge's Hotel. Gaaah! Gaaah! GAAAAA-AAAAH! Wedding is in forty-five minutes and have just spilt enormous splodge of Rouge Noir nail varnish down front of dress.

What am I doing? Weddings are insane torture concept. Torture-victim guests (though not, obviously, on same scale as Amnesty International clients) dressed up to nines in weird things such would never wear normally e.g. white tights, having to get out of bed practically in middle of night on Saturday morning, run round house shouting 'Fuck! fuck! fuck!' trying to find old bits of wrapping paper with silver on, wrap up bizarre unnecessary gifts in manner of ice cream- or bread-makers (destined for endless recycling amongst Smug Marrieds, as who wants to lurch home at the end of the evening and spend an hour sieving ingredients into giant plastic machine, so when wake up in morning can consume entire giant loaf of bread on way to work instead of buying chocolate croissant when get cappuccino?), then drive 400 miles, eating petrol-station wine gums, vomit in car and be unable to find church? Look at me! Why me, Lord? Why? Looks as if have started period in weird backwards-way-round way on dress.

11.20 a.m. Thank God. Shazzer just came back to room and we have decided best thing is to *cut out* the nail varnish patch from the dress as material so stiff, shiny and sticky-outy that has not gone through to lining underneath, which is same colour and can hold bouquet in front.

Yes, sure that will be fine. No one will notice. Might even think it part of design. As if whole dress is part of extremely large piece of lace.

Good. Calm and poised. Inner poise. Presence or otherwise of hole in dress is not point of occasion, which is to do with other things. Fortunately. Sure it will all be serene and fine. Shaz was really far gone last night. Hope she is going to get through it today.

Later. Blimey! Arrived at church only twenty minutes late and immediately looked for Mark. Could tell he was tense just from back of head. Then the organ started up and he turned round, saw me and, unfortunately, looked as if he were going to burst out laughing. Could not blame him really as dressed not as sofa but as giant puffball.

We set off in stately procession down the aisle. God, Shaz looked rough. Had that air of intense concentration to prevent anyone noticing hangover. Walk seemed to go on for ever to the tune of:

Here comes the bride
Sixty inches wide.
See how she wa-ddles from side unto side.

I mean, why oh why?

'Bridget. Your foot,' hissed Shaz.

Looked down. Shazzer's Agent Provocateur lilac bra with fur on was attached to the heel of my satin kitten-heel shoe. Considered kicking it off but then bra would be left lying tellingly in aisle throughout ceremony. Instead tried unsuccessfully to flip it under my dress causing brief interlude of awkward leaping gait with little result. Was blessed relief when got to front and could pick bra up and stuff it behind bouquet during hymn. Vile Richard looked great, really confident. He was just wearing an ordinary suit which was nice – not all dressed up in some insane morning suit-style outfit as if one of the extras from the film *Oliver* singing 'Who Will Buy This Wonderful Morning?' and doing a high-kicking formation dance.

Unfortunately, Jude had made the – it was already beginning to seem – crucial mistake of not excluding tiny children from the wedding. Just as the actual wedding ceremony began, a baby started crying at the back of the church. It was top-level crying, of the sort when they start it off, then there's a pause while they draw breath like waiting for the thunder to come after the lightning, then a huge primal scream follows. Cannot believe middle-class modern mothers. Looked round to see this woman was jigging the baby up and down, rolling her eyes smugly at everyone as if to say 'Durrrr!'. It didn't seem to enter her head that it might be nice to take the baby out so the audience could hear Jude and Vile Richard pledge their souls together for a lifetime as one. A swish of long shiny hair at the back of the church caught my eye: Rebecca. She was wearing an immaculate soft grey suit and craning her neck in the direction of Mark. Beside her was a glum-looking Giles Benwick, holding a present with a bow on top.

'Richard Wilfred Albert Paul . . .' said the vicar in a resounding tone. Had no idea Vile Richard had so many Vile names. What were his parents thinking of?

'. . . Wilt thou love her, cherish her . . .'

Mmmm. Love the wedding ceremony. V. heart-warming.

'. . . Comfort and keep her . . .'

Dumph. A football crashed down the aisle into the back of Jude's dress.

'. . . For better, for worse . . .'

Two tiny boys, wearing, I swear, tap-dancing shoes, broke free from their pews and tore after the ball.

'. . . So long as you both shall live?'

There was a muffled noise, then the two boys started having an increasingly loud whispered gibberish conversation while the baby started crying again.

Above the din could faintly hear Vile Richard say 'I will', though could possibly have been 'I won't' apart from the fact that he and Jude were beaming at each other gooily.

'Judith Caroline Jonquil . . .'

How come I have only got two names? Has everyone except me got great long lists of gibberish after their name?

'. . . Wilt thou take Richard Wilfred Albert Paul . . .'

Was vaguely aware of Sharon's prayer book starting to sway out of the corner of my left eye.

'. . . Hapag . . .'

Shazzer's prayer book was definitely swaying now.

Looked round in alarm, just in time to see Simon, in full morning dress, rush forward. Shazzer's legs started to fold under her in a slow-motion-type curtsey and she collapsed in a heap, straight into Simon's arms.

'. . . Wilt thou love him, cherish him . . .'

Simon was now dragging Shazzer shiftily towards the vestry, her feet trailing along the ground out of the lilac puffball as if she were a dead body.

'. . . Honour and obey . . .'

Obey Vile Richard? Briefly considered following Shazzer into the vestry to see if she was OK but what would Jude think if she turned round now in her worst hour of need, to find Shazzer and I had buggered off?

'. . . So long as you both shall live?'

There was a series of bumps as Simon manhandled Shazzer into the vestry.

'I will.'

The vestry door slammed shut behind them.

'I now declare you . . .'

The two little boys emerged from the font area and set off back down the aisle. God, the baby was really yelling now.

The vicar paused and cleared his throat. Turned round to see the boys kicking the football against the pews. Caught Mark's eye. Suddenly he put down his prayer book, stepped out of the pew, picked one of the boys up under each arm and marched them out of the church.

'I now declare you man and wife.'

The whole church burst into applause and Jude and Richard beamed happily.

By the time we emerged from signing the register the atmosphere amongst the under-fives was positively festive. There was, effectively, a children's party going on in front of the altar and we walked back down the aisle behind a furious Magda carrying a screaming Constance out of the church going 'Mummy will smack, she will smack, she will smack.'

As we emerged into freezing rain and high winds, I overheard the mother of the footballing boys saying nastily to a bemused Mark, 'But it's wonderful having children just being themselves at a wedding. I mean that's what a wedding is all about, isn't it?'

'I wouldn't know,' said Mark cheerfully. 'Couldn't hear a bloody thing.'

Returned to Claridge's to find Jude's parents had unbridledly pushed the boat out and the ballroom was festooned with bronzed, be-leaved and be-fruited streamer things and copper-coloured pyramids of fruit and cherubs the size of donkeys.

All you could hear, when walked in, was people going:

'Two hundred and fifty grand.'

'Oh come on. It must have been at least £300,000.'

'Are you kidding? Claridge's? Half a million.'

Caught sight of Rebecca, looking frantically round the room with a fixed smile like a toy with a head on a stick. Giles was nervously following her, his hand hovering round her waist.

Jude's father, Sir Ralph Russell, a booming 'don't worry, everyone, I'm a fantastically rich and successful businessman', was shaking Sharon's hand in the line.

'Ah, Sarah,' he roared. 'Feeling better?'

'Sharon,' corrected Jude, radiantly.

'Oh yes, thank you,' said Shaz, a hand delicately fluttering to her throat. 'It was just the heat . . .'

Nearly spurted out laughing considering it was so fridge-like that everyone was wearing thermal underwear.

'Are you sure it wasn't the tightness of your stays against the Chardonnay, Shaz?' said Mark, at which she stuck a finger up at him, laughing.

Jude's mother smiled icily. She was stick thin in some sort of encrusted Escada nightmare with unexplained fins sticking out around the hips, presumably to make it look as if she had some. (Oh joyous deception to be in need of!)

'Giles, don't put your wallet in your trouser pocket, darling, it makes your thighs look big,' snapped Rebecca.

'Now you're being co-dependent, darling,' said Giles, putting his hand towards her waist.

'I'm not!' said Rebecca, brushing his hand away crossly, then putting back the smile. 'Mark!' she cried. She looked at him as if she thought the crowd had parted, time had stopped still and the Glen Miller Band was going to strike up with 'It Had to be You'.

'Oh hi,' said Mark, casually. 'Giles, old boy! Never thought I'd see you in a waistcoat!'

'Hello, Bridget,' said Giles, giving me a smacking kiss. 'Lovely dress.'

'Apart from the hole,' said Rebecca.

I looked away in exasperation and spotted Magda at the edge of the room looking agonized, obsessively pushing a non-existent strand of hair from her face.

'Oh that's part of the design,' Mark was saying, smiling proudly. 'It's a Yurdish fertility symbol.'

'Excuse me,' I said. Then reached up and whispered in Mark's ear, 'There's something wrong with Magda.'

Found Magda so upset she could hardly speak. 'Stop it, darling, stop it,' she was saying vaguely as Constance tried messily to push a chocolate lolly into the pocket of her pistachio suit.

'What's wrong?'

'That . . . that . . . witch who had the affair with Jeremy last year. She's here! If he so much as dares fucking speak to her . . .'

'Hey, Constance? Did you enjoy the wedding?' It was Mark, holding out a glass of champagne for Magda.

'What?' said Constance, looking up at Mark with round eyes.

'The wedding? In the church?'

'The parpy?'

'Yes,' he said laughing, 'the party in the church.'

'Well, Mummy took me out,' she said, looking at him as if he were an imbecile.

'Fucking bitch!' said Magda.

'It was supposed to be a parpy,' Constance said darkly.

'Can you take her away?' I whispered to Mark.

'Come on, Constance, let's go find the football.'

To my surprise, Constance took his hand and happily pottered off with him.

'Fucking bitch. I'm gonna kill 'er, I'm gonna . . .'

I followed Magda's gaze to where a young girl, dressed in pink, was in animated conversation with Jude. It was the same girl I'd seen Jeremy with last year in a restaurant in Portobello and again outside The Ivy one night, getting into a taxi.

'What's Jude doing inviting her?' said Magda, furiously.

'Well, how would Jude know it was her?' I said,

watching them. 'Maybe she works with her or something.'

'Weddings! Keep you only to her! Oh God, Bridge.' Magda started crying and trying to fumble for a tissue. 'I'm sorry.'

Saw Shaz spot the crisis and start hurrying towards us.

'Come on, girls, come on!' Jude, oblivious, surrounded by enraptured friends of her parents, was about to chuck the bouquet. She started ploughing her way loudly towards us, followed by the entourage. 'Here we go. Ready now, Bridget.'

As if in slow motion, I saw the bouquet fly through the air towards me, half caught it, took one look at Magda's tear-stained face and chucked it at Shazzer, who dropped it on the floor.

'Ladies and gentlemen.' A ludicrous be-knickerbockered butler was banging a cherub-shaped hammer on a bronze flower-decked lectern. 'Will you please be silent and upstanding as the wedding party makes its way to the top table.'

Fuck! Top table! Where was *my* bouquet? I bent down, picked up Jude's from Shazzer's feet and, with a gay fixed grin, held it up in front of the hole in my dress.

'It was when we moved to Great Missenden that Judith's outstanding gifts in the freestyle and butterfly strokes . . .'

By 5 o'clock Sir Ralph had already been talking for twenty-five minutes.

'. . . Became *strongly* apparent not only to us, her admittedly *biased*' – he looked up to elicit a dutiful faint ripple of pretend laughter – 'parents, but to the entire South Buckinghamshire region. It was a year in which Judith not only attained *first place* for the butterfly and freestyle sections in three consecutive tournaments in the South Buckinghamshire Under-Twelves Dolphin League but obtained her Gold Personal Survival Medal just three weeks before her first year exams! . . .'

'What's going on with you and Simon?' I hissed to Shaz.

'Nothing,' she hissed back, staring straight ahead at the audience.

'. . . In that same very busy year Judith obtained a distinction in her Grade II Associated Board Examinations on the clarinet – an early indication of the rounded "Famma Universale" she was to become . . .'

'But he must have been watching you in church otherwise he wouldn't have rushed up in time to catch you.'

'I know, but I was sick in his hand in the vestry.'

'. . . Keen and accomplished swimmer, deputy head girl – and frankly this, as the headmistress privately admitted to me, was an error of judgement since Karen Jenkins' performance as head girl was . . . well. This is a day for celebration, not for regret, and I know Karen's, er, *father* is with us today . . .'

Caught Mark's eye and thought was going to explode. Jude was a model of detachment, beaming at everyone, stroking Vile Richard's knee and giving him little kisses for all the world as if the cauchemarish cacophony were not happening and she had not, on so many occasions, slumped drunkenly on my floor incanting 'Commitment-phobic bastard. Vile by name, and Vile by nature, 'ere, 'ave we run out of wine?'

'. . . Second lead clarinetist in the school orchestra, keen trapezer, Judith was and is a prize *beyond rubies* . . .'

Could see where all this was leading. Unfortunately it took a further thirty-five-minute trawl through Jude's gap year, Cambridge triumph, and meteoric rise through the corridors of the financial world to get there.

'. . . And finally, it only remains for me to hope that, er . . .'

Everyone held their breath as Sir Ralph looked down at his notes for really beyond all sense, beyond all reason, beyond all decorum and good English manners, too long.

'*Richard!*' he said finally, 'is suitably grateful for this priceless gift, this jewel, which has today been so graciously bestowed upon him.'

Richard, rather wittily, rolled his eyes, and the room broke into relieved applause. Sir Ralph seemed inclined to continue with another forty pages, but mercifully gave up when the applause didn't.

Vile Richard then gave a short and rather endearing speech, and read out a selection of telegrams, which were all as dull as bricks apart from one from Tom in San Francisco, which unfortunately read: 'CONGRATULATIONS: MAY IT BE THE FIRST OF MANY.'

Then Jude got to her feet. She said a few very nice words of thanks and then – hurrah! – started reading out the bit that me and Shaz had done with her last night. This is what she said. As follows. Hurrah.

'Today I bade farewell to being a Singleton. But although I am now a Married I promise not to be a Smug one. I promise never to torment any Singletons in the world by asking them why they're still not married, or ever say "How's your love life?" Instead, I will always respect that that is as much their private business as whether I am still having sex with my husband.'

'I promise she will still be having sex with her husband,' said Vile Richard and everyone laughed.

'I promise never to suggest that Singletondom is a mistake, or that because someone is a Singleton there is anything wrong with them. For, as we all know, Singletondom is a normal state in the modern world, all of us are single at different times in our lives and the state is every bit as worthy of respect as Holy Wedlock.'

There was a ripple of appreciation. (At least I think that's what it was.)

'I promise also to keep in constant contact with my best friends, Bridget and Sharon, who are living proof that the Urban Singleton Family is just as strong and supportive, just as there for you, as anyone's blood family.'

I grinned sheepishly as Shazzer dug her toe into mine under the table. Jude looked round at us and raised her glass.

'And now I'd like to raise a toast to Bridget and Shazzer: the best friends a girl could have in the whole world.'

(I wrote that bit.)

'Ladies and gentlemen – the bridesmaids.'

There was a huge roar of applause. Love Jude, love Shaz, I thought as everyone rose to their feet.

'The bridesmaids,' said everyone. Was marvellous having all the attention. Saw Simon beaming at Shaz and looked across at Mark to see him beaming at me too.

*

Was all a bit hazy after that, but remember seeing Magda and Jeremy laughing together in a corner and catching her afterwards.

'What's going on?'

Turned out the trollop works in Jude's company. Jude told Magda all she knew was that the girl had had this distraught affair with a man who was still in love with his wife. She nearly died when Magda told her it was Jeremy, but all agreed we should not be horrible to the girl because it was really Jeremy who had been the fuckwit.

'Bloody old bugger. Anyway, he's learned his lesson now. Nobody's perfect and I love the old fart really.'

'Well, look at Jackie Onassis,' I said encouragingly.

'Well, exactly,' said Magda.

'Or Hilary Clinton.'

We both looked at each other uncertainly then started laughing.

Best bit was when I went out to the loo. Simon was snogging Shazzer with his hand up her bridesmaid dress!

There are sometimes those relationships that once you see them starting you just know, click: that's it, it's perfect, it's going to work, they'll go for the long haul – usually the sort of relationships you see starting between your immediate ex, who you were hoping to get back with, and somebody else.

I slipped back into the reception before Sharon and Simon saw me, and smiled. Good old Shaz. She deserves it, I thought, then stopped in my tracks. Rebecca was clutching Mark's lapel, talking passionately to him. I darted behind a pillar and listened.

'Don't you think,' she was saying. 'Don't you think it's

perfectly possible for two people who ought to be together, a perfect match in every way – in intellect, in physique, in education, in position – to be kept apart, through misunderstanding, through defensiveness, through pride, through . . .' She paused, then rasped darkly, 'the interference of others and end up with the wrong partners. Don't you?'

'Well yes,' murmured Mark. 'Though I'm not quite sure about your list of . . .'

'Do you? Do you?' She sounded drunk.

'It so nearly happened with Bridget and me.'

'I know! I know. She's wrong for you, darling, as Giles is for me . . . Oh, Mark. I only went to Giles to make you realize what you feel for me. Perhaps it was wrong but . . . they're not our equals!'

'Um . . .' said Mark.

'I know, I know. I can sense how trapped you feel. But it's your life! You can't live it with someone who thinks Rimbaud was played by Sylvester Stallone, you need stimulus, you need . . .'

'Rebecca,' said Mark quietly, 'I need Bridget.'

At this, Rebecca let out a horrifying noise, which was something between a pissed wail and an angry bellow.

Gently determined not to feel any shallow sense of triumph, nor gloating, unspiritual glee that the two-faced, stick-insect-legged snooty bitch from Bogoffland had got her comeuppance, I glided away, beaming smugly all over my face.

Ended up leaning against a pillar by the dance floor, watching Magda and Jeremy locked in an embrace, bodies moving together in a ten-year-old practised dance, Magda's head on Jeremy's shoulder, eyes closed, peaceful,

Jeremy's hand roaming idly over her bottom. He whispered something to her and she laughed without opening her eyes.

Felt a hand slip round my waist. It was Mark, looking at Magda and Jeremy too. 'Want to dance?' he said.

15

Excess Christmas Spirit

Monday 15 December

9st 3 (seems, alas to be true that weight finds own level), cards sent 0, presents purchased 0, improvement in hole in wall since originally made: single holly sprig.

6.30 p.m. Everything is lovely. Usually, week before Christmas, am hungover and hysterical, furious with self for not escaping to tiny woodman's cottage deep in forest to sit quietly by fire; instead of waking up in huge, throbbing, mountingly hysterical city with population gnawing off entire fists at thought of work/cards/present deadlines, getting trussed up like chickens in order to sit in grid-locked streets bellowing like bears at newly employed mini-cab drivers for trying to locate Soho Square using a map of central Addis Ababa, then arrive at parties to be greeted by same group of people have seen for last three nights only three times more drunk and hungover and want to shout 'WILL YOU ALL JUST SOD OFF!' and go home.

That attitude is both negative and wrong. At last have found way to live peaceful, pure and good life, hardly smoking at all and only a bit pissed once at Jude's wedding. Even drunk man at party on Friday did not really disturb equilibrium when called me and Sharon 'glib media whores'.

Also got brilliant mail today, including postcard from Mum and Dad in Kenya saying Dad has been having a whale of a time on Wellington's jet-ski and did the limbo with a Masai girl on buffet night and they hoped Mark and I won't be too lonely without them at Christmas. Then a PS from Dad saying, 'We haven't got twins, it's well over six foot and more than satisfactory on the bouncy front! *Hakuna Matata.*'

Hurrah! Everyone is happy and at peace. Tonight, for example, am going to write Christmas cards not with reluctance but with joy! – for as it says in *Buddhism: The Drama of the Moneyed Monk*, the secret of spiritual happiness is not doing the washing up in order to get the washing up done but to do the washing up. Is exactly the same with Christmas cards.

6.40 p.m. Bit of a boring idea though, just sitting in all evening writing Christmas cards when is Christmas.

6.45 p.m. Maybe will have one of chocolate tree decorations.

6.46 p.m. Maybe – too – will just have little festive glass of wine to celebrate Christmas.

6.50 p.m. Mmm. Wine is delicious. Maybe will have one cigarette also. Just one.

6.51 p.m. Mmm. Cigarette is lovely. I mean self-discipline isn't everything. Look at Pol Pot.

6.55 p.m. Will start cards in a minute when have finished wine. Maybe will just read letter again.

Cinnamon Productions

Sit Up Britain   FiveAlive   Blind Snog

From the Desk of Grant D. Pike, Chief Executive

Dear Bridget,

As you may have been aware, a Staf-trak programme has been under way during the last year monitoring staff performance and the flow of ideas throughout Cinnamon Productions.

You will be delighted to hear that 68 per cent of the fun 'And finally' end of programme items on Sit Up Britain have originated with you. Congratulations!

We understand that your resignation in September arose through disagreements with Sit Up Britain's Executive Producer Richard Finch. Richard, as I'm sure you have heard, was suspended from his position in October due to 'personal difficulties'.

We are currently re-organizing the staffing on the show and would like to invite you to rejoin the team, either promoted to Assistant Producer or in consultatory capacity, providing a flow of ideas on a freelance basis. The period since your resignation would be considered as paid leave.

We believe that – injected with new positive energy and get up and go – Sit Up, as the flagship of Cinnamon Productions, has a great future in the twenty-first century. We hope that you will be a major creative force in our new revamped team. If you will telephone my secretary to arrange an appointment I will be delighted to discuss revised terms and conditions with you.

Yours,

Grant D. Pike

Chief Executive, Cinnamon Productions

You see! You see! Also Michael from the *Independent* says I can have another go at a celebrity interview as they got quite a few letters after the Mr Darcy interview. As he said, anything that gets letters is good no matter how bad it is. So I can be a freelance. Hurrah! And then I never have to be late. Think will have a top up to celebrate. Ooh goody, doorbell!

Goody, goody. Is arrival of Christmas tree. You see! *Really* on top of Christmas. Mark is coming round tomorrow and will find Christmas Casbah!

8 p.m. As tree men staggered upstairs, grunting and gasping, feared may have underestimated largeness of tree, especially when terrifyingly filled entire doorway then burst through, branches flapping like invasion of Macduff in woods of Dunsinane. A spray of soil and two youths followed going, 'It's a fucking big 'un, where do you wan' it?'

'By the fire,' I said. Unfortunately, however, tree would no way fit, some branches poking into flames, others forced up vertically by sofa and rest burgeoning into middle of room while top of tree bent at odd angle against ceiling.

'Can you try it over there?' I said. 'What's that smell by the way?'

Claiming it was some Finnish invention to stop the needles dropping, rather than the obvious fact that the tree had gone off, the boys struggled to place tree between bedroom and bathroom doors at which branches sprang out totally blocking both.

'Try the middle of the room?' I said with tremendous dignity.

The boys sniggered at each other and manhandled tree monster into the centre of the room. At this point I couldn't see either of them any more. 'That's fine, thank you,' I said in a high, strangled voice, and they departed giggling all the way down the stairs.

8.05 p.m. Hmm.

8.10 p.m. Well, is no problem. Will simply detach from issue of tree and write cards.

8.20 p.m. Mmm. Love the lovely wine. Question is, does it matter if you don't send Christmas cards? Sure there are people from whom have never in my life received a Christmas card. Is this rude? Always seems faintly ridiculous to send e.g. Jude or Shazzer a Christmas card when see them every other day. But then how can one expect cards in return? Except that, of course, sending cards never yields fruit until following year, unless send cards in first week of December but would be unthinkable, Bored-Married-style behaviour. Hmm. Maybe should do list of pros and cons of sending cards.

8.25 p.m. Think will just have little look at Christmas *Vogue* first.

8.40 p.m. Attracted yet massively undermined by *Vogue* world of Christmas. Realize own fashion look and gift ideas grimly outdated and ought to be cycling, wearing slippy Dosa petticoat with eiderdown on top and puppy slung over shoulder, posing at parties with pre-pubescent model daughter and planning to buy friends pashmina hot-water bottle covers, fragrant stuff to put in laundry instead of usual stench from service wash, silver flash-lights from Asprey – with Christmas tree lights meanwhile reflecting sparklingly off teeth.

Am not going to take any notice. Is v. unspiritual. Just imagine if Pompeii-style volcano erupted south of Slough, and everyone was preserved in stone on bicycles wearing puppies, eiderdowns and daughters, future generations would come and laugh at spiritual emptiness of it. Also reject mindless luxury gifts, which say more about showy-offiness of giver than thought for receiver.

9 p.m. Would quite like pashmina hot-water bottle for self though.

9.15 p.m. Christmas gift list:

Mum – pashmina hot-water bottle cover.
Dad – pashmina hot-water bottle cover.

Oh God. Cannot ignore tree-pong any longer: is pungent and repulsively reminiscent of pine-scented shoe insole that has been worn for several months penetrating walls and solid hardwood door. Bloody tree. Only way to traverse room now would be to snuffle under tree in manner of wild boar. Think will read Christmas card from Gary again. Was great. Card was rolled up in shape of bullet and 'Sorry!' on it. Inside it said:

Dear Bridget,

Sorry about the bullet. I do not know what come over me but things have not gone good for me with money and the fishing incident. Bridget, it was special between us. It really meant something. I was going to finish the infill when the money came through. When that solicitor's letter come it was that wanky I was gutted and lost a grip on myself.

Then there was a copy of *Angler's Mail* opened at page 10. Opposite a page headed 'Carp World' with an article on 'Pick of the Pellet Feeds' were six pictures of fishermen all holding big slimy grey fish, including one of Gary with a pretend stamp across saying 'Disqualified' and a column underneath headed:

BOILING MAD

Three times East Hendon champion Gary Wilshaw has been suspended from East Hendon AA after a fish switching incident. Wilshaw, 37, of West Elm Drive, took first place with this 32lb 12oz common carp allegedly on a size 4 hook to a 15lb snake-bite hook link and 14mm boilie.

It later emerged, through a tip off, that the carp was a farmed fish from East Sheen, probably planted on the size 4 overnight.

A spokesman for East Hendon AA said, 'This kind of practice brings the entire sport of reservoir coarse fishing into disrepute and cannot be tolerated by the East Hendon AA.'

9.25 p.m. You see, felt powerless like Daniel. Poor Gary with his fish. Humiliated. He loves fish. Poor Daniel. Men at risk.

9.30 p.m. Mmm. Wines delicious. Is festive party on

own. Think of all lovely people who have been in life syear, even ones who did bad things. Feel nothing but love and forgiveness. Holding on to resentment juss eesaway at one.

9.45 p.m. Swil write carsnow. Will do liss.

11.20 p.m. Dunnit. Off to postssbox now.

11.30 p.m. Backinfla. Blurry tree. I know. Wllget scissors.

Midnight. Yurs. Berrer. Oof. Sleepynow. Oops. Tumbled over.

Tuesday 16 December

9st 12, alcohol units 6, cigarettes 45, calories 5,732, chocolate tree decorations 132, cards sent – oh God, hell, beelzebub and all his sub-poltergeists.

8.30 a.m. Bit confused. Has just taken an hour and seven minutes to get dressed and am still not dressed, having realized there is splodge on front of skirt.

8.45 a.m. Have got skirt off now. Will put grey one on instead, but where the fuck is it? Oof. Head hurts. Right, am not going to drink again for . . . Oh, maybe skirt is in living room.

9 a.m. In living room now, but everything is such a mess. Think will have some toast. Cigarettes are evil poison.

9.15 a.m. Gaah! Have just seen tree.

9.30 a.m. Gaah! Gaah! Have just found card that got missed. This is what says:

Happy Christmas to my dearest, dearest Ken. I have so appreciated all your kindness this year. You are a wonderful, wonderful person, so strong, and clear-sighted and good with figures. Although we have had our ups and downs, it is so important not to hold on to resentment if one is to grow. I feel very close to you now, both as a professional, and as a man.

With real love,

Bridget

Who is Ken? Gaaah! Ken is accountant. Have only met him once and then we had row about sending my VAT in late. Oh my God. Must find list.

Gaaah! As well as Jude, Shazzer, Magda, Tom etc. list includes:

The Assistant to the British Consul, Bangkok
The British Ambassador to Thailand
Rt Hon. Sir Hugo Boynton
Admiral Darcy
DI Kirby
Colin Firth
Richard Finch
The Foreign Secretary
Jed
Michael at the *Independent*
Grant D. Pike
Tony Blair

Cards are at large in the world and do not know what have put in them.

Wednesday 17 December

No feedback from cards. Maybe the others were fine actually and Ken's was throwback freak.

Thursday 18 December

9.30 a.m. Was just on way out when phone rang.

'Bridget, it's Gary!'

'Oh hi!' I trilled hysterically. 'Where are you?'

'In the nick, aren't I? Thanks for the card. That was sweet. Sweet. It really means the world.'

'Oh, hahahaha,' I laughed nervously.

'So are you going to come to see me today?'

'What?'

'You know . . . the card.'

'Uuuum?' I said in a high, strangled voice. 'I can't quite remember what I put. Do you . . . ?'

'I'll read it to you, shall I?' he said shyly. Then proceeded to read, stumbling over the words.

> *Dearest Gary,*
>
> *I know that your job as a builder is very different from mine. But I totally respect that, because it is a real craft. You make things with your hands and get up very early in the mornings and together – even though the infill extension isn't finished – we have built something great and beautiful, as a team. Two very different people, and even though the hole in the wall is still there – after nearly eight months! – I can see the growth of the project through it. Which is wonderful. I know that you are in prison, serving your dues, but soon the*

time of that will be over. Thank you for your card about the bullet and the fishing and I really, really forgive you.

I feel very close to you now, both as a craftsman, and as a man. And if anyone deserves joy and a real creative charge in the coming year – even in prison – it is you.

With love,

Bridget

'Creative charge,' he said in a throaty voice. Managed to get away by explaining was late for work but . . . Oh God. Who have I sent them to?

7 p.m. Back home. Went in for first consultancy meeting in office, which went really quite well, actually – especially since Horrible Harold has been demoted to fact-checker for being boring – until Patchouli yelled that she'd got a call from Richard Finch in the Priory, she was putting it on speaker phone and everyone had to listen.

'Hello team!' he said. 'Just called to spread a little festive spirit as it's the only sort I'm allowed. I'd like to read you something.' He cleared his throat. '"A merry, merry Christmas, dearest Richard." Isn't that nice?' There was a spurt of laughter. '"I know our relationship has had its ups and downs. But now it is Christmas I realize it is very strong – challenging, vigorous, honest and true. You are a fascinating, fascinating man, full of vigour and contradiction. I feel very close to you now it is Christmas – both as a producer and as a man. With love, Bridget."'

Oh, oh, it was just . . . Gaah! Doorbell.

11 p.m. It was Mark. With a very odd expression on his face. He came into the flat and looked around in consternation. 'What's that strange smell? What in the name of arse is that?'

I followed his gaze. Christmas tree in truth did not look as good as remembered. Had chopped off top and tried to trim rest into traditional triangular shape but now, in middle of room, was tall thin shorn thing with blunt edges like very bad cheap pretend tree from discount store.

'It was a bit . . .' I started to explain.

'A bit what?' he said with a mixture of amusement and incredulity.

'Big,' I said lamely.

'Big, eh? I see. Well, never mind that for now. Can I read something to you?' he said, taking a card out of his pocket.

'OK,' I said resignedly, sinking down on the sofa. Mark cleared his throat.

'"My dear, dear Nigel,"' he began. 'You remember my colleague, Nigel, do you, Bridget? Senior partner in the company. The fat one who isn't Giles?' He cleared his throat again. '"My dear, dear Nigel. I know we have only met once at Rebecca's when you pulled her out of the lake. But now it is Christmas, I realize, through being Mark's closest colleague, you have in a strange way been close to me all year too. I feel"' – Mark paused and gave me a look – '"very close to you now. You are a wonderful man: fit, attractive," – this, I remind you, is Fat Nigel we're talking about – "vigorous"' – he paused and raised his eyebrows – '"brilliant creatively, because being a lawyer is actually a very creative job, I will always think fondly of you, glistening"' – he was laughing now – '"glistening . . . glistening *bravely* in the sunlight and the water. Merry Christmas to my dear, dear Nigel. Bridget."'

I slumped on the sofa.

'Now come on,' grinned Mark. 'Everyone will know you were pissed. It's funny.'

'I'm going to have to go away,' I said sorrowfully. 'I'm going to have to leave the country.'

'Well, actually,' he said, kneeling in front of me and taking my hands, 'it's interesting you should say that. I've been asked to go to LA for five months. To work on the Mexican Calabreras case.'

'What?' It was all getting worse and worse.

'Don't look so traumatized. I was going to ask you . . . Will you come with me?'

I thought hard. I thought about Jude and Shazzer, and Agnès B on Westbourne Grove, and cappuccinos in Coins, and Oxford Street.

'Bridget?' he said gently. 'It's very warm and sunny there and they have swimming pools.'

'Oh,' I said, eyes darting interestedly from one side to the other.

'I'll wash up,' he promised.

I thought about bullets and fish, and drug smugglers and Richard Finch and my mum and the hole in the wall and the Christmas cards.

'You can smoke in the house.'

I looked at him, so earnest and solemn and sweet and thought that wherever he was, I didn't want to be without him.

'Yes,' I said happily, 'I'd love to come.'

Friday 19 December

11 a.m. Hurrah! Am going to America to start again, like the early pioneers. The land of the free. Was really good fun last night. Mark and me got out scissors again and did festive topiary turning tree into tiny Xmas cracker. Also we have made list and are going to do shopping tomorrow. Love Christmas. Celebration of good fun life, surely not perfection. Hurrah! Will be fantastic in California with sunshine and millions of self-help books – though will eschew all dating books – and Zen and sushi and all healthy stuff like green . . . Ooh goody, telephone!

'Er, Bridget. It's Mark.' His voice did not sound good. 'There's been a bit of a change of plan. The Calabreras case has been put back till June. But there is another job I quite fancy taking on and, er, I was wondering . . .'

'Yes?' I said suspiciously.

'How would you feel about . . .'

'About what?'

'Thailand?'

Think will just have a little glass of wine and a cigarette.

THE END